Speed

Speed

A NOVEL BY

MARK HARRIS

DONALD I. FINE, INC.
New York

Harris, Mark, 1922–
Speed / by Mark Harris.
p.   cm.
ISBN 1-55611-180-0
I. Title.
PS3515.A757S64   1990
813′.54—dc20
90-55028
CIP

Manufactured in the United States of America
10 9 8 7 6 5 4 3 2

Designed by Irving Perkins Associates

This book is a novel. Fiction first to last. It is not a memoir, not
autobiography, nor any other sort of non-fiction. Its structure follows not the
course of actual events but the strategic direction of the plot's suspense. Its
characters, though they are sometimes drawn from the suggestions of my
memory, depart from life to serve the invented plot.

Four lines beginning "Who can pass a district school . . ." are from Vachel
Lindsay, "A Gospel of Beauty," the Macmillan Company.

For Josephine, Tom, and Lawrence

. . . the more I squeeze the sponge of memory the more its stored secretions flow . . .
—HENRY JAMES
A Small Boy and Others

I write for myself and for strangers.
—Attributed to Gertrude Stein

". . . a stammering man is never a worthless one. Physiology can tell you why. It is an excess of delicacy, excess of sensibility to the presence of his fellow-creature, that makes him stammer."
—CARLYLE TO EMERSON,
quoted by JOHN UPDIKE in
Self-Consciousness: Memoirs

How unfair is life.
—HOLLY WIGGEN to her husband in
Bang the Drum Slowly

Part One

CHAPTER ONE

ONE DAY in our tiny rented winter cottage in Florida my brother Speed and I were in the kitchen and my mother and Babe Ruth were in the other room when from that other room came a terrible, frightening, awful commotion, as of persons fighting, and Babe Ruth shouted above it all, "I'll bust his chops." Were those father's chops the Babe was threatening to bust? Perhaps so. Father was back home in Mount Vernon, New York. Mother and her two charming boy babies were wintering in Florida.

At the height of the shouting and commotion and screaming and yelling my brother Speed fell or jumped or dived or was pushed from the kitchen table and smashed to the floor on his head. He lay stunned or unconscious on the floor, and my mother in the midst of this excitement came running from the other room and saw what I had done, or what she so logically suspected I had done, and whacked me with her open hand across the head and addressed me in a voice I recognized as truth, "You pushed him off the table, you disgusting stinking skunk." She had never struck me before. She never struck me again.

Her saying I had pushed him made me suspect it was true. I knew there was no sense denying it. I had called to her, "Speed fell off the table," but I saw now that my power to deceive my mother was less than I had thought, that if she had not actually seen me

3

push my brother from the table she had seen through me to my character, to my relationship to my brother and its logical outcome, detecting motives I had thought invisible.

On the other hand, I might not really have pushed him. Mother could not have been certain and neither could I and neither could Speed and neither could Babe Ruth. Understand, I loved my brother, we were then and afterward frequently friends and companions and athletic teammates and mutual defenders, but it had been necessary for me to push him off the table—if in fact I *had* pushed him off the table. I don't know. We don't know. I had pushed him off tables before, nobody had complained, not even he, and I would push him off more tables yet, so to speak, before we were done.

Mother, Speed, and I had sojourned for the month of March at St. Petersburg, Florida, where at a certain baseball field Babe Ruth picked me up and asked me my name, and when I replied said to my mother, "What a smart little boy you've got there." An achievement to know one's own name!

When he asked me my religion I replied, "Mother is Lutheran but father's too busy," and he swung around to the laughing crowd in the grandstand and held me high, exhibiting me, and told them one and all, "You never heard a little kid as smart as this," and he threw me again into the air and caught me coming down.

Babe Ruth's holding me aloft and praising my little brain arose not really so much from his admiration for my brain as from his admiration for mother's body. This I explored later in life in low conversation with my brother Speed, taunting him with the proposition that he was Babe Ruth's *bastard bastard bastard* son by our beloved mother.

We had gone that March to Florida for mother's health and the health of her babes. Grandfather paid for the trip. We traveled south and home again on the splendid luxurious Orange Blossom Special.

In Florida the cars had license plates only at the rear. Back home in New York cars had license plates front and rear. Since I thought all laws were universal I watched with a kind of horror all the one-plate cars go by. Was nobody outraged but me? I counted the

4

number of illegal cars passing before my eyes and reported these facts in a letter to father, urging him to come down to Florida and arrest all these people, shoot them, put them in jail, bawl them out, electrocute them in the electric chair at Sing Sing. They deserved it. Father had the authority to arrest people. Some months afterward I saw my letter posted on his office wall down the station, and there it remained for years.

Having said all this I must tell you that it might not have been Babe Ruth at all in our little tiny winter shack. It might have been Doc Duffy shouting at mother in the other room, might have been Doc Duffy in his naked skin at the door between the rooms.

Officially, Doc Duffy was missing in action in France in World War One five years before I was born. He was presumed dead. But he might never have been killed, he might have wandered back to America and settled somewhere far from Mount Vernon and kept a rendezvous with mother in our little cottage in Florida.

Doc Duffy earnestly loved mother and declared his intention to marry her if only she would have him (which she would, yes). Toward mother he was always exceedingly respectful, affectionate, and courteous. He treated her "like a sister," mother said.

Mother, father, and Aunt Ember agreed that Doc Duffy had always been a perfect boy, a handsome boy, a laughing boy, a true and loyal and wholesome boy. He was clean and responsible. His parents were poor Irish immigrants, like father's.

Doc, like father, earned his own way as soon as he could. He gathered good marks at Mount Vernon High School, where his name may be found on the wall among the names of many other sweet boys dead or presumed dead in several wars.

Father and Doc Duffy commuted together one year by trolley car and elevated train to Fordham University in the Bronx. They were two Irish kids trying to lift themselves in life. Doc intended to be a physician. He advanced as far as the nickname. Father intended to be a lawyer. Instead they went to war, from which father returned to the Mount Vernon police and married mother in a spectacularly lavish ceremony at her home, Walk a Mile House, with the agreement or understanding between the bride and the groom, however, that if, or ever, late or soon, mother's truest love on earth Doc Duffy returned from the war father would consent to their instantly annulling their marriage so that she might marry Doc Duffy. Father agreed with mother to this. Did I ever lay eyes on Doc Duffy? How could I, since he was presumed dead five years before I was born? Unless, of course, he was the gent in his naked skin in Florida when my brother Speed jumped, dived, fell, or was pushed from the table.

What am I to make of the long automobile ride in father's police car from Pennsylvania Station in New York to the Sheridan Gardens Apartments in Mount Vernon on the day we returned from Florida, of father and Aunt Ember singing as we rode happy joyful popular songs from the recent war in which father had served? Or of father's private use of the public car? The police of Mount Vernon were not so accountable then. When father became Police Chief the police became accountable. Meanwhile he drove the public car to his private destination.

It was as if father and Aunt Ember had sung together often before, as if they had been singing together all the month of March when mother and Speed and I were gone. I had the distinct feeling as they sang, child that I was, that this moment for father and Aunt Ember arose from a journey that they, too, had enjoyed while we were gone.

I heard it said that father had a "crush," as it was called, on Aunt Ember, a daring woman, mother's idol but not her model, for Aunt Ember was flamboyant, risqué, elegant, and conspicuous, while mother was shy. If Aunt *Ember* had gone to bed with Babe Ruth she'd have let all us baseball fans know it.

Aunt Ember was a party person. She even enjoyed children's parties and arranged as many as she could to celebrate all sorts of occasions, not alone for the amusement of the children but for the amusement of their parents, whom she entertained with jokes and stories. We children sat watching our parents laugh. One pantomime I vividly recall: Aunt Ember's charade entitled "Herbert

Hoover wiping his—." I missed the political point of the humor but I caught the naughtiness.

Mother and father discussed nobody so much or so often in our house as they discussed Aunt Ember. Mother never conceded that Aunt Ember had ever—what shall I call it?—misbehaved. Mother never denied that her sister "went out" with all sorts of men, sometimes with men who were other women's husbands, but that was actually harmless—to a restaurant, to dance a little, Ember loved dancing and had loved dancing "since she was a little girl, as long as I can remember," mother said.

"Loving dancing from childhood doesn't clear her from the charges," said father. "Men don't take women to hoity-toity restaurants to dance a little." Poor mother, how was she to know why men took women to restaurants? She was no worldly policeman. "Men want only one thing," said father. By "men" he meant all the men of the world except him. "Do you know what dancing is?" Oh, yes, we knew what dancing was, for we had heard it many times from father who reeled it off and smacked his palms and looked hard at us boys to see if we knew what he was getting at. "Dancing-is-the-vertical-manifestation-of-a-horizontal-desire," he recited, laughing to beat the band.

Our memorable ride in the police car from Penn Station to Mount Vernon ended at a fabulous destination. Father had carried us to the Sheridan Gardens Apartments, for that was where Aunt Ember in all her foresight had taken him. Mother was surprised. Her own father was bound to have, she said, "a thousand fits" to hear of our landing there in the midst of the Jews.

One day while we had been away in the south father had stood with Aunt Ember at the vestibule bells and mailboxes of House D, Sheridan Gardens Apartments. "Kikes and sheenies," he said, reading the names in the boxes, "almost nobody here but kikes and sheenies and you're expecting me to live here and raise my kids. You've got a screw loose if you're asking me."

"Keep your voice down somewhat," Aunt Ember said, "and consider the advantages," which were, as she viewed them, a neighborhood where people cared for law and order, for getting

7

ahead, for religion, for good schools, for saving money, for keeping the streets clean.

These things he could have elsewhere, too, father argued, but he had already weakened because Ember was a smart smart girl and because, above all, she was there already, installed in House B, right across the courtyard. He may have imagined himself in the role of the lover crossing the courtyard in the night affectionately to visit his lovely wife's lovely sister. Did father ever go to bed with Aunt Ember? I have no idea. I wouldn't be surprised if he did and I wouldn't be surprised if he didn't. This book is not about that.

It wasn't that Aunt Ember was lovelier than mother, but that she was lovely in a different way, she was interesting and stimulating and fashionable and original. She knew things. If she didn't know things she found them out. She was smart, shrewd, she was up to the hour on medical matters, financial matters, slants on education, books, she went frequently to New York to the theater, museums, concerts. Aunt Ember introduced mother to birth-control devices once she had introduced mother to birth control. She knew things for what they were. She knew an apartment house occupied mainly by middle-income upward-striving second-generation Jews was going to be a good safe place to live.

Aunt Ember deepened father as she had already over a lifetime deepened mother. So there was father, immigrant kid, family of his own, his ambition sharply increasing as his ignorance began to dissolve, standing with Aunt Ember at the doorbells of House D reading down that list of names and in his perplexity and indecision frowning at her whose beauty and wisdom had captured him for one lonesome month while his wife was away. He demanded of Aunt Ember one more time, "Do you really mean you're planting me in here with all these—?"

"You'll learn not to say it," she said, and when he turned from the doorbells to the mailboxes she said to him, "It's not going to be any different in the mailboxes either," and he said to her, "Ember, you're a witch, you're destroying me in my own eyes." He slammed the vestibule door behind him and stood in the courtyard looking for somewhere to run, and Aunt Ember followed him and said,

"The doorbells and the mailboxes aren't going to be any different in House A or B or C either, you'll never do better for yourself and your family as long as you live. Grow up. Come on I'll go with you to the agent's office and see you sign the lease." All my boyhood I lived in House D.

Father persuaded mother, as Aunt Ember had persuaded him, that this was going to be all for the best, that he had made a scientific study of it, that the Jews were O.K., that they were—this he said five hundred times in my short life—"just as much American citizens as you and I." Father detected Jewish faults and quirks. Jews were afraid of dogs. Jews never bought Fords. Jews ate different food. Jews spoke foreign languages and had foreign ideas. Jews yelled out of the window. Jews were law-abiding—"we never see them down the station," by which he meant Jews were seldom in police trouble in Mount Vernon, seldom arrested.

Often I wondered how Aunt Ember knew so much. She had an answer to every question, and if she had no answer she said, "I'll ask my palmist." By analyzing the lines of the palms of Aunt Ember's hands her palmist advised her how to live. Her palmist foretold the future and retrieved the past. Her palmist knew the right and wise thing to do when in doubt.

Aunt Ember said "My palmist says . . ." as other people said "I saw it in the newspaper." Skeptical of religion, she believed in her palmist. Her palmist was the authority on the conduct of life, as the dictionary was the authority on words, as the doctor was the authority on health, as the World Almanac was the authority on *facts*.

When as boys Speed or I said to Aunt Ember "This palmistry is bunk" she persuaded us to look hard at her palms. But there where her palmist saw the world revealed Speed and I saw only the lines of her hands.

Who was this palmist and where did she live or hold her sessions? I never saw Aunt Ember *go* to her palmist. I never heard the *name* of her palmist. I never picked up the ringing phone at Aunt Ember's and heard somebody say, "This is the palmist."

Aunt Ember's palmist had advised her that "marriage makes

9

grass grow under your feet." Therefore, on the advice of her palmist, she remained unmarried though seldom unattached, living
here and there in other parts of the world. Whenever she was
briefly gone from the Sheridan Gardens Apartments I collected her
mail, watered her plants, and gazed at nude pictures in her books.

Mother would have preferred to live near grandmother and grandfather in Walk a Mile House. But father believed, or pretended to
believe, that mother's true desire was to live as close as possible to
Aunt Ember. So you see he had done *mother* a favor by locating us
all in the Sheridan Gardens Apartments, it had never been he so
much as *mother* who yearned to live near Aunt Ember, it was
mother who crossed the courtyard to be with Aunt Ember ten
million times a day. "You're Ember's prisoner," father said, "you
can't move two steps without asking her advice on the next newest
thing down the road."

"You consult more with Ember than I ever do," mother said.
"Let's keep track some time, dear. Let's make a chart up here on
the wall and see who goes over to Ember's actually how many
times per week or month."

Mother for the sake of happiness and harmony with father, whom
she loved through all his sins, would have moved anywhere, gone
anywhere, served as policeman's wife anywhere in the world his
whimsy led him, and indeed strolled off with him in the end arm
in arm into his exile.

East or west, Mount Vernon was best. Mother was born in Walk a
Mile House. That great house, still standing in all its sprawling
charm, was named to commemorate the cigarette slogan "I'd Walk
a Mile for a Camel," which grandfather had composed and for which
he had received a great deal of money. The laborers who came from
a distance to build his house charged him as much as a dollar a day.

Mother thought herself fabulously fortunate to live just where
she lived. She could never imagine living anywhere else. When
mother was a girl Mount Vernon was a distant suburb of New York.
The little town was dusty, windswept, and remote. The train barely

stopped at the station. Neither shops nor theaters nor physicians had come to town. Few streets had yet been paved. There was no hospital: mother was born in grandmother's bed.

Walk a Mile House was then the only grand house in town, rising in its absurd isolation on the strength of grandfather's current conviction that sooner or later, when people started moving out from the city, he'd be at the center of things.

How could anybody not live in Mount Vernon, New York? We were "next to the biggest city in the country." That is to say, we were the first city north of New York. But that was our trouble, too, our lost dignity. Our name fell from the map, travelers by train thought when they stopped at Mount Vernon they were still in the city, and the Boston train did not condescend to stop at all, speeding through on the fast track all lights ablaze, nobody looking out. People have always said to me, "Oh, yes, I know where it is, I pass through on the train." We became a parkway off-ramp. Mount Vernon was so close to New York Speed and I seldom went there. Father never took us. "There's nothing down there I care to see any more," he said.

When father was hardly more than a boy he went to work for grandfather. He adored grandfather and grandmother and their daughter, too, whom he married as soon as it appeared likely that Doc Duffy would never return from the war.

Grandfather was blind. Father was grandfather's eyes, his valet, his chauffeur, his bodyguard, his drug connection. Father cleared the path of dogs, for grandfather feared and condemned dogs and believed in their extermination. When he heard a report of anyone's being bitten by a dog he warned me, "Don't go anywhere near a dog. If you see a dog coming toward you run across the street. Carry a stick with you. Carry a brick. If a dog comes anywhere near you throw the brick at him." When Speed and I were little boys we owned a dog named Rin Tin Tin the Second. This was our humor. Rin Tin Tin the Second was one-tenth the size of the famous moving-picture dog Rin Tin Tin, but suddenly our dog was gone. Later we learned that grandfather had assigned his faithful black servant Mary Washington to kidnap and kill our dog, and so she did. Mary Washington, who worked for grandfather for sixty years, inherited Walk a Mile House when he died.

Another of father's main tasks was to go about the house protecting grandfather from the blind man's nemesis—doors ajar. Almost from infancy I too learned that every door in Walk a Mile House must be either wholly open or wholly shut. Father read the New York *Times* to grandfather at breakfast.

Every morning father laid out grandfather's clothes and the objects of his pockets, his money, his cigars, his pencils, his pink memorandum pads, his keys, his handkerchiefs, his eyedrops, and when grandmother so kindly or affectionately told grandfather how fine he looked he contemptuously ignored her, as if to ask "Why shouldn't I look as good as any other man?" Father drove grandfather to the railroad station and accompanied him to his office in Manhattan. Grandfather insisted that visitors to his office were often unaware that he was blind. "I stare them right in the eye," grandfather said, but I afterward knew from my own experience of grandfather that when he thought he was staring me in the eye he was often staring somewhere else.

He was never more than a step from his cigars, which he lit with high-flaring matches. He was proof, if anyone cared, that a smoker need not see his own smoke to love smoking. "Is it lit?" he asked, shaking out the match. Sometimes he burned his fingers.

He wrote checks with the same confident flair. "Wouldn't you think a man that wrote this check had a hundred percent perfect sight?" He was proud of his mastery. He served himself as his own proof of the theory that in America every man could succeed if only he cultivated guts, gumption, energy, imagination, good morals, good habits.

The first day I ran out to play in that wonderland surrounding the Sheridan Gardens Apartments I was accidentally knocked to the ground by a big boy playing ball, who as he helped me to my feet comforted me with a stunning witticism. "Don't worry, kid," he said, "you'll be a man before your mother," and as soon as possible I said this to my brother Speed.

*   *   *

I learned to tie my shoelaces sitting on the floor of our living-room in Apartment 2–D of the Sheridan Gardens Apartments in Mount Vernon, New York, and the person who taught me was father.

Father was under the impression that the thing troubling me was the fact that all the children but me knew how to tie their shoes. But here is a truth father never knew. It was not the children at school who unnerved me, but Speed, who had for some time been tying his shoes. Yet he was a year younger than I. How could such unfairness be?

Speed was the master of mechanical things. He could take things apart and put them together again. He could repair broken objects, bang a nail straight in six blows.

Speed was also a very good writer. I could write passably well, but never with Speed's grace or confidence, never against the pressure of a deadline, as he could. Sometimes Speed wrote a school composition for me, rescued me from the desert of my mind. Above my signature he wrote several love letters for me, as occasions required, and in time, as you will see, he wrote my letter to my lover proposing marriage. In the hour of father's deepest travail Speed the scribe took charge of things and skillfully composed a curriculum vitae rescuing father from the disaster of unemployment. Speed wrote poetry, and eventually a precocious novel called *Love Never Surrenders*.

Yet everyone believed that I was the superior brother. I alone knew Speed's value. I alone knew the ways in which he was superior to me. The idea that Speed could do so many things so much better than I at first enraged me, infuriated me, kept me awake. I seethed. But the power of my longing for fairness enabled me to see beyond Speed to the larger world which God had made—so we were informed—and caused me to challenge God and doubt His existence. How could God have made the world so stupid that it missed the true virtue of Speed?

The problem was, of course, Speed's stuttering. Speed was a stutterer while I was a fluent rapid-fire speaker. The world therefore believed I was superior to Speed. Speed's speech was labori-

13

ous. He was unable to express long or complicated ideas regardless of how expressive he may have been with his brilliant hands and his brilliant inventive creative mind.

Father favored me, for father was of the world. My shoelaces tied tight, often on Sunday morning I accompanied father on his long walk up and down the glorious peaceful sweet-smelling streets of Mount Vernon, up the hill from the Sheridan Gardens Apartments past the Esplanade Gardens Apartments, down Lincoln Avenue to the Boston Westchester railroad station for father's New York *Daily Mirror* and his pack of smokes, and perhaps across the line into Pelham—

No, not *into* Pelham, not far, only inches and feet into Pelham, for the whole thrilling point of it was to pause on that spot of earth on the sidewalk beneath the railroad bridge to confront the directional sign "Entering Pelham," or, when you turned about again, "Entering Mount Vernon." Poised between the signs I was then by father's calculation half in Pelham, half in Mount Vernon. "Look at this miracle kid," father exhorted a grandstand never so real as Babe Ruth's, "look at this unbelievable boy."

There I stood in my own amazement, neither wholly in one town nor the other, a miracle boy in two towns, a little boy gone alone and unaccompanied to another town, yet only an arm's reach from his father. Then with a leap father and I exchanged places, reversing towns, so that I was in father's and father in mine. Then back together to Mount Vernon.

Along the way we stopped to talk to many people. This I did not enjoy, although I understood it was important to father. Father was appointed by the mayor, and these were the mayor's constituents. I would have preferred moving forward ceaselessly to the goodies that were in it for me as my reward for my forbearance, to candy and ice cream and orange juice and ice-cold soda and grandmother's bosom and song at Walk a Mile House at the end of the line.

If I were to be with father I wanted father to myself. Speed of course was out of the question. Speed was slow. That had always been grandfather's word for him—slow, Speed was slow. He was an embarrassment, a signal of father's weakness or failure, not the sort of thing father cared to advertise on these Sunday morning political tours. If Speed were with us people struggled by main force to bring forth speech from him, and when they failed they looked upon father sympathetically, telling him of cures for stuttering of which they had heard, of doctors who cured stuttering in a minute. Had he tried?

Yes, of course, we were trying all the time, said father, "always running back and forth to that big place in Delaware." He had taken Speed once to a medical facility in Delaware. But he had given up, he wasn't really trying any more, partly because it looked hopeless and if it wasn't hopeless it was certainly expensive. This I now see was my father's fatal flaw: his primitive idea that Speed was incurably doomed forever.

People were eager to pause along the way to talk to father. They saw him through their windows and came down the walks out of their houses. They shook his hand. They saluted him from passing cars. They flattered him by admiring his miracle son. They loved father's lingering brogue, his formidable muscle and brawn, his beef, his respectable presence. If you, Mr. Citizen, were talking to my father you were talking to the law, you were a friend of the law, you stood in shared space with the man who could have pinched you if he cared to, could have shot you dead on the spot if he cared to—no questions asked, "I thought the guy was going for a gun"—but he did not shoot you dead because you were a law-abiding citizen standing right here face to face with your good neighbor the police himself.

Sometimes father wore his off-duty uniform. Joke, no such thing existed, it was his duty uniform, and by wearing it he violated regulations. He wore it nonetheless as it pleased him to do so until he himself became chief, whereupon he enforced the rule he had broken. On these Sunday walks he shook hands, he shook hands, he shook hands. My feet hurt. He shuffled his claims. "Of course I'm Irish but I'm living in a Jewish street aren't I?" Or again, "True, I live in a Jewish street but I'm as Irish as you," or once again, face to face with a Protestant, "I'll never deny I was born an Irishman, we can't help what we were born, but what counts with me is the wife is Lutheran." He claimed to have been born in Mount Vernon, he claimed to have been born in New York City, he claimed to have been born in Ireland, he claimed to have been born on shipboard in passage from Ireland to America.

Words, words, words, words, how boring for me to listen to the talking! My feet hurt and my throat was parched. I endured it for father, all this jawing week in week out on whatever streets we walked, the same talk over and over, considerations of the beauty of the day, the health of the family, the state of the world, money, automobiles, race, religion, taxes, and I was condemned to stand waiting until they completed their conversation, which was never. It was all one conversation, and it was endless, I hated the sight of the next talking man in our path. When one man stopped the next began, and every man patted me on the head.

Father informed me that some of these men were wise men to whom I might listen with profit, but I did not care how wise they were, I was not ready for wisdom.

At last we arrived at Walk a Mile House where lived the wisest man of all. Father idolized him. Grandfather was rich, smart, shrewd, he was the man in command. So he certainly appeared. "When you consider what he's done blind," said father, "imagine what he would have done if he wasn't, he would have torn up the world. Listen to your grandfather. Everything he ever says is wisdom. Put it to use and it'll earn you money. He's the smartest man you'll ever meet."

How was grandfather smart? Grandfather had a hundred memory tricks. He carried five hundred phone numbers in his head and he could dial them in a flash. *Dial*, I'm talking *dial*, I'm not talking push-button Touch-Tone telephones forty years in the future. Grandfather carried in his head the names and addresses of one thousand top executives at one thousand top American companies and he could recite them for anyone who cared to flatter him by asking him to recite them. I played that flattery game. "Grandfather, tell me the names of some company presidents." And so he would. Speed deplored that streak in me. He said, "You're a d-d-d-d-d-d-d-d-d-d-d-d-d-d-d . . . "

16

"I'm a dirty little whore, am I?" But I pressed my silver coins to my palms and held them out for Speed to see.

How else was grandfather smart? "Men come to him," said father, "he don't go to other men."

That was a Sunday feature, the men who came to Walk a Mile House to meet with grandfather. They met in the west wing of Walk a Mile House, in the sun parlor so perfectly named when the sun was out. They laughed, they shouted, they swore, they sweated, they called one another by the names of famous financiers, they shrieked, they gasped, they choked in their own smoke, they spit into grandfather's spittoon, and they coughed a ceaseless chorus in spite of grandfather's famous worldwide slogan of cigarette safety: "Old Gold. Not a cough in a carload."

How could that be? Very early in life I heard Aunt Ember argue against this paradox in grandfather. Could grandfather be a liar, could he write one thing and cough another? To whom could I report this, as I had reported Florida license plates to father?

Father's presence in the uniform of the law endorsed the righteousness of the men in the sun parlor at Walk a Mile House. The sun parlor was a room almost circular, whose tall windows were bolted closed. It was airless—free, at least, of *fresh* air. That was the point. In the airtight sun parlor two or three times a day grandfather set fire to the contents of a vial of powder in a shallow pan and inhaled a substance informally named by me in baby talk: "burney-burney" for the relief of the terrible pressure symptomatic of his blindness. ("Burney-burney for the relief of glaucoma"—do you feel that advertising pulse? "Sal Hepatica for the Smile of Health . . . Ipana for the Smile of Beauty"—those too were grandfather's national poems.) I loved the smell of those burney-burney fumes. When I smelled it again thirty-five years later at the height of the era of the hippies it was not known as grandfather's "burney-burney" but as marijuana.

The airless hothouse sun parlor had an underworld feeling to it, the odor of a pool hall, the haze of a gaming den. Here were grandfather's toll-free illegal telephones with New York exchanges, robbing the telephone company of hundreds of dollars. His illicit phones impressed his visitors. If he loved the telephone company so much why did he rob it? Here were file cabinets I was not to open, although their sliding drawers were tempting, speeding along on tracks, in and out, open and shut.

Men came to grandfather with their dreams of money, to attach themselves to grandfather's projects or schemes, to be permitted to invest money in grandfather so that he might favor them by investing it elsewhere and in the end return their money to them not doubled or trebled or quadrupled but multiplied beyond even the contemplation of the English language, which has no word for money doubled or trebled or quadrupled over and over and over and over repeatedly and endlessly and infinitely until the modest investor and his chums have captured nothing less than the wealth of the universe.

The more the men smoked the more they laughed and shouted and cheered and applauded and clapped their hands and leaped from their chairs in optimistic excitement. Grandfather had sold the world Camel cigarettes and Victrola. Hadn't he? Well, no, not exactly. He had sold the *slogans*, words, catch phrases. At that sort of thing down grandfather's side of the family we were very good. Grandfather was a clever man of clever words. But Grandfather had not manufactured new products, as he now intended to do. These men of faith were prepared to wait, though not forever, as we shall see. Meanwhile they knew that grandfather was the rich and deserving author of "There's a Ford in Your Future . . . Santa Fe All the Way," that Grandfather gave birth to Chessie the Chesapeake Railway cat. Grandfather gave breakfast food "Snap, crackle, and pop . . . the Breakfast of champions . . . they're crisper." From grandfather came Coca-Cola, the drink you drink, "the Pause that Refreshes." Grandfather the bard sang not only of Camels and Old Gold but of Lucky Strikes, "They Satisfy."

"Time to Retire?" Fisk Rubber, you bet you. "Nibble a Nab for a Nickel," yes, there again was grandfather with his alliterative genius, filling the American stomach with Nabs: for a period of time every American man woman and child ate two tons of Nabs *per* day (estimate).

I was reminded some time ago by Aunt Ember, to whom I have gone for family information, that I had seldom been admitted to the sun parlor. "You couldn't have seen those men up close," she said. "The door was shut tight against children. You wouldn't have been let in."

"I saw them from the garden," I said.

"There were curtains on the windows," Aunt Ember said. "It was a steambath. No, it was an oven where they cooked up their schemes. Your grandfather was the chef and your poor father was the kitchen boy."

I saw them from the garden with grandmother," I said.

"When the weather was good," Aunt Ember said.

Grandmother made the weather good. In the garden I rocked with grandmother in her chair. We watched her tulips grow. Sometimes I fell asleep, my head upon her breast. She sang to me.

When I think of grandmother's music I think first of that comic old song which may have been suggested to her thought by the men behind the curtains in the airtight room in the smoke above.

> Willie, Willie, oh so silly,
> Smoked a big cigar.
> Took a puff, that's enough,
> Silly boy you are.
> They had to call the doctor in because it made him ill.

I've never known if that last line belongs. Surely it does not *look* as if it belongs. Grandmother would not have cared. She improvised. Petty correctness was nothing to her.

In Walk a Mile House scarcely an hour of the day passed free of flame and smoke and the sight of the men fussing, puffing, the fabulous shapes of blue smoke curling to the ceiling, the knocking of pipes, and the varieties of fragrance. Grandmother could have anticipated this historical note: of the men of the family residing for various periods at Walk a Mile House—grandfather's brothers, grandmother's brothers, nephews, cousins, sons-in-law, say thirty altogether—twenty died of cigarettes.

She rose early, worked hard all day, and retired late, keeping the peace if possible among the men of the house, pacifying all warring parties and factions, protecting all children from the worst sounds of dispute. She took upon herself every duty, yet she was always available, surely one of the world's great mute humanitarians, who could never issue a stern command to a black maid though she be lectured a thousand times by her husband on the inferiority of blacks and her duty to make them sweat.

Grandmother never engaged in dinner-table discussions of history, grammar, politics. Her thoughts were elsewhere. Although grandfather kept the radio very loud at dinner she ignored it, she was lost in her own head. She never laughed at anything any comedian ever said, and she never appeared to respond to the most catastrophic news events as they were brought to us by Gabriel Heatter and Lowell Thomas. She cared nothing for statistics, facts. Whose head was on which coin or bill? Grandmother cared nothing for that. She was never, like grandfather, moralistic, she never bored me with sermons, never forced me to pretend to be interested in anything I was not interested in, never described to me some future world I'd better be aware of.

Aunt Ember once told me I seemed as a boy to prefer women to men, and I think this must have been true. Mother and grandmother made more sense to me than their husbands. Rocking in grandmother's arms in her chair in the garden was a thousand times more delightful to me than tramping the streets with father, shaking hands. Grandmother's softness engaged me, her breasts were dreamland itself, to which I departed without leaving her arms soon after her music began.

She was an abused person. Grandfather took mistresses—took them, indeed, directly into the sun parlor, though not on Sunday when his visiting investors were already sufficiently excited. She had nursed grandfather for years through the physical and spiritual agony of his fading eyesight, but they had not for years engaged in conversation.

Grandmother and I walked out to see sad moving pictures. She assured me the film was only make-believe—"it's not really happening"—but it was she who was weeping, not I. She wept to read sad novels, too, and told the plots to mother on the telephone. As time went on she spoke more and more freely to mother of her distaste for grandfather, of her plan to flee, to live somewhere alone, however humbly, but those were flights of her fancy only.

I felt her oppression in her behalf, and I often wondered why she obeyed him so loyally. When he called her name he expected her to hurry to him wherever she was. Wherever she was, she always heard him call. Often I wished she might have pretended otherwise. He often called out, "Are you in the room?" She needn't have answered. He wouldn't have known. I played that trick on him myself. But though I sometimes took hope from an instant of her hesitation she quickly so softly replied, "What do you need?"

I saw her only once exploit his blindness. That was a moment in the garden, too. Guests stood about with glasses in their hands. At some signal everyone rather quickly passed from the garden to the house. For some reason grandfather had not received the signal. Grandmother saw from the kitchen that he had been left alone, and she knew, as I did, that when he discovered what had happened he would erupt in a fury of embarrassment. I saw in her face her temptation to go to him, to rescue him, but she chose not to do so. She assumed an expression of regretful sorrow, of pride, as if to say, "I know my duty to you, but you have failed yours to me, I'll just leave you there."

I had thought of grandmother as a fleshy, heavy person, no doubt because, when I sank to sleep on her bosom in the garden, I felt myself enveloped by her flesh, I was blissfully aware of the *feel* of her beyond the sight of her. Then, too, I vividly *saw* her flesh, too, her thigh, the bare white flesh of her thigh when, to pay the iceman or the grocer's delivery boy, she turned slightly away from all eyes, lifted her skirt, lowered the top of her stocking, and in a flash withdrew her modest roll of dollar bills. Five, six, eight. Not much. What you saw was what she had.

One Sunday at Walk a Mile House a grand ceremony occurred, not in the sun parlor but in a large room in the attic suite. This was a day of supreme importance to me, the day of the installation of

Walk a Mile Railway. Men owned automobiles. Grandfather also owned a railroad. He cut a ribbon to celebrate the occasion, and all the men cheered who had adjourned for the moment from the sun parlor to the attic suite to raise their glasses to "the greatest little railroad in the world."

Walk a Mile Railway had been under construction for many weeks, and I as a ranking and favored child was thought by grandfather to have been following the event with interest. I don't remember doing so. I had been invited to come to watch the men build it, and I think I once went for an hour or less, but I really did not care for a railroad merely in progress.

It was situated on a waist-high table on powerful legs. The table so filled the room we could not walk around it. To cross from one side of the table to the other the life-sized human trainman, woman, boy, girl, was required to crawl beneath the table. This discouraged the participation of adults, who did not like to crawl. I did not mind crawling, but I disliked the extensive network of tangled wires beneath the table. I did not wish to be shocked. Life was shocking enough.

At the great opening of the railway grandfather's admiring men up from the sun parlor were loud and outspoken and probably sincere in their admiration for the layout. The table was a town—houses, streets, automobiles, human figures, animal figures. At its center was a railroad station. All tracks led to the railroad station, and all tracks led away, in a complex arrangement of comings and goings. I always expected that at any moment a collision would end all operations, but in reality every track was an independent line, and the railroad was therefore a *model* railroad: no collision ever occurred, nobody was ever hurt. The mountaintops were capped with cotton snow.

In motion the rumbling of the trains drowned conversation, bells rang, sirens sounded, warning signals flashed, and somewhere in the countryside at the far end of the table a pasteboard cow periodically called "Moo-oo." Of all the mechanical marvels-in-motion on the table—hundreds of pieces—the mechanization of the cow delighted me most.

For some years after the installation of Walk a Mile Railway I had no interest in it. I barely remembered it was there. Speed, who might have enjoyed it, avoided Walk a Mile Railway as he avoided Walk a Mile House, and for the same reason: every symbol of grandfather depressed him. Grandfather, on the other hand, was depressed by Speed. "Speed is missing out on the power and glory of railroading," grandfather said. "He can't deny credit where credit is due, railroads changed the face of the nation. If he'd study the railroad he'd learn the lesson of America."

I do not know if I learned the lesson I was expected to learn. I learned that cows were as loud and as large as steam engines from which, in fact, no steam emanated. Walk a Mile Railroad was supposed to teach us children how to buy and sell railroad tickets and spell the names of difficult places like Chautauqua, Genesee, Niagara, Onondaga, and Syracuse (this was a New York State railroad), and it was supposed to acquaint us with electrical principles, but all of this I either soon learned on my own—how to buy a railway ticket, how to spell—or never learned or cared to learn: electrical principles.

Grandfather never visited the only railroad he ever owned. He hated to climb stairs. As for myself, for years I was distant from it. When at last, after the passage of time, I returned to it everything appeared to be in place, exactly as I had seen it on the first day of its operation, as if no one had been there since. I flipped the switch and everything resumed, the trains gained speed, the giant cow moo-ed, houses lit up all over town, signals flashed, whistles sounded, and I began my long, educational, erotic, sensational association with that railroad. When you hear about the railroad phase of my life I think you'll wish you'd been me.

23

CHAPTER TWO

OUR LIVES as boys were never more bleak for Speed and me than when we compared the Sheridan Gardens Apartments to the Esplanade Gardens Apartments. The Esplanade was seven stories high, crowned with gargoyles and conical towers. Sheridan Gardens Apartments, to which father had taken us, was only four stories high and flat-roofed. Speed and I wished it otherwise. G-men with machine guns on the roof of the Esplanade Gardens Apartments firing down on the Sheridan Gardens Apartments could have wiped us out in twenty minutes. In every way we lacked the class of the Esplanade.

Gardens? What gardens? There were never any gardens.

Sheridan Gardens Apartments had four wings, called A, B, C, and D, and four apartments on each of the four floors of each wing, 1,2,3,4. Father, mother, Speed, and I lived in the second apartment on the ground floor of wing D. Thus, 2–D. The apartment above us was 22–D. Above that 32–D. Above that, 42–D. Above that the roof of baking, steaming, sticking tar in summer, where we were forbidden to go in every season for fear of our falling over the side or of our being hurled to our deaths by perverts.

Esplanade Gardens, *seven* stories high, was divided as the Sheridan Gardens Apartments was, into four parts, four Houses, but within each of its houses nestled *five* apartments to a floor. The arithmetic was unanswerable: *seven* stories multiplied by four wings multiplied by *five* apartments achieved a total for the enemy of one hundred and forty apartments, whereas we down the hill in the Sheridan Gardens Apartments could muster forces numbering only four by four by four to a shameful sixty-four.

These numbers said to me that the people of the Esplanade were richer and finer than we by a ratio of one hundred and forty to sixty-four. They were also closer to the East Lincoln Avenue bus line.

The bitterest medicine may have been this, that the Sheridan Gardens Apartments was a walk-up, no elevators, whereas the Esplanade had an elevator in each wing. Each Esplanade elevator was individual and distinct. Blindfold me, thrust me into any elevator, I could have told you where I was. I could tell you today, I think. I knew each of those elevators by the song of its cables. Speed and I discovered elevator tricks, how to make the thing go with the gate open, how to make it go with the lights off. Up and down we went in the dark elevator, gate open, light off, defying the tenants waiting at each floor. They screamed, they called, they shook their fists, they condemned the "super"—an immigrant wretch thirty days off the boat huddled with his famished family in rooms in the cellar.

Speed and I clung like monkeys to the overhead grillwork, lifting ourselves from the elevator floor, deceiving the mechanism which, thinking itself weightless, responded to the tenants' relentless angry ringing of the call bell. Thus Speed and I were carried to the floor to which we were summoned, where the tenant opening the door to the sight of two hanging boys scared himself to death.

One winter day in an Esplanade elevator I maneuvered myself into intimate contact with a girl named Clara Baum, embraced her and knew despite the thicknesses of our intervening winter garments the excitement of her body and advised my brother to try the same thing first chance he got.

Sheridan Gardens Apartments, low and vulnerable, could have been invaded at any hour of the night by the children of the Wartburg orphan asylum. This was a near and present danger about which Speed and I deliberated in our early years. We were especially frightened of orphans since we had never seen any. "The Wart" was an institution hidden from our view by heavy woods, but what we never saw we sometimes heard through our open windows when dusk was balmy, for at that hour the orphanage band played "The Star-Spangled Banner" for the lowering of the flag.

The question arose in father's mind whether, hearing the anthem through the window, we were required to stand. I am amazed now to recall that he thought we should. If we did not stand for the anthem our patriotism lay in doubt, at least in father's own mind. Father was not yet at ease in a neighborhood of Jews. He had weathered some more or less good-natured ribbing from his colleagues down the station—had he given up pork? had he gone to the temple to be circumcised?—and he felt himself properly under suspicion as an anti-Christ anti-American. He felt he may have made a mistake in following Aunt Ember's advice. He worried about a hypothetical passerby, a foe who might, by looking into our window, catch us languidly, defiantly sitting down just at the moment the anthem was playing, as if we cared nothing for America.

Mother ridiculed his fear. "I feel like a moron standing up for the music in my own house," she said.

"How do you know those rules?" father asked.

"Dear," she said, "it's common sense."

For a while, however, apart from mother's common sense, we stood when the anthem was played by the Wartburg band. We rose from dinner. We rose from our places before the radio. Our silly practice continued at least until father became sufficiently secure of himself as police chief to reinterpret the law, overrule himself, and remain seated in his own house.

Sometimes father came gliding through the neighborhood in a squad car, pausing among us boys to see whether we were behaving ourselves. When he came on us behind the Esplanade we begged him to throw a ball to the roof. Father could throw a ball seven floors to the roof of the Esplanade Gardens. Not many fathers could throw a ball anywhere. I judged a boy's character by his father's throwing style. A father who could not throw hard and gracefully placed his son in doubt.

Father was graceful and strong, his arms were powerfully muscled. He stepped from his squad car. He removed his hat, his uniform jacket. He unbelted his revolver. He loosened his necktie, he rolled his sleeve above his elbow, he took the ball, he eyed the roof, he bounced the ball hard to test it. He asked, "What have you boys been thinking you're doing?" Nothing, just playing around, we said. "Not getting in no mischief," he said. "No sir, no sir." "I better not hear about any." "No sir, no sir, you won't." No other father was "sir." But then, no other father was police chief. Other fathers were merchants, bookkeepers, accountants, shopkeepers, petty clerks, drivers, slaves of the offices of the city to which they commuted on the New Haven and the Central or, for some years, on the ambitious New York Westchester & Boston Railway crashing into bankruptcy three hundred miles south of Boston.

Few fathers could throw a ball to the roof. Few? Who else? Offhand I cannot remember another. Few fathers glided by with guns on their hips in the middle of the afternoon, and no fathers at all were members of the police force. Policemen lived in another part of town, with firemen.

Father reared back, he threw, and the ball rocketed to the sky, much higher than the Esplanade, nine, ten stories high before it gave out, fell to the roof. "Lost ball," he said. We knew his meaning—we were not to retrieve the ball from the roof. But of course when father's squad car was out of sight we did.

Father's power delighted me, thrilled me, but Speed's power humiliated me. Soon Speed, too, could throw a ball to the Esplanade roof, seven stories high at nine years old. I was a year older than he and I could not quite throw the damn ball to the dirty fuckin bastard sonofabitchin roof. My throws grazed the seventh-floor ledge and fell back.

I hated Speed for his prowess, his ease, the confidence with which he wound up and twirled, not with father's show of strength, simply with Speed's own ease, not so much hurling it as tossing it, gazing with interest and without much doubt and with essential confidence at the arc of the ball as it cleared the ledge and fell silently to the roof.

He had not given it much to spare. He had not rocketed it high as father had, nor had he meant to. He had given it only power enough. His fundamental power remained in reserve for the next time, for tomorrow, for whenever he might care again to throw to the roof.

At some moments I truly hated him. I wished his arm would fall off. He may have known my agony, but he never taunted me, never teased me, never flaunted the profound idea that he, one year younger than I, could throw a ball day after day higher than I could throw it. I envied not alone his art and accuracy, not alone the power of his throwing but almost above all the invisible power he held in reserve, the power lying always unexpended and latent within him. He was the athlete. I died a thousand deaths.

Father said Jews loved money. So did I. Once a young man named John Didakis came to the neighborhood in a battered old Essex looking for boys (girls were out of the question) to sell the *Saturday Evening Post*. Stacked on the rear seat of his car were hundreds of copies of the *Post* tied with tough cord in packages of five.

A magazine "route" was said to be an enviable possession. One had it like a grant from a king. I do not know who declared John Didakis king, but he managed it royally—he was a shrewd king stingy with his grants lest they devalue themselves in the public mind.

I wanted a route. Speed wanted a route. John Didakis saw in us, I think, boys with a reliable look who might very well prove to be dependable long-term salesman for him and the Curtis Publishing Company of Philadelphia. John's problem was whether to choose Speed or me. It never entered his head or ours that Speed and I might sell as *partners*. No, the code of the age called for one or the other.

To settle the matter he handed each of us a copy of the current issue of the *Post*, gave us a few minutes to "look it over," and, holding a nickel between two fingers in the air, challenged us to sell it to him with a "spiel." "Study it and give me a spiel," he said. "Give me an argument why this magazine is worth my nickel. My nickels are precious. I've got a family to feed." With his free hand he introduced us to the panoramic spectacle of the Sheridan Gardens Apartments, "sixty-four apartments in there with sixty-four men with families to feed." Sixty-three, he meant. Aunt Ember lived alone.

I studied the magazine. *This* was something to read. This was my first appreciation of professional journalism. *This* was a magazine. I was amazed, flabbergasted, inspired. Look at this marvelous thing! How did they put so much genius in here? I deeply inhaled the odor of it. I caressed its silken page. I returned to John Didakis with my spiel. He held his nickel in his hand. "Mr. Customer," I began, displaying the magazine before me, "this here magazine is going to keep you reading for hours and I'm standing at your door telling you now why you want to buy it from me with your hard-earned nickel. Just the advertisements alone have got more colors in them than anything you ever saw, and helpful, too, and the jokes are funny and the cartoons will keep you rolling in the aisles. Here's stories and true articles for the whole family no matter who you are—"

"That's enough, good enough," said John Didakis, "it may be the best I ever heard," and he said to Speed, "Now you, let's hear your spiel," but Speed was incapable of delivering a spiel to celebrate the wonders of the *Saturday Evening Post*. I remember his beginning his effort quite as if he truly expected a spiel to come forth. In the excitement of possibility—profits every week in money and merchandise—he had for a moment assumed a world so abundant with pleasure no man would stutter. I too had forgotten that Speed could not spiel. On that day he could not even stutter. He was simply unable to speak. He held the magazine before him like a shield, but he was mute, nothing came from his mouth at all, no sound.

Language he had, but not speech. On paper he was very good. Beginning early in life he was a superb writer. But he was no speaker, no spieler, and John Didakis, who was, after all, a busy king with an Essex loaded with *Saturday Evening Posts*, ended the contest swiftly and decisively with his royal edict: "O.K., you," meaning O.K., me. He never looked at Speed again.

I was now a salesman for the *Saturday Evening Post*, founded by Benjamin Franklin. I never delivered a spiel to a customer. Everybody knew the *Saturday Evening Post*. It was then the outstanding popular magazine of America and continued to be so for years. John Didakis gave me five copies of the *Post*, a shoulder bag to carry them in, and a catalogue of prizes and premiums in merchandise waiting in Philadelphia for a high-flying salesman like me. He took my telephone number and my address, grunted a message of luck, and in his clattering Essex departed.

During my first week I sold five copies easily. It was as nothing, no challenge. My route was grandfather, Aunt Ember, my Uncle Kevin (who was also a policeman), my Uncle Wilhelm who lived on Summit Avenue, and father. Father had no use for a magazine, but when he saw that I had sold four *Post*s he bought the fifth. Through all the years I sold the *Post* he bought a copy every week without ever opening one. Mother read the stories "complete in this issue," scorning serials which were "nothing but a trick to make you buy it next week."

The magazine cost five cents a copy. The boy who sold it received a commission of a penny and a half. For every five magazines a boy sold he received one green gift coupon. Five green coupons were equal to one brown coupon, exchangeable for valuable objects for pleasure and use.

I did all my Christmas shopping with Curtis Publishing Company brownies and greenies, for I was one of those rare boys who could plan for Christmas in June. I supplied myself with most of the athletic equipment I was ever to need. It was cheap shopping.

I loved those brown and green coupons because they were money. I also loved my brother except when I felt compelled to hurt him. I was never so filled with satisfaction as when I was writing out orders and sending off coupons for shining gifts for myself. I felt that each gift aroused my brother's envy, although I think now that I might have been wrong, that it may have aroused only his contempt for my thinking so well of myself that I should present myself with so many gifts. Gifts, brownies, greenies, it was all money and I loved money. I accumulated money. Speed never accumulated money. The greatest sum he ever held in his hand he lost within an hour in a sexual quest. We will arrive there.

After my first week I asked John Didakis to increase me from five to ten magazines so I might begin selling to strangers. Soon I was selling twenty a week, thirty, and finally sixty, earning a profit of ninety cents, two brown stamps, and two green stamps per week.

My route, my grant from the king, was the Sheridan Gardens Apartments, the Esplanade Gardens Apartments, the Bailey Park Apartments, Franklin Towers, and side streets I can name to this day though I've been back to the neighborhood for only two hours these fifty years. What was a route? It was only what one made it. It wasn't anything. If you had a few customers on Magnolia Avenue and a few more in House Three of the Esplanade, that was your route. The king was an illusion.

If my *Saturday Evening Post* career was a victory over Speed I paid for it in the misery of weekly discomfort. I hated rising at dawn, tramping up and down the apartment-house stairs, strangled in the strap of my heavy bag of magazines. To avoid harsh weather I could pass from wing to wing of the apartment houses through the connecting warm basements, but the basements were frightening, too, bad things happened there, in the basement of the Esplanade Gardens Apartments a man had been murdered.

I hated dawn ever afterward. Anticipation was worse than the experience. I dreamed bad dreams of dark dawns and bloody basements every week of my boy's life, usually the night before *Post* day. At dawn at each customer's door I rolled a copy of the *Post* to insert between the knob and the wall, or I slid it under the door. How I knew those air spaces under the doors! No room, jam it in the knob. But in the knob it could be stolen, the customer could claim he never got it. Under the door was a sure thing. In the hand was best of all, I could ask for my nickel then and there. "Later I'll

31

give it to you, come back." "Ma'am, I'm going to be awfully busy later." "You got change of a five then?" "Change of a five?" Translation: Fuck you change of a five, where does a boy get change of a five, go in your change purse and find me a nickel you old hag. "Give me a minute, I'll look," and she made me wait, too, until she came shuffling back with a nickel.

I kept meticulous records. I knew who paid what for how many issues, who owed what, and to whom I owed change. I never forgot, on the theory that my customer never forgot, either.

And the odor of food through those doors! Coffee in the morning. Collecting my money at night I learned the meaning of the phrase *his mouth watered*. The customer came to the door napkin in hand, food in the mouth, cheeks swelling with food, chewing his food, licking his lips; food frying, hissing, boiling, somebody slicing cake on the breadboard, tea darkening in the glass.

From apartment to apartment I followed the radio. I waited at the door for the comedians' jokes—stalled with my foot in the door until I heard Eddie Cantor's punchline, stalled with my foot in the door during "Amateur Hour" to hear Major Bowes's verdict on the contestant, stalled with my foot in the door for the ball scores in season.

I collected a nickel apiece from my customers if I was lucky. Not everybody was home, at least to me—some people were home but chose not to answer the door. I could hear their radios, the bastards. Door-to-door collecting was agony, hideous, the nadir of every week of my boyhood. Everyone was dining but me. Everyone was at home listening to the radio but me. Dogs barked at me. People became angry at me for waking them up. I never really earned ninety cents a week. Ninety cents was theory only. Stolen magazines and bad debts diminished my profits.

Not many years had passed since the night I learned on the floor of our living-room to tie my shoelaces, and here I was again, on a Sunday night, struggling in the midst of another crisis. Now, however, I was sitting on the sofa, not on the floor.

Once I had been desperate to tie my shoes by Monday. Now I

was desperate to decide by tomorrow what "My Occupational Life Intention" was. That was the title of the composition I was required to write for Mrs. Packard-Steinberg for Occupational Guidance.

Mrs. Packard-Steinberg was the only schoolteacher ever to live in the Sheridan Gardens Apartments. She taught her course, Occupational Guidance, with all her energy over a period of many years in declining health (mental) to protect the children of our school from squandering their lives. She worried about us. In class she wept or seemed to weep at the possibility of the misery lying ahead for us, she held her head in her hands, she turned her face to the wall in despair when she described to us the hideous conditions of the job marketplace. She provided us with—entertained us with, one might say—vivid, lurid accounts of young men and women gone wrong, wandering bereft and poverty-stricken across the planet looking for work. (Certain of those bereft girls "ready to do anything" I wished I could meet, for at that age I was becoming sexual.) She was always cold. She wore sweaters of the brightest primary colors. A teacher wearing a sweater was unusual in those days.

Mrs. Packard-Steinberg in her classroom could always illustrate everything with something else. She showed us pictures and read us more or less relevant stories and poems and delivered more or less relevant Shakespearean soliloquies to dramatize the plight of the American worker in the twentieth century. She maneuvered the arts into Occupational Guidance.

She made things especially interesting by setting up the movie screen for films and slides. Once she showed us a wonderful animated cartoon about a rare bird. Its fresh-laid egg would hatch a new automobile. She danced around, calling out with excitement, as if she had never seen this film, "I'm rich, I'm rich, I'm rich, my bird will lay me a new automobile every day." Of course she had seen the cartoon fifty times, but we boys and girls were there for the first time. She sang and jumped about to the music of the film. The role she created for herself she played in the jolliest liveliest way *ensemble* with the animated cartoon. But at the end—tragedy, serious disappointment. The bird could produce only one automobile in her lifetime, and she had just done it. Today's egg was the last. "Every bird in this life gets one chance," Mrs. Packard-Steinberg told us. "Take it when it comes. There's no waiting around for miracles."

Mrs. Packard-Steinberg was not thinking just of *jobs.* She was an idealist. She viewed her own work, too, as more than a bread-and-butter job. To teach children, to guide them—to be the guidance teacher—was a mission, a calling, a divine opportunity never consciously mingled with purely secular objectives. "I want everybody in this class to become famous and worthwhile," she said. She told us her dream for the children of Wilson School in the form of a few lines of poetry so moving to her she could never recite them without struggling for breath.

> Who can pass a district school
> Without the hope that there may wait
> Some baby-heart the books shall flame
> With zeal to make his playmates great . . .

"Do you see what I'm saying? I'm the poet and who are you? I am the person passing the district school and you are the baby-hearts. You are the somebody in here who is going to work hard and make us famous, lift us up high in the world, make the world better than it used to be."

It was her devout wish that we make our families proud of us eternally, that we send our names down the years into history, that we uplift mankind, set the slaves free, as Lincoln had done, and if there were no slaves to set free *find some.*

To prepare for our essays we prepared "life profiles." We answered questionnaires.

What would I do in life?
I did not know.
How would I feed myself if I were "left to my own devices"?
I loved the phrase but I did not know the answer.
What skills did I have?
Selling the *Saturday Evening Post* to sixty families a week in sev-

eral apartment houses and up and down several side streets of Mount Vernon, New York, among them the family of Mrs. Packard-Steinberg herself, Apartment 24–B, Sheridan Gardens Apartments.

How much money did I earn by the use of those skills?

Ninety cents per week in theory, less in actuality.

Would that sum be sufficient to support me when I became an adult?

No.

Had I given this matter much thought?

Never until the composition was assigned by Mrs. Packard-Steinberg.

What plans had I made for my occupational future?

None.

She had frightened me. She told us of men and women, some of them graduates of our own school, who, *neglecting to present her with a composition entitled "My Occupational Life Intention,"* had gone forth unready into the cruel unsympathetic world without skills, without plan. The future was Monday, in Mrs. Packard-Steinberg's classroom at eleven o'clock when the composition was due. Children of the past who had failed their crucial assignment had ended by sleeping in the gutters, begging for crusts in the windswept service alleys behind the kitchens of glamorous hotels. Did I want to end that way?

No.

"That's a lot of you-know-what hogwash," father said. "What makes you think everybody else in the whole class know what they're going to do for an occupation?"

"They said so."

"They told you so?"

"They raised their hand."

"Anybody can raise their hand," said father. "Look at me, I'm raising my hand. Anybody can raise their hand Friday afternoon and tell you they're going to know something by Monday. It's a long time from Friday till Monday."

"Nobody really knows what they're going to do in life," said mother comfortingly.

"Any kid that knows what they're going to do in life in the ninth grade is a goddamn liar," father said. He was not angry. He was presenting facts.

"But, dear," said mother to me, "she's right to start you thinking about it. I have a suggestion. I think it's a perfectly good one, too. Think up an occupation and write about it and hand it in. You're good at thinking up things like that, out of your imagination."

"I'm not supposed to imagine it, it's supposed to be real, something I've got the facts about, the conditions of the work and the skills it takes."

"Write about the police," said father.

"You don't want me to be a policeman."

"You can write about one without being one."

"Did you ever think seriously about any kind of work to do in life?" mother asked.

"I've thought about being a mailman," I said. The idea of being a mailman had lately tempted me and I'll tell you why. Don't laugh. Tolerate my boyhood. It was sexual, romantic. I had begun to imagine women alone in their houses. A mailman (always mail-*man* in those days) walked around in residential neighborhoods from which all the men were gone all day. Only the women remained in their houses pining to exhibit themselves naked to boys like me. That was the job description as I saw it.

"That's not a bad idea," mother said.

"It's a lousy idea," father said.

"Dear," said mother, "it's not a bad idea to *write* about."

"Why would you want to be a letter-carrier?" father asked.

"It's steady work, it's within my abilities and interests, it's good health in the outdoors, and it performs a service for mankind," I said. Those were among Mrs. Packard-Steinberg's criteria.

"You won't get rich," father said.

"Just write it up," mother suggested.

"It's just crazy nonsense," father said. "A boy doesn't have to decide such a thing by tomorrow. What time tomorrow?"

"By eleven o'clock," I said.

"Holy Christ," said father, "then you better get to work."

*   *   *

We had in our living-room a "secretary," as we called it, an out-sized ancient object which may have been intended as a desk, may have been intended as a bureau, and was in any case a confused creation, at one moment a rolltop desk with a flat surface for writing, at another moment a chest of drawers for the seasonal storage of garments—gloves, hats, shawls, scarves, ear muffs, and woollen socks.

At that useless beauty that night I began to write my little composition. It went poorly, slowly, and finally not at all. I was thinking too hard about naked ladies waiting for their mail. My page, too, was naked. Once during that long evening mother passed through the living-room to find me sitting there idle. "Don't you think Mrs. Packard-Steinberg might let you speak this composition instead of writing it?" she asked. "You're such a good speaker. It seems only fair, dear."

"No, it wouldn't be fair. The other kids are all writing their composition. Nobody's speaking."

"It's only that you're so good at talking," mother said.

"She'd never let me."

"We don't know what she might accept. She's a warm and open-hearted person."

"She's crazy," I said.

"A little *peculiar*, dear, yes, she might be that, but we don't want to call people crazy too soon. And a lot of people are crazy besides her. Maybe I can speak to her for you."

"In the middle of the night?"

Mother left our apartment for a moment. Winter rushed in. I knew where she was going. She went to the window of the stairway landing to see if the Packard-Steinbergs' light was on. She returned. "Their light is on."

"Still no," I said.

"I value you for your honesty," said mother, and she kissed me on the top of my head. "But if you change your mind I'll call her first thing in the morning."

I had the feeling there at midnight, dreaming of bed, that to fail the composition was to fail not the composition alone but all the future as well, to become a derelict, a wanderer, a starvation case on the streets of big cities. The whole thing was imminent. In eleven hours the future began. Every bird in this life gets one chance, and I had had mine. Don't wait around for miracles. I was a goner. My future was past. I fell asleep at the secretary.

Soon I awoke. When I awoke I found lying there at my elbow an essay entitled according to instructions "My Occupational Life Intention," composed by Speed on his own Durable Tablet notepaper colored differently from mine to avoid dispute between us.

I did not read it. At eleven o'clock in the morning in our class in Occupational Guidance we passed our compositions to the front of the room. When Mrs. Packard-Steinberg swept my composition into her arms with all the rest the matter departed my mind. Composition done, the future was settled. The whole idea of the postal service also departed my mind, naked ladies, good health, chance for promotion and all. I did not hold those pieces of paper in my hand again for twenty years, when I read them for the first time.

Three days later Mrs. Packard-Steinberg was sitting in our living-room in her overcoat. Beneath her coat she wore two of her bright classroom sweaters. She had never been in our apartment and I wished she were not there now. When I entered, Mrs. Packard-Steinberg stood, as if I were a divinity. She had been thinking of me for two days, and at night she had been admitting me to her dreams. "I've been telling your mother what a wonderful boy you are," she said.

"I've been telling my mother the same thing for years."

"He's clever," said Mrs. Packard-Steinberg.

"I try," said I.

"You try and you succeed," she said. "Your composition was the most wonderful any pupil has ever turned in in all the years I've been teaching."

"I gave it my best," I said.

"He did," said mother, "He sat there half the night with it. Right there at the secretary."

"Half the night," said Mrs. Packard-Steinberg with admiration. She could not get over it. It was wonderful. "You're a boy who's thinking far out ahead of yourself," she said. "If only we had thousands and thousands of young people like you all our problems would be solved. You have a special skill, a special mercy I think I'll say, I see that you are going to be a very big man in your time."

"I'm already five-feet-ten," I said.

Oh how she laughed at my wit! "It's not as if you're too serious, either," she said, "you've got a real live-wire sense of humor and that's going to carry you far when you have dark moments, too, because a boy like you, as smart and as brainy and as generous in his heart as you is going to have dark moments out there in the future. I can tell you that."

"But it's not going to be an all-dark future, then," said mother.

"Oh no, it's going to be more bright than dark," said Mrs. Packard-Steinberg.

"He was worried about your class," said mother.

"Of course he was worried. That's a big part of his conscientiousness, that he worried, that he sat up late with this great work"—she was presenting mother with the composition Speed had written—"that's how it's done, that's how great men proceed. I've read the biographies of great men and there you are, you have one right in front of you in your own house."

"Ember's palmist says he's going to get rich talking," mother said. "With his mouth. It's only now that he's breaking through with his writing."

Mrs. Packard-Steinberg scowled at me a little. "Do you go to palmists?"

"Aunt Ember goes to palmists."

"Better. I didn't think you would. You're too scientific, you're too far-seeing and visionary, you have the mind of a great man. Where do your ideas come from?"

"I get a lot of them from my brother," I said.

"Your brother," she said a little doubtfully. "He's the boy who—"

39

"Stutters," I said.

"He has a slight speech defect," said mother.

"I'll have your brother next year," she said, "but he'll never equal you. How can anyone equal you?" Now she plunged across the room and kissed me and I had had enough of that.

Speed's composition (technically *my* composition) begins:

Money is such a great thing too bad there's not enough to go around. We keep it all in one place instead of spreading it around. My occupational life intention is to work as hard as I can, work my fingers to the bone if I must, to spread the wealth around to all the people everywhere. I intend to be a lifelong worker employed by the Share the Wealth movement, making it the biggest movement in the world, as it deserves to be. One of these days you will see Share the Wealth headquarters on every street corner. Here in Mount Vernon Share the Wealth will take over the whole building Proctor's Theater now is in. The starving people of China will be things of the past. We have all seen pictures of the starving children on the streets of China. At least we have if we read the newspapers, which we should daily. Some people have too little and others have too much. This would not occur if we shared the wealth. I say to you, "Share the Wealth," follow me along the paths of the world to newer and greater prosperity for all. How? By sharing the wealth, by giving every person what they need to live in a comfortable house protected against the weather with food for the whole family, a radio, electric lights, ice box or refrigerator, and all other necessities.

Mrs. Packard-Steinberg marked those pages in the margins. She wrote "Wow!" and "Yes!"and "Good!" and "Great!" and "Young man, you are superb!!!" She forgave punctuation errors, she loved the work for its message, as readers do.

Speed in the later paragraphs of my composition is sensible and reasonable, imaginative—creative, we say. Fifty years later a cartoon in The New Yorker portrayed two bloated clubmen in fine leather chairs, drinks in hand, cigars in hand, one man saying to the other, "Everybody loves money. Too bad there isn't enough to go around." When I came across it I felt that the cartoon artist, one

Bernard Schoenbaum, had stolen the idea from my brother Speed.

Mother read my essay on the telephone to grandfather who in the course of time invited me to dinner. Of all the nights of my life this was to be of more importance to me than almost any other, not because of anything grandfather said to me, oh no, not that at all, but because of something else so wonderful I can hardly wait to tell you about it.

We were three for dinner, grandmother, grandfather, and I. This dinner was for me. Later we were to go, grandfather and I, to the sun parlor man to man. Then I would learn the reason for my invitation.

But grandmother counted for me, if not for him. He could not see the smiles she and I exchanged at table, nor her reaching for my hand. She said to me once, "I wonder what will become of you, my dear child, when I am dead and gone." Of the thousands of sentences grandfather spoke to me none was so loving as that. He could not see—because he could not *see*—that even as he was delivering several consecutive after-dinner addresses my eyes were wandering, inattentive. From time to time I said, as grandmother did, "Yes, I understand, I think you're certainly right," but I may not have truly heard him.

Since grandmother and I offered no resistance to grandfather's thoughts he must have begun that evening in a lower key than usual. Sometimes, when his brothers, his nephews, his sons-in-law came to dinner they disputed him and caused him to shout. He was a shouter and a table-banger. Often, impatient with me and with others, with our stupidity, our lack of initiative, our deadened sense of invention, our ignorance of geography, our deficiency in mental arithmetic, our inability to draw from history exactly the conclusions he had drawn, grandfather pounded the table to drive home his points, pounded plates, cups, saucers, pounded tines of forks and sent the forks flying through the air. We children retrieved the forks from the floor. I hated that pounding bit. I hated seeing it coming, watching him feeling about, running his hands over the tablecloth, seeking a clear space to pound away without overturning soup, cups, and glasses. We children often rushed to remove objects from the path of his anger, but we were not always successful.

First, of course, "Amos 'n' Andy," grandfather's favorite radio program, America's beloved radio show, as the *Saturday Evening Post* was America's beloved magazine. Nobody dared to speak when "Amos 'n' Andy" was on the radio. It was a crime. Silence. No rattling the silverware, no clinking the glasses, off the hook with the telephone lest grandfather miss a single syllable. Nobody could escape from "Amos 'n' Andy" and the Fresh Air Taxi Company. I had no desire to escape. I loved the language of "Amos 'n' Andy." I did not catch all the jokes of "Amos 'n' Andy" but I loved the tricks of language, the volume of the radio enveloped me, and if the radio thwarted conversation there was a certain safety in that, too, in grandfather's being too far diverted by his laughter to challenge anyone with hard questions for which, in any case, nobody had the answers but him.

The nightly comedy of "Amos 'n' Andy" was provided by two white men playing the roles of lazy, ignorant, ingenious, scheming Negroes—"blacks" as we would say now; "niggers" as grandfather said then. Grandfather drew from "Amos 'n' Andy" broad conclusions about mankind. The program seemed to teach him in fifteen minutes every night that if you were lazy and sat around all day in your Fresh-Air Taxicab you'd end up as poor as you began, you'd never get ahead. "Amos 'n' Andy" reminded grandfather to remind anyone within the sound of his voice how not to live, how not to be. "Amos 'n' Andy" gave him a good feeling about his own character, revealing him as everything Amos and Andy were not, beginning with his speech, which he thought of as precise and correctly pronounced, exhibiting proof that wealth arose from virtue, for if grandfather were as indolent as the people of "Amos 'n' Andy" he would be as poor as they. Would he not?

I had understood from mother that grandfather intended to congratulate me for my essay—Speed's essay. Father was delighted. "You go over there and have a good time," father said. "Him inviting you alone means you're crossing a boundary. He's reaching out to you man to man. I wouldn't be at all surprised if him and you end up over coffee in the sun parlor and the next thing you know you'll be smoking a cigar."

I had crossed a boundary line. The child was passing to adult. Could this be? How suddenly it had come! In the past, when dinner was over at Walk a Mile House, we children glided to the pantry where a glass camel stood full of candy. Remove the camel's hump and eat your candy. Of course grandmother had filled the camel for us, but we children thought we were stealing the candy, and we much preferred it that way. Tonight, however, I felt how inappropriate that camel candy was. Tonight was coffee, liqueur, for grandfather invited me to the sun parlor, as father predicted he would. No boy entered the sun parlor. Therefore I was no longer a boy. I followed grandfather into his domain.

Afterward from time to time a maid came to replenish our cups, bringing with her one of the great luxuries of civilization—grandmother's fudge rum balls rolled in cocoa, candy a thousand times more delicious than any the glass camel ever held, not a child's candy but an adult's candy. Now and then I find this delicacy in a shop and seize it. It is not grandmother's. Nevertheless, let a fudge rum ball rolled in cocoa melt in my mouth and my mind flies through space to this evening, one of the turnings of my life.

Grandfather struck a match, felt, smelled, heat, flame, dipped it into his dish of burney-burney. The fumes relaxed him and relieved his eyes. When the burney-burney expired he lit his cigar. He asked me if I smoked. I said I did not smoke. In fact Speed and I had tried a few cigarettes, but we had not yet acquired the habit.

"Several weeks ago," said grandfather, "your mother read me that essay you wrote for class. It was certainly extremely interesting and well-written because you've got the inherited flair for writing that runs in our family." Speed's essay he meant, of course, not mine. "However, your little essay leaves much to be desired because it is based on certain false assumptions and we've got to clear some of them up before we proceed." Grandfather took his writing tablet from his table, his pen from his pocket, and in his blindness drew, as I had seen him so swiftly and artistically draw often be-

43

fore, a map of the world, or at least of that part of the world he considered important—America (i.e., the United States) and Europe. In those days grandfather left out Asia and Africa, as he left out grandmother.

I had often seen him prove or illustrate theories by drawing the map he drew for me in the sun parlor. Everyone marveled at his accuracy. Few sighted people could so genuinely have produced the United States and Europe. He drew national boundaries, rivers, trade routes. He located the principal cities of the United States, among them Mount Vernon, New York—"next to the biggest city in the country." He sketched crowns here and there in Europe to show monarchies, little cocked hats of the American Revolution to show democracy.

The maid stepped through the door with our coffee. Grandfather waited until she was gone before he continued.

"Now the reason I'm going into this map is the result of your mother's calling me up and reading your class composition. It was a wonderfully written composition, you use words very well, you have an expanding vocabulary. You have inherited writing talent from the Schneck side of the family. I say talent. I don't say genius. Do you know what genius is?"

"A terrifically smart person is a genius."

"According to Thomas Edison genius in the application of the seat of the pants to the seat of the chair. Genius is one percent inspiration and ninety-nine percent perspiration. Did you know that?"

"Not until just now," I said. This was that obliging part of me Speed so deeply hated.

"The only thing I disliked about your essay was that it was all very wrong in its thinking," said grandfather. "I was ashamed of it."

"The teacher liked it," I said.

"That's why she's only a teacher," said grandfather. "Do you know your teacher's annual salary? Are you aware that her salary is two thousand dollars a year?"

"No sir," I said, "I wasn't aware of that," and I did not know, either, with much certainty, whether grandfather was saying two thousand was good or bad. It sounded very good to me. "It sounds like a good salary to me," I said, "my own income is only ninety cents a week."

"Your income is going to be a lot more than ninety cents a week when you get yourself geared up for action," grandfather said, "and the way we get ourselves geared up is by listening to great men. After I digested your essay on the phone from your mother I sat myself right down and I drew a little map of the world and I added up the number of people in the world, and after I added up the number of people I took a close estimate of the wealth of the world in American dollars, and I divided the wealth of the world in dollars by the number of people in the world. My answer was this: if you shared the wealth among all the people of the world each and every person would receive as his share—how much do you suppose?"

"I don't know, grandfather."

"You should have sat down and arrived at the quotient before you wrote the essay," he said. "You should have checked your facts and figures before you wrote it. You'd have come out at a different place. The sad fact is that if you shared the wealth among the people of the world everybody would end up with only twenty-nine cents."

"I didn't say anything about sharing the wealth," I said.

"Your whole essay was about sharing the wealth."

"It was supposed to be about being a mailman," I said.

"I'm talking about your sharing-the-wealth essay," said grandfather. "How much good is it going to do the people of the world to give everybody twenty-nine cents?"

"It's not much," I said. "It's a Sunday *Mirror* and a pack of smokes and four pennies left over."

"I thought you don't smoke."

"Father smokes."

"I didn't want you to take my word for it," grandfather said, "and I don't want you to take my word for it now. Therefore I want to tell you what I did. I wrote a letter to the smartest man in the world. Can you tell me who the smartest man in the world is?"

"Thomas Edison?"

"Is there anyone in the world who doesn't know who Mr. Henry Ford is?" grandfather asked.

I did not like answering rhetorical questions. I replied with an evasion. "I haven't met anyone," I said.

"Mr. Henry Ford is the smartest man in the world," said grandfather. "You've got to agree to that, haven't you?"

"I honestly don't really know," I said.

"Mr. Henry Ford is the smartest man in the world, and that's why I went to him to check on the facts in your essay. What did I ask him?"

"Are you asking me?"

"Yes, what did I ask him?"

"I don't know, grandfather."

"I wrote him the following letter." From his memory grandfather brought forth his letter.

Dear Mr. Henry Ford,

You will remember me from several occasions of our meeting in one matter and another. My grandson has written a school essay in favor of sharing the wealth. In earnest conversation with him I demonstrated that if all the wealth of the world were distributed among all its inhabitants each man, woman, and child on the whole globe would receive only twenty-nine cents apiece. This would by no means solve the problems of poverty in the world. Poverty is solved by the daring investment of capital. My grandson and I have agreed to present this question to the man whom we believe is the smartest man in the world. That man is you, Mr. Henry Ford. Will you be so kind as to tell us your opinion of my opinion that sharing the wealth is the wrong way to solve the world's problems?

"I don't remember that we talked this over," I said.

"We have just talked it over," said grandfather. "Where did you ever hear about sharing the wealth?"

"I never heard about it."

"You wrote about it."

46

"I heard about it from Speed."

"It's all irrelevant now because I have here a reply from Mr. Henry Ford." Grandfather shook out a piece of paper. "I think this is it. Is this it?"

"Yes, sir, that's it."

"You may examine it if you wish."

"I wonder if this is his genuine signature," I said.

"I was reasonably confident Mr. Henry Ford would answer me," grandfather said. "He's no slouch. Tell me what his letter says."

Henry Ford's letter said:

Dear Mr. Schneck:

Everything you have told your promising grandson is perfectly right.

Yours very truly,

Henry Ford

Once again the maid entered the sun parlor. She removed our coffee cups and replaced them with two liqueur glasses, a small bottle of liqueur, and a plate of six fudge rum balls rolled in cocoa. Grandfather asked me what she had brought us, but I did not know the names of the things she had brought us, and he called her back and asked her what she had brought us. She did not know the names of the things, either. She said she would find out. Named or not, I ate my share of fudge rum balls rolled in cocoa, and sipped my liqueur.

"I'm sure you never saw a letter from Mr. Henry Ford before," said grandfather. "I can tell you that Mr. Henry Ford earns more than ninety cents a week and you, too, have got to get moving. You can't go on selling the *Saturday Evening Post*. Selling magazines is for little boys, and you're too old for that now. You've got to get on to bigger things. I'm telling you all this for your own good, and I am telling it to you because of the special family considerations. Do you understand me?"

47

"I'm not sure I do, sir. What special family considerations are those?"

"Because in view of your brother Speed it's you who have got to be the special brains of the family over there."

"Speed is a very brainy kid," I said.

"Speed may have *character*," said grandfather. "That may be what you're thinking of. Speed has character but he does not have a fine brain. Some of us have fine brains. I have a fine brain and your father worked for me, you know, and has a fine brain now, and you have a fine brain and a way of getting along with everybody. Speed, unfortunately, has a slow and somewhat sluggish brain with missing connections."

Grandfather could never get over the idea that Speed was slow and sluggish. Nothing could have been further from the truth. "Missing connections. That's why he stammers. He has a motor difficulty. I know all about these things. I worked on a method to cure stammering. It might still come to something if we can raise the capital. I love Speed. We all love Speed, but Speed is a victim of circumstances we can't do anything about, can we? If we could do anything about it we would. Therefore it's all up to you. You're going to have to raise your sights. You're going to have to think beyond ninety cents a week."

"Ninety cents is really working out quite fine with me," I said. "Mother packs my lunch."

Grandfather lost a little patience with me. He had intended to give me the letter from Henry Ford, but he retrieved it from the table, as if he weren't so sure I deserved it. He began to grow angry, and his sightless eyes rolled in his head. He lit his burney-burney again and breathed it in deeply to regain his good nature.

"I don't like to hear you say it's working out quite fine with you," he said. "Nothing can be working out very fine at ninety cents a week. Anything can work out fine enough if a person resigns himself to it. A pig doesn't object to the smell of the pigpen. Anybody can get accustomed to bad conditions of work and low starvation wages and go along without complaining. All you have to do is cringe and abase yourself and lower your sights. All you have to do is look down instead of up. You are past the age when you ought to be accepting ninety cents a week. You ought to be out there earning anywhere from six to eight dollars somewhere after school."

"I've got lots of schoolwork," I said.

"My God, a dollar a day is not too much to ask. My God, that ninety cents a week that you accept so cheerfully is a lot less than we even pay that dirty smelly nigger girl out there in the kitchen," who, to my embarrassment, was not in the kitchen but standing in the doorway listening.

CHAPTER THREE

HER NAME was Champrain Johnson. This may seem to you to be an unusual name, but there's nothing unusual about it when you recall that during a certain decade in America many black people were swept along by the fad of naming their children for cities and lakes of the Northeast and Upper Middle West. This is a fact any linguistic regional specialist will confirm for you.

For some reason never entirely clear, even to the linguists, the parents so committed to the practice—the mothers and fathers of the Champrains, the Adilondacks, the Salanacs, the Toredos, the Tolontos, etc.—in plucking the name from the Rand McNally map altered it slightly to make it their own, often by changing the letter *r* to *l* as in, let us say, the conversion of Racine to Lacine.

Black maids with all sorts of unusual names came over the years to Walk a Mile House. They remained either for years or for days, or so it seemed, for that, too, was said to be one of the peculiarities of black folk, who remained on a job twenty minutes or twenty years. With black folk it was all or nothing, fly-by-night or stay forever. They were "members of the family," one said, although they did not dine with us, sit with us, share our bathrooms, talk as equals with us, or in other basic ways share with us as members of the family. To this rule Mary Washington was the only exception:

she worked in Walk a Mile House for sixty years. When grandfather died she inherited it.

Three or four black women were always employed there. They
lived in tiny rooms in the east wing, counterpart of grandfather's
single large sun parlor in the west. At certain times at Walk a Mile
House, when black women outnumbered the rooms allotted to
them, she whose status was lowest was assigned a room considered
least desirable because of the arduous climb to reach it in the attic
suite. There Champrain Johnson lived in her high little space beside Walk a Mile Railway.

I had already committed one crime against her. I had stolen a
quarter from the pocket of her apron hanging on a hook beside
the ice tongs on the back of the kitchen door. I had not even
intended to steal it. I had simply, in walking past, stuck my hand
into the warm pocket and found there a good old United States
quarter. I had not expected to find anything. When I felt my
hand in the apron pocket come into contact with a quarter I
seized the coin, clutched it, palmed it, withdrew it exulting, and
transferred it without half a second's conscience or hesitation to
my own pocket.

Subsequently I spent it or saved it, I cannot remember, but in
either case it entered into the service of my own fortune. Not a
great deal of money, you say, even with fifty years' interest ac-
crued, but it was a great deal to me then, and to Champrain
Johnson, too, who informed grandmother that a quarter had been
stolen from her apron pocket. One moment it had been there and
the next moment not. She made no accusation against me. She had
her opinion, however.

Grandmother said to me, "The girl Champrain is missing some
money from her apron. Her apron was hanging on the door back
there."

"I didn't see any apron," I said.

"I wonder if her money might have fallen into your hand as you
passed by."

"No money fell into my hand," I said, which was certainly true.

"My sweet boy, you know I'm not asking you if it did or if it didn't. I know that if it did you'll want to return it to Champrain somehow some way or another at your next opportunity."

"I never touched anybody's quarter," I self-righteously said to grandmother.

"Of course you didn't if you say so," she said. "Oh, did I say it was a quarter? All right, if that's what it was I'll give her another out of my own pocket."

I did not return it. She got it back, didn't she? Grandmother gave her another, didn't she? And who was out anything? Wasn't grandmother's husband a rich man? Hadn't grandmother herself a stocking full of dollar bills?

Moreover, Champrain had had no emotion about the whole thing. She could not have been hurt. She did not cry. I concluded therefore that she had felt nothing, that she was without emotion about her loss. Her money was gone and would come again, and since she clearly felt nothing I was certainly under no obligation to feel anything myself. If she didn't care why should I? Therefore I did not care, or so I must have believed. When I turned confidently from grandmother I dismissed the matter forever. I was wrong, however. Soon I began to feel it as a sin and prayed for forgiveness.

Months afterward, on the night of my momentous meeting with grandfather in the sun parlor, I had really quite forgotten it. I did not think of Champrain as the girl I had stolen the quarter from but only as the most recent of many black maids in the long parade of black maids through Walk a Mile House.

In the moment, however, of grandfather's insulting her I saw how keenly she had felt what she had heard. Her jaw dropped when she heard what he had said, and she turned her eyes to me to beseech me to rescue her from this insult, to ask *me* what she ought to do about it (though I was as mortified as she), to ask *me* whether she was altogether bound now to give him the information she had obtained for us—the name of grandmother's candy. She saw that grandfather's unkindness had embarrassed me, that I was embarrassed for myself and for her, too, that I was then in my final moment of a certain kind of innocence, believing that she was without feeling, believing that she would hardly have heard him or that if she heard him she would hardly have cared, that she was quite accustomed to being called a dirty smelly nigger, it did not cause her pain as it would have caused *me* pain. Suddenly I knew what I had theretofore never paused to consider, that a black girl might be essentially quite like white girls whom I was expected to respect and honor, that this Champrain, black as she was, was nevertheless as sensitive as anyone else to pain and insult, that she was not to be insulted and not to be stolen from. She did not smell. She was not dirty. And where in this did I stand? Her eyes were upon me, seeking my answer.

"Who's there?" grandfather asked, for he had heard someone at the sun parlor door. I could not reply. Therefore he raised his voice and addressed the doorway instead. He was enraged. He knew that he was being deceived, humiliated by his blindness. "Answer me, who's there?" And when I was still too paralyzed to speak he roared again, not quite at me, "Answer me, you son of a bitch."

"Nobody's there," I said.

He regained control of himself. "Are you sure?" he asked. "I thought I heard somebody."

"No, sir, dead sure," said I, and thus by allying myself in this small way with Champrain Johnson I joined her in feeling.

Then, too, when I saw the pain and hope and anger in her eyes I was overcome by a surge of sexual feeling I had never known, never imagined, and was deeply ashamed of now in my new breathless bliss. My mouth went dry, my organ enlarged and almost burst, and I deeply hated grandfather who was detaining me there, talking on and on about my duty to my family when I should so much have preferred to leap from my chair and pursue Champrain and seize her and in apology and passion cover her face with kisses, with kiss after kiss after kiss pending the time we should have heard from someone how to behave when our kisses were exhausted. Champrain turned from us without giving us the information she had gone for—the name of grandmother's candy, rum fudge balls rolled in cocoa—and I did not see her again that night or for some weeks thereafter. I made up my mind to do so. Sometimes, of course, boys burn with determination for minutes only. That happened often to me, in and out of love overnight.

Speed and I had not yet much experience of girls. We threw snowballs at them. We tried to get close to them in the elevators at the Esplanade Gardens Apartments. At night from a distance we studied the drawn shades of girls' lighted bedrooms in the hope of a revealing silhouette.

Aunt Ember perceived in the lines and configurations of our palms a great deal of evidence that we would soon find girls to make us happy. And we would make girls happy, too. "Don't despair," she said, "you're both awfully nice boys no matter what anybody says, you're tall and good-looking and you have handsome, sturdy bodies."

A handsome *body*. Now there was something to think about. She was the first adult authority from whom we had heard the idea that bodies were considerations quite as important as religion or character. Her opinion assisted us by relieving us. Something about the body mattered, though we were not certain why or what and we were too shy to ask Aunt Ember too much, though she'd have given us a straight answer.

Soon Speed and I were discussing the body endlessly. We decided that the route to elucidation lay through the roller-skating rink on West Lincoln Avenue. If we were to take two girls there and skate with them awhile other things would develop.

But where were two girls who would have us? One afternoon in the library we spied a girl who seemed right, sitting at a high table. We saw by a tag above her heart that she was one Miss Boland, an employee of the library. She was copying information from one set of cards to another. Now and again with a charming gesture she moistened the corners of her lips with her tongue.

Speed and I conferred. We thought to ask her to go with us to the roller-skating rink. She would have a friend, a sister, who might care to come along. We deliberated for a long time how to put this interesting proposition to her. It seemed to us that since our first sentences to her would be crucial we must prepare them well. In encounters of this kind we had already through life arrived at a natural strategy. I was the speaker, of course. Speed stood by. I was the brother of words. My speech was quick and glib. Speed, on the other hand, I now confess, was handsomer. Girls, women even, often talked with me while gazing at Speed.

For half an hour we crafted our sentences, deciding at last that I should say to Miss Boland, "My brother Speed and I have been wondering if you're a roller-skater. We were only thinking that in case you were a roller-skater we could go roller-skating Saturday night, you and I and my brother and maybe somebody else such as another girl you might have in mind."

"No," Miss Boland replied, "I'm afraid I really don't."

In her manner of answering me, and even in her way of looking beyond me to Speed, it was clear she was prepared to be friendly to us. She was not saying no to us forever on all subjects, she cared to be cordial, she was open to us, she smiled, all this time so charmingly touching the tip of her tongue to the corners of her lips.

I did not know what to say next, whether to suggest an alternative plan or to leave her for an alternative girl. Speed and I retreated to confer. And when we did we saw from the distance a pair of crutches beneath Miss Boland's high table. Her legs were in steel braces. She was undoubtedly a victim of the disease we called in those days infantile paralysis. But worse, what were Speed and I to do?

"Let's get out of here," I said.

"We can't," said Speed. "We've got to g-g-g-g-g-g-g-g . . ."

"Go back to her?" I asked him. "Why? If you ask me what we've got to do is get out of here," and I would have fled from the library had he not held my arm.

"We can't just r-r-r-r-r-r-r-r-r-r-r-r-r-r . . ." he said.

"Run," I said. "I can run. I'd rather run than waste a whole night on a crippled girl."

"We can suggest s-s-s-s-s-s-s-s-s-s-s . . ." Speed said.

"Something else? Like what?" I asked. "What are you going to suggest to a crippled girl?"

"Why do you k-k-k-k-k-k-k-k-k-k-k-k . . ."

"Why do I keep calling her a crippled girl? Because she's crippled."

"You have no feeling," he said. He often accused me of deficiency of feeling, which was to say especially, I suppose, deficiency of feeling toward *him*. At the worst moments of our brotherhood he thought me intolerant toward him, unfeeling for his affliction, unsympathetic generally, untrustworthy. "We can d-d-d-d-d-d-d-d-d-d-d . . ."

"Do what? Tell me what."

"Do something else besides s-s-s-s-s-s-s-s-s . . ."

"Something besides skating? Tell me what." I was ready to do anything to get to the point of the thing—parlor games, read books, recite poetry, listen to the radio, oh yes, there were lots of things we could do before we touched, but touch we must. In our handsome bodies we knew that at some point the touching was the object of the evening. We had discussed it a thousand times, the touching, the touching, whatever it was or came to, however it began or ended.

All that was left to discover. Aunt Ember observed by our palms that we would discover it, too, but one thing I knew from the beginning without help from Aunt Ember was that my discovery could never occur with a girl whose legs were tied by steel braces, lovely as she may have appeared at her high desk in the library from her waist to her golden hair.

"President R-R-R-R-R-R-R-R-R-R-R . . ." said Speed, pleading with me to re-examine my values.

"President Roosevelt's in steel braces, too" I said. "I'm not going skating with President Roosevelt."

"You're going with a g-g-g-g-g . . ." said Speed.

"Right."

I went away from Miss Boland's table. I went elsewhere in the library. From time to time I saw Speed still beside Miss Boland, standing at her table, leaning with his elbows on her table talking earnestly with her. They were in long, deep conversation—any conversation with Speed was bound to be long—because Speed felt an obligation to Miss Boland not to flee, not to abandon her. He had begun at this time of his life to acquire a conscious vested interest in viewing people whole beyond their defects, as he would have had people view him. Miss Boland's body was defective, but so was his. If she could not walk well he could not speak well.

As high-school boys Speed and I sometimes took a trip to New York on the subway which ended (or began) at 241st Street and White Plains Road, where the city of Mount Vernon met the borough of the Bronx. Aunt Ember, who highly recommended the Metropolitan Museum of Art, gave us her current copy of Patron News, and Speed and I told ourselves we were headed for the museum one zero winter day, although we may have known we were destined to end up not at the Metropolitan Museum of Art but at the peep shows on 42nd Street.

On the sidewalk before the peep show the barker announced three girls in a basket to be run through with knives. This was something Speed and I had to see. We paid twenty cents each to be admitted. It was a lot of money. With twenty cents I could have bought two hot dogs and two cups of steaming chocolate.

Still, if we saw what we thought we'd see it wasn't much to pay at all—not the girls run through with knives, we knew they couldn't do that, even on 42nd Street, but the girls in the basket *naked*, that was what we were paying twenty cents to see. That was how it was advertised.

Up onstage before our very eyes three girls in shorts and halters climbed into the straw basket, sinking down and out of sight. They tossed their shorts and halters back over the side of the basket. The man with the long knives (on the sidewalk he'd been the barker, indoors he was the knife-wielder) ran them through, and the three lovely girls shrieked and squealed as the man of knives plunged knife after knife into the basket.

If they were not dead they were certainly naked. Hadn't we seen them enter the deep basket and throw their clothes behind? For only an additional fifty cents (each) Speed and I were permitted to climb onstage and see for ourselves how the girls in the basket had fared, whether they were alive, and if they were alive whether they were naked. It was our lunch money. We were to have had a grand lunch at a restaurant, perhaps a Horn & Hardart Automat, perhaps Chinese.

We saw in the basket below the knife blades three girls entwined with one another, a featureless expanse of flesh.

On our long hungry subway ride back to Mount Vernon Speed and I were angry at each other. We had not only been fools but worse, fools in each other's sight, we had paid half a dollar apiece to see nothing. In the bitter wind of a snowstorm, I think as a kind of self-immolation, trolley fare and bus fare still in our pockets, we walked all the way home from the end of the subway line. At dinner I reported to mother and father many details of the Metropolitan Museum of Art. I had studied Aunt Ember's Patron News. I astounded Speed, who marveled at my describing wonders of the world we had not seen at the great museum to which we had not been.

Speed himself could not have spoken in such a way even had he not stuttered. He was not a boy of speech but a boy of writing, author of many fine poems, stories, and of the excellent controversial composition "My Occupational Life Intention." He declined in any case to lie if it was at all possible to tell the truth, although he was often filled with admiration for my eloquent inventions, my exotic vocabulary, my assembling of data, facts, figures, statistics. Father said, "I'm glad to hear you boys went to the museum, you didn't hang out in none of those peep shows or anything like that."

I had not forgotten Champrain. I planned my opening address to her, as Speed and I had planned my opening address to Miss Boland in the library. I intended to begin with the question of the quarter I had stolen from her apron pocket, and to trace for her a dual line of thought: "Lovely Champrain," I would say—for she *was* lovely, a sturdy, slender girl of my age with very white teeth and very white whites of her eyes and magnificent long black hair in profusion worn upswept to give her, she thought, the look of an older woman—"I want to apologize to you more deeply than any words can transmit to you my apologies for having stolen that

58

quarter from you from your apron pocket hanging on the kitchen door, and secondly I want to return it to you. Here it is." For this occasion I had shined up a quarter and prepared a harmless lie—this, I would say, was the same quarter I had stolen from her, so you see I stole it not for greedy use but as a souvenir of a girl I admired.

In preparation I had imagined Champrain's role, too. I had given her speeches as clear as my own. She had carried in her heart, she said, our shared mortification at the sun parlor door. It had been for her a supreme moment of her brief existence, as she supposed it had been for me, too. We had that moment together she and I, when my eye had caught hers and hers caught mine and we saw in each other's eyes that we were united in silence against grandfather. We believed together in our divine and democratic connection of spirit.

How then to find out if this would happen as I hoped? How to see her? Several times I rang the telephone at Walk a Mile House in the hope she would pick it up, but it was never she who answered. I hung up. I wanted to see her again but I did not know how to see her without returning to the complications of Walk a Mile House.

I did not want to sit long hours receiving instruction from grandfather on living my life. My life pleased me as it was, though I would have been happier with more money for my pocket, would have been happier if Speed and I could have had separate bedrooms, would have been happier if I had been a more formidable athlete, would have been happier if I had been more certain of my occupational life intention—

That was it! There it was! My occupational life intention! I would become a railroad man.

Therefore soon in the role of apprentice railroad man I made my first exploratory visit to Walk a Mile House to survey Walk a Mile Railway, to observe how a railroad ran so that I too could venture forth to run a great railroad for which grandfather might write slogans to catch the eyes and ears of America. Grandfather said he had not recently heard of any idea so admirable, so practical, so exemplary as my buckling down at last to something serious. "And it's something that works Speed in, too," grandfather said. "You'll always be able to find jobs for Speed. Lots of railroad jobs don't require any speech. I can see a slow boy like Speed fitting in quite well."

"He'll be coming over with me," I assured grandfather, but Speed never came. I never invited him. It was a long time before I even told him where I went—"Two's company and three's a crowd," we Mount Vernon High School boys and girls always said.

I climbed the stairs to the attic suite. The railroad room smelled musty. An adult would have opened a window. If anyone had been there running Walk a Mile Railway he had not been there often. The railroad town was silent, dark, motionless. The passengers waiting on the platform and the stationmaster and the porters frozen at their tasks were exactly where I had left them, like Buck Rogers and his girl Wilma and their foe Killer Kane on the radio in "suspended animation."

When I flipped the switches, when everything resumed, when the trains began to grind down the track, when the silly freak pasteboard cow began to moo-oo-oo, when lights, whistles, sirens, bells, and honking horns all touched the town with reality I, too, having put so much noise into motion, sweating with life, glided like a phantom in the night from my study of railroad operations to Champrain's room next door.

She was at her bath. Her door was shut. She sang with her Philco radio. I heard my trains in the room behind me. She must have heard them, too, and she may also have overheard downstairs that the studious trainman was coming to the railroad room to enlarge his understanding. The idea, however, that she might be awaiting me as eagerly as I sought her was at that hour of my life beyond my experience. When I thought I heard her rising from her tub I fled from her door soaked in my guilt, back to my trains. I cooled, and my heart slowed. Round and round went the engines and the cars, passengers, freight, and caboose of Walk a Mile Railway. I sat awhile at the railroad table and watched my railroad go. I had escaped, returned to a safe place from the post I had taken outside her bath, where I had been protected only by a single door from the sight of sinful nakedness. I decided to retire from railroading, to put away this animal nonsense, to go home and attend my schoolbooks and my friends and my family and my brother—

No, I would do no such thing. This was something I was going to have to face sooner or later. I would not retire from railroading, I would try again, I would show courage, I would make myself do it. This bestial thing must happen to me as it happened some time to every man (sometimes when they were only boys). Therefore why not up there in the attic suite on the right-of-way of the Walk a Mile Railway with Champrain Johnson named for a lake? Night after night for several weeks I returned to run my railroad, and night after night she sang in her bath to the music of her radio.

The life of Champrain Johnson as far as I knew was uncomplicated by calendars or plans. We never met anywhere in life but in Walk a Mile House, where she was the fourth maid and I was the favored grandson. She kept no calendar, received no mail, no telephone calls. In affluent neighborhoods of Mount Vernon every Thursday night was "maid's night out." Champrain went home to black Mount Vernon, I assumed. Her street and house I never knew. On Sunday afternoon she was at liberty again, gone presumably to church. She left Walk a Mile House in slick black high-heeled shoes for the trolley line. Along the curb before Walk a Mile House were parked idle automobiles belonging to my uncles and my cousins for whom she had prepared and served midday dinner, not one of whom even in the worst weather ever thought to drive her to her church. I despised those men. She carried a shining slick black purse to match her shoes, and a Bible.

What did anyone make of my addiction to my railroad? Walk a Mile House was often occupied by guests, in many cases distraught aunts and uncles beached between marriages, in ill health, unemployed, frequently all three, for whom grandfather provided haven or shelter and kept a close record of it, too, mentioning to me the habits and personalities of ungrateful relations who, having fed at his table, complained of his will to domination. I was not always clear whom he had in mind. My memories of most of my aunts and uncles remain indistinct. I never heard the outcomes of the plots of their lives—who finally married whom, what the trouble had been, where they had come from, where history took them.

If they carried into their future with them any memory of me it is likely to have been grandfather's account of the ambitious boy in the attic cranking up to make a mint of money. For grandfather, his own suggestions became his own realities. That boy upstairs was on his way to becoming a notable trainman. Think how natural it was, too, in light of the powerful railroad connection already in the family: grandfather's stirring advertising challenge on the billboards of America. "A hog can cross the country without changing trains—why can't you . . . Santa Fe All the Way." Those were grandfather's.

Beginning low with mere models that boy would soon work his way up into the annals of railroading, up, up, ticket-taker, conductor, electrician, engineer, executive, director of advertising, vice-president in charge of everything, chairman of the board, that kid would own the whole road some day.

Meanwhile unknown to grandfather and my cousins and my uncles and my aunts I stalked for weeks with singleminded desire under cover of engine whistles the girl at her bath behind the closed door. I did not know I had only to knock.

You may not have thought of me as a person of prayer but I was a person of prayer nonetheless. I had a modest and essentially unselfish repertoire of prayers. For some years I prayed three prayers for the future and one for forgiveness. To my repertoire I now added a fourth prayer for the future and a second for forgiveness, to wit:

Prayer Four for the Future: "Dear God, please make Champrain white."

Prayer Two for Forgiveness: "Dear God, please forgive me for stealing Champrain's quarter from her apron."

The older I grew the less my praying reflected the growth of my soul. When I served up my prayers I reverted in my speech to the little boy's tumbling haste of delivery. When I listen now to the prayers inside my head I hear the accents of our speech as children in Mount Vernon, New York. I hear the sound of myself and the depth of the things I believed. It never occurred to me to reciprocate the favors of God. Hell, God made me, I didn't ask to be born, did I? I didn't visit these miseries on myself, God did. It was His fault. What you break you pay for.

Each night's brief session of prayer was a reversion to earliest childhood. My maturing logic prohibited me from reciting my small-boy's prayers in an adult voice. I gave off the sound of my most childlike self. Moreover, it struck me that if God were to believe in me I should sound maximally innocent, as if I for my part believed in Him.

My oldest prayer, my first, was as self-denying as a prayer can be. With the first word I gave away my guileless character. "God!" I began—a demand, a call for His undivided attention, as if He were my constant loving grandmother delighted at any moment to whip out a dollar from her stocking for me.

But then and always I paused, caught hold of myself. Let's have a little humility. "Hey, where do you get off *demanding* things of God? Try *beseeching* God, try tact. You wouldn't talk to one of your *Saturday Evening Post* customers as rudely as you talk to God." Therefore in my ritual I revoked the imperious "God!" and slid as gracefully as I could into humility:

Prayer One for the Future: "God, please see to it that my poor blind grandfather may have sight and not have to live the rest of his life in darkness."

In my earliest days of prayer I knelt beside my bed, hands before my face, head bowed. On the coldest nights I kept my knees from touching the floor. God would not notice. In a good cause He'd not stoop to measuring inches. Over the years God grew more rational along with me. I reached at last a point of such elevated reason that I did not kneel at all, but prayed in bed, on my side. My knees were *bent*, however, in the angle of kneeling.

Toward religion mother and father seemed indifferent. Once in a while we went to church. Father preferred St. Ursula's because it was nearer than St. Catherine's. Mother went once in a while to

a Lutheran church which burned down and was never rebuilt.
Mother was Lutheran and father was busy—Babe Ruth got a kick
out of that, unless, of course, the laughing man in Florida was not
Babe Ruth but mother's lost lover Doc Duffy.

The only God I could imagine looked like grandfather, except
that He was not blind: indeed, *All-seeing*, He could look right into
your bedroom and measure the distance of your knees from the
floor. In exchange for obedience, in exchange for my appearing
sufficiently to agree with authority, in exchange for my seeming to
accept respectable evidence, as in the matter of grandfather's in-
quiry to Henry Ford, God who was more or less made in the image
of grandfather would grant me my needs as I identified them.

Speed hated both God and grandfather and never prayed. He
enjoyed the music of the Catholic church, but he felt hypocritical
for taking pleasure without repayment in conviction. Earlier than
I he was an atheist, but then he was everything earlier than I. The
great teacher of my life was a year younger than I. Our sharing a
bedroom for so many years was a slight problem for me since I
prayed aloud. But one prayer, which was for him, I learned to
whisper only for God, as I whispered also its companion forgiveness prayer:

Prayer Three for the Future: "Dear God, fix Speed's stuttering
so he could talk normal like the rest of us."

Prayer One for Forgiveness: "Dear God, I don't really know if I
pushed Speed off the table in Florida. Maybe he jumped or fell or
dived. If it was an act of God it was Your fault, right? If it was me
that pushed him off please forgive me forevermore."

My second prayer for the future was my Doc Duffy prayer. I
observe as I listen to it now in that trouble-free recorder in my
head that I upgraded my salutation from "God" to "Dear God":

Prayer Two for the Future: "Dear God, please make sure Doc
Duffy stays dead as we do not want him here in this apartment."

Who were *we*? *We* were Speed and I, I suppose. According to
the family legend mother wanted Doc Duffy home and live. As for
father, he had no choice: it was an article of his marital agreement.
If Doc Duffy showed up, father was out. Unjust it may have been,

but we had always understood from father himself that a contract was a contract, subject to change but never to unilateral defiance.

The photograph of Doc Duffy most familiar to Speed and me shows father and Doc Duffy in soldier suits, arms linked with mother's, on the west lawn of Walk a Mile House beneath the old chestnut tree. There grandmother sang to me. The camera's eye catches behind them grandfather's sun parlor windows shut tight against the fresh air. The year is 1917.

The striking detail of the picture is the sun sparkling on Doc Duffy's eyeglasses. From that detail Speed and I had formed the impression of a somewhat weak-eyed man who groped his way to war, leaving mother behind, breaking her heart, and who intended at his leisure to grope his way back again. Since he was built like Babe Ruth he was powerful, he could command even the Mount Vernon police chief to vacate Apartment 2–D at the Sheridan Gardens Apartments, he could simply, tired of being missing in Europe, wander into our lives, demanding of us everything we had formerly granted to father only.

But Doc Duffy had no right to return. Surely God in His justice saw that as the overriding argument supporting Prayer Two. Mother may once on the eve of battle have issued Doc Duffy a permanent invitation to return, but Speed and I had not.

We visualized his returning and taking us over house and children, ousting father, moving right into Apartment 2–D, the man with sparkling eyeglasses, shaving with father's shaving gear, stepping into our lives as if he'd been there all the time, sleeping in mother's bed with mother in it, and then, worst of all, most embarrassing of all, *sitting on our toilet* where father had sat. He would try to kiss us. "Come here, kid, give us a kiss, I'm your father now." A strange man, a man I'd never seen before, and I was supposed to trot over and kiss him and call him dad! No way. Oh, God, think of that!

Poor father, where would he go if he were forced to live up to his agreement to leave? Was this agreement legal to begin with? Could it be challenged in the courts? After all, nothing had been written, no contract, no letter-agreement. I would certainly testify to the effect that I wished to have the agreement nullified and abrogated and declared null and void, and Speed was in this with me all the way.

What objects of the house would father take with him? Which things of our home were his and which were Speed's and mine? The modern-day property settlement was foreign to us. Children heard little of divorce in those days. Father said that if Doc Duffy returned he'd move himself down the station and live in a cell, and at times he appeared even to welcome the possibility. When father was angry with mother he said, "Doc Duffy got off lucky."

Yet I must have been basically less fearful than Speed, basically more secure because less gullible. I had no older brother to confuse me. In spite of Doc Duffy's being every inch obnoxious, unspeakable, I apparently expected to live at home with him if he returned.

Speed did not. His hatred for Doc Duffy was constant, obscene, and extreme. Often Speed said he would kill him, frequently in a specific and symbolic way emphasizing Doc's death as retribution for his having displaced father—shoot him on the toilet, stab him shaving at the sink with father's gear, crown him with a hammer at father's place at the dinner table to the tune of the Wartburg orphan asylum band playing "The Star-Spangled Banner."

At times Speed followed a different course. He would not kill Doc Duffy. He would simply leave home, pack his bags and go. "It'll be him or m-m-m-m-m-m-m-m-m-m-m-m . . . ," Speed or Doc Duffy but never both. He would run away. Where? "You'd never know," he said, but he offered me a spread of possibilities, and I remember most often Pikes Peak, the Rocky Mountains generally, Grand Canyon, Yosemite—"The West," he said, which in those days appeared to us remote beyond belief. A man gone west could never be found. In time, as the size of the world contracted for Speed as for all of us he announced overseas destinations to which he would flee, to Share the Wealth socialist paradises in Russia and middle Europe, ascetic spiritual retreats in Asia.

If Doc Duffy appeared at the Sheridan Gardens Apartments Speed would be gone in an hour. "I wouldn't sh-sh-sh-sh . . ."—

wouldn't shit one shit with Doc Duffy in the house, shave one shave, bathe one bath. Mother could choose. It was him or Doc Duffy.

For a while when we were very young I had persuaded Speed that he was the son—*bastard bastard bastard* son you understand, which made his character even worse—of Babe Ruth, conceived once upon a time in March when mother wintered in Florida. The arithmetic followed: Speed's birthday was in December.

Or if he was not the son of Babe Ruth he was the son of Doc Duffy, who had either appeared on mother's scene in Florida or had impregnated her years earlier with delayed sperm. Speed, who had scarcely yet heard of sperm itself, easily believed in delayed sperm. Champrain Johnson, when she was seventeen, still believed in it long after I had invented it to taunt my brother Speed. I drove him half out of his mind with this bedtime theory— slow-acting, persistent, stubborn, indefatigable, indestructible delayed sperm commonly identified by headline scientists in post-mortems on big Irishmen like Babe Ruth and Doc Duffy—sperm fighting its way upstream through the wombs of women, causing eventual pregnancies and stuttering babies. Speed insisted my theory was bunk, he had consulted Aunt Ember and other people, I was "shouting up a h-h-h-h-h-h-h-h-h . . ."—shouting up a horse's ass—but time and again he begged me to review it, which I happily did, lecturing persuasively from bed to bed in the dark.

Sometimes I was afraid I would never get up the nerve to try for Champrain again. I had once reached her door but no farther. I could bring myself to the door but I could not knock. I began to think I might leave well enough alone. I settled in some contentment in my railroad village. At moments I thought I might even take that place grandfather was reserving for me as one of your powerful American railroaders, though I knew nothing more about railroads than how to throw switches on the control board in the room in the attic suite, how to get the cars rolling with all their noise up, how to tiptoe every little while to Champrain's door to hear what I could hear of the excitement of her splashing in her bath, hear her singing the songs of the "Hit Parade." What long baths she took! I wondered why. Was she that dirty? Grandfather had called her dirty, smelly, but she did not look dirty to me and she smelled very good, too, of the soaps and cleansers she worked in all day. Girls in any case were cleaner than boys in body and mind. We all knew that.

I waited, I sweated, the train came down the track into my eyes, negotiated its curve, blew its whistle, slowed for the station filled with people standing there reading their newspapers, pushing their baby carriages, walking arm in arm, loading baggage onto a cart, raised a puff of smoke as real as any puff of smoke you'd ever see.

One summer night while I was at my trains there occurred a fabulous thunderstorm which seemed not so much to douse the lights—though it certainly did that, darkening half of Mount Vernon—as to produce a unique heavenly silence. All sound died. My trains rolled to a stop in the darkened village. I saw nothing, I heard nothing. Beyond the wall of the railroad room Champrain's radio was silent, and Champrain had stopped singing and in her sweet voice addressed an unknown presence. "What you do?"

That said, she took matters into her own hands. Her instinct saved us. She ran water into her tub. I heard the rushing of the water louder and clearer than I had ever heard it—water running, if this were possible, angrily, impatiently— and I felt that it was a message to me, the rushing water talking to me as Champrain had talked a moment ago to an unknown presence, and the water said to me, or so I hear it now in her melodious voice half a century after that stormy night, *Light off, train off, radio off, now what we going to do when the time come at last?* and in the darkness of the attic suite I stole to her bathroom door.

The first time I'd been there I had lost my courage. I feared I would lose it now again. I persuaded myself of my honorable mission, pinching between two fingers the quarter I'd shined up for her, which was legally hers, which I had for some weeks intended to return to her, waiting only for an opportune moment, as, for example, now. When I rapped on her door with my quarter she turned off the water, but she did not speak. I rapped on the door again and said, "I want to return something to you that belongs to you."

"Carry it in," she said.

I opened that forbidding door. Her bathroom was moist and warm with steam, suddenly lit for the fraction of a second by lightning at the window, but that was too little time for me to see her. I was thankful for that. This was going to be terribly embarrassing, just the two of us here in this sealed space. The storm at its height protected me. It was a frightening storm and I wished the world would end and spare me this confusion. Where was she? I did not know and I did not really want to find out, and I reached for her but I did not touch her. "Where are you?"

"Hear me speaking," she said, and I moved toward the sound of her speaking. She was sitting on the edge of the tub. She had not been in the tub. She had only been running the water, sending her message to me by water signal. She wore a cotton robe, afterward to become familiar to me as white, frayed at the elbows. Now when we touched she recoiled from me, as if she were as shocked as I by all this that was happening to us, but that was the only time she ever recoiled from me, and even then she instantly returned to me and embarrassed me unspeakably, groping in the dark for me and finding a major part of me enlarged in my trousers, and she said, "What's that there?"

"That's my flashlight," I said.

"Why didn't you put it on when the lights gone out?" she said, laughing in a way that made me know she knew what it really was. At first I could not believe she truly knew. I had not known what that old thing meant to girls. Ever afterward in our love play we called it my flashlight.

There were moments, before I knew Champrain better, when I feared or fantasized her cutting my flashlight off, when I saw her not as she was but as the creature of grandfather's imagination, a girl with an arsenal of knives. At those moments I felt that this railroading wasn't worth it after all. I imagined that she was waiting only for the convenient moment, and when it came she'd slice away my flashlight with a stroke of a knife from the treasure of knives she kept hidden in her attic room.

"Sit down and take a low off your feet," she said. She had trouble with the letter *d*.

"I'm not supposed to be here," I said.

"Where you suppose to be?"

"Running my trains."

"You already ran them."

"I've got to run them some more. I can't stay. The reason I came to your door," I said, "was because I wanted to tell you who stole your quarter from your apron that time. It was me who stole your quarter and I want to give it back to you." In the dark I held it out to her.

"I thought you probably was the one," said she. "I forgave you."

"Here it is," I said.

"This is not the time to give me money," she said.

"I'm going to give it to you anyway."

"Then give it to me," she said, and she must have held out her hand, but in the darkness our hands missed the connection and I did not try hard enough to find her. I don't know why. I think I was angry that she had guessed me for the thief all along and ruined my chance at confession when I had so *wanted* to confess. Then, too, a quarter was a quarter. My commission on sixteen *Saturday Evening Posts* was twenty-four cents. And so I kept it, that is to say, of course, spent it, but not on her, just as I never bought her a new white robe although I often intended to do so. I was a tightwad kid. I hated to give anything away. I was an insatiable collector of everything of hard value, a fanatical money-clutcher, a desperate hoarder of fortune. That may have been part of the trouble at last between Speed and me.

"I'll see your train," she said. "I never saw them ran."

"I can't run them until the electric goes back on," I said.

"We watch them stand still," she said.

"We can't see them in the dark," I said.

"If I don't see them I never miss them," she said.

We held hands. In the hallway she led me first, however, to the balustrade. We looked down. Far below, the well of the house was in almost total darkness. Grandmother had lit candles and the odor of paraffin drifted up to us. We heard grandfather's voice indistinctly. "He blaming her for the storm," Champrain said. "It knock out his radio."

She loved grandmother as deeply as she disliked grandfather, and we always had that together, she and I, we loved and disliked the same people in the same way, we always agreed upon people. The only person we did not agree upon was me. She loved me better than I deserved.

Hand in hand we entered my train room. Champrain's presence changed the whole meaning of the room. This was no longer a model railroad. We were passengers preparing to go somewhere, waiting at the station, sheltered from the raging storm. Life would never be better than it was at that moment, with all the power off and everything ready to happen. I knew it could not long remain that way, but since it had been given to us we accepted it as the gift it was. Champrain was barefoot. She remembered something. She returned to her room for her brush and comb and came to the train room again and sat in my engineer's chair at the dead switches and I combed and brushed her hair for her, blissfully drawing the comb and brush hundreds of times down through her long black shining hair. Now and then the action of the comb produced a spark, and always it produced exclamations of gratitude from Champrain, who took extraordinary pleasure from my luxurious attention. I thought then—I told her this—I might become a hairdresser, not a railroad tycoon, not a mailman but a hairdresser, yes, that would solve the problem of my occupational life intention. "You wouldn't like stranger ladies all day long," she said, for she knew the boredom of daily work as I had not yet experienced it. Of course she was right. I loved to comb and brush her hair, and I did it often, sometimes for hours and hours at a time, but I would never have cared for hairdressing as my life, and I think Mrs. Packard-Steinberg would have said it was beneath me.

CHAPTER FOUR

IN MY sophomore year at Mount Vernon High School I was one of a hundred and fifty boys trying out for fifteen spaces on the varsity basketball team—"under the watchful eye of the coach," the sportswriters might have said. The coach was Mr. Cabot, whom we called "Mr." as boys did in those days. I suited up in sneakers and shorts, socks and jock, and scrimmaged for a week in a series of cross-court games under the watchful eye of Mr. Cabot.

After the first week of practice Mr. Cabot posted on the bulletin board a "cut list" of boys who need not return. My name was not on it. I hadn't expected it to be. He had reduced one hundred and fifty boys to fifty. After the second week he posted a second cut list reducing fifty to twenty-five and still my name did not appear. I began to think he was making a mistake. I could have ranked among fifty but I did not think I ranked among twenty-five. I knew how good I was and wasn't. I knew myself well. I knew I was a generous, kind, loving, wholesome, brave, healthy, devoted boy inclined also toward jealousy, envy, meanness, unkindness, lying, selfishness, and cowardice.

Three weeks into practice we were issued uniforms. Somebody handed me maroon pants and a maroon shirt numbered fifty-five. Mount Vernon High was the Maroons. Just before practice, dressed in my uniform, I dropped into the coach's office where a sentence I meant to be declarative came out interrogative. "Mr. Cabot, I see that you're still keeping me on the squad?"

His reply was absurd. "Aren't you the police chief's son?"

He had been afraid to cut the son of the chief. He thought father would throw him in jail if he did not make a place for me on the squad. Mr. Cabot's idea of justice had never been well-developed, although he spoke often of fair play and sportsmanship. Speed played for him afterward and distinguished himself, but Speed thought of the coach as a mental infant. Once when Speed asked him what he meant by "fair play" Mr. Cabot replied, "No spitting." I turned in my uniform. I had worn it half an hour.

But if I could not play on my high-school team I could form my own. I organized a team drawn from boys in the Sheridan Gardens Apartments (Phil Shopsin, Norman Hirsch, Froo Gross, and I), the Esplanade Gardens Apartments (Ed Selkowitz, Bernie Wolf, and Jerry Hazan), and from elsewhere in the near neighborhood (Seth Koretz and David Marks). We had played basketball for years together on the Wilson School playground. We knew each other's style of play. On the whole we liked each other. We unanimously adopted my suggestion that we call ourselves the Mount Vernon Police Revolvers. Our fathers paid for our uniforms. The police department gave us fifty dollars.

We played in the Mount Vernon recreation department leagues. We also traveled a bit. I did our booking, hanging on the telephone, calendar in hand, making dates with likely teams in the county. Once we played in Long Island. Once we played in West New York. Once we played in Stamford, Connecticut.

I was the bellwether boy who rounded up the others, who made sure there were five or six of us for every date—just enough, not too many, nobody wanted to sit it out. In three years I never missed a game. Nobody else was as attached as I to the experience. In our second year I gave up my *Saturday Evening Post* route. I had suffered that damn thing eight years.

It was I who coordinated transportation, found a driver— somebody's father, older brother; sometimes somebody's mother, though mothers weren't so often drivers then as now; county bus; train.

I was treasurer, too, for hot dogs and hamburgers and ice-cold Cokes after the game, when we sat earnestly at diner counters reviewing our performances. I was our recordkeeper, kept conscientious scorebooks on the whole. Yet if it were necessary to bring individual scoring into agreement with our game score I gave myself a point or two.

Early in the first year of our collective life, when officers down the station saw our lineup in the Mount Vernon *Daily Argus*, they complained to father that we had no right to call ourselves the Mount Vernon Police Revolvers. The team, except for me, was unconnected to the police. A note to father from one of his men said our team was "strictly a phoney collection eighty percent kikes and sheenies." Our mothers unstitched the word *Police* from our shirts and we were now the Mount Vernon Revolvers.

Mother said to me one day, "Dear, do you know what I'm hoping you'll do?"

"Be a millionaire," I said.

"Not exactly," she said.

"Learn to shave without cutting myself," I said.

"Not exactly that, either," said mother. "Dear, what I have in mind is this. I know that when I butt into you boys' business you think I'm butting in, and I don't pretend to be a sporting expert, but I think you should make your brother a part of your basketball team."

"I don't," I said, "because he's a year younger than the rest of us are and it's not right. I don't want to insult the other Revolvers by dumping a young kid on them."

"You could make a place for him," she said. "I know that when I mention sports you think I don't know what I'm talking about. But I know for a fact that your team boys wouldn't be insulted. Speed is a wonderful basketball player and all your teammates would be glad to have him."

"Who said that? Whose mother were you talking to?"

"I was simply told so," she said.

"Who said he's a wonderful basketball player?" I asked. That had stung me. I hated whoever had said it. The worst of it was that I knew it was true. Speed was a wonderful basketball player and I was less than wonderful. There was no disputing that, but mother would not reveal who said those heart-sinking things. Maybe father said them. I spent more time trying to figure out who said those things than addressing myself to the truth of the situation.

On this issue through the whole first winter of the life of the Revolvers my principal antagonist was Ed Selkowitz. Ed hinted several times, soon coming out more and more broadly with it, that Speed could provide a dimension our Revolvers really needed.

When I think of Ed Selkowitz I think of a sweet, sincere, honest, fair-minded boy with wrists so powerful he shot baskets long range with his hands high over his head. When he passed the ball he passed bullets, and he passed fairly, too—*fairness* was his quality. He played no favorites, he passed to the right person in the right place. He was a team player all the way. Ed didn't care who scored just so long as the *Revolvers* scored. He never stopped playing, he played every game to the last second, and we all knew how he rescued us ten, twenty times a game from bad situations.

I wished only that he'd let the truth die. But he could never cease campaigning for Speed. Ed knew a sterling basketball player when he saw one, he'd played with Speed for years on the Wilson School playground, and he knew how Speed could help us.

Maybe the more Ed Selkowitz played beside me the more he admired my brother. I was a reasonably helpful player with serious deficiencies. My greatest asset was my skill at the center-jump. I was a tall boy and a very good center-jump. In those days the center-jump was extremely important because the game came back to the jump after every basket. My timing was perfect, I could spring high into the air, take good control with my fingertips, and thereby give the Revolvers possession six times in ten.

Unfortunately, however, once we started down the floor, I had an incurable tendency to retain possession of the ball rather than to pass it or shoot it. In the service of some anxiety of my own I coveted the ball and I wanted to keep it. I did not want anybody else to touch it. It was mine. But that was not the point of the game. The point was either to score a basket or pass the ball to someone among your teammates who had the will to do so, to score more than the other team, and win.

My anxious reasoning seemed to hold that if we never relinquished the ball the other team could never score. But neither could we. All games would end zero-zero. I was all form. I was a splendid ball-handler—indeed, too good. "The trouble with you," Ed Selkowitz told me often, "is you dribble too good, you dribble your way into a crowd and come out the other side and nobody touched the ball but you. That gets us absolutely no place. All you accomplished was you kept the ball you had in the first place. Why don't you pass the ball to the rest of us and let us score some points? Why don't you sink it in the basket? Why don't you pass it out to another human being? What have you got against us? Why not pass it out to one of us guys and let us see if we can sink a few if you don't mind? Why is the ball so precious to you that you want to hang on to it all your life?"

He asked me those questions a thousand times, before every game and during the game and after the game in the greasy diner at our midnight supper. If things had come down to it Ed Selkowitz and the Revolvers would rather have had Speed than me. I gave in.

Speed played with us all our second year and that was far and away our best year, and mother was pleased. We played about fifty games and won about thirty.

Speed was becoming a very distinguished basketball player indeed. One of his most powerful attributes was his skill in shooting from the corners. He was phenomenal. He almost couldn't miss. Boys' teams didn't bother to guard shooters in the corners and he scored ten or twelve points a game before the other guys woke up to what he was doing to them. Twelve points was a hot hand in those days—I'm talking now about 50–40 games, 45–35 games, we didn't shoot so much then as now, and of course the center-jump slowed the game.

Then when the other team finally put the guard on Speed in the corners he came out of the corners onto the floor and in the most spectacular and unprecedented manner violated all the coaching wisdom anybody had ever heard—he fired one-handed jump shots.

Nobody in America was shooting one-handed jump shots in those days except some colored boys in some colored colleges down south and the Harlem Globetrotters up north. People watching Speed for the first time gasped and said it couldn't be, nobody *threw* the ball at the basket like that, it wasn't the done thing. He was defying all the books, all the manuals, everything that passed for the wisdom of basketball.

When Speed played for Mr. Cabot at the high school the following year Mr. Cabot tried to prohibit him from shooting one-handed. Coach Cabot told Speed it wasn't done, nobody shot one-handed, and Speed said, "I do it my way or I g-g-g-g-g-g-g-g-g-g . . ."—do it his way or he'd go back and play with the Revolvers. Mr. Cabot remembered that the first son of the police chief had turned his suit in. He wasn't going to be so foolish as to allow this improved second son to do the same. "All right, then, shoot with one hand if you must," he said, and Speed shooting one-handed set county scoring records that stood for many years. All around the county coaches and players said they intended to take up one-handed shooting, too, but it was a quarter of a century before anybody seriously did it. Then *everybody* did it.

Alas! in the same year my Revolvers fell apart. All the boys but me had become trapped in their parents' demands that they forgo basketball and focus on their studies. More and more they were dropping out, seeming to grow faster than I, dropping out of basketball and taking up studies—aspiring to lives of business, law, medicine. My playmates had been warned of the future, brought to earth. I neglected my schoolwork for the sake of our team, but that was a sacrifice my fellow Revolvers were unwilling to make. In most of my school subjects my grades sank to F.

Sometimes I found it almost impossible to gather five boys to present to opponents who took basketball more seriously than we. My teammates had grown sullen on the telephone, pleading all sorts of excuses why they could not leave home, they were worried about their grades, worried about their college entrance applications. They had fallen from the dreams of boyhood into the fantasies of realistic life.

On one of the dreariest, saddest nights of my life I rode a streetcar in the rain with Froo Gross, Ed Selkowitz, and Phil Shopsin somewhere into Yonkers for a game at a high school. A fifth Revolver was to have met us there. I forget who. He never showed up. The janitor did not show up, either, to unlock the building. The other team arrived, piling out of two cars, shouting and laughing and screaming as we Revolvers used to do. These kids struck me as awfully young and childish. They offered us one of their players to make our fifth, but we couldn't see ourselves playing that way, we'd been nine Revolvers from the beginning, we were ten the year Speed was with us, and we were four of us now dripping in the rain somewhere at a darkened school in Yonkers where we had never been and would never come again and to which, in any case, the janitor never arrived. That was the last game I booked.

Back in Mount Vernon that night the high school was lit from top to bottom. A critical game was in progress. Cars were parked for a mile up and down Gramatan Avenue. Froo, Ed, Phil, and I couldn't even get in. Inside the school, on the basketball court, my brother Speed was popping shots from the corners and from the center floor. He was the hero of the night. The sight of his photograph in the Mount Vernon *Daily Argus* was intolerable to me. The first time I saw his name in big headlines I almost expired of rage and self-pity.

If in the midst of things—if in the midst of the busiest possible day of all days, Thanksgiving, Christmas, Easter, never mind what—I dropped by Walk a Mile House to see my trains Champrain ran upstairs from the kitchen to join me, so devoted was she to me, so suspenseful and so painful was my absence to her.

One evening I dropped by Walk a Mile House in the midst of the grandest dinner party of important capital investors and their women to check my trains and how they ran, and as I sat there at Walk a Mile Railway Champrain appeared in her black-and-white starched serving-girl uniform, calling to me as breathless as a quarter-miler from having run those flights of stairs, "Keep that engine flying down the track, follow me to the observation car," and when I arrived in the observation car I observed her uniform hung on the bedpost and her happy body bouncing on her back on the bed and we made love on the straightaway at sixty m.p.h. Sixty m.p.h. was considered high speed in those days. Then we threw everything into reverse—she snatched her uniform from the bedpost and dashed from her room, patting down her starched skirt to make it look again as fresh and as starched as ever (at least to the casual eye), down the stairs to the important moneyed men and women dining below who had not noticed that she'd been gone.

On another occasion, in the midst of a dinner party, when I dropped by Walk a Mile House to check little technical details (about which I was totally ignorant) on the Walk a Mile Railway she ran to me breathless again between courses and threw herself down beneath the train table where in our heedless passion we entangled our legs in the railroad wires and blew every last fuse of Walk a Mile House. I could have been a headline in the Mount Vernon *Daily Argus:* BOY ELECTROCUTED WHILE PLAYING WITH TRAINS. Could have been, but luckily wasn't, could have been BOY AND GIRL BLOW UP HOUSE WHILE MAKING LOVE UNDER THE RAILROAD RIGHT OF WAY. We learned to care less and less for consequences. I would have loved to have had our supreme life known to all people everywhere, this life of joy I led with Champrain. To every other eye she was a servant and I was family. In fact, however, she and I were family. Certainly we were closer than grandmother and grandfather, who never kissed. But we were not discovered by the United States Census. We were outcast family, although we never felt outcast, we felt on the other hand privileged, special, secluded, superior. Everyone else was outcast, not us. Nobody knew our bliss but us. She was mine and I was hers and we enjoyed each other in every way known to man and woman as soon as we figured out how.

No consequences could have equaled or erased or diminished the pleasures we knew. Only great good happened between us and almost nothing bad—a few blown fuses: grandmother lit candles and replaced the fuses and grandfather condemned the West-chester Lighting Company.

Sometimes mother, father, Speed, and I walked across town for Sunday dinner at Walk a Mile House. In time, as his conscience and his moral indignation deepened, Speed refused to go, but mother and father and I continued to go, and Champrain served our meal, gliding back and forth between dining-room and kitchen.

When her eye caught mine she smiled without smiling. We had a secret. We pretended not to know each other. I spoke of her to others as "the girl." That amused us and had its practical value, too, establishing my distance from servants, as if I believed that servants were so far beneath me they did not even have names—"Ask the girl for more meat . . . tell the girl to tell the cook . . ."

Champrain was unkind to grandfather. One of her tasks was to tell him which plates she was setting before him, but often she told him wrong, told him carrots for beans, hot for cold, sweet for sour, slid the salt to him when he had asked for pepper, handed him water for wine, wine for beer, confirming his belief that she was not only smelly and dirty but stupid. She made life harder for him than it needed to have been, avenging herself as well as she could for the insult with which he had wounded her.

On the subject of race I was always tense at dinner at Walk a Mile House. Every evening episode of "Amos 'n' Andy," for which we were held as captive audience, opened the whole subject all over again in grandfather's mind. Moreover, grandfather at this time had taken a strong dislike to the black prizefighter Joe Louis. Listening to Louis's fights on the radio grandfather winced as if he himself were the victim of each blow Louis landed on a white opponent. He rooted for Schmeling, Sharkey, Braddock, Tommy Farr, Two-Ton Tony Galento against Louis, and even for Buddy Baer, though Baer was a Jew. Whenever prizefight time approached I feared grandfather's breaking out with new racial epithets insulting my defenseless Champrain.

Consider. I have nine grandchildren. Whenever I am tempted to offer one of them a pious lecture on the wise life I remember this: that of all the thousands or millions of words grandfather ever spoke to me, of all the sermons he delivered in the hope of teaching me the rules of the jungle and how to dominate the pack, of all the maps of the world he drew to illustrate his theories, of all the tales of heroic men he presented to me for my emulation—Washington, Ben Franklin, Andrew Carnegie, and his superhero Henry Ford—almost the only passage of his collected speeches I remember was his fleeting insult of Champrain, his having called her one night within her own hearing and mine a dirty smelly, etc.

That was the best thing he ever did for me, his greatest boon to my life. Nothing he ever said so beautifully assisted me as that darting attack upon Champrain, for if he had not spoken as he did she and I might never in turn have met with our eyes. She might have remained for me forever only the girl who had brought us grandmother's candy. Thus grandfather with his few immortal words *did* change my life, not at all as he intended.

Only I knew who she was, and only she knew me. She and I adored that game of make-believe: make believe you are the serving girl and I am the prince of Walk a Mile House. I suppose other serving girls and other princes have played that game the world over, but in view of our never having heard of them this felt like our heaven alone. As she served the table I alone saw that she was smiling. To other guests she appeared remote or withdrawn, nondescript. When at last I mentioned her to Speed he could not quite place her. Then he said, "Oh, the s-s-s-s-s-straight-faced girl?" Yes, you could say that, the straight-faced girl.

Sometimes as she served us her bare arm came close to my cheek, the heat of her flesh was on me. Of course she did it to make my scalp tingle, make my pecker jump, destroy my appetite for food, send my mind wandering. On her circuit of the big dinner table sometimes unobserved she touched a finger to the back of my neck, her face all the while impassive, straight, unsmiling. Her touch unnerved me.

Let's invent statistics, as people do. Champrain and I traveled once-and-a-half from here to the moon and back on the Walk a Mile Railway. Sometimes we rode under the table, sometimes in the observation car. We were the only two riders in the history of the road. I was the engineer and she was the passenger. Sometimes the railroad ran itself and we were both passengers. We had no Jim Crow car on that train—the engineer and sole passenger desegregated together. We used the same rest room. Also same bathtub, same sleeping compartment. Simultaneously. No other railroad provided such friendly services. The engineer permitted the passenger to be engineer if she wished, and he became passenger. They exchanged positions. They assumed whichever position was fun. In spite of the engineer's distraction the railroad had the best safety record in America. Never an accident. Once, however, the passenger bit the engineer's nose so hard she drew blood. The engineer told his mother his bruise had been suffered during a Revolvers basketball game, and his mother thought it was odd—"A bite, dear, do the boys bite at basketball?" The bite left a small scar at the tip of his nose he would carry with him to the end of his days.

Walk a Mile Railway traveled only through New York State. Those were the tickets supplied by the manufacturer—the cities of the Hudson and the western expanse of the state, Kingston, Albany, Schenectady, Amsterdam, Utica, Rome, Syracuse, Auburn, Ithaca, Buffalo, Binghamton. At the end of the route was Niagara Falls, often called "the honeymoon capital of the world."

Sixty-seven years old, sitting here writing my memories of Champrain Johnson, I develop at my desk an erection like new. "Such is the power and glory of railroading, which changed the face of the nation."

After years of delay and diversion grandfather turned his attention again to his *One-Volume World Encyclopedia of Sexual Health & Information*. For many years grandfather's unborn book had stood on his sun parlor shelf. It was a sturdy, pretty book, bound in red buckram with the overgrown title and the publisher's somewhat redundant name in gold on the spine: *Walk a Mile House Press*. It was five hundred pages long, all blank. Word one had yet to be written.

I may have been his inspiration for the revival of this project. My teenage presence, my deepening voice, my sprouting beard, the very smell of me recommended the idea. He made me a part of it. On several Sunday mornings he summoned me to the sun parlor of Walk a Mile House to discuss from the point of view of innocent boyhood the whole question of sexual health.

I was his stooge and dummy. I didn't mind. I enjoyed it. My audience was his assembled hopeful friends and investors, his laughing, joking, boisterous, smoking choking coughing men calling one another Mr. Morgan Mr. Rockefeller Mr. Astor Mr. Carnegie in their airtight space. I entered his parlor with the convincing air, I know, of a boy who hadn't the slightest idea in the world why he'd been asked to come. It was as if someone having just noticed me strolling past the window had on the impulse asked me in.

"We've been talking something over," grandfather said, "and we need your current slant on our idea." He introduced me to his visitors, naming them in order as he pointed round the room. Here and there he named a man wrong, but the marvel of his having named them on the whole so right redeemed his occasional error. He was impressive, to be sure.

"I'll give you what I can," I said.

"I happened to think of my grandson because I know something about his ignorance," grandfather said. The men of the room gazed upon me as the model of ignorance. It was all in a good cause. "Our book will dispel my grandson's ignorance," grandfather said. "This is a boy whose whole generation is waiting to be set free."

It was grandfather's belief, he told his potential investors, that out there in the wide wide world a vast market of ready young lonesome boys and girls milled ever so restlessly, longing for information about sexual life. Their blood was up but their knowledge was down. At high-school dances they sat more or less idle along the wall, girls on one side of the room, boys on the other, awaiting grandfather's *Encyclopedia* to guide them into the night. The book would lead the child. That was his theory.

Playing this game was thrilling to me. It was fun, I did it easily. We love those games we're good at.

Speed said it was foul lying, crooked stuff, charlatanism, a fraud, like knifing naked girls in a basket. No, I replied, it was an art, a kind of stage-acting, it was money-earning in a good family cause. It was keeping the peace with grandfather. If I didn't keep it who would? I gave grandfather what I knew he wanted. It was the best way to deal with him.

Speed dealt with him another way. Speed boycotted Walk a Mile House and thought I should have remained away, too. Speed believed I was a hypocrite for hanging around as I did, for lending myself to grandfather's purpose. He called me an "ass-kissing kiss-asser," and he shocked me when he said to me, "You sometimes sound m-m-m-m-m-m-m-m-m-m-m-m-m-m-m . . ."—I sometimes sounded more like grandfather than grandfather. That was something for me to think over. I have been thinking it over ever since.

Grandfather fired the questions. I was the specimen witness. He laid the groundwork. He described the general intention of his book—*their* book. "How do you think boys and girls in Mount Vernon High School are going to react to this book?"

"Of course I can't speak for girls," I shyly said, "but I know that the boys are going to leap at a book like that."

"Tell us a bit about boys then, it's been a long time since we were boys in this room, tell us what boys your age actually *know* about sexual health and information?"

"I regret to say we're ignorant," I said. "We just exchange all our misinformation."

"Tell us," he said—I knew what he meant me to tell. He fired up his burney-burney, filled the sun parlor with its tranquilizing fumes, set himself afloat, and relaxed his associates, too. Their faces in relaxation turned earnestly toward me. Grandfather uncapped his pen, folded back the cover of his writing tablet. "Tell us," he said, "give us some sort of an idea what a boy of your age and condition thinks about the opposite sex. Tell us this, do you have a female friend who's a—very special friend of yours?"

"Well, there's mother," I slyly said.

"I don't mean your mother."

"I know you don't mean mother," I said. He always said *your mother*, never *mother*. "Or grandmother. I know you're asking if I have a girlfriend yet, but no, sir, I don't have a girlfriend, I'm probably not ready for a girlfriend yet between my ignorance, my nervousness, my fear, my not knowing how to go about things."

"Yes. Of course. Very well put," he said. "But you do have some girls who are friends, don't you?"

"No, grandfather, I really don't."

"You don't go to dances? You don't go to parties? You don't belong to clubs at schools—the French Club, the Philately Club, the Railroad Club, clubs of that sort?"

"Oh, yes, we do those things, but they're not the same—"

"Not the same as what?"

"They only make things worse."

"You have no feeling about girls at all?" he asked. This worried him, or at least he made it appear so. He frowned, as if this problem might actually be too real even for his *Encyclopedia* to solve.

"*Feelings* about girls, yes, I have them," I said, "as all boys do—at least all *healthy* boys, or so we're told, we're told it's all very healthy to think about girls as much as we like, as long as we do our schoolwork first, but in many ways we don't even have the preparation to think about them—"

"The vocabulary?" grandfather asked. A principal feature of his *Encyclopedia* was to be its comprehensive section of vocabulary.

"That's certainly part of it. Boys lack the vocabulary."

"Do girls have the vocabulary?"

"Maybe they do. I don't know girls well enough to know what they have."

The men laughed at my unwitting double meaning. Grandfather wrapped his own secret smile around his cigar. "I'd conclude from what you're saying that if a book came on the market that would help you acquaint yourself with girls and their vocabularies you'd welcome such a book."

"I'd buy it right up," I said.

"At seven dollars and fifty cents?" he asked.

"I guess I should have asked the price first," I said. Grandfather's price-conscious men laughed again. "No, I wouldn't be able to pay that much for a book, nobody would except Henry Ford—"

"Then we've got here a great big book at seven-fifty that you and your friends are clamoring to buy, hundreds and hundreds of boys looking for the book that's not yet written, the good book not available to them, out of their desperate reach. Now what are you going to do? How are you going to read such a book even when it comes on the market? No boy can buy a book at seven-fifty."

"They'd have it in the school library, " I said. "I can see the kids crowding around."

"Reading it together," he said. "Of course the school's got to *buy* it in the first place." This was his master stroke, key and kernel of his plan. Every high-school library in America would own a copy of his book. On his tablet he drew the map of America, the forty-eight states, and by mental arithmetic this sightless genius astounded his associates by multiplying the number of states by the number of high schools in each state and the number of high schools in each state by seven dollars and fifty cents, arriving at a number not only correct but vastly satisfying to him and his men. He had been visualizing an expanded library scene, he saw dozens of kids all in a circle awed by the book, all of us more or less reading it together, dancing around it as if it were a bonfire, a pep rally. "Tell us," he said, "what do boys and girls talk about when they're together. Would boys and girls read this book together?"

"It would help if we could," I said.

"Do you wish you had a girlfriend? When I was your age I already had girlfriends."

"If I knew how to go ahead with a girlfriend I'd have one."

"You feel that if only you had more information you'd be able to get along better with the opposite sex. But when I was a boy we didn't have all that trouble. I didn't need a lot of information to get myself all dressed up and go down the street and wait for a girl to come by and tip my cap to her."

"That's just not how it's done any more," I said. "I think kids are more nervous now. A modern-day kid might have an idea he wants to say hello to a certain girl living nearby, maybe in the next house, but a boy can't just go over there and knock on her door—"

"Why not? What's the matter with you?"

"Boys are too nervous."

"Boys in my generation were nervous, too, but we worked up our courage until at last we could at least go over and knock on the girl's door. But I think I see what you're saying. Nowadays, with all our respect for information we think we need information and vocabulary to begin our acquaintance, we need more information to proceed. Boys don't understand the other sex and the other sex doesn't understand the boys."

"It's a vicious cycle," I said.

"Have you ever—then you've never engaged in, let us say, anything like an intimacy with a girl?"

Our audience was attentive to this. It was what they cared to hear, for they were curious about me, as if I were their son. It was almost as interesting to them as grandfather's projection of vast and satisfying numbers. I kept them awhile in suspense. I was learning how to tell a story. "I'm not totally sure what you mean by an intimacy."

"Hasn't your dad told you anything? This is surprising to me."

"Lots of dads don't tell their boys very much," I said. This hit home to these assembled dads. These dads before us in grandfather's sun parlor had not told their sons very much. "Boys' fathers don't tell them anything any more. They don't know how. They don't have the information. They don't have the—I don't know how to say it—we boys crave books to tell us these things, but there really aren't a lot of books on the subject as far as I know."

"Aren't *any*," said grandfather. "There aren't *any* books that tell boys and girls about intimacy. I've been telling people for years there have got to be books to tell these things—I mean one big book, one standard work on the subject, one volume in everybody's house or library. Do you think a book like this would profit from pictures in it?"

"I'd love pictures," I said.

"Pictures of intimacy," he said.

"Kids would go wild," I said.

"Let them go wild," grandfather said.

"Maybe drawings would be easier to handle," I said. "A book of pictures I don't know—I see the kids tearing a book of pictures to tatters."

"The library will order another," grandfather said.

"Yes, yes, pictures, not drawings," came a voice from the assembled men.

"I think all of us boys underneath are more anxious than we ever let on for health and information—"

"All right," said grandfather, "now you're going to find out what you don't know from a well-prepared and well-researched and scholarly and yet attractive and colorful popular easy-to-read book which is going to give you the knowledge of procedures. No high-school library is going to dare to be without it. Torn to tatters and reordered, there's the ticket."

Grandfather would provide all youth with the elements of Nature lately eroded by modern life. History told him he had struck upon a sound idea. What was Henry Ford's automobile but the merest boost to Nature! Man was here, wheels were here, the desire to travel faster was here, all grandfather claimed to provide was a vehicle offering a faster ride. He wasn't claiming his book would solve life any more than the Ford car had solved life. "I hate it when people call me a dreamer," grandfather said. "I'm a practical man, I'm a realist." His confidence soared with his conviction. People required his *One-Volume World Encyclopedia of Sexual Health & Information* as crucially as they required the Ford car.

Grandfather was delighted with my way of handling myself during those Sunday meetings, prouder of me, more pleased, more satisfied with me than he had ever imagined himself becoming. In a family divided I could be counted on the reliable side. His daughter Ember was a whore. His grandson Speed was slow. Railroading had done wonders for me.

Why should Speed have objected to my supporting grandfather in a business cause? Weren't we all better off when grandfather was happy and optimistic, when he felt the world was at the point of beating a pathway to his door? Ask grandmother. She knew better than anyone how important it was to help grandfather think he was making progress. With my Sunday assistance grandfather gathered boundless new energy and confident enthusiasm with which he soon raised thousands of dollars presumably to publish his marvelous book.

And yet, I who was stooge, dummy, specimen witness, proved in real life the other side of the case. I had no need for his book. When from the balustrade Champrain and I hand in hand gazed down into the well of the darkened house, and in our heaven's perch received the drifting aroma of paraffin, we required no volume to explain us to ourselves. We wouldn't have paid two cents for a book. We could not have used a book as a gift. When the lights blew, Champrain ran the water in her tub, and when I heard her water run I went to her, not to the high-school library.

Grandfather, inspired creator of the *One-Volume World Encyclopedia of Sexual Health & Information,* was also, at that very period of our lives, Champrain's admirer.

When nobody was about the house at breakfast to read the New York *Times* to grandfather Champrain read it to him. She was the best of all readers. Champrain, by reading the news, taught me how to read it ever after. She got the surrealism of it into her low, strong voice. I read any newspaper today in the voice of Champrain Johnson. Over the years I have watched other women, "anchors" as they are called, give the news on the television, reading it word for word, vacant of sympathy, drenched with sentiment, getting hold of the facts, missing the dreadful truth. Anchors indeed, dead weights. Nobody ever delivered the news like Champrain.

Grandfather did not know I sat there listening. I smell his toast, eggs, coffee. I marvel at the gusto of his attack on his grapefruit halves. He scoops, he slurps. Champrain cannot resist watching him. He quickens her own appetite. I hear his taxicab blowing its horn.

Pick a day. Pick a single day of the past. Champrain is reading. Hear her voice: "Singing toe is ruled by three hundred foreigners."

Grandfather said, "Spell it." Champrain spelled it. "Tsingtao," he said, "go on."

"Mayor and police flee before Japanese advance curbs on looting are remove invaders continue gains defeatist tone of the Chinese statements believe to be propaganda for surrender Admiral Chinese name the mayor of Singing toe like you say his chief of police and all members of the police force have fled from the port leaving the maintenance of law and order in the hand of three hundred foreigners who are arm only with clubs I feel sorry for them three hundred has got to try and keep the whole town peaceful."

"Next," said grandfather.

"Victory at Teruel is hailed with job in insurgent Spain troops order to pursue retreating Loyalists to consolate triumph reports rebel garrison still besiege though conceding loss of strategic hill all that war blood over a hill I don't believe it insurgent leaders hail the action as one of the most decisive defeats inflict on the government in the seventeen months old war seventeen months them fools been fighting."

"Next," said grandfather.

"Order restrains fixing of prices federation of dealer groups is told to cease unlawful practice in sales control—"

"Next."

"France to refuse to arm old alleys a virtual bargo order on armament supplies to Rumania and Slavia flirting by the two nations with Germany and Italy held cause for action whatever they mean by flirting officials said tonight that the French government have order a virtual bargo on armament shipments to their alleys—"

"Allies," said grandfather.

"Because of their growing friendship with Germany and Italy members of the chamber of deputies said that a long funny Frenchy name done order the suppression of government license—"

"Next," said grandfather.

"Relief to be added to job insurance where state checks are under substitute level—"

"Spell it," said grandfather. Champrain spelled it. "Subsistence," he said.

"Then the city will make up the difference all eligibles must file welfare authorities expect large savings without hardship on needy thank goodness."

"Next."

"President authorize new eligible for navy bids will be let soon for three million dollar craft."

"Authorizes a new what?" grandfather asked.

"President authorize new eligible," said Champrain.

"Spell it." Champrain spelled it. "Dirigible," grandfather said.

"The announcement mark the end of a period of uncertainty as to whether the government would experiment further with the lighter than air type of aircraft—"

"Next," said grandfather.

Champrain did not sit at table with grandfather. No, she was required to stand. She spread the newspaper on the dining-room table and stood before it, bent at the waist, her elbows on the table, forearms upright. Now and then with her bright red tongue she lubricated her lips. Grandfather required—or thought he required—a lot of news as fast as possible. Therefore she read to him very fast. To demonstrate his appreciation for her reading he sometimes (I saw this with my own eyes) reached for her and seized her hip, thinking to get a feel of what he could not see, and when he touched her she pulled away from him and ceased to read, not as a rebuke, I think, but as a way of collecting her thoughts in this matter, like time-out in basketball. Grandfather, too, ceased. He did not pursue her. When he seemed to be ready for listening again she continued. She was not moralistic about it, pious, or proper. No, she just did not like grandfather.

"Four murders laid to thug held here," Champrain read. "Detroit gangster and woman trap in apartment with thirty thousand dollars in narcotics call kidnapper too, police say he kill woman witness against him at trial in Missouri I don't know if I testify against a gangster myself I don't know if it be worth it to me to do it police place a member of the Detroit Purple Gang and his woman friend in the line-up in their pocket the police say they found a loaded twenty-five caliber automatic but automatic what—"

"Gun," said grandfather.

"That's right the suspect was handcuff and a search was made the police say they found fifty pounds of sugar morphine and cocaine

91

the usual method of mixing before making a sale it was value at thirty thousand in underwhirl trade—"

"Next," said grandfather.

"Pepper hits big business going from sugar to pepper Florida senator opens his campaign praising President Rofell opening a campaign for re-election Senator Claude Pepper criticize big business as the rotten apple in the business barrel—"

"Next."

"Split threatens in student union convention ends with mutterings of I don't know what."

"Spell it." Champrain spelled it. "Schism," said grandfather.

"Mutterings of schism delegates declare opposition to sending war supplies to Japan and rebel Spain—"

"Next."

"Brilliant Paris doctor unask as a lunatic—"

"Doctor what?" grandfather asked.

"I see now he unmask as a lunatic not unask my mistake nobody ask him nothing one of the capital's brilliant young doctors who had lately manage to get a following in fashionable circles has been unmask as a carpenter who escaped from an insane asylum sounds like some doctors right here in Mount Vernon he is man with a French name twenty-four years old who last February escape from the municipal asylum in the suburb of French name set up a doctor's office in Paris and his engaging personality soon attract a great number of patients he was able to inspire confidence not only with his patients but also with druggists and some medical men I bet he was good-looking too if he fool all them people like that I bet a lot of his patients was Frenchy women—"

"Continue," said grandfather somewhat impatiently.

"Sure enough just what I say," said Champrain, "one physician sent his wife to be treated by Frenchy name—"

"Next."

"Seabiscuit breaks track record to win earnings reach three hundred and forty million four hundred and eighty thousand—"

"How much?"

"Three four nought four eight nought."

"That's not millions."

"It's a lot for only a horse Seabiscuit defeat War Admiral amid scenes of frantic enthusiasm of a record crowd of forty million persons smashing the track record—"

"I'm sure it's forty thousand, not million," grandfather said. "Next."

"News and notes of the advertising field. Mutual billings hit new high, Pontiac utilizes radio scare, accounts, personnel, notes, Hanson joins J. Walter Thompson—"

"What's Hanson's name?"

"Maurice F. Hanson for the last five years account executive—"

"Bums one and all," said grandfather. "Next."

Champrain turned the page and resumed. "Swing viewed as musical Hitlerism professor sees fans ripe for dictatorship the greatest error in western intelligent culture is the separation of reason and emotion professor Harry D. Gideonse declare in an address—"

"Western what? Spell it." Champrain spelled it. "Western intellectual culture," said grandfather.

"I thought I say that."

"Next."

"King writes Rofell *Daily Herald* said today that a letter from King George accepting President Rofell's invitation to pay a visit to Washington next summer was en route to the White House."

"Next."

"First lady's trick dress three in one evening gown was a big help on her recent lecture tour says Mrs. Franklin D. Rofell the dress was of uncrushable black velvet with a long skirt oh my I bet she look pretty a jacket with a long sleeve was added for dinner wear to vary the appearance in the evening she sometime add a long sash that trail off into a brocade train a ruff around the neck provide another change Mrs. Rofell told a press conference—"

"Next."

"Boy three killed by smoke sister four overcome in closet where they hid from fire I see what's coming now these little children be black sure enough a three year old Negro was suffocate and his sister four was overcome yesterday when terrify by a smoky fire that start in their apartment they lock themselves in a closet the children were alone in the apartment when the fire start from some cause that Deputy Chief Thomas McCoy was unable to learn and before it could be brought under control eaten its way across the entire floor and down to the floor beneath. Southboun traffic along Seventh Avenue was reroute between a hundred and forty sixth street and a hundred and forty second street for nearly an hour now wasn't that too bad about the people that got held up in the traffic by these mean children burn up alive in the fire."

"Next," said grandfather.

Champrain composed herself and resumed. "Hitler held guided by stars in Czech crisis astrologer advise date for the venture Chancellor Adolf Hitler of Germany was inspire to maintain the firm stand he assume during the negotiations over the partition of Czechoslava by a favorable conjunction of the stars and planets report to him by his favorite astrologer according to reports current in formed circles in Berlin—"

Grandfather's breakfasts seldom varied. He scooped half a grapefruit, ate one soft-boiled egg, one slice of toast. His napkin was tucked for protection into his collar. He listened to his reader with the close attention of a child listening to a bedtime story. He drank one cup of coffee very quickly, removed his napkin, stood at his place, and tied his necktie. Sometimes he tied it well, sometime he tied it poorly, but in either case we were never to tell him he had not tied it well. He buttoned his vest and coat, counted his cigars and dropped them into his breast pocket. His reader continued all the while. If time remained, grandfather drank a second cup of coffee as carefully as he could to avoid its spilling, but he seldom finished his second cup. His taxicab arrived. His reader threw down the newspaper (later she would clip and save "Today's Radio Listings"), helped grandfather into his overcoat, handed him his hat, escorted him to his cab at the curb, and returned swiftly to the kitchen inspired to enjoy her breakfast as much as he had enjoyed his.

If grandmother were standing close he said a cool goodbye to her, but in later years she never even came downstairs to see him off. She watched for his cab from her window, and when it rolled away she descended for breakfast with Champrain.

Grandmother and Champrain shared their distaste for him. The less they relished him the more they loved each other. At the door he said to his reader, "I expect I'll be home for dinner," and the reader passed the word to grandmother. But if he decided during the day not to come home for dinner he was too thoughtless even to notify her by telephone. She took dinner with the black women as she had taken breakfast.

CHAPTER FIVE

FATHER OFTEN SAID, "Police work taught me that anybody that's got a secret also got somebody he wants to let it out to."

I had a secret and her name was Champrain and the thing I wanted to do most in this world was to tell Speed about Champrain and me. For a long time I had worried that people would know about Champrain and me, I did everything I could possibly do to keep it secret, and I perfectly succeeded. Now all of a sudden I wanted to share this secret I had kept so close.

I wanted to make Speed envious. He was a great basketball star and I wanted him to know that being a great basketball star was a fine enough thing but might not be as fine a thing as being as happy as I. I wanted Speed to understand that if he lived in a world of fame (by *world* I then meant the universe extending on four lines to infinity from Apartment 2–D of the Sheridan Gardens Apartments to the Pelham line, to the Bronxville line, to the Yonkers line, to 241st Street and White Plains Road in the Bronx) I on the other hand lived in a world of serenest bliss, a world of love and delight confined to two rooms in the attic suite of Walk a Mile House. I wanted him to know that I was not simply what I must have looked like to him, that I was not the mere anonymous unsung boy he thought I was, that I was unlike anybody he knew, that I was far more than just another kid plodding on through school, muddling his marks, slinking off in the afternoon to run his trains.

I wanted Speed to understand that Champrain for me was the first and foremost topmost and most stupendous thing in life, compared to whom even the most illustrious basketball career was nothing. I wanted Speed to know what he was missing. I wanted him to know I would not have traded Champrain for the glory of becoming the outstanding scorer in the history of Mount Vernon basketball. I think I believed that, too. Of course I hadn't been given the choice.

I wanted Speed to know that a certain young woman of my life whose name he hardly knew, to whom he had hardly ever spoken, whom he thought of as only a straight-faced black girl appearing now and again out of the kitchen, had shown me more than anyone had ever shown me of love and tenderness and sweetness and bliss and wisdom and good sense and hilarity.

I wanted my brother to know that the romance all the boys were always talking about I already *had*. I had it now and I had had it for a long time and they had never had it nor had anything like it. It made me laugh inside myself to hear boys boast of their conquests. After hours and hours of driving all over Westchester County trying to learn to drink, spending all their money on girls and gasoline, they managed finally by dawn's early light to place their hands on a girl's breast. This passed as some sort of achievement. In my eyes those boys were infantile. I wanted Speed to know that the experience all the boys yearned for with every cell of their straining bodies I *had*, that what all the infantile boys on the basketball team were thinking about all night and talking about all day I was *living*. If Speed were to know those things about me his respect for me would increase and draw us closer.

This did not immediately happen. I was uncertain how to approach Speed in the matter. For some weeks it occurred to me that if I could not bring myself to tell my secret to Speed I might be able to share it with Aunt Ember. What would Aunt Ember say? In my mind I gave her a speech in response to my disclosure—"Why not, a boy with a handsome body and a girl with a handsome body—I trust she has a handsome body, too . . ."

Then too, the question of color. I was unable to decide where Aunt Ember would stand if I told her Champrain was black. Sometimes it seemed to me the color difference might be O.K. with her. At other times I feared the possible consequences. How insane of me to risk Champrain and everything she so wonderfully represented for the questionable pleasure of admitting Aunt Ember to our secret!

But I did not know Aunt Ember as well then as I know her now, years after she is gone, and clearly I did not know Speed, either, who would have applauded me, praised me, supported me with his poet's soul. Speed the stutterer was himself of course an outcast, he would have embraced Champrain as a sister. I know this now, having been blessed by good fortune with years to think it over. But my mind was not then so acute with analogies.

At last, one night, I made a kind of decision. I would, so to speak, test the waters. In a confidential mood, in the dark, bed to bed, I approached Speed with the whole matter in a somewhat oblique way. I said to Speed across that no-man's-land between our beds, "I'll tell you something I heard if you swear you won't tell anybody I told you." Of course he agreed to that. "One of grandmother's maids—" I began.

"Did what?"

"Well, it wasn't so much what she did. She was done to."

"Which maid?" he asked.

"The youngest one," I said. "I can't remember her name."

"The s-s-s-s-s-s-s-s-s-s-s-s-s-s-s . . .?"

"Right," I said, "the straight-faced girl, I can hardly believe this myself, I don't know why I'm telling you."

"Keep going now that you s-s-s-s-s . . ." said Speed.

"I heard that grandfather tried to cop a feel from her."

Speed mildly swore, but his oath told me nothing. "So what?" he said.

"She was reading the newspaper to him and he kept edging over more and more toward her, closer and closer and saying, 'Come over here closer to me,' and she answered him, 'I'll read it louder from over here,' and he kept following her around the table until she ended up throwing down the newspaper and running away and squealing on him to Mary Washington and grandmother. What do you think about a thing like this happening? Do you have any opinion on it?"

Speed said, "I wouldn't p-p-p-p-p-p-p-p-p-p . . ."—wouldn't put it past him. "What opinion?"

"Opinion of grandfather doing a thing like this. Opinion of her being black," I said.

"Black or white's the s-s-s-s-s-s-s . . ."

Black or white the same. Yes, I needn't have been surprised, that was about the way Speed would have viewed it. "But what about such an old man doing it?" I asked. "Don't you think grandfather's being awfully horny at his age?"

"Men are h-h-h-h-h-h-h-horny at all ages," Speed said, but now he swore again, a somewhat more feeling oath than he had sworn a moment before. There was something here he was groping for, something more to all this than blackness or horniness. Speed had developed in his mind a more complex meaning to grandfather's copping a feel from a maid. For Speed it went deeper than my eye saw. It was something much more than ordinary mischief because whatever grandfather undertook was bound to be more deeply wicked than it first appeared. "That old bastard," said Speed.

He believed without much verification that anything bad about grandfather was bound to be true, that grandfather was base, that grandfather was guilty, guilty. Speed, in this case only, reversed the order of the law. He began with an assumption of grandfather's guilt on any charge brought against him, and he found in his own verdict corroboration of grandfather's bad character. In this case the thing that grandfather had done wrong was not that he had felt or stroked or caressed the maid, not that he had sneaked up on her from behind and got his hands on her, from whose clutch she had squirmed away and run and told grandmother, but that he had unloosed his whole evil character upon her, tainted her, poisoned her, contaminated her. Speed accelerated the rage and violence of his obscenity to a level so fierce I was shocked.

Why did Speed so violently swear? "What makes you so mad?" I asked. "He's just an old lecher."

"I don't care about l-l-l-l-l-l-l-l-l-l-l-l-l . . ." he said. He did not care about lechery, he did not care about race. It was the question of fairness which concerned Speed. It was always fairness he cared about. No, Speed did not care especially if grandfather were an old lecherous beast. Did Speed swear because grandfather was mingling the races? No, no, "Who the hell c-c-c-c-c . . ."—cares about the purity of the races? Not Speed. "It's not fair," said Speed. That was what he objected to, that it was not fair, that the poor girl whoever she was, whatever her name was, "the straight-faced girl," as he called her, was defenseless against grandfather, that grandfather had all the power over this girl and she had none over him, that she had everything to lose and he had nothing to lose, that if she resisted him he could fire her from her job with the snap of his fingers. "He could k-k-k-k-k-k-k-k-k-k-k-k-k . . ."—he could *kill* her if he wished, and who then would arrest and convict him? His son-in-law the chief of police? He could make her pregnant and disclaim her, she was without recourse, he had made a slave of her, a person without rights.

"I hadn't thought about it from that angle," I said.

"It's the only angle," he said. "The f-f-f-f-f-f-f . . ."

The fairness of it! Speed knew unfairness. That was Speed's way of coming at things, through the question of fairness, of justice, not sex or color but fairness and justice, and he lay there swearing far into the night.

I withdrew my idea of telling him about Champrain and me. My moment was gone. I saw that I'd need to hold on to my secret for a while. I saw that if I told my secret to Speed he would see me, too, as being in grandfather's position. If Champrain could not reject the king she could not reject the king's grandson, either. I could not at that moment have persuaded Speed that Champrain loved me, that we were in love now genuinely beyond doubt, free of all coercion. But in that moment he would have been unable to believe it. I was a kind of prince, after all. If Speed saw me as a drudge with a bad report card he saw me also as a prince of the estate from which he had been excluded by the king himself, who had declared him slow and stupid, useless because speechless.

I had not thought about the *fairness* of it all. Sex and color, yes, I had thought about them, but I had not yet arrived at fairness. Speed was ahead of me. He had always been ahead of me. He was younger but older. Do you follow?

We grew closer than we had ever been. We seemed to forgive each other everything. We began to walk to school together. We had not walked to school together since we'd been little kids, and now one day, all of a sudden, we fell into step together and walked to school, and mother said to me, apparently on the assumption that the decision had been mine, "You'll never realize what a beautiful sight it is to see my two boys walking to school together. Nothing has ever pleased me more in all my life."

I replied to mother, "As soon as we're out of your sight we have a fistfight and go different ways."

"No," cried Speed in the most alarmed manner. "No, no." He did not want mother to hear such a thing, even as a joke, and she was quick to reassure him, saying, "Dear, don't be so serious-minded, I know your brother's only fooling."

And why not? Why *not* walk to school with Speed? I had never wanted to be seen with Speed and his friends. They had always been too young for me, they had always seemed to me to be ignorant of the world. They were all virgins. God, if they knew what I knew—but they did not. And yet we had started out together one morning, Speed and I, fallen into step, as I have said, up the Sheridan Avenue hill to East Lincoln where, I supposed, other kids would join us, Speed would merge with friends of his own, and I with mine.

But nobody joined us. Everyone respected our privacy. Everyone assumed that this privacy was the thing we wanted, we two rugged independent brothers, Speed the silent basketball star and his big but smaller brother. I had the reputation then of being a sort of

101

secret lone operative—Speed's *mentor*, really, Speed's guide to life, Speed's one-man entourage aloof from the peasants, straight-arming the world, keeping all mankind at a distance. Nobody called to us, spoke to us, waved to us from passing cars, and so we walked all the way to school together, nobody but Speed and me.

Now for a while Speed was not only a brother but also a friend. Think how wonderful it was to have a friend right there in the house! The lives that we had always lived apart we could now live together in a kind of dual solitude in which we alone existed at the highest level of thought, as indifferent as possible to the boys we knew, and sometimes even contemptuous of them for their bad grammar and their low literary taste. We became inseparable.

Speed and I required privacy. We did not wish to be overheard. We sought the streets, walking in every weather. We walked miles and miles, up every street and avenue, down every lane and cul-de-sac in the city of Mount Vernon, New York. Nobody would ever know the streets of this city better than we. I can draw you a perfect map of Mount Vernon—a far more accurate map than grandfather's map of the world—even as I can recite the order of the streets, although I have been back to that holy city for only one day in fifty years.

We took up coffee-drinking and cigarette-smoking. We learned to drink coffee cup after cup, sitting in one or another of the little cafeterias on Fourth Avenue, the busy business street of Mount Vernon—Bickford's was one cafeteria, the Waldorf was another—loading our cups with sugar and cream and drinking the night away.

We compared our feelings on every subject. We talked about the books and magazines we read. We had become extremely conscious of our grammar. We had discovered the New Yorker and the New York *Times*. We abandoned Street & Smith pulp sports magazines, and we were contemptuous of the New York tabloids, the *News* and the *Mirror*, and of our unlettered ignorant father the policeman, who read the scandals in the tabloids and the news in the Mount Vernon *Daily Argus* and that was all he read and all he had ever read, whose character and motives we interminably discussed in the hope of discovering our own souls and our own vocations.

Much of our education occurred in Loew's and Proctor's first-run moviehouses, and after we had seen the first-run films we selected those which had challenged our minds and saw them again at the Bunny, the Parkway, the Embassy. With those films in common between us we sharpened and exercised our intellects in a ceaseless duel of comrades debating the nature of the world, the nature of mankind, the nature of God, religion, our grandparents, our friends, our teachers, our cousins and our aunts and our uncles all over town.

Walking the streets of Mount Vernon we honed our logic. We lay upon green lawns to contemplate the heavens. We leaned. Yes, we were always *leaning*. Speed required time to gather his thoughts for quick, precise delivery, to keep his stuttering minimal. We leaned against fences, houses, telephone poles, storefronts, cars, while Speed rallied his ideas within the limits of his speech. We corrected each other's fallacious thinking minute by minute, ever alert, sharpening ourselves with our exchanges, we debated, we clashed, we disputed, we thrashed out all the great ideas we had read in books or heard on radio.

We took policy positions on current issues. We had a policy position on everything—on Nazism, fascism, communism, isolationism, interventionism, unionism, racism, free trade, euthanasia, vivisection, capital punishment, and the admission of Alaska.

We plotted our schoolwork. One of my classes in my senior year was called Current Events. My teacher was a somewhat silly troubled man named Mr. Moore. I took as my subject for my term paper "Intermarriage," by which we mainly meant in those days marriage between a black person and a white person.

I had then no plan to marry Champrain or anyone else black or white. Not surprisingly, however, I was interested in the subject. Speed and I, walking the streets of Mount Vernon, hammered out our policy position. It was this: we favored intermarriage for people who cared to intermarry. We upheld the law of New York State, which permitted intermarriage. We felt it was an individual matter for each person to decide for himself or herself. I wrote this out. My brother corrected and expanded it. I corrected and refined his corrections and expansions. I supplied additions adapted from scattered library information. Speed supplied additions of his own gathered from library sources of his own. We mingled and merged our additions, we checked my spelling, we debated my punctuation.

My Current Events teacher Mr. Moore was delighted with the *style* of my paper, he approved the logic, admired the documentation, but he absurdly deducted a letter grade on the grounds that he did not expect black people and white people ever to marry across the color line. In the margin of the paper he wrote, "You're jumping the gun."

Speed ground his teeth to see the grade *B*. He was disgusted with Mr. Moore. "F-F-F-F-F-F-F-F-F-F-F-F . . ."—Fuck Moore's jumping gun, he meant. Speed knew intermarriage would come. Speed knew the future. He foresaw many events other people called impossible, and indeed almost everything he foresaw has arrived, much of it so long ago it has already passed to history, like the one-handed jump shot.

All right, now this seemed like the right time to tell Speed about Champrain. Yet I still could not do so. I held my secret close to me, concealed within me, urging Champrain to do the same, as I am sure she did. I now knew Speed so well and had become with him so wonderfully close and confidential that I knew he would cheer my news if only I told it to him. Yet I continued to withhold myself. I was somehow still unready or unable to tell him my most precious truth.

We discussed what we were going to be in life, what we were going to do with our futures. Speed's stuttering eliminated many possible jobs for him. Both of us knew we did not intend to go down the station, nor had father ever encouraged us to do so. I had never been serious about a career in the Share the Wealth program, as Speed had described it for me in my paper for Mrs. Packard-Steinberg, but Speed thought himself fit for such a career.

He regretted that society was organized to concentrate wealth rather than to share it, and by his eloquence I was converted to spiritual collectivism, theoretical socialism, even as I dreamed of being rich enough to be generous to the poor. I had abandoned plans to be a mailman, hairdresser, railroad man.

We discussed many girls and admired them and speculated about them, about their prospects as wives, and about the obligations of marriage. Speed loved girls and the girls would have loved him more easily but for his stuttering.

He had become taller than I. Worse than that, he was handsomer than I. In the past I had been superior to him in every department of life, but lately the evidence of my superiority had fallen away. He was now a far better athlete than I, and we knew it. He was as good a writer as I. But he did not realize that he was also handsomer than I. His sense of his own attractiveness had been cast into doubt for him by his lack of social success. If he was so handsome why wasn't he rich in girls?

He should have known how handsome he was by the way the girls on the street sized us up, looking from me to him, him to— him again, make a choice, pick a boy, lingering finally on him, never on me, dwelling on him, ignoring me. They might have given him their confidence except that as soon as he tried to engage in conversation with girls he lost through stuttering all the advantage he had gained through beauty and bearing.

Young women first meeting him thought he was having a heart attack, that he was choking on a fishbone. More sophisticated women thought he was having an orgasm right out there in the middle of the sidewalk. They had no way of knowing that Speed was as brilliant as he was handsome, a genius of written words. He writhed, he panted, his teeth clattered, sometimes he bit his tongue. His jaws froze. When he began to speak, tried to speak, girls turned from him to me as from a lost cause, as if to say, "Well, all right then, how about you?"

Speed traveled on two or three occasions to a notable institution of speech correction in Delaware, where he remained for a few days to be examined and treated. He came home resolved to attend to the matters revealed to him. He read books about stuttering. He read a book about the lives of famous men who stuttered—I was surprised to learn how many of the world's movers and shakers accomplished their great deeds in spite of their impediments. Speed attempted to acquire habits and develop attitudes thought to assist the stuttering victim to escape his condition. These suggestions often assisted him in life generally, but they did nothing to relieve his stuttering. Of the literature on stuttering he brought home from Delaware I remember nothing much but the word *disfluency*, which I have used in my writing as opportunity arose.

You must understand that Speed's stutter or stammer was not simply a moment's delay. It was a silence. Strangers unaware of the cause of his silence did not know whether Speed intended to speak at all. If not, why not? Speed learned to avoid confusion by maintaining a friendly face, a good smile. His smile enhanced his charm, but all he gained he soon lost when he tried to speak. One Mrs. Mullen, a tenant at the Sheridan Gardens Apartments, once referred to him as "the handsomest idiot who ever lived."

Try this experiment. Take a watch with a second hand. Speak aloud a simple sentence. Say, for example, "Let's go to the library," or "Have you had breakfast yet?" or "Please tell me the phone number of the Joneses on Smith Street." Say, "Mother, I'm going out to play." How long has it taken you? These sentences can be spoken in two seconds, three seconds, four. For Speed, a sentence made difficult by the double presence of the letter *L*—"Let's go to the library"—required of him half a minute or more unless in despair he chose not to complete it at all. The sentence "Please tell me the phone number of the Joneses on Smith Street" he would never have undertaken. Early in life he knew he could never master the telephone. He told me often that the severest penalty of his speech defect was his inability to reach girls by phone.

What was the cause of Speed's stuttering? Grandfather once believed that Speed at a young age had been frightened by a mad dog. Nobody could remember such an incident.

Alternatively grandfather held to the view that Speed's stuttering was the result of his having fallen, jumped, dived, or been pushed from the table in St. Petersburg, Florida. In my mind I denied that this had been the case since it was I who might have caused that fall in the near presence of Babe Ruth, unless the man of flesh I seem to remember was not Babe Ruth but mother's lost lover Doc Duffy.

During the time of our walking a million miles or more around and around the streets of Mount Vernon my brother Speed became deeply addicted to motorcycles. For several months the first plan of his life was to build for himself the motorcycle of his dreams. He declared that if only he owned his own homemade motorcycle he would be happy. We argued whether a motorcycle could bring a man happiness. I argued no and Speed argued yes and we never settled it.

Speed had gone gaga. Any discussion of any subject could be interrupted by the roar of a motorcycle speeding by. A motorcycle parked at the curb detained us indefinitely. We were obliged to pause and examine every feature of it. By the time we resumed our walking we had forgotten the subject of our conversation. He told me hundreds of things about motorcycles I had never demanded to know, how much they cost, how much they weighed, how many cyclinders they had, how much horsepower. I learned the meaning of loop frames, fork suspensions, leaf springs. I came to understand electrical systems. I became conversant with the ideas of counter-shaft gearboxes, chain drives, valves per cylinder, suspension characteristics, frames, carburetors, magnetos.

When Speed talked motorcycles he lost contact with me. This was uncharacteristic of him, for on all other topics he was conscientiously aware of my limits. He compared the features of one model of motorcycle with the features of another, trying to persuade me to share his conviction in matters toward which I was utterly indifferent. In this he reminded me at moments of grandfather arguing with me about the world economic system or the philosophy of Henry Ford, never noticing that I cared for neither.

To build his motorcycle Speed saved his money as he could. It was not much. Cash was scarce at our house. But he had no intention of surrendering his scheme. Now and then he bought parts and tools as his funds permitted. In his sleep he made motorcycle sounds. He collected some photographs of motorcycles famous for one reason or another, among these a red Indian he extravagantly admired but did not often see.

He acquired a contempt for automobiles, which he referred to as "four-wheeled vehicles," as if they were freaks of the road. But in fact, at that time, the motorcycle, not the car, was the freak, the odd thing—noisy, dangerous, threatening, immense, awkward, usually Harley-Davidson machines recklessly driven by irresponsible men destined for jail. Harley-Davidson's only American competitor was the red, trim, slim, lithe, light, graceful Indian, soon to disappear.

One bright April Sunday afternoon Speed's motorcycle plans abruptly changed, and in a way our lives changed too. As we were walking we turned a quiet corner into Summit Avenue and came upon an Indian parked glistening in the sun. It was even lovelier than its photographs. Indeed, lovely, only a motorcycle, but lovely. We approached it. Speed caressed it, sighed, spoke to it, fell in love with it, one might say—yes, fell in love with the Indian motorcycle if it were possible for a man to fall in love with a motorcycle. Intermarriage.

As I recall, after Speed had examined the machine we went up and down Summit Avenue ringing doorbells, seeking its owner. Uncle Wilhelm lived on Summit. We stopped at his house for help, but he had no idea who owned the Indian. "I don't notice motorcycles," said Uncle Wilhelm. Speed left a note taped to the machine, offering to buy it "at any price," although he hadn't fifty dollars to his name. He asked the owner to telephone him, but no call ever came.

No matter. If it was not to be that Indian it would be another. On the spot Speed declared his new plan. Instead of building his own motorcycle he would buy an old Indian somewhere, "customize" it, make it *his*, make it unlike any motorcycle anyone had ever owned anywhere or ever would and live happily forever after.

CHAPTER SIX

GRANDFATHER'S PROBLEM at this season of our lives was well-defined. He was in terrible trouble and required all his resourcefulness. He could have gone to jail. I could not imagine grandfather in jail. Who would dare to order him into a cell and slam the door behind him? Who could make him mop a floor, scrub a toilet? Accustomed as grandfather was to luxury and personal service he would never tolerate the discomfort of a jail.

The solution was uncomplicated. Grandfather and his lawyers formed a corporation to discourage litigation. *Our* corporation (for I became part of it) was known forever after as the Mount Vernon Venue Investment Corporation (MVVIC). We gathered together—Messrs. Dagger and Church (I do not invent names), grandfather, father, mother who was a heroine this day, a stenographer, and I—to convey grandfather's money to our newborn corporation, of which grandmother was named president, mother vice-president, and I accounts payable manager.

I think grandfather must have assumed that his incorporated money would remain within his control. He could not really believe it was leaving him. Although the very idea of the corporation was to insulate him from his enemies by detaching him from his holdings, he privately believed that when everything had cooled President Grandmother and Vice-president Mother would drop it all back in his lap. He thought of them as acquiescent. Grandmother declined to appear in the sun parlor. "President not present," said Mr. Dagger the word-playing attorney. Grandfather said she would appear in the course of the day, but she did not.

Nor did Speed appear. Grandfather had not included him. Speed was not acquiescent, as I was. In the division of things grandfather conveyed nothing to Speed, nothing to Aunt Ember. Speed was slow—that had always been grandfather's opinion—and Aunt Ember was a whore.

Grandfather had retained Messrs. Dagger and Church from time to time to preserve him from the intricacies of the law. Their greater mission now was to keep him out of jail. I was much entertained by Mr. Dagger, who was something of a punster, who spoke melodiously and rhythmically, as if speech were metered poetry. This was especially interesting to me, coming just at the time Speed and I were fervently engrossed by questions of language and writing.

Mr. Dagger's partner Mr. Church wore a coat and vest at all hours, even when the going was hottest and hardest in grandfather's steaming sun parlor. The month was June and the day was sultry. In two weeks I would graduate from high school. Mr. Church, unlike Mr. Dagger, was mainly silent, seldom looking up from papers on which he kept a close record of our proceedings. He appeared to have much more respect for grandfather than Mr. Dagger had. It might have been their strategy to keep grandfather in line by alternating Mr. Dagger's cutting frankness with Mr. Church's consoling respect. Mr. Church admired grandfather's having achieved so great a success in life in spite of his handicap (fortune must be counted success however ill-got) and he commended grandfather several times for his quick apprehension of the law. Grandfather thought up all sorts of angles his lawyers overlooked. They flattered him that he often knew other people's business better than people knew it themselves.

Grandfather had received money from many men coming at one time or another to Walk a Mile House to smoke and talk and laugh and inhale his burney-burney and convey to him sums large and small for grandfather ever so kindly to invest for them in fail-proof schemes like reusable stationery, unlosable golf balls, the telephonogram, the world's most powerful dog poison, ringless bells, and the *One-Volume World Encyclopedia of Sexual Health & Information*. Even at this very moment, when his troubles were raining upon him, he was engaged in a plan to establish a New York daily newspaper to tell the absolute truth about everything every day, and a sister picture magazine to tell it every week.

Grandfather claimed to have spent every dollar to develop the project for which it was assigned—for research, promotion, advertising, trademarks, patents, office expenses, and stationery. The stationery I certainly knew to be real enough. Grandfather's first step in the development of a project was always the design and production of new stationery. His letterhead featured his name, address, telephone numbers, his motto "A Promise Made Is a Promise Kept," and a delicate sketch of Walk a Mile House by an artist unknown, inaccurately representing the windows of the attic suite as if a third room existed between Champrain's and Walk a Mile Railway.

However, grandfather's tabulation of expenses fell tons and tons short of the money he had taken in. Somewhere or other fifty thousand dollars had dropped from view. He was unaccountable. He could account only in hundreds for dollars which had come to him in thousands. With his lawyers he had drawn long lists of credible disbursements for which, however, he could offer no proof of payment.

In the course of outlining our strategy Mr. Dagger was able to describe grandfather's crimes with eloquent candor. He relished detail, emphasizing to grandfather how guilty he was and how well his lawyers knew it. "To a rational mind it might appear that much of the money which came to you," said Mr. Dagger, "self-dissipated."

I could not keep from laughing at this. Mr. Dagger glanced at me quickly, seeming to ask, "What did I say to make the boy laugh?" Then he smiled a congratulatory smile at me for my appreciative ear. "Well might this smart lad laugh at self-dissipating money.

Well might a jury laugh, too. Take, for example, your admirable uplifting scheme to publish for the edification of the world your *One-Volume World Encyclopedia of Sexual Health & Information.* You became so diverted by the satisfying adventure of the money-raising itself that you allowed the money to disappear without accounting. You became more transfixed by money than by sex. It appears to be your figmentary claim," said Mr. Dagger to grandfather, "that money dissipates itself, that it has a conscious will, that money performs autonomous operations upon itself like the doctor in the newsreel last week with a knife and a hand-held mirror slicing out his own appendix."

Self-dissipating money! I loved it. I laughed for days and days, and Speed laughed with me. Grandfather's money had been resting itself in a safe place, and on this day it was to become the capital of the Mount Vernon Venue Investment Corporation, even as grandmother, mother, and I were to become the corporation's officers.

Truly grandfather's money had a life of its own after all. It had come to him magically. Easy come easy go. Now it departed from him to join the corporation, to trick the army of enemies, those men who had so recently begged to be joined with him as his hopeful associates, who so boasted of him to their own friends, who tried to flatter him by saying, "We're already enriched just standing in your presence," although, as things turned out, it was really not presence but money they sought, those men who had sent him gifts and praised the splendor of Walk a Mile House and admired the swiftness of grandfather's brain. "If I'm guilty of anything," grandfather bitterly said, "I'm guilty of being too kind." These plans which other men called deceptions grandfather had viewed as works-in-progress.

On his own terms Mr. Dagger concurred. He saw that I enjoyed his style. Grandfather, too, as a man of words, was amused by Mr. Dagger's ironic way of putting things. To amuse us he sang on at unusual length. "These men threatening suit against you to recover their self-dissipated money are unreasonable in their disappointment," he said. "Their anger derives from their gullible greed.

After all, you always told them what stuff you were made of. You told them over and over again that you were a tricky man, Mr. Schneck. They should not have expected you to be any less tricky with their money than with anybody else's. You promised them that you were a moneymaker, and so you were, and it was *their* money you were making. They had had grand hopes of your multiplying their dollars endlessly. And so you would if they had given you a chance. It is only that your creations have not yet been created, they are simply unrealized, they have taken the temporary form of a mountain of embossed stationery. Your announcement of the unlosable golf ball is different only in degree from the materiality of the unlosable golf ball itself. These litigants are prematurely angry, short of patience. They were not deceived by *you*, Mr. Schneck, but by themselves, by their having intoxicated themselves with hope. This is a poor situation into which they have forced us. To protect ourselves from them we have insulated ourselves within this corporation."

But when the time came for us to sign binding documents mother rebelled, crying out, "I'm not going to sign any of your damn documents," and she tightened her jaws on what she had said, refusing at first to give her reasons.

"Is that my daughter I hear?" grandfather asked. He was astonished at mother's new boldness. She had never resisted him. She had never spoken so fearlessly in his presence. I thought it was wonderful, rather thrilling, really. She frightened even herself.

In gentle tones Mr. Dagger said to mother more than once, "Madame, do give us your reason," and at last she was able to gather herself to do so. "I won't stand for one of my boys being officers of the corporation and the other not. I won't have Speed excluded. Both my boys should be officers or neither of them should be, but not one without the other. It's not fair. I never played favorites with either of my boys in all their lives. Life is hard enough for Speed."

"Who is Speed?" asked Mr. Church.

"The other grandson," said grandfather.

"My other son," said mother.

"He fell on his head when he was a baby," grandfather told Mr. Dagger. "He's slow."

"Speed is as fast as anybody else," said mother, "faster than most. It's only his speech that's slow. What you can all of you do is leave me out and put Speed in."

"Never," said grandfather. "I'll go to jail before I put him in. He's not responsible."

"He's responsible," said mother. "He's the most responsible boy in the world, he's more responsible than anybody I'm looking at anywhere in this room right this minute."

"He's the captain of the high-school basketball team," father quietly said. "He's on the honor roll." Father came across the room to mother and sat beside her and took her hand, both encouraging her and restraining her. He was fearful of her challenging grandfather, and perhaps he was embarrassed, too, for having left to her the fight he ought to have fought himself. "You've got to sign it," he said, not less gently than Mr. Dagger had spoken. "It's all for the best."

"All for the worst, dear, that's what you mean," said mother.

"You don't want to be left out," said father.

"I don't want to be in, either," mother replied. "We've got to take care of Speed."

"It's only money." This sounded funny coming from grandfather.

"It's only money I want," mother said. "Not for myself but for my boys, for both my boys, not for one boy and not the other. Speed is my boy, too."

"These little differences of opinion occur in the best of families," said Mr. Dagger the lawyer. "Let me suggest that those of us who can bring ourselves to sign these pages do so, and we who sign will continue to pray for the guidance of the others."

"We require another witness," said his partner Mr. Church.

"A witness, yes," said Mr. Dagger.

"Send the vice-president to fetch a maid as witness," said grandfather.

But now mother roused her will as never before. "I'm not running vice-president errands," she said. "I'm not the vice-president. I haven't agreed to any of this and I don't know if I ever will."

"The vice-president declines to run," quipped Mr. Dagger.

"Then ask my daughter."

Oh, that was different! Poor mother. As his daughter she had always dashed here and there as grandfather required. What was one more dash? Away she flew, returning soon with Champrain.

How I should have loved the novelty of Champrain's having signed as corporation witness. That would have been a precious souvenir, a single page eventually bearing grandmother's signature, mother's, mine, father's twice (once as witness to mine, once as "enabling agent"), and Champrain's.

When Champrain entered the sun parlor Mr. Dagger was arrested for a moment by her beauty, collected himself, and asked her, "Have you, young lady, yet seen your twenty-first birthday?" Her eyes met mine to ask whether a simple question so formally phrased meant what it sounded like. "No, sir, I have not seen it."

She was eighteen, as I was, and therefore, somewhat to her disappointment, I think, disqualified as witness and sent away to bring us an older woman. Thus not Champrain's signature but the signature of Mary Washington appears with the stenographer's as witnesses to the corporation papers. At the hour she signed, however, she had witnessed nothing. She witnessed blank spaces. Grandmother had not yet signed—she had not even come to the sun parlor. Mother had not signed. I had not signed.

The first person to sign was father, in his role as enabling agent, for which he received a "fee" of five thousand dollars for duties unspecified. This was a gift to him from grandfather. In his life father had never received so large a sum at once, nor would he ever again. I appreciate its magnitude when I remember that our rent for 2–D at the Sheridan Gardens Apartments was twenty-eight dollars a month.

"Now," said Mr. Dagger, "to conclude these arrangements with the happiest thought, it has come to my mind to arrive at a family agreement in the following way. Here is the most successful thing we can do to please mother and grandfather. We can permit one grandson to represent both."

What was this? What did he mean by this? He meant that we

should do as he and grandfather had decided to do. I should accept my title as accounts payable manager, but at the same time, said Mr. Dagger to me, "to please mother and to make all these arrangements fair all around in every direction, you will promise to share your duties with your brother Speed."

"Share the duties and also the money, dear," mother said to me.

"For a family so loving and trusting these paper-signings hardly seem appropriate," said Mr. Dagger, holding a document with his fingertips to express his disgust. "We're above this. I see that I'm right. One grandson might sign for both. This boy will share his situation with his brother."

"We share everything," I said.

"Do you really?" mother asked me. "Will you share the money as well as the situation? Do you promise, dear?"

"I promise," I said. "Of course I promise. I'll share everything in the world with Speed."

"Mother's mind is easy to hear that," said Mr. Dagger. "You are an exemplary son."

"I hope we'll write this down," said mother.

"Indeed we'll write this down," said Mr. Dagger.

"And sign it," mother said.

"Of course," said Mr. Dagger, "we'll write it down and sign it and that will be the agreement between the two grandsons, your two fine sons, this son here and your honor-roll son called—"

"Speed," said mother, but with effort. Her encounter had exhausted her, moved her, and exhilarated her. She had won few enough victories in her life, and until this day never against grandfather.

With the signing of the papers the Mount Vernon Venue Investment Corporation (MVVIC) assumed from grandfather a sum slightly less than fifty thousand dollars (but a very great sum in its time) to be administered by the woman he had abused for years, my own beloved grandmother upon whose bosom I drifted to blissful sleep in the garden of Walk a Mile House; by my mother, who had always feared her father and cringed before him; and by me when I came of age.

It was a ceremonial signing. Everyone sipped a bit of whiskey except Mary Washington, who had left the room. Father watched me closely as I drank. I pretended to shudder at the acrid sting of the whiskey, as if I had never tasted it, although Speed and I had nipped from time to time at father's supply, and Champrain and I at grandfather's. When everyone laughed at my innocence grandfather asked what was funny. "They're laughing at me," I said, slurring my words as if I were becoming intoxicated.

"Don't laugh at him," grandfather said, "this is something for the *Daily Argus*, a boy becomes a corporation officer when he's only eighteen, he never drank a sniff of whiskey in his life and he's an accounts payable manager, we're talking about a boy who's got the stuff," but Mr. Dagger cautioned us all that the less said about this to the *Daily Argus* the better.

Mary Washington, servant, one of the witnesses to the signing of our corporation papers, had been a maid at Walk a Mile House for as long as I could remember—*longer* than I could remember, for she had been there before I was born.

She almost never left the house. Somebody once told me she owned no street shoes. When I was twenty years old I left Mount Vernon to go and succeed in the world. She was there when I returned for a day's visit twenty years later, and she was still there when grandfather died at ninety.

How admirably she protected grandmother and grandfather from everything! So people said. But as my own psychological intelligence advanced I saw that it was Mary Washington she protected. In the beginning her province was the cellar laundry. She washed and hung and ironed a million tons of everybody's dirty laundry. She was also somewhat of a plumber, she kept the flow flowing.

Very early in life I liked to wander to the cellar to watch her at the tubs and boards in steam and suds. Once I came upon her smoking a cigarette. She was the first woman I ever saw smoking. Later in life she smoked freely all over the house. In the cellar she

bravely killed rats as they dared to appear. She killed neighborhood dogs by whom grandfather felt threatened, neighborhood
cats if they kept him awake. It was she who on grandfather's orders
kidnapped and destroyed Speed's and my beloved little dog, Rin
Tin Tin the Second.

Once I heard grandmother say, "She's not like us," but
whether she meant "Negroes are not like us" or "Mary Washington is not like us" I do not know. To test the proposition I
touched Mary Washington's bare arm, and I recall being surprised to discover that her flesh was similar to mine. She once
confused me further by seeming to tell me (or so my mind received it) that the color of her skin was a kind of error made by
Genung's department store on Fourth Avenue, that she was
really white, that Genung's had delivered the wrong order, that
she would exchange this mistaken brown skin for her own as soon
as she got around to it.

She was the reigning maid, queen of the maids, chief maid by far
in seniority, longest in point of service, unchallenged resident forever. She had nowhere else to go, no family, no home away from
Walk a Mile House, no friend finally but grandfather. The maids of
the house feared her and tried never to offend her. Grandfather
hired and fired maids on her recommendation. He thought she
could manage everything better than grandmother could, as perhaps she did. Even before grandmother's death Mary Washington
was essentially steward of Walk a Mile House.

She was grandfather's eyes as he depended upon her to be,
guarding him from the abuse of maids and tradesmen who would
serve him dishonestly, shirk their duties, steal his property. "If you
get the hang of Mary Washington," Aunt Ember said, "you get the
hang of slavery. There must have always been one slave in every
house who sold out the others." As Mary Washington had been
plumber and rat-killer and kidnapper and murderer of dogs so was
she also spy and informer, self-appointed guardian of the peace of
Walk a Mile House. With a single action she altered my life sig-
nificantly, as every reader will discover in the pages ahead.

*   *   *

Now that father had forged ahead somewhat in the money department he arrived at a decision bringing joy to Speed's heart and mine. He would spend a small portion of his new money expanding our apartment. He would rent the apartment next door and "smash a door through" our living-room wall into the living-room of 3–D.

Thereby we would double ourselves. Speed would have a bedroom of his own, and so would I. Our four-and-a-half-room apartment would become a nine-room apartment, we'd be the biggest apartment anywhere, we'd have two of everything—two dumbwaiters, no longer one; two mailboxes, no longer one; two bathrooms; two kitchens; two fire escapes; two doorbells; everything everybody else had but twice as much. I thought how superior I would feel.

Father signed the lease for our new territory. The Sheridan Gardens Apartments rental agent came to see what we planned to do. "We plan to smash a door through the wall," father said.

Speed said no, don't smash a door through. "Build an archway," he said.

"I never heard of an archway through," said the rental agent.

"You're hearing now," said Speed. "It's the simplest thing in the w-w-w-w-w-w-w-w-w-w-w-w-w-w-w . . ."

"I can't see going to the trouble," said the agent.

"It'll be more b-b-b-b-b-b-b-b-b-b-b-b-b-b . . ."

"Beautiful," I said.

"Nobody cares about that," said father. "All we want's a wood door to just pass through to the other apartment. An old-fashioned door's enough. Nobody can build an archway anyhow. You need a skill for that."

"An archway could be t-t-t-t-t-t-t . . ." said Speed, demonstrating with his arms.

"Twice the width of a door," I said.

Father replied, "We're not running parades through the joint. For a fancy job like you're talking about we'll need an extra-fancy carpenter and there's nobody we can get."

"Get me," said Speed, who'd do a job of beauty, he said, he could be had cheaper than a door and more for the love than the money.

Father was sold on the savings if not the beauty, but the Sher-

119

idan Gardens Apartments agent said, "You can't do it, it's a load-bearing wall."

"It's not a load-b-b-b-b-b-b-b-b-b . . ." Speed said. He had given the whole matter a lot more thought than the agent had.

"It's got electric wires all through it," the agent said. "You'll set two apartments on fire instead of one."

"I won't s-s-s-s-s-s-s-s-s-s-s . . ."

"Speed won't set anything on fire," I said.

And so it was agreed that Speed would do the work. How patiently, how carefully, how slowly and thoroughly he went at it! With a wax pencil and a tethered string he began by tracing an oval archway on the wall. There he let his sketch remain for several days, to ripen in his mind. Father feared that Speed had abandoned the work, forgotten it, "bit off more than he can chew," several times offering to bring in a run-of-the-mill carpenter hungering for a job. But Speed had not abandoned it. He was only thinking.

Speed was then at an extremely difficult, stubborn period of his life. If father pressed him to hurry with the job Speed curled his lip and asked, "What's your g-g-g-g-g-g . . . ?"

"I wish you wouldn't swear so in the house," said mother.

"He's so slow," father said.

"But p-p-p-p-p-p-p-p-p-p . . ." said Speed.

"But perfect," I said.

"Better know what you're doing b-b-b-b-b-b-b-b-b-b . . ."

"Better know what you're doing before you go cutting holes in a wall," I said.

"You said it," said Speed.

He sawed through plaster and wood along the lines of his sketch. Day by day he punched out the wall. He considered every blow. The archway took shape before our eyes, not speedily but certainly. Speed would never be hurried, on that job or any other. He was a perfectionist, a genius, and a true artist. Even the chief of police dared not bark orders at Speed. Father saw that the job was at a critical stage—I mean to say critical for father himself, who could not now afford to irritate Speed. One cross word from father and Speed might very well walk off, leaving a hole in the wall.

And yet again, this time for more than a week, the project seemed to have died away. Speed had left the scene. The guts of the wall hung bare to the world. Why didn't he tell father where he had gone? He never cared to tell us where he was going or why. He just went.

In fact he had gone in search of flexible wood to support the oval crown of his archway. This was an errand for which he required time to travel from shop to shop to find exactly the wood he needed. This was nothing a stuttering boy could accomplish by telephone, even with the help of his ignorant brother. When Speed found the wood he needed he resumed his labor. He had not been swift but he had been confident.

He plastered.

Then he was gone again to search for matching paint, and once again poor helpless frustrated father felt that in his moodiness Speed had abandoned the job, walked off, gone on strike without telling us. Speed would explain nothing to us. This was his job. Only he understood it, and when at last he had begun to paint, father's fears vanished, Speed's mood lifted, mother smiled with satisfaction, and we saw that the work was done. It was perfect, it was beautiful, masterful, not only fine craftsmanship but uplifting in the way it offered space and light to those rooms as no plain square door could have done. When the Sheridan Gardens Apartments rental agent viewed the work he nodded his head up and down, admitting that he had been of little faith, and as he left he shook Speed's hand and forgot he had shaken it and came back and shook it again.

On the evening the work was done father said to Speed at dinner, the odor of paint so fresh in the house, "That's the best-looking job I ever saw, you'd make a great carpenter," and mother concurred and kissed her son and congratulated her husband on his having been so patient all along. We never knew a better moment than that.

It was a graceful connecting archway. It seemed to be in motion, to flow. We had now expanded, or Speed had expanded us, from four and a half rooms to nine. In that luxury of space we lived liberated as long as we remained a family. Speed's archway would flow forever, offering lightness and grace. So I believed.

121

CHAPTER SEVEN

O N THE FIRST of July Speed and I went away together to work at a farm called Brookside Bough. This farm was also a modest retreat for visitors from New York City, boarding six or eight guests a weekend. Speed and I would be weekday farmers and weekend kitchen boys. We would sleep in the hayloft.

Mr. and Mrs. Kyrene were the owners of Brookside Bough. They were new at this work and in the end not very good at it. They lost money through inexperience and generosity. Before long Mr. Kyrene gave up farming and returned to police work. He had once worked for father down the station.

He had written us a letter telling us what our wages would be. "Your wages can be whatever we end up agreeing you are worth," he wrote, "because we never had boys working for us before and we don't know how things are going to come out for us. So let's try it and see how it works out." Father knew Mr. Kyrene to be a fair-minded man, and that was good enough for Speed and me. We were excited. We could make some money. Speed could come home with enough money to buy an Indian motorcycle.

Grandfather was angry. His mismanagement of his own affairs never so far humbled him that he withheld his advice from me. He argued in the following way: "In the business world people agree beforehand how much they're paying you for whatever goods or services you're giving them. You'll be making these farmers rich all summer and you'll come home worked to the bone and exhausted and empty-handed. Those crooked farmers in the country will say you were good for nothing and pay you accordingly." He was "outraged," he said. "You an honor-roll high-school graduate"—I had never been on the honor roll, *Speed* was on the honor roll—"are going to spend your summer scouring pots and pans and waiting on tables like the smelly dirty nigger girl out there in the kitchen." Those old familiar phrases froze me and I should have had the courage to challenge him. Speed would have challenged him. Speed had more courage than I. And yet those phrases had been lucky for me, too, hadn't they? They had brought Champrain and me together into our friendship.

On the other hand grandfather became enthusiastic about the possibility of Speed's actually becoming a farmer and making a prosperous living of it. On this subject he spoke to me confidentially. "A farmer doesn't need the powers of speech," grandfather said. "This work is perfect for a slow boy like Speed who can't talk. On a farm full of pigs and animals all he's got to do is grunt at them while the trees and crops grow without any talking to." His vision of our summer changed for the better. Instead of seeing us returning from the farm weary and broke he saw good things happening to Speed. "He's a natural farmer," grandfather said. With what evidence he spoke I cannot say, for Speed had never grown anything in the ground or raised any animals. The only dog we had ever had Mary Washington kidnapped. Grandfather gave me five dollars for my pocket. He gave Speed nothing.

This was my first long-distance train trip. I had never gone far by train except once-and-a-half to the moon on Walk a Mile Railway. Brookside Bough was located up the Hudson River valley north of Perkinsville, New York. Speed and I went into Perkinsville once or twice that summer to swim in the public pool. I remember thinking to myself, "My God, the *whiteness* of these girls." I'd forgotten how white white girls were. Some black folk walked the streets of

Perkinsville, but I was disappointed to see that no black girls swam at the pool.

We went once to town to buy a radio for our hayloft, and a very good radio it was, too. It cost us three dollars and played on for many years.

One day in Perkinsville Speed discovered the motorcycle of his dreams on an elevated sell-or-swap exhibit platform in front of Cameron's Wheel Shop. He was ecstatic, out of his skin with excitement. It was a bright red Indian Scout selling for two hundred dollars used. At the height of his motorcycle dream Speed had imagined himself owning only a lowly Indian Pony. But now a Scout! It was beyond belief. The shift was on the right, the throttle was on the left. In this way the Indian differed from every motorcycle ever made in the history of the universe. This may not mean much to you and me, but it meant everything to my brother Speed.

Mr. Cameron of the Cameron Wheel Shop agreed to hold the machine until the end of the summer, for a deposit of twenty dollars. Speed asked if he might "test drive around the block." Sure, said Mr. Cameron, and away flew Speed, his hair in the wind, and he disappeared from our view. He was gone a long time. "Did he say around the block or around the world?" said Mr. Cameron, and we became more and more apprehensive until at last Speed returned with a twenty-dollar bill in his teeth. He had sped in clouds of dust on unpaved country roads all the way to Brookside Bough to borrow the twenty from Mr. Kyrene.

Speed and I did our real swimming that summer in a brook which *bubbled*—no other word can do it—through Brookside Bough. Mrs. Kyrene frequently said, "Boys will be boys beside the bubbling brook at Brookside Bough." Speed and I found her repetition tiresome, but of course we did not complain. There we were in our own private chilled bubbling brook, a corner of paradise at the end of a hot day.

Speed fervently wished for girls instead of a brother to swim with in the bubbling brook at Brookside Bough, and indeed one Saturday afternoon two young women in a car drove into the farm and looked around and were disgusted to notice that the guests were married couples. However, when they strolled beside the brook and saw Speed and me they decided to stay. They asked us how the water was and I said, "Great, strip yourselves stark naked and jump in," and they said they might. They went back to the house and paid Mrs. Kyrene for a room and returned to the brook in their swimsuits with their towels on their arms, and they touched their toes to the water.

But after they tried to talk to Speed they decided not to remain after all. They demanded that Mrs. Kyrene give them their money back. They were angry, as if something had been falsely represented to them. A few minutes afterward lightning struck the water. I scrambled out of that bubbling lightning-struck brook in a hurry, but Speed remained in the exhilarating water, daring God to strike again.

Speed feared there was no girl for him as far as he knew anywhere in the world. Never mind love, he said, he was just looking for some physical girl who'd rather screw than have a billion dollars, any old girl, young or old, big or little, pretty or not. He thought there must certainly be a house of prostitution nearby. As soon as he owned his motorcycle he would drive himself to such a place no matter how far away. Meanwhile he complained constantly of painful testicles. In those days boys called that malady "blue balls." I don't know what boys call it now. I suppose they call it the same thing. I had long been free of it. Champrain kept my testicles well.

He envied me my sexual relaxation, my peace of mind, my seeming lack of lust for girls. I had still been unable to confide in him about Champrain, much as I yearned to do so, and for a while he must have interpreted my ease as evidence of my superiority, my greater restraint, my willpower, the power of my mental faculties to conquer my merely animal thrust. "Jesus God," he said. He meant those girls who came and went. "They didn't give me a ch-ch-ch-ch-ch-ch-ch-ch-ch-ch . . ." A chance.

"Listen, Speed, the right girl will come along for you. Be patient and give it time."

"My balls ache," my poor brother said.

"Think lofty thoughts," I said. "Think about the babbling of this beautiful brook, think about Nature, think about beautiful poetry, think about ideas for your epic poem." He was at that time writing an epic poem, which he soon abandoned for his novel.

"I'm thinking a-b-b-b-b-b-b-b-b-b-b-b . . ." he said. About ass, he meant.

"You'll get hold of yourself," I said

Speed worked tirelessly, ceaselessly, mowing and hoeing, fixing up, patching up, one day a mason, one day a carpenter, one day raking hay in the meadow. He learned to milk cows. The cows seemed small to me. Mr. Kyrene laughed. "No, those are normal-sized cows," he said, and Speed and I realized we had never seen cows. The only cow of my acquaintance was the pasteboard cow in the meadow along the roadbed of Walk a Mile Railway, and she was bigger than a locomotive. Speed drove the tractor, operated the dairy separator, the power saw. He sawed and piled wood for the winter, he picked fruit so fast he would have earned a fortune had he been paid by the basket, he dug a cesspool. In the fury of the work he planned his writing, and it was also for him a great relief from speech, quite as grandfather had hinted. He grew brown and stronger than ever that summer.

As for me, I disliked farm work and hid myself from it as much as I could. I suppose I did not like *any* sort of work, on or off the farm. I wanted things to come easy for me, like my elevation to accounts payable manager of the Mount Vernon Venue Investment Corporation. Assuredly I hated rising at dawn. I had hated it ever since my *Saturday Evening Post* days, when I struggled at dawn strangling in my magazine bag up and down the stairways of the apartment houses and through the dark dangerous cellars where perverts lurked.

The weekend was better than the week. Guests came up from New York and Speed and I waited tables and assisted Mrs. Kyrene in the kitchen. I preferred indoors to outdoors, kitchen to fields, though it was hot in the kitchen and I spent so much time standing in front of the electric fan that Mrs. Kyrene, sweet as she was, nevertheless took to calling me testily Fan Boy. One day she fired me. Speed said to her, "If you f-f-f-f-f-f . . ."—if you fire my brother you fire me, too. On the spot she rehired me. The Kyrenes could not have survived that summer without Speed. Once she said to me, "Fan Boy, why in the aitch did you come up here if you didn't intend to work?" I made a witticism: "I like to watch my brother work," I said. Well, at least I thought it was a witticism, I kept smiling to myself all day, and here it is still making me smile half a century later.

I learned to mix cocktails for the guests and became swift and efficient at all sorts of drinks I had myself yet to taste. The guests at Brookside Bough went in a big way for punches and flings and almost anything mixed in a shaker. I loved the cold feel of the silver cocktail shaker. I preferred the fragrance of the guests to the odor of the hogs. The guests were professional people on the rise whom I envied for their indoor New York City lives. I did not intend to become a farmer. Speed could become a farmer if he wished.

By the end of the summer I had begun to consume more liquor than was good for me. Later, when I became a writer, I drank between books. I became known in the trade as one of those extraordinarily productive genius drunks.

Speed at this time was writing an epic poem for which he had a title I now forget, though I remember the brand name of the pad he wrote it on: Durable Tablet. This was the same Durable Tablet on which we had collaborated on my essay "Intermarriage" for Mr. Moore in Current Events.

He wrote almost without lifting his eyes from his paper for an hour or more every night in the hayloft where we slept. After he had written for an hour he read me his new lines, and sometimes on the following night he read me revisions of the lines he had read me the night before. I always agreed that it was an improvement but I could not be sure. His epic poem was in a state of evolution, as you will see.

His hero was a young man "yclept by all who knew him" Americus the Modest whose mission was to roam the earth pacifying and reforming savage Hitlerian dictators wherever he found them. In general, however, the adventures of Americus the Modest led him not so often to the realms of dictators as to countries about which Speed happened to possess accurate fragments of information. Scotchmen wore kilts, Japanese lived in paper houses, China was overpopulated, India revered the cow. When Speed's knowledge was depleted in one place Americus the Modest took off on his horse for another.

However, after a series of adventures the epic poem began to evolve from its medieval setting to the city of Pittsburgh, Pa., to which, of course, Speed had never been. He emphasized smoke and steel. The hero is now called not Americus the Modest but Amiel Melvin, and he has exchanged his horse for a motorcycle.

Amiel suffers an affliction—he is deaf. Nevertheless he has heard enough about life to know that many young beautiful charming women of Pittsburgh are abused by rich old lecherous steel magnates conducting illicit seductions on "screened porches" resembling in some details the sun parlor in the western wing of Walk a Mile House.

This epic poem, evolving from medieval to modern, horse to motorcycle, was marked in its progression not alone by radical changes of plan but by the author's frantic transitions from pencil to pencil. As each pencil wore down he took up another. I see him now, hurling the exhausted pencil into the hay below our loft, furiously sharpening a new pencil with his knife, and resuming with all possible urgency his tale of Amiel Melvin pursuing fairness and justice for women, punishment and disgrace for lecherous steel magnates.

Speed never completed either of these major versions of his epic poem. The villain was never apprehended, the girl was never rescued, and the hero on his Indian Pony (motorcycle) never received the reward he desired. It was the moral question of the hero's reward that stopped Speed. His logical, desirable reward was the girl herself, to whom in the hero's imagination he had made love all over Pittsburgh, but Speed recognized in this the impurity of the motives of the creator who, it seemed, had not rescued the girl or condemned the villain so much in the interest of justice or fairness as in the lecherous spirit of the steel magnate. The hero was only a lecherous steel magnate in hero's clothing.

Speed forever monitored his own moral position. He did not call it that. "Being fair"—that was what he called it. He couldn't let it alone. Everything had to be *fair* from every possible point of view. This put a heavy burden on his telling of the tale. He worried endlessly. I often said to him, "My God, why can't the hero punish the villain and win the girl besides—mix a little pleasure with business?" but Speed rejected such compromise. Yet the thing was done all the time in a thousand movies and epic poems since Time began—a thousand generations of mankind have gobbled up epic poems by poets who themselves had the morality of rapists. Well, said Speed, that was *them.*

He demanded too much of himself. We discussed this intensely, and he would have found his way out of the problem, but by the end of the summer he passed from his epic poem to his modern novel. His transition to novel is commemorated on the Durable Tablet below the last few feeble lines of his abandoned epic poem. One comes upon the passage with something of a shock since it seems for an instant to flow from the continuity of the text itself thus *fuck this, I'm abandoning this, turn over and start novel.*

Indeed, when I "turn over' the Durable Tablet I come upon the first words of the novel begun by Speed in the hayloft. This new work was published some years afterward under the boyish title *Love Never Surrenders.* It exists as my brother's only published work. The manuscript or writing pad called Durable Tablet itself, one side epic poem, reverse side *Love Never Surrenders,* may be examined by interested persons in the archive of the Sheridan Gardens Apartments Authors Memorial Shrine at Mount Vernon, New York.

Several days after our arrival at Brookside Bough I received a penny postcard postmarked Mount Vernon whose whole message was this:

Hope you having fun kiss your brother. Your sweetheart.

Then again, after several days, I received another from the same place in the same hand whose message was this:

Miss my ride on the railrow train raining like cats and dogs kiss your brother. Your sweetheart.

Then again, a week or ten days later, I received another postcard from the same place in the same hand which said:

So hot the house burning down feel like. Your sweetheart.

Or after a passage of days again:

Got the stomach cramp today but they go away tomorrow. Your sweetheart.

Or again:

Come home and see how my hair been did. Your sweetheart.

Or once again:

I'm glad to see time gone by and one more month till you be home. Kiss your brother. Your sweetheart.

Speed argued that it was my duty to reveal to him the meaning of these cards; that is to say, to tell him instantly who the writer was. Nothing should be secret between us. Wasn't that so? Well, yes, but I could not yet divulge my secret. Speed had been hard on grandfather for copping a feel from the defenseless girl—turned grandfather into a ruthless lecherous Pittsburgh steel magnate— and I thought he'd view me as he viewed grandfather.

He occupied himself with logical guessing, deductive reasoning. The cards had come from Mount Vernon from a girl pretending low literacy, someone who knew Speed, too, well enough to send him a peck of a kiss. Speed mulled those postcards, speculating on the writer. He guessed cousins and schoolmates, somebody who loved to play with language. He studied the postmarks. The cards were always mailed on Thursdays and Sundays, and I was surprised that he did not make more of that than he did: maids' days off in Mount Vernon.

One afternoon as I swam in the brook Speed arrived with the latest postcard in the mail. Triumphantly he held it up and called to me, "Now I know it's the s-s-s-s-s-s-s-s-s-s . . ."—the straight-faced girl who worked for grandmother, who read the New York *Times* to grandfather while he tried to cop a feel from her. "You know her b-b-b-b-b-b-b-b . . ." he said—I knew her better, he meant, than I had let on, for on this day the card which arrived was a good deal more confidential or intimate than any of her previous cards.

Grandfar try and feel me most every day while I'm reading him the paper but I slip a way and stay out of the reach of his hand. Kiss your brother. Your sweetheart.

Yes, I eagerly confessed, I knew her better than I had told him I knew her, we were even in a small way verging, I said, on the outer limits of a kind of limited intimacy—

"You f-f-f-f-f-f-f-f-f-f . . ."

Fucked her, well, yes, now that he'd mentioned it, more than once, more than we could count. At first we counted and then we stopped counting, lost track. "I'm glad to be telling you this," I said, "because I've been wanting to tell it to you for a long time."

"Why d-d-d-d-d-d-d-d . . .?" But he did not require my answer, he had begun to put it all together. He laughed very hard and rolled on the ground on the bank of the brook, laughed so hard he fell into the brook. "I never b-b-b-b-b-believed," he said, "never believed those fucking t-t-t-t-t-t-t-t-t . . ."—never believed in my interest in the trains, always dimly suspected that I was up to something actually unrelated to Walk a Mile Railway. He laughed so hard he forgot the pain of his testicles. He splashed across the brook and up the farther bank and executed a backward somersault in the grass, laughing and whooping and jumping up and clapping his hands. He had not laughed with such joy in a long time. I joined him at his laughing.

"You've got to marry her," said Speed.

I stopped laughing.

Oh yes, he said, she was plainly in love with me and I had plainly taken every advantage of her love to satisfy my aching testicles—

"*You* have aching testicles," I said. "Not I."

"You'd have them if it w-w-w-w-w-w-w-w-w . . ."—I'd have had them, too, if it weren't for Champrain, he said. These postcards, he argued, revealed her love for me. This was love. This was more than copping a feel. This called for marriage. This wasn't grandfather's case at all. Grandfather did not love her, he only exerted control over her, held her as prisoner and slave, but this was altogether different.

"I'm not ready to get married yet."

"Why not? Remember your ess-ess-ess-ess-ess-ess . . ."

"Essay on intermarriage?"

He was extremely proud of me for having handled myself so well in this matter, for having had a steady girl all along, for having conquered the sexual mystery. His respect for me soared. I was a winner, a lover, a winner at love. Possibly I was the first of the Mount Vernon Revolvers to have triumphed in this way. Speed was simply delighted, that's all there was to it, he was delighted, pleased, proud. "I c-c-c-c-c-c-c-c . . ."—can't wait to get home to meet her, embrace her, welcome her as his sister, see this one-time maid now sister in the new light of all that had been revealed to him on this perfect day, that's what he was saying.

He would not rest or be silent until he knew everything about her. Night and day we talked of her. Did *she* have a sister? Where were my photographs of her? I had none? Why not? I should have had a dozen of her. He seemed to be saying it was some sort of deficiency in me not to have a photograph of her.

I could not satisfy all his questions, but I could tell him things I did know, and he took it all in with the deepest interest. One day soon afterward he wrote a poem—sonnet, not epic—called "The Balustrade," based on the moment Champrain and I stood by the balustrade of the attic suite peering down into the house darkened by the storm. Speed injected into the poem a tingling sense, I thought, of the odor of paraffin rising "to the black girl nose, to the white boy nose," as he phrased it in his poem.

In our conversations Speed speculated joyfully and gravely on the consequences of my making known my intention to marry Champrain. He visualized mother and father and grandmother and grandfather and ten dozen conventional uncles and aunts and cousins all over Mount Vernon and five hundred friends and acquaintances and one thousand high-school students and father's cops and detectives down the station.

He saw my wedding plans on the society page of the *Daily Argus*. With his lips he wrote it up. The son of the police chief was worth an article, a photograph, and his financée, too, if she were white. But nobody had ever seen a non-white bride on the society page of the *Daily Argus* and nobody expected we would. He shook my hand repeatedly, as if my marriage had been announced, and he as my best man talked of the bride night and day. For me it was a splendid feeling to be able at last to share my secret. I should have done it sooner, but these things take time, and I was the happier for it, and Speed was happier, too, and our brotherhood was deeper and closer than ever.

One guest who came for a couple of weekends to Brookside Bough was a banker from New York named Mr. Hollis Jones. I was shocked and disgusted to overhear him say, "I tell you, this is a bad time for a young person just going out in the world. I pity young people these days." He predicted war and devastation and a worse economic depression than we could imagine. His schedule called for everybody's falling deep into poverty until at least the middle of the twenty-first century. I didn't like to hear him speak that way. "I tell you," said the banker Mr. Jones, "half the boys graduating high school in the next five years will be killed overseas by nineteen-fifty."

Speed and I wrote him off as a "vile pessimist." Our policy position was optimism. We did not like to think of the future in terms Mr. Jones had described it. We were glad to see him drive away to New York Sunday evening. I vowed to Speed that if I ever again met Mr. Jones I would challenge his opinions. He was a man of little faith.

Then we heard that he was returning, and my mind went to work rallying arguments to present to him if I dared to speak up. I was only a table-waiter and I wasn't supposed to discuss worldly matters with guests. To my surprise I seemed to have no arguments of my own. Everything I arrived at came right out of grandfather's mouth, and I saw that whether I liked it or not I was much more grandfather's boy than I would have cared to confess. Grandfather had sold me optimism, persuading me that these were the best of times if only one seized them.

Grandfather taught me contempt for complainers and whiners like Mr. Jones the banker. "Did you ever hear me complain of my blindness?" grandfather asked. No matter what befell the world we who were bright young fellows flourished independently of external events, grandfather said. Strength was virtue, we strong boys seized whatever opportunities came our way. Depression, prosperity, war, and peace were all the same to us, we turned every event to sound business and grew richer and richer and thrived on faith.

Look at me! I had become accounts payable manager of the Mount Vernon Venue Investment Corporation (MVVIC) without trying. My corporation—I as the highest-ranking male officer began to think of it as mine—had fifty thousand dollars in the bank and interest accruing daily. That was what I called seizing opportunity, moving right along, up the ladder from *Saturday Evening Post*. Was this good fortune simply accidental? No, grandfather trusted me, and when his lawyers looked me over they trusted me, too. I had an honest open expression and I was tall and straight and my hair was slicked into place. People had confidence in me. I was well-spoken, articulate, I could rattle off ideas. I was clean-cut and had a bright smile. "Sal Hepatica for the Smile of Health . . . Ipana for the Smile of Beauty"—but would you believe that although grandfather wrote those million-dollar lines I brushed my teeth with Kolynos whose battle cry I never knew?

Even so, for the moment I was only a weekend table-waiter at a small farm. I was tense with frustration to think I could not talk back to Mr. Hollis Jones the banker. When he returned for a second weekend at Brookside Bough the sight of him enraged me. I could barely contain myself. Friday evening I mixed the cocktail he requested, but when I passed the icy glass to him I addressed him in an argumentative voice.

To my surprise, however, I did not say at all the things I had intended to say. On the contrary, my first words were of grand-father. "Mr. Jones," I said, "if my grandfather were here he'd oppose everything you said two weeks ago."

Mr. Jones was startled to hear me speak so forthrightly. He had known me only as a bartender, table-waiter. "Tell me what I said two weeks ago," he said. "Two weeks is a frightfully long time."

"You said nothing is ahead but bad times and war."

"And your grandfather sees it differently, does he?"

"My grandfather says people have always been pessimistic in the past but there are always ways for young men to make a lot of money if they keep their eyes open for the opportunities."

Mr. Jones raised his glass in a toast, whether to me or to grand-father I did not know. Perhaps to both. "You've just graduated from high school," he said, "you're headed out into the world. Listen to your grandfather. Ignore me."

Two other guests at Brookside Bough were a young couple named Bob and Marianne Chakerian who engaged Speed and me in con-versation every chance they had. At first Speed and I had the feeling that Bob was hanging around too close to us, and we wor-ried that he was one of those extremely queer homos who carried his wife about as his cover-up. We were beginning to become aware of that side of life.

Bob Chakerian, too, like the banker Mr. Jones, lectured the guests on the state of the world, but when the guests seemed indifferent to him he lectured Speed and me and taught us a great deal in a short space. Since Bob and Marianne were much younger than Mr. Jones my brother and I were readier for them than we were for the banker. And though Marianne was remote from us, and in the practical sense unattainable, we were from time to time able to draw close enough to her actually to touch her flesh. This occurred most memorably on several successive nights when we four went strolling and singing down the moonlit country road. It was far from the complete experience of love and flesh Speed desired but it was better than nothing at all—"better than a stick in the eye," as people said in Mount Vernon—and its clear restricted options relaxed his testicles.

Millions of people share with us the memory of the wonderful song they taught us. If you do not thrill to that song you are dead. Sing along if you wish. Everyone knows this inspiring tune.

> I dreamed I saw Joe Hill last night,
> Alive as you and me.
> Says I, but Joe you're ten years dead,
> I never died, says he.
> I never died, says he.
>
> The copper bosses killed you Joe,
> They shot you Joe says I.
> Takes more than guns to kill a man,
> Says Joe, I didn't die,
> Says Joe, I didn't die.
>
> Says Joe, what they forgot to kill
> Went on to organize,
> Went on to organize.
>
> Where working men defend their rights
> It's there you'll find my Joe,
> It's there you'll find my Joe.
> I never died, says he,
> I never died, says he.

Down the country road we walked late at night, kicking up the dust, singing that song about the union man executed by the bosses. On the spot we were converted to the union movement. How could I have wept and sung at once? My tears filled my eyes, my blood surged, my heart pumped and thumped and jumped and bumped and clumped, and the sweat rolled down my fiery body.

The Chakerians gave us a bag of magazines to read—a paper bag from Gristede's grocery in New York. I assumed this loaded bag was a loan: we *Saturday Evening Post* salesmen never gave away *magazines.* But no, the Chakerians meant us to keep them forever. They also prepared a list of books they urged us to withdraw from the library as soon as we got home. My mind's eye sees the list but I cannot name any of the titles and I do not remember if I read the books.

I conclude the obvious, that the Chakerians were left-wing, liberal, socialist, perhaps Marxist enthusiasts. I remember nothing very specific. The single sentence I remember Bob speaking rises above doctrine: "The great man is the man who insists that everybody has the same privileges he has." This appealed mightily to Speed's sense of universal fairness.

Speed identified himself passionately with Joe Hill, speaking of Joe Hill as if he had known him well, in his mind raising him from the dead, setting out together to organize the working classes, completing the work Joe Hill began. I could see headlines in the Mount Vernon *Daily Argus*, POLICE CHIEF'S SON LEADS INTERNATIONAL WORKING-CLASS REVOLUTION TO SUCCESS, SAVES WORLD. Wouldn't grandfather have loved that? And yet, deeply embedded as this is in my memory, our experience of the Chakerians was ended in hours. My image of the working-class revolution is of a stunning young raven-haired woman whose hand I held down a moonlit country road while my brother held the other. My sense of myself as a working man defending my rights sustained itself only a few nights of a powerful weekend. Joe Hill was only a song.

Speed abandoned his epic poem because it could not match the reality of Champrain and me. Her story and mine was so wonderful, so close to him, so real, so available to him in its detail, that he hung up his epic-poet's hat and donned the novelist's.

137

Of course, to make a novel of my romance with Champrain, Speed undertook to alter facts to meet his dramatic needs. This he brilliantly accomplished laboring night after night in our hayloft. Beside him our three-dollar radio inspired him with the popular music Champrain Johnson was presumably listening to at that very minute as she soaked in her tub at Walk a Mile House one hundred miles south of Brookside Bough.

Here let me outline as briefly as possible the premise of the novel afterward entitled *Love Never Surrenders:*

A Negro lad named Deeps has won a position as manservant at the home of the wealthy white family, the Brooksides, in Verne Mountain, New York. Deeps is eighteen years old and has just graduated from high school.

His new employer, Mrs. Brookside, is the wife of Hollis Brookside, a wealthy New York banker. Mrs. Brookside is reactionary, racist. Deeps presents himself to her as a young man we have not quite liked. He is somewhat of a sycophant, he fawns, he scrapes, seemingly indifferent to his own dignity. Mrs. Brookside approves of him and hires him immediately.

The Brooksides' daughter, Thiwest, like Deeps a recent high-school graduate, impatient of wealth, impatient of idleness, has spurned the idea of college to "find herself" as a weaver. Her several precious looms are the state of the art. Thiwest is the namesake, we are told, of her mother's admired heroine of the Scandinavian epic poem *Thiwest and Leif.* This is Speed's fun: in truth her name is only an anagram for the word *whitest. Deeps,* as many readers perceive, spells *Speed* backwards. So much for wordplay. A young writer who could not speak words mastered them in play when he could, and triumphed over his stuttering.

Mrs. Brookside leads Deeps up the long flights of stairs to the room he will occupy at the top of the house. Although the room is hardly bigger than a closet Deeps expresses his delight with these "commodious quarters." Mrs. Brookside loves his excessive humility. She parts from Deeps, leaving him to unpack his bag. A few seconds after he has closed the door behind her he explodes in his privacy with a venomous oath condemning her race and her class.

Readers who know the reality from which my brother adapted his tale will hardly be surprised to hear that Thiwest, attracted by Deeps's appearance, drawn to his virtuous rage, creates her opportunity to establish her valuable looms in her new weaver's headquarters in a room in the attic suite not far from his . . . and there I leave you.

As Speed's creation evolved beneath his hand from medieval poem to modern novel he inevitably dwelled in his mind on Champrain and me. We were his working models. But as Deeps and Thiwest emerged as Speed's independent creations he began to see more and more clearly the truest motives of the models from which he had departed. In this process I came off badly. He increasingly felt that I was not doing right by Champrain. I should by now have announced my engagement to marry her. He demanded to know why I had not done so.

"Well," I said, "one reason I haven't done so is I haven't consulted Champrain herself."

"You consulted her p-p-p-p-p-p-p-p-p . . ."—consulted her plenty on the train, he meant.

"On what train? Never. We never discussed marriage."

"On the train to Niagara F-F-F-F-F-F-F-F-F-F . . ."

"What train to Niagara Falls? You're crazy, you're driving yourself looney on the farm."

"On Walk a Mile R-R-R-R-R-R-R-R-R . . ."

Oh, I saw what he meant, on Walk a Mile Railway we often rode the train to Niagara Falls, that was what he meant, all aboard for Niagara Falls, New York, honeymoon capital of the world. There we were on the way to Niagara Falls: this, said Speed, was my implicit promise to Champrain, this was my coy way of saying I would marry her.

"Boys say that to girls," I said. "It doesn't mean a damn thing. I love apples, I love grapes, I don't marry them."

You said it, you must mean it, said my brother to me. Where did I think I was living? Did I think I was living in a moral cesspool?

Then of course it was his turn to accuse *me* of the worst possible thing: he accused me of resembling grandfather, of living down

139

there in a moral swamp with grandfather, in a moral cesspool, of imprisoning Champrain even as grandfather himself imprisoned Champrain, copping a feel from her when he pleased, and in spite of her objections, while she was herself defenseless, powerless to resist, indebted to him for her job, forced to be servile and slavish.

"Your analogy is mad," I replied, "I forced her to nothing, you're getting my story confused with your fiction. Don't you remember? It was Champrain who ran the water in the bathtub that made me come . . . Remember?"

"Come, yeah," said Speed, that was what it was about, after all, it wasn't love, it was come, come, come, it was a rotten love affair, it was all sperm and no love, it never left the bedroom. "Your p-p-p-p-p-p-p-p-p . . ." said Speed.

"What about it?"

"That was all you ever g-g-g-g-g-g-g-g . . ." All I ever gave her was my prick, he said. Love? Never. Anything else? Did I ever make her a present of anything besides my prick? Did I ever repay her the quarter I owed her? Imagine that, he said, a man steals a quarter from his lover out of her apron pocket and never pays her back. Did I ever buy her a white robe to replace the white robe she wore all the time with the frayed elbows? Did I ever buy her a comb or a brush, though I knew how important her hair was to her? Imagine a man who doesn't even carry a photograph of his beloved, who has never taken a picture of her, never carried pictures of her in his wallet.

"She's your w-w-w-w-w-w-w-w-w-w . . ."

"She's not my wife. A person has to be married before he has a wife."

"I consider her so," said Speed.

She was my wife but I had failed her. That was his thesis. I was a brute, a beast, I had not fully borne my share of the burden of the relationship. I was a foul and negligent husband in the way I was a foul and lazy farmer boy, letting the other person do the work. "Fan Boy," he called me, in imitation of Mrs. Kyrene, lazy fan boy standing in front of the breeze all day. I wanted all the pleasure of Champrain but I offered her none of the devotion of marriage. As her husband I had failed her. I should have escorted her down the streets of Mount Vernon. I should have taken her to high-school dances. That would have been a "Maroon first." (Maroon was our high-school color.)

Speed compared me to a young man living in slavery days. I was one who celebrated the underground railroad, leading slaves to freedom. I believed in emancipation. I was a volunteer locomotive engineer on the underground railroad. However, when the moment came to start the train I'd forget, I'd have spied a nice brown girl to fuck, and all my stranded passengers would be captured and returned to the slaveholders. That was me, a betrayer.

Where was I on her afternoons off, Speed asked. "Did you ever g-g-g-g-g-g-g-g-g . . .?"—did I ever on a Sunday afternoon get one of our lazy shithead snoring uncles sleeping off their midday dinners on every bed and couch in Walk a Mile House to drive her home for her few hours with her family?

And by the way, had I ever met her family?

No. I did not even know where she lived.

Well, had I ever even made the slightest *effort* to meet her family? Did I ever even on a rainy day escort her under an umbrella to the trolley line? Did I ever take her *anywhere* except to bed?

"No, no, I realize this," I said. "We never met anywhere outside of Walk a Mile."

"You're a s-s-s-s-s-s-s-s-s . . ." I was a scurvy bastard, he said, I was wicked. Did I ever try to negotiate a salary raise for her with grandfather? I could sing all night about Joe Hill who *died* for union rights but I didn't dare to confront grandfather to try to get a few dollars extra for the woman I claimed to love, for the woman who was my wife. "I consider her your wife," he said. That was final. He accused me of having done only one thing in life for her. "You kept your great big old f-f-f-f-f-f-f-f-f-f . . ."—kept my flashlight charged, kept my batteries up. We laughed at that. We laughed even as we argued. The author of *Love Never Surrenders* was a man of humor.

And now the time had come, said Speed, for me to atone, for me

141

to begin to do right by Champrain. I agreed to begin by carrying a gift for her when we went home. I would present her with the radio Speed and I had bought for our hayloft. Speed applauded that, but he reminded me that the radio would be a hand-me-down, I was passing used stuff down to the Negro, I was still like most white people looking upon the Negroes as our garbage cans.

Driven by the force of Speed's moral logic I tried to fall in love with Champrain as I had not been in love with her before. I adopted as my model Thiwest in *Love Never Surrenders*. For Thiwest at first it was Deeps's body alone which charmed her, but as time went by she became devoted to his whole soul. I liked myself better in my brother's book than in my own life.

Speed, to keep my commitment warm for me, as I might not have done for myself, wrote in my behalf a letter proposing my marriage to Champrain. I copied it from his page of Durable Tablet to a page of my own verbatim except that I attached to the end of each paragraph a qualifying sentence to serve, I thought, as a brake against this headlong train ride to marriage.

That was mid-August. I handed my letter to Mr. Kyrene, who mailed it from the Perkinsville post office on his run to town.

Sweetheart Champrain,

The time has come to speak the truth and to say everything which, though it has been in my heart, has been lying below the surface. Do I love you? I have said so often that I do. But have I meant it, or was my saying "I love you" only the power of carnal desire speaking in me? It may have been the latter.

In fifteen calendar days I shall see you again, and as soon as possible thereafter we shall be married in spite of all the obstacles my family or our society might deem proper to place in our way. Of course I suppose there may be some obstacles we will not be able to overcome.

But we can make miracles, we who are in love. We will transcend all obstacles, for we are in love, in love, in love, and we will marry, for this I promise and pledge to you now. Anyhow, this will give us plenty to talk over, won't it?

Please tell me that you have received this letter, and tell me, too, what you think of it. Are we absolutely sure we want to do this sort of thing?

Your husband-to-be (?),

As Speed and I approached the date we had set to leave the farm Speed had two immediate objectives. He intended to purchase the Indian Scout from the Cameron Wheel Shop in Perkinsville and he intended to get laid by a prostitute somewhere between Perkinsville and Mount Vernon. He did not know where, but he was determined to make it happen and get this thing over with once and for all.

Of course he had no idea where he might locate a prostitute, no idea how to go about it. We imagined you might find one under a lamppost at night. He was certain he would find her somewhere between Perkinsville and Mount Vernon. After all, he was a problem-solver. On his newly acquired Indian Scout we'd follow the map. In Kingston, Poughkeepsie, maybe Newburgh, there was bound to be some sort of small-town brothel, nothing too fancy, he was just a beginner. If necessary we could even swing over to Danbury, Connecticut. "You can j-j-j-j-j-j-j-j-j-j-j . . ."

"Join you? I don't think I'll join you," I said.

"You have your l-l-l-l-l-l-l . . ."

"Little sweetheart back home," I said.

"Little *wife*," he said.

Well, perhaps so, but Champrain had not replied to my letter proposing marriage. I hoped this meant that she had rejected the whole idea. I saw too many problems ahead. When Mount Vernon heard the news of my engagement we would find ourselves standing alone against our family—Speed and Aunt Ember and I. And I wasn't so sure of Aunt Ember. I wasn't so sure of myself, either. The only person I was sure of was Speed, about whom one could be sure at all times. When Speed took a position he stood by it. If he changed his position he told you.

But why was it right or morally O.K. for Speed to lay a prostitute in New York or Connecticut or anywhere else and get up and walk

143

away without marrying her while I, on the other hand, was under obligation to marry Champrain? He had thought this through. Because, he said, the business of the prostitute was acknowledged, the relationship between the prostitute and her customer was agreed upon, this was a matter not of love but of money. It was not, said Speed—now indulging his favorite sarcasm—as if he had subtly planted in her mind pipedream marital expectations formed on make-believe train trips on model railroads to Niagara Falls, New York, honeymoon capital of the world.

Consider the energy of youth. The night before our departure from Brookside Bough Speed and I, working by the light of an old oil lantern, picked the last of the summer's raspberries. Speed worked hard and fast. Picking in the poor light he badly tore up his hands, but he felt good about saving the crop for the Kyrenes. About midnight we trotted down to the brook for one last brisk swim, and when we returned to our hayloft Speed wrote awhile to the end of a new chapter of *Love Never Surrenders* and read the whole chapter to me. I loved it. I followed it perfectly. Its modern idiom was much more compatible to my ear than the old-fashioned verses of his epic poem. His book at this point was half-done.

We turned out our light at two and we were up at six o'clock Saturday morning. Mrs. Kyrene served us a wonderful breakfast. I taste it yet. That was the only meal we ate in the dining-room. I remember the luxurious feeling of that kind lady's waiting on us as if we were guests. We made jokes as we ate, condemning the table service of those lazy Mount Vernon boys.

Soon Mr. Kyrene returned from town with our money in two envelopes. Was there mail at the P.O. for us? The mail was more on my mind than money. No, he was sorry to say, there had been no mail for us. "I know you're anxious to hear from your sweetie-pie," he said to me. My wife-to-be. When we told the Kyrenes of my engagement Mrs. Kyrene felt that she understood at last my poor working habits on the farm. "It's no wonder," she said, "your head has been floating up there in cloud-distraction-land."

We had not mentioned to Mr. and Mrs. Kyrene that Champrain

was black. Our fears masqueraded as conviction. We said to ourselves, *Her being a Negro is not important, it doesn't matter, that's
why we don't mention it, right?* but our hesitation arose obviously
from the fact that it precisely *did* matter. We knew we were in for
it. I saw my wedding attended by Speed and Aunt Ember and
some of the left-wing crackpot super-intellectual high-school kids
from the World Relations Club, and Bob and Marianne Chakerian
if we could find out their address from the Kyrenes. What was
grandfather going to say about my marrying "the dirty smelly nigger girl in the kitchen"? He was going to say, "Yes, and in the
kitchen is where you'll marry her and afterward we'll have your
grand reception in the bathroom."

If I married Champrain would grandfather remove me as accounts payable manager of the MVVIC? Could he? Did he have
that power? If not, who had the power? Maybe that was something
I ought to be inquiring into. During the summer the idea of the
corporation had begun to assume interest for me. I was soon to
become a working man. What in the world could I do? I had no
skills. How was I to earn a living? I wished I had given it some
serious thought back in the days of Occupational Guidance under
Mrs. Packard-Steinberg. A lot of good this Share the Wealth shit
was doing me now. Maybe my corporate connection could help me
out. Maybe this corporate connection was worth cash to me, too.
The corporation had fifty thousand dollars in the bank. Suppose my
funds ran low while I was on the hunt for a job. Could I borrow
from the corporation? It was a summer thought, wasn't it?

Mr. Kyrene laid the money envelopes on the table before us,
and he said, "You remember we agreed we would pay you what
you were worth." What had he thought we were worth? The envelopes contained the secret of our value. "How much do you boys
think you're worth?" he asked.

I had thought about that. For sixty days' labor I thought to
myself I was worth sixty dollars. And yet, considering, for example,
how heartily I had eaten three meals a day and how much fun I had
had in one way or another, and how often, in fact—to be honest
with myself on the negative side of things—I had really quite

literally lain down on the job or sneaked off to sleep or rest or read a book I was ready to deduct fifteen dollars from my sixty and go home feeling rich with forty-five. "Forty-five dollars," I said. "Am I close?"

"Very close," said Mr. Kyrene. With his eyes he consulted his wife. She turned to Speed. "How about you, Speed, what are you worth?" He was scowling angrily, not at first trusting himself to speak or even to try until he was confident he could manage an entire sentence. Then he burst out, "A goddamn lot more than forty-five." He rested a moment from speech and then he tried again, but this time he had less success with his sentence. "My m-m-m-m-m-m-m-m-m-m-m-m-m . . ."

"His motorcycle alone is going to cost him a hundred," I said.

"Maybe my b-b-b-b-b-b-b-b-b . . ."

I translated. "He says, 'Maybe my brother thinks *he's* worth only forty-five, but not me.' "

"I'm w-w-w-w-w-w-w-w-w-w-w-w-w . . ."

"He's worth a lot more," I said. "That's what he's saying."

Mr. Kyrene fondled the envelopes on the table. He and Mrs. Kyrene nodded their heads. They, too, had agreed that Speed was worth a lot more than I. Mr. Kyrene asked me, "How much more is Speed worth than you?" but it was Speed whose reply was ready. "Five times more," he firmly said.

He knew me. He knew what I was all about and what I was worth and what I was good for and what I was not good for. If I was worth forty-five Speed was worth two hundred and twenty-five. All right, I could buy that. Often in the past, under similar circumstances, I argued that I was a year older than he and therefore worth more. Wasn't my vaster experience of life worth something? On the other hand, one might ask to what use I had applied my vaster experience. None. To lying in the shade. To cleaning my dinner plate. To sampling the liquor. To standing as much as possible in the way of the breezes of the kitchen fan. I knew in my heart that one Speed was worth five me. At farming I hadn't really been worth anything. At the kitchen work I'd been slow and slovenly. At table-waiting I was lousy, as the guests must have agreed, for they left tips for Speed and almost nothing for me, and they said to Speed they hoped to see him next year. Nobody said that to me. One guest left Speed a note praising his "unfailing everyday good cheer and dignity."

"I did pretty good bartending," I said.

"It's remarkable how we all agree," said Mr. Kyrene, sliding one envelope across the table to Speed, and the other to me. We opened our envelopes. My envelope contained fifty dollars. Speed's contained two hundred and fifty. He peeled off a twenty-dollar bill and repaid Mr. Kyrene for the loan for the deposit on the Indian Scout, and Mrs. Kyrene embraced Speed and said, "Even this isn't what we really think you're worth. We think you're worth much more than this but this is all we've got. You saved our lives this summer and we're going to make it worth your while to come back next summer, too," and she embraced him again, holding him even closer than before, and she kissed him all over his face, and when at last we left the room Mr. Kyrene remembered to shake my hand.

Let me give you an idea how much two hundred dollars was worth in Perkinsville or Mount Vernon or America on that August day. A great big ice cream cone was a nickel. A package of gum with five sticks was a nickel. A Hershey's chocolate candy bar was a nickel. A package of cigarettes was twelve cents. A gallon of gasoline was fifteen cents. Haircut twenty cents. Shave ten cents. Shoeshine five cents. Decent breakfast thirty cents. Pretty good lunch thirty-five cents. Dinner half a buck. Daily newspaper three cents. The Sunday New York *Times*, complete with the big brown rotogravure section and all the domestic news and all the news of foreign affairs, sports, books, theater, music, business, and a million miles of classified advertising, ten cents. Let's get dressed. My best suit cost eighteen dollars. My best shoes cost six. My best necktie cost ninety-five cents. Father's prescription-ground eyeglasses cost five dollars. He could have bought them cheaper but he always said, "You don't grow new eyes," so he squandered.

Our hayloft radio had cost us three dollars in Perkinsville. I took it home as a gift for Champrain with a card "For my sweetheart, music for her ears." That three-dollar radio played on for years and years. Catch up on your mail. Postcards a penny. Regular mail three cents, goes anywhere in the country. We didn't send much by air mail in those days, but when we did it was a nickel.

I was homeward bound with my brother whose plan it was to purchase in Perkinsville the motorcycle to which he had committed himself. Then we would hurry to Mount Vernon, perhaps with a pause for Speed's sexual gratification at a small-town brothel lying in wait along our route. I may not have been as good a farm worker as Speed, but I had long ago conquered the problem of virginity. Speed's turn had come.

First, however, condoms. Speed intended to protect himself from disease and the prostitute from pregnancy. It was Speed's character to care for himself and to care for others, too. He was a social man, a community man, a team man in life even as he was at basketball.

In those days, purchasing condoms was a nerve-wracking task. Now, of course, all America is *encouraged* to purchase condoms, the shelves of the stores are loaded with condoms attractively packaged in scenes of flesh-colored romance, advertised and promoted in clever language sparkling with double entendre. The lovely schoolgirl clerk sells health-preserving condoms without a blush, like toothpaste. Every large pharmacy sells hundreds of these enticing packages every day to men, women, and children.

In the old days, however, the mood was different. To begin with, one did not know if one's favorite drugstore carried the product. If it did would the clerk sell it to *you*? In Mount Vernon my condom connection was Proctor Pharmacy at Prospect and Gramatan Avenues, far from the Sheridan Gardens Apartments, although even then, before making my purchase, I surveyed the whole outdoors to be sure no one was watching me—no friend of my mother, no sharp-eyed police officer from down the station. Before seeking the condom clerk I pretended to have come for a magazine, for ice cream or candy, always with my eye upon the door, drifting at last to the druggist himself—a man with a toothpick in his mouth, one

Mr. Kiefer; I'd have turned round and gone home before I'd have bought a condom from a woman. I presented myself to Mr. Kiefer as one who had never been here before, an outsider, a visitor from a distant place, like Mars. I spoke in a faltering voice, dry with anxiety, "Do you by any chance sell—?"

"Sell what, son?" As if he had not recognized me.

"Condoms."

"You bet."

"How much are they?"

They were fifty cents a package. The druggist with an air of unconcern, distracted, glancing about the store, keeping track of comings and goings, pretending boredom, perhaps, to put his young customer at ease, slipped a package of three condoms into a small, plain paper bag, shook it down, folded over the top of the bag, and handed the package to me. Quickly, with a sense of relief, I slid it into my pocket. And only then, once more free and clear, once more having survived detection by mother's women and father's police, did I begin to savor the anticipation of my pleasure soon to be shared with Champrain.

Speed in Perkinsville in front of Rexall Drugs, like me at Prospect and Gramatan before Proctor Pharmacy, surveyed the street before entering. He ordered me to wait on the sidewalk with our bags. I was to be lookout, though I could not imagine whom I was looking out for—we did not know a soul in Perkinsville or in all the country round.

After Speed entered Rexall Drugs he instantly returned, as if for a fresh breath. "I thought I s-s-s-s-s-s-s-s-s-s-s . . ." he said.

"Saw nobody," I said, "you saw citizens of Perkinsville. Who else could you have seen?"

"Here I go again," he said, breathing deep as if he were diving to the bottom of the sea. He re-entered the drug store. I waited on the sidewalk. Speed was inside the store for five minutes. People came and went.

When Speed emerged from the store he was breathless, he was as white as this paper before me this minute, staring beyond me at a point in the sky, bursting to speak, to cry, to scream. He was choking like a drowning man. His hands were at his throat. I called to him, I ran to him, I cried to him, "What happened to you? What happened? What can I do? What happened?" Something had happened profounder than a boy's embarrassment. His legs would not support him. He could not stand. He slumped to the curb beside our bags, his fists clenched, his hands inexplicably freshly bleeding from last night's raspberry picking, his eyes wild, his body writhing. Suddenly, with the most strenuous contortion, he vomited into the gutter. Was that all? Was he merely ill? I wish that that had been all. It was not. In the drugstore, to pay fifty cents for a package of condoms, he had taken a dollar bill from his wallet and placed his wallet for a moment on the counter, and when he next looked his wallet was gone.

CHAPTER EIGHT

NOT BY Indian motorcycle but by Greyhound bus we made our way home from Perkinsville. I paid our fares. The bus was slow. To accommodate passengers it often left the highway and wound its way along secondary roads, but it made no local stops at small-town brothels.

At home Speed sank to his bed, where he lay the first twenty-four hours in his traveling clothes without speaking or eating. He who had worked so hard so long during the broiling summer for two months came home with nothing—no, correction, came home with the dollar bill he had been about to pay Rexall Drugs for condoms. I who had hardly worked at all came home with fifty dollars.

His hands were mashed and raw and seeping or bleeding from berry-picking. Mother brought him bowls of hot water, and he soaked his hands in epsom salts. The salts stung him, and he winced. The doctor came and said the hands were infected. "Go on soaking them in epsom salts." For that he charged us two dollars, the bastard. Speed was a shattered boy. "Two hundred and fifty dollars," he said. Over and over he said it, "Two hundred and fifty dollars," though it was only two hundred and thirty, he was forgetting he'd repaid Mr. Kyrene twenty for the motorcycle loan. He was in a state of shock, I think, and the doctor thought so, too.

When he began to recover, mother and father and I sat with him in his new private bedroom in apartment 3–D, to which good old apartment 2–D was now connected by Speed's brilliant arched doorway. His new bedroom was off at a distance from us, and that felt good to him, he liked the idea of being able to get away from us when he could. We tried to remember all the families who had lived in 3–D over the years. We made a list.

Speed dug his manuscript out of his travel bag and gave it to me to read to mother and father, but after six pages he asked me to stop, he was too affected to listen, it reminded him too much of his long summer of happy labor ruined by its short quick tragic end.

"Don't think of it as tragic," father said—whose own deep troubles he concealed from us boys for the moment—"think of anything that happens as only the makings of your next book. You'll make thousands of dollars like that lady from Atlanta." *Gone With the Wind* was such a big book that year even father had heard of it. He comforted Speed, sitting beside his bed, running his fingers through Speed's hair. "You'll be back on your feet," father said. "You'll laugh at all this some day."

"I'll never l-l-l-l-l-l-l-l-l-l-l . . ." said Speed. During this week of his life he could not see any future for himself. He talked of quitting school, getting some sort of job, he had a friend who could get him in as stock boy at Genung's. Coach Cabot came to the house one afternoon to persuade him not to quit school, at least until after basketball season. Speed was sunk and discouraged, lying on his back with his hands up in the air to keep his wounds from throbbing.

He was still on the lookout for a title for his book. *Love Never Surrenders* had not yet crossed his mind. Mother and father offered bizarre suggestions at which Speed and I laughed—*Two Farm Boys. Two Boys on a Farm. Home from the Farm. Home at Last.* How could they have heard even the first six pages and still believed it was a tale of two boys on a farm? "Well, dear," said mother to Speed, "I'm not a literary expert but I'm glad to see you laughing, laughter is the best medicine," and to me she said, "You and I know, dear, what will help Speed get better the soonest possible, don't we?"

"No, mother, what?"

"We don't have to be talking about that now," said father.

"Now's the best time of any," said mother, "while we're all here together. Speed will get better the fastest in body and spirit as soon as we sign the paper including him as part of our corporation." She was obsessed by the idea of our signing a paper bringing Speed into the Mount Vernon Venue Investment Corporation (MVVIC). What paper? Grandfather's lawyer, Mr. Dagger, was to have drawn up a paper bringing Speed into the corporation, but we had heard nothing from him.

"We'll do it," I said. "If we don't hear from Mr. Dagger he'll hear from us."

"That's the spirit," mother said, "I know you're going to do it, I know I can depend on you, and Speed knows he can depend on you, too. We don't doubt you for a minute."

But she could not really speak for Speed. Speed doubted me even if mother did not. He doubted me before I even doubted myself. That was plain enough to see. I saw by his eyes that Speed did not believe me, that mother was going to have to pursue me for a long time before she got me to sign the paper she wanted me to sign, if ever she did, if ever in fact the paper ever came in the first place from Mr. Dagger.

Speed heard me reassure mother, heard mother praise my spirit, but he suspected that this was a sickbed promise, that I was trying to comfort him as he lay there wept dry for his lost fortune, his lost Indian Scout. He knew that when his swollen hands returned to their normal size and his spirits were restored, and he was up and about going on the rounds of his life again I'd be able with my quick-talking mouth to find some excuse for not signing over half my share to my stuttering brother.

I saw in Speed's eyes a reflection of my character. Speed's eyes were a perfect mirror of my soul. He knew me. He had known me all his life. He had known me since the day he fell or dived or jumped or was pushed from the table in Florida. In Sheridan Gardens Apartments all our lives we had shared a bedroom. Brothers get to know each other well enough, and if they are astute, as

Speed was, if they are big watchers and lookers and studiers, as opposed to big talkers and bullshitters, they see a lot of things nobody else sees. Since I did not fully perceive my own slippery character Speed perceived it for me.

As far as I knew I intended to keep my promise. On the other hand, consider this. If I were to share this corporation with mother and grandmother was it not my obligation to assume a true adult responsibility for the corporation and all its holdings? Had Speed proved himself responsible? I did not think so. He was still too young. Wasn't it reasonable to wait a year or two or even more for Speed to prove himself? These thoughts crossed my mind often. I argued them in my head. Speed had lost money of his own because of his impetuousness, carelessness, his erratic control of his passions. All right, he had a right to be wanton with his own money, but corporation money was something else and my responsibility toward it was in the nature of a sacred charge. Was it not? Speed had had big money in his hand and allowed it to slip away. Self-vanishing money, like self-dissipating money. The Indian Scout motorcycle he had adored, that too was gone—he had ridden it one day from the Cameron Wheel Shop to Brookside Bough and back, and that was all the use he ever got of his two-hundred-dollar motorcycle. Everything gone. Gone with the wind for a package of condoms.

He saw what I was thinking. His eyes were a mirror of my character. He knew long before I knew that I was not now inclined to keep my promise—that I had made my promise in the burney-burney aura of grandfather's sun parlor and at that moment intended to keep it, that at that hour of my young and ignorant life I did not know I cared for money, but since that day I had graduated from high school and worked on the farm and I was beginning to see the reality ahead.

He said, "You've got sh-sh-sh-sh-sh-sh-sh-sh-sh-sh . . ."

I translated. "I've got shit between my teeth," I said. It was an old Mount Vernon expression.

"Dear," said mother to Speed, "that's not a nice thing to say to your brother."

154

*   *   *

The day after Speed and I returned home from Brookside Bough I strolled over to Walk a Mile House to visit my trains. I carried the radio for Champrain, "For my sweetheart, music for her ears." It was afternoon. Grandmother sat on the front porch with her fan in her hand, but she was not fanning herself. She said she was happy to see me. I said I hoped she was happy generally. I fear she was not. She asked me how I had enjoyed my summer. Had I been well? What were my job prospects?

I remembered to ask grandmother courteous questions, too, for I was growing older and more mature, more diplomatic, sounding more than ever like father, too, working his way down the long checklist of gentle inquiries he put to the men on the streets on those boring Sunday mornings of my childhood—How have *you* been, grandmother, you're looking very well, and how is grandfather, how is everybody, was Mount Vernon too hot this summer?

I asked her if she knew the song "Joe Hill." Yes, she had heard it, she hummed it a little, and I moved her by telling her that one of the finest memories of my life was of her singing to me under the chestnut tree. We agreed that I was now, however, rather too big to sit on her lap with my head on her breast, wasn't I? "You could sit on mine," I said.

"I don't sit on gentlemen's laps any more," she said. She said I looked healthy and sunburned as if I had worked hard on the farm, and I told her how much we had learned about farming and animals and Nature, how we loved swimming in the bubbling brook after a hard day's work, and how many interesting people we had met. I did not tell her how my morbid thoughts had lately been leading me to visions of her death and its effect on the corporate structure of the Mount Vernon Venue Investment Corporation.

"But poor Speed lost his wages," grandmother said.

"Yes, that was an awful thing," I said. "He laid his wallet on the counter in the drugstore. He just went in to buy some cough drops."

"Did you notify the police?" grandmother asked.

"Oh, yes," I said, for grandmother had faith in the police—her son-in-law, after all, was the police chief of Mount Vernon, New York—but we had not notified the police. We knew the police could have done nothing.

"I wish Speed would come over and see me," she said. "I haven't seen him for a long time."

Respectful boy that I was, I faked leisure in a rocking-chair on the porch inquiring about grandmother's summer. In my head I had an explanation for the radio under my arm, but she did not ask for any. In my trousers my flashlight glowed—a guy's got a hard-on sitting on the porch with his grandmother! Couldn't be helped. I hid it with the radio on my lap. She saw that I was impatient to visit my trains, and when she freed me I hurried into the house and up the stairs with the serious expression of a man off to business.

But beyond the second landing I climbed extremely slowly, to savor the moment, to torture myself, to have fun before the fun even began, to pretend that I was nobody but some silly boy climbing the stairs to run his electric trains when as a matter of fact I was a hot-blooded boy who within a few minutes would be clinging to his sweetheart, his bride-to-be, committing her life and his to all sorts of difficult complications. But I was going to be an honest man about it, I was going to see it through. I had made a promise. That was what Niagara Falls was all about, whether I admitted it or not. I agreed with Speed, railroad trips to Niagara Falls were promises of marriage, I was obliged to see it through. "A promise made is a promise kept," said grandfather's stationery.

When I reached the attic suite I was four stories closer than grandmother to heaven. But it was too silent there. We always loved sound to cover the excitement of our love. Champrain's door was closed.

I went to my train room. In no time at all I had everything on the move again, speeding in every direction at top noise, engines and cars rumbling, whistles blowing, and my old pal the pasteboard cow standing taller than the engines, calling "Moo-moo-ooo-oooo." I knew that cow was a fraud now, having seen real cows all summer, but she was my pal all the same, she was my favorite railroad figure except for my favorite passenger Champrain Johnson on the night train to Niagara Falls, New York.

I knocked at her door. She was taking her siesta, sleeping with her radio beside her head. So I imagined. I heard her old scratchy radio. I imagined that, too. How she'd love this new one! Softly I knocked again. I smiled to visualize the smile she'd smile when she opened the door and it was me. Actually, she did not reply to my soft knock. Why was that—today was not Thursday. She should be there. Softly I knocked for the third time, but still she did not reply. In my pants my flashlight glowed. Speed had nothing on me with his aching testicles. I was becoming activated again. Perhaps she was asleep. Perhaps I should knock louder. She loved my waking her. When I awakened her she would not let me kiss her until she'd rinsed her mouth with Listerine.

I knocked louder. She did not answer. She had turned off her radio. I had clearly heard her radio and now it was silent. Why was that? Perhaps I had not heard it in the first place. Perhaps Champrain was not in her room. That moment of mystery was unbearable, but I feared that if I opened her door I should see a sight worse yet—Champrain would be gone. I opened the door and she was gone.

I don't mean gone for the day but gone forever. It was not as if she might have stepped out for the afternoon, to the doctor, to the dentist, for in those days such appointments lay beyond the hopes of black maids. Champrain had no doctor, no dentist, no sick time, no vacation days, no insurance of any kind, no unemployment compensation, and not even Social Security, for grandfather refused to impose upon himself the backbreaking burden of deducting sixty cents a month from Champrain's pay and adding to it sixty cents of his own and filling out a simple form and sending the form with one dollar and twenty cents in a postpaid envelope to the government of the United States. Everything was gone with her, her few poor flowered cotton dresses, her aprons, her white robe frayed at the elbows, her overshoes, her parasol, her Bible, her magazines, her pictures on the wall, her scratchy old radio, nothing remaining of Champrain Johnson but the odor of Woolworth perfume, Fairy soap, and Listerine.

I returned to Walk a Mile Railway. I pulled the plug. I never saw those trains again. Life for me was changing very quickly. I carried my radio downstairs and sat again on the porch with grandmother. "You didn't stay long," she said. Had grandmother seen any good movies during the summer? No, she had not gone much to the movies this summer. Did she remember she used to take me to the movies? Of course she remembered. Did she remember she used to keep her movie money in her stocking? Yes, of course she remembered, she kept *all* her money in her stocking. Still did. Had she heard many good radio programs this summer? I asked her how Mary Washington was. She was fine, she was always fine, queen of the kingdom. Then there was another maid, her name was Joan, how was she? She was fine, too, they were all fine, it was thoughtful of me to ask. "And how is what's-her-name?" I asked. Grandmother asked who. "What's her-name," I said, "the girl upstairs."

"She's gone," said grandmother.

"Where did she go?" I inquired without apparent interest.

"Grandfather fired her," she said.

"Why did grandfather fire her?" I asked.

"You'll have to ask grandfather," grandmother said.

Easy enough to say, isn't it? Ask your grandfather. Fat chance of my asking grandfather. How could I bring the matter round? On the following night I went to him. Half a block away I spotted him on the porch by the glow of his cigar, and I knew, too, that as I approached Walk a Mile House the sound of his radio would rise to greet me. I climbed the steps with noisy shoes so he could hear me. "Who's there?" he said. I sat in the same chair I had sat with grandmother yesterday.

He turned his radio down, but even as we talked he half-heard his news, keeping up with Lowell Thomas and Gabriel Heatter, whom he imitated very well and poked fun at but without whom he could not live, either. "I was wondering when you'd come over," he said. "Have you lost interest in your trains?"

"I only got back in town a couple of days ago," I said. That sounded extremely mature and grown-up, didn't it?—*only got back in town a couple of days ago*, as if I were an executive on the go from New York to Chicago. Still, a boy who was ready to marry was mature and grown-up enough. I did not approach him as frontally or as boldly as I had intended to do, but rather timidly. I said to him, "I was just wondering about one of the maids that lives upstairs, and when I came over here yesterday I mentioned it to grandmother." Fine boy, blaming it somehow on grandmother. "I noticed she cleared out of that room up there near the trains, you know, and I was just wondering why she might have left. Grandmother mentioned you fired her and I was just wondering why."

"You were just wondering," he said.

"Yes I was."

"Now that you're a big shot back from out of town have a cigar. Get started," and he gave me a cigar. "Fired who?" he asked.

"The girl upstairs," I said.

"Don't you even know her name?"

"Know whose name?" I asked.

"Oh, come on," grandfather said.

"I knew it but I forgot it. I'm wondering why she was fired because I wanted to be in touch with her because I wrote her a letter." In *touch* with her, indeed—grandfather had tried touching her, too, *but I slip a way and stay out of the reach of his hand.*

"You must have known her name when you wrote her the letter."

"I remembered it when I wrote it. That was several weeks ago. I've forgotten it since."

"That's terrible," said grandfather. "I hope that racketeering farmer didn't end up paying you what you were worth." He laughed with pleasure at his own joke and I laughed too as soon as I caught on to it. "I hear that he paid Speed twice as much money as he paid you," grandfather said, but this was not part of the joke, grandfather did not laugh, he had been angry to hear that Speed had been paid twice as much as I.

Now I made it worse. "Five times as much," I said.

"God help us all," said grandfather, "and you just let them do that to you, did you? Didn't you fight back? If you don't claim what's rightfully yours who's going to claim it for you? Nobody. Where do you think you're going to get in the world taking things lying down?"

"It sort of doesn't seem to matter now that we're home," I said.

"You actually wrote that girl a letter," grandfather said.

It was clear to me that he had not heard of my letter to Champrain. I was relieved. My letter to Champrain had gone astray. That appeared clear. Had she received it she would have responded to it. She might have said No I can't marry you I'm betrothed to another, but she would not simply have remained silent. She would have made an effort to reach me. Champrain identified deeply with people in love.

"Yes I did," I replied.

"What was the occasion?"

"I just sent her some recipes from the farmer's wife. She was a great cook, that farmer's wife, and she said if the farmer's wife had any good recipes I should send them on."

"Recipes aren't a letter," he said. "So you didn't write her a letter, you just sent her some recipes. I didn't know she cooked."

"Probably she cooks at home."

"I don't think she had a home. If she's got any sort of an address Mary Washington can give it to you."

"She wants to get married and cook," I said.

"Or whatever it is they do that we call marrying," grandfather said.

"Why did you fire her?" I asked. "What were the charges against her?"

"Disobedience."

"No kidding? She didn't seem like a disobedient type to me."

"Well, she seemed like a disobedient type to Mary Washington," grandfather said, "and Mary's the one that has to work with her. I don't ask questions. You and I don't know about these things. You and I are men of the world. Are you smoking that cigar?"

160

"I'm lighting it," I said. "I'm wondering what she did that was disobedient."

"I have no idea," grandfather said.

"I'm just wondering."

"Don't bother your head wondering. Wonder about big things. We're not hick farmers in the country who hire people and tell them we'll pay them what they're worth. We know in advance what the person's supposed to do and what we're paying her for doing it. If she can't do it out she goes. *Five times as much as you!* My God, you must be feeling ashamed and insulted." That was a phrase he often used to apply to many situations in life, "ashamed and insulted." "What are you going to do with your money, little as it was? Give it to me and I'll double it for you in no time. What's Speed going to do with his money? How much was it? I suppose it wasn't much. Five times as much as practically nothing probably wasn't much, was it?"

"I got fifty and he got two-fifty," I said.

"God help us all," said grandfather. If he had had his little writing pads out there on the porch with him he'd have drawn a map of the U.S. and Europe and done some arithmetic across the Great Plains and the Atlantic Ocean to arrive at the sums he now announced to me. "You worked sixty days for fifty dollars or eighty-three-cents-and-a-thirdperdaythoughyou'reahigh-school-graduate-honor-roll student. Let's say you worked twelve hours a day or dawn to dusk for eighty-three cents or a little under seven cents an hour. You know what you ought to do? You ought to paint your face black and rent yourself out as a slave."

"Grandfather," I said, "I was never on the honor roll. Speed was on the honor roll." I was pleased with myself for correcting him as I did. "I don't feel ashamed and insulted," I said. "He deserved five times as much as I. I learned a lot about a lot of things you can't add up to in money, it was a fabulous summer and there was plenty of food at every meal, very big helpings, meals that would have cost us fifty cents in a restaurant."

"Speed should buy a farm," grandfather said. "Maybe I'll buy him a farm in the country and set him up in business. Farming is perfect for a slow boy like Speed who can't talk, all he's got to do is work and work and leave the trees and the pigs to themselves and they'll give off fruit and grow fat on your garbage. You know you've got to hand it to the money-loving Hebes, they don't eat garbage-eating pigs."

I couldn't let him say *Hebes* like that. Speed and I had a policy position on this. We agreed the right thing to do was to answer back to all racial prejudice. "We have a lot of Jewish friends and neighbors," I said, "and a lot of them eat bacon and ham, you know. Pigs."

"Over there in the Sheridan Gardens Apartments," grandfather said—he had never been to the Sheridan Gardens Apartments—"they'll eat anything, and as for your recipe correspondent in the kitchen, she's gone."

"That's all right," I said, "I was just wondering, just a bit curious. This is a fine cigar," I said. It was virtually the first cigar I had ever smoked. "I'll be heading upstairs to the railroad."

But I headed instead to the kitchen, where Mary Washington, too, was sitting smoking. She was reading the *Argus*. Fat chance of my asking Mary Washington anything, either. I had always been afraid of her. Among my earliest memories of her is my memory of her killing a rat in the cellar, heaving a skillet at him, picking him up by the tail: "Excuse me, young fellow."

Of course she knew exactly what I had come for. "Out of the kitchen with that cigar," she said. I carried my cigar to another room and parked it in an ashtray and returned to the kitchen. She offered me a cigarette and I took it and I sat at the table with her and asked her what was new in the *Argus*, and I said to her, "Grandfather says you'll give me Champrain Johnson's address."

"I got no idea of Champrain Johnson's address," said Mary Washington.

"I wrote her a letter and I'm just wondering if she's planning to answer it."

"*Did* you write her a letter?" she asked.

"I'm sure she would have answered my letter," I said. "It was very important. Very personal."

"Everybody don't answer everybody's letter," she said.

"Why did you fire her?" I asked.

"Fire her? I didn't fire her," she said.

"Grandfather said you fired her."

"I don't fire people. Grandfather fired her," she said. "My boy, I just work here." She smiled a slightly saucy smile at me, implying secret knowledge, making me think that perhaps it had something to do with his copping a feel after all.

"Why does one person tell me one thing and another person tell me another?"

"I don't know," she said. "Ask your grandfather."

She was cool. Cool, calm, and collected, we used to say. She knew all about my letter to Champrain. She had read it. She and Speed and I were the only people in the world who had read it. She asked me if I'd like a piece of pie and a cup of coffee and I declined. I was really eager to finish my cigarette and get back to my cigar. I was uneasy. I felt that I was sitting in the presence of truth and hadn't a chance in the world of finding it out.

The facts were these, as I learned in time from Aunt Ember. I had written a letter to Champrain proposing to marry her. When Mary Washington saw my envelope in the mailbox addressed to Champrain postmarked Perkinsville she plucked it out and read my letter and tore it in half and dropped it into the wastepaper basket and shortly proceeded, after one supportive consultation, to prevent this awful matter from going forward.

She viewed my letter, no doubt correctly, as an incendiary document threatening the peace and serenity of Walk a Mile House and everybody in it and dozens or scores of relations for miles around. Her consultation was by telephone with Aunt Ember, to whom she presented the facts of the matter with the conviction that of all the women of the family only Ember had mind enough to see the issue clear. It was her plan, she told Aunt Ember, to take the law into her own hands. She wasn't asking, she was telling. She was going to do what she was going to do, and she wanted Ember to share this knowledge with her.

Aunt Ember asked for thirty minutes to consult her palmist. It was half-past eleven in the morning. "By noon," said Mary Washington. Aunt Ember consulted her own heart. She was amused and pleased by the spectacle of her surprising nephew, but she was disappointed that she could not quite call to mind the body of Champrain Johnson. She was sorry she hadn't paid more *particular* attention at the time. She would always remember Champrain in a general way as being (these are her words) "tall and slender, with long black shining hair flowing down her brown body like waves of darkness."

She saw the correctness of Mary Washington's course. On the telephone Aunt Ember had for a moment misunderstood only one thing. "You didn't say it was Speed who wrote the letter," she said. "No, not Speed." "I'd have guessed Speed," Aunt Ember said. "Well," replied Mary Washington, "it wasn't Speed fell for the electric trains."

So serious was this threat to the peace of Mary Washington's world that she would tell grandfather nothing so grave as the truth, which would only inspire him with a thousand opportunities for oratory, the grandest pageant of family drama even as he punished everybody within sight. And the boy (I was the boy) would thereafter go and do the same mad thing all over again as soon as he could find another willing girl black or white to attract so much attention with.

Best in any case, the two women agreed, weighing the cost of one poor girl's pain and confusion against the cost of years of bitter family turmoil, to say nothing to grandfather except that the upstairs girl would never do, she must be fired, she was smelly and dirty (*there* was a phrase he'd go for), dishonest and lazy and rebellious and sneaky and not worth by half what we're paying her. "I'll get you a better girl by next week for the same money," said Mary Washington to grandfather, who replied, "Of course, do it, don't bother me with trifles, get rid of her, then."

Mary Washington expressed to Champrain Johnson regrets and apologies for grandfather's unfair decision. "Because I slip away from him and stay out of the reach of his dirty old hand," said Champrain. "I suppose that's it," said Mary Washington, warning the girl that the old man in his violent anger spoke of getting the police after her—his son-in-law, you know, is the chief of police—if ever she showed her face hereabouts, he was a bad-tempered guilty man and his grandson no better. She gave the forlorn girl one week's extra wages and a letter of reference avoiding any mention of her crimes, which Champrain in shock carried away with her among her garments and magazines and scratchy old Philco radio when she cleared out of Walk a Mile House.

"Isn't there any way I can find out her address?" I asked Mary Washington.

"There might not be," she said. "I'll call people. I'll try. But I know ahead of time what I'm going to tell you"—nothing could have been more perfectly true—"I feel she left town. From all I hear I'm sure she's far away. She got a lot of bad things in her record, and the worst is this from grandfather now. If she's smart she left Mount Vernon."

"I can't imagine what she could have done," I said.

"Of course you can't," she said. "You're a nice boy no matter what you think, you haven't lived long enough to imagine everything, and Speed, too. I wish I see him more but he seldom comes over."

Speed never worried so much *why* Champrain was gone as *where* she had gone and how we might find her. In spite of his own misfortune he turned immediately to the task. "We'll find her," he said, as full of confidence as anyone could be, and we set out, two tall slender white boys tramping up and down the streets of the Negro ghetto of Mount Vernon searching for a black girl named Champrain Johnson. I don't think anybody in Mount Vernon called it *ghetto* then. But that was what it was. We walked up and down streets I'd never known existed. Often the streets felt unsafe, and I was sorry I was there, but I was young and beyond danger. I would not go there now.

As politely as we could we stopped men and women of all ages, and asked them, "Do you by any chance know a young woman named Champrain Johnson?" and they looked from me to Speed, first wondering why we were looking for her, and wondering then why Speed did not speak. Sometimes I explained, "My brother stutters," and sometimes they accepted that; sometimes my saying so only deepened their suspicions, and they insisted on carrying on the conversation with Speed himself, to see what his stuttering was like. Sometimes they thought he was faking it, thought it was some kind of stunt.

If people weren't nasty or suspicious they were helpful. They gave us long complicated directions heading us in the direction of a girl they thought *might just be* named Champrain Johnson, *might just be her from the way you describe her*, but nobody guaranteed anything, and sometimes people just gave us directions, I think, because they thought we'd rather have wrong directions than no directions at all, and children especially played games with us, giving us difficult directions and following us up and down the streets to see how much complication we could take.

After we had searched for a week I was ready to give up. Speed was not ready to give up. This was my *wife* we were looking for. He insisted so. He was determined to find her. "If only we had a a m-m-m-m-m-m-m-m-m-m . . ." If only we had a what? If only we had a motorcycle we could have found her, it would have speeded up our search, Speed believed, it didn't have to be an Indian Scout, either, it could be a plain old "moron bourgeois middle-class Harley."

But we would not have found her by motorcycle no matter what brand. Something in me told me, made me know, made me understand and accept that Champrain was not to be found in Mount Vernon and may not have been anywhere in the county or the state or for all I knew the world, earth, she might have been dead. She *felt* dead.

"Never surrender. Love never s-s-s-s-s-s-s-s-s . . ." said Speed— and there he had it! Had what? He jumped into the air and clapped his hands with exultation at the corner of Eleventh Avenue and First Street, where he came not upon Champrain Johnson but his title for his novel, *Love Never Surrenders*. From that moment forward we called his manuscript by that name.

The telephone book was filled with Johnsons. We spent a week calling them from the Shopsins' apartment—Phil had been one of our Revolvers. Speed fed me numbers from the phone book, and in a way it was kind of fun until the fun wore off and this, too, became as fatiguing as walking the streets of the ghetto. He kept me at it. My throat wore out. The sound of my voice repeating itself oppressed me—"Hello, Sir (Madame), I am trying to locate a young woman named Champrain Johnson." I said this over and over a hundred times or more, waiting for the reply we sought that never came, dreaming of help from every voice on the phone, but never receiving it. At one point of my fatigue I felt myself doing this as a favor to him, as if this search were not mine but his.

Hard to tell from the directory who was black and who was white. In my methodical way I went down the list Johnson by Johnson, asking for Champrain. When a number answered, Speed checked it off. Night after night I kept trying because Speed would not let me give up. He began to think he loved her more than I loved her. He was sure he would have felt about her more strongly than I, had she been his wife not mine.

Some people were extremely rude to me on the phone. A Negro man said to me, "Piece of honky white shit, do you mean to marry her when you find her? Do you think colored girls are nothing but a free fuck?" White men were not less rude to me than Negro men. "It sounds to me like you're trying to locate a nigger," one white man said, "so if you're saying I'm a nigger come over here and tell me so to my face and I'll knock your ass off." A black woman said she knew where Champrain was, she'd give me Champrain's address if I told her the story behind my search. I told her my story as candidly as I dared, and when I had finished telling it to her she said, "I'll tell you where she is. She ain't in church."

When we had come to the end of the uses of the streets and the telephone and we still had not found Champrain I began to be convinced we never would. Speed was determined to continue to try. "Try," he said. "Keep t-t-t-t-t-t-t-t . . ." We weren't trying hard enough, he said.

"How long can we go on trying?" I asked.

"All your life," he said. He meant what he said, too. He expected me to spend my life searching for Champrain. It was only what he would do or what he thought he would do if he were I. He deplored my defeatism. I was giving up on her, he said.

The time had come to give up the search. That was my position. I was callous. That was Speed's position. The milk of human kindness had dried up in me. "You're always giving up t-t-t-t-t-t-t-t-t-t . . ."—too easily. I undervalued people I pretended to love, I was a bit of a hypocrite, a bit of a fair-weather friend, I was thinking about running around looking for a job, putting the question of my employment above the welfare of my lost wife.

That was his general condemnation of me. It made him begin to suspect that I was not a good brother, either, that I was ready to give up on him, too, ready to abandon him, just as I was ready to abandon our search for Champrain.

Maybe she was dead. If she was dead we weren't abandoning her, were we? Speed thought she might have committed suicide. I did not think so. She had never talked of suicide, never talked morbidly, she always talked as if life were out ahead of her and she was eager to try it and see how things came out.

Then, too, if she had committed suicide she'd have left her body behind, right? Not necessarily, said Speed: if he were to commit suicide he'd get on a boat and sail out in the ocean and toss himself overboard to prevent his body from being found.

More than likely, said Speed, if she hadn't committed suicide she had simply run away from the complications of our relationship, she'd have logically gone out west to the Rocky Mountains, that was where she'd have gone, found a small town, settled in one of those undeveloped little cities such as Albuquerque, Denver, maybe taken a place up in the mountains, poked around Pikes Peak, that's what Speed would do if he took it into his head to run away out west.

How would she have got out west? She didn't have a dollar to her name.

She'd have hitchhiked, gone most of the way with a nice guy

high up in the cab of a great big cross-country truck, maybe if she was lucky got a lift on a motorcycle, ridden out west hanging on with both hands to a guy's belt.

"What make motorcycle?" I asked Speed.

"Some moron b-b-b-b-b-b-b-b-b . . ."—bourgeois Harley-Davidson, he said, but I knew that in his head it wasn't a Harley-Davidson he saw, it was himself he saw on the Indian Scout he had almost bought, and Champrain behind him hanging to his belt all the way west.

Some of Speed's speculations came amazingly close to the truth as I heard it eventually from Aunt Ember. He imagined that grandfather had killed her—didn't actually kill her with his own hand but sent Mary Washington to fling a skillet at her head. Grandfather had sent Mary Washington once to kidnap Rin Tin Tin the Second, and after a man's passion permits him to kill one living thing it permits him to kill another and another and another, killing becomes policy, killing becomes easier and easier, a killer moves up the line on the scale of living things from dogs to humans. History demonstrates this, said Speed. Mankind depressed him. Mary Washington had fished my letter to Champrain from Champrain's apron pocket hanging on the kitchen door, "that same p-p-p-p-p-p-p-p-p-p-p-p-p . . ."—that same pocket, Speed said, from which I had once stolen Champrain's quarter—and she read it and ran with it to grandfather, and grandfather said to Mary Washington, "Go ahead."

Or Champrain threatened to tell grandmother that grandfather kept trying to cop a feel at breakfast over the New York *Times*. Or Champrain did tell grandmother. Or Champrain did tell Mary Washington. Whatever the course of events, it might all have been irrelevant to my letter, which she may or may not have received, which Mr. Kyrene may or may not even have remembered to mail at the Perkinsville post office—did it ever occur to me, Speed asked, that my letter proposing marriage to Champrain Johnson might be lying this minute on the floor under the driver's seat of Mr. and Mrs. Kyrene's car?

On the theory that Champrain might be dead, Speed and I went over to the *Daily Argus* office to read the obituary notices. We were supplied with the newspapers for July and August by a helpful man who had the idea we were on police business for father. We read them thoroughly but we did not find her and we did not find anybody else we knew. We were not yet of an age to find our friends on the obituary page. There was no news of Champrain Johnson on any other page, either, of her having either died or lived while we were gone, no murders, no suicides, no reports of missing persons of her description.

But something quite different happened in the *Daily Argus* office at the table where Speed and I sat for several cool September days. We discovered the pleasures of reading newspapers back beyond yesterday. They gave us a sense of our having lived in history. True, it was only the history of the summer just ended, but it charmed us all the same with the impression it gave of its being as remote as if it had been not weeks ago but years ago. We agreed that all eras were the same, only the names and the styles were different.

Speed and I decided we would establish a historypaper. This was the same sort of thing old-fashioned folk called a newspaper except that ours would carry only brilliant articles superior in their intelligence, ignoring all petty data, focusing only on long-range historical considerations.

I knew we could do it, too. I had no doubt of it. We excited ourselves. How easy it had been! We had wondered for weeks—for years: ever since Mrs. Packard-Steinberg's classes in Occupational Guidance—what jobs we would possibly be able to assume to support and distinguish ourselves through life, to keep ourselves from perishing on the streets. How well we had taken to heart the lesson of that pet bird laying an egg with an automobile in it: only one egg to a bird. "Every bird in this life gets one chance."

Right, and here we were, we had stumbled on our one and only chance almost without looking for it. After years of worrying, we had dissolved our crisis. We had merely to establish our historypaper and begin. I with my corporate experience would direct the business end of things while amassing a vast library of history books, Speed would run the writing end, train the youngsters coming up, and between the two of us we would produce the best-written, profoundest, most profitable daily historypaper in America. That at least was our idea.

The case against grandfather and grandfather's "conspirators and heirs," brought against him by his formerly friendly investment associates, was defeated in court in White Plains by the lawyers Messrs. Dagger and Church. His adversaries declined to appeal the decision when they learned that he was penniless, that his elusive self-dissipating money lay beyond his reach in the treasury of the Mount Vernon Venue Investment Corporation, grandmother president, mother vice-president, and I the accounts payable manager.

When father came home from court on the final day he said, "O.K., praise the Lord I'm not locked up, mother and I we'll take a vacation cruise to the Bahamas"—*Baharmers* he pronounced it— "and lay in a deck chair."

But they never went near the water. A tragic consequence developed after the trial. Soon father would lose his job. When grandfather's financial activities were reported in the *Argus*, if not with the stately rhythms of Gibbon or Wells at least with decent accuracy, father was through down the station—not a convicted crook but a suspected crook. The mayor could not reappoint him. The mayor was extremely fond of father and knew him to be honest and kind and efficient. Yet people were wary of a police chief who appeared to have been investing other people's money in his own pocket.

Of course that wasn't at all what he had done. He had accepted five thousand dollars from grandfather as an "enabling fee" in the formation of the MVVIC. It looked bad, sounded bad, and, as Speed said, "*was* bad, *is* bad, if you c-c-c-c-c-c-c-c-c-c-c . . ."—if you can't explain what services you performed for a sum of money the money's not yours. That was Speed's view.

Father had no idea how he would earn his living. He said he'd rest awhile. But without income his rest could never be restful. He said he'd economize. "We'll re-plaster up the archway and squeeze back in one apartment and half the rent," he said, but mother said she'd rather die than re-plaster Speed's beautiful arched doorway.

He expected daily that somebody would offer him a chief's job in Westchester County. He said he would never leave that area. But when nobody in any police department offered him work he reduced his requirements. He agreed he need not go as chief. He'd go as an ordinary officer, he'd walk a beat, ride a beat, clerk a station, any damn thing, and rise again to chief in time anyhow. He was a natural chief. He was a long time losing confidence.

Now he was prepared to go anywhere. He thought to send a "national letter" around the country. He tried to write it. I remember his sitting at our secretary, struggling with the letter. His hands sweated at the secretary. He was the image of our handsome Speed bending over his manuscript in the hayloft at Brookside Bough. Speed resembled father. (I resembled grandfather.) The difference between father and Speed was that father could translate almost nothing from head to paper.

In preparation for his "national letter" father made notes for a capsule outline of his life which I paraphrase here in a manner as faithfully as possible reflecting their mood.

Of the several versions of his birth he chose this: he had been brought to "the blessed United States of America" from Ireland as "a babe in arms" and had grown up in a house near the corner of Langdon Terrace and Fourth Street in Mount Vernon, New York.

When he was a senior in high school he had gone to work as aide and bodyguard for a "notable and distinguished blind advertising executive with offices in New York" who encouraged him to pursue legal and police work and assisted him in attending college. With his friend Doc Duffy he attended Fordham University for "about one year." Unfortunately "due to the intervention of the war" he and the aforementioned Duffy had gone to war, and when Doc Duffy "unfortunately did not return from the world conflagration" father ended by marrying Duffy's fiancée, daughter of the advertising executive aforementioned.

In view of his new family responsibilities he abandoned his law career, for which many people thought him highly qualified, and accepted work down the station. From beat patrolman he rose in the ranks, was subsequently appointed chief by one Mayor Berg and moved to his permanent residence, the Sheridan Gardens Apartments, with his wife and his two delightful sons.

His career was "successful in every way." Annually he was re-appointed chief.

But at length an event occurred which "made me look bad in the eyes of the public." In gratitude for many kindnesses in the past father had recently "obliged my father-in-law" by serving as his "enabling agent . . . safeguarding sums for him in the name of one business account or another." These sums were later alleged to be the property of other persons. A trial followed. Charges against both grandfather and father were dismissed in court in White Plains, New York, county seat of Westchester. Here he supplied the judge's name, trial dates, and file numbers of case documents.

By agreement with the mayor of Mount Vernon, whose highly enthusiastic letter of reference was herewith enclosed, father re-signed as chief to seek "greener pastures elsewhere." He and his wife had "always longed to travel away from Mount Vernon to begin life anew."

There ends father's autobiographical capsule. The mayor to whom he refers was named Berg, whom Speed and I snobbishly ridiculed for pronouncing his own name "Boig" and the city he governed "Mount Voinon."

From these notes father attempted to draft his "national letter," for which he had assembled a curriculum vitae loaded with statis-tics, a long list of his fraternal memberships, and letters of endorse-ment from mayors and other well-known Mount Vernonites. One sentence of his draft remains in my mind: "I never did a dishonest thing." But in his next sentence he extended his career at Fordham University from one year with Doc Duffy to four years culminating in "a regular law degree with special honors."

In his chair before the secretary he was paralyzed. His affection-ate, sympathetic, talented son Speed, unable to bear the sight of his father's torment, undertook to compose his father's national letter. As Speed presented the image beyond the statistics it was this: father had never boasted of being a great policeman. He admired certain great policemen about whom he had heard, but he had never appeared to himself outstanding. Yet as he now in his "autumnal years" (he was forty-five) looked back upon his achievement, he saw that he had maintained peace with justice for many years in Mount Vernon. Unlike many other policemen, he had never broken the law in the interest of accomplishing a police objective, never mindlessly run up big numbers of arrests or apprehensions, never beaten a suspect, and never abused prisoners, not even Negroes.

He explained his recent difficulties with frankness. The worst court charge against him was not even that he had received stolen money but that he kept no records. That was true. "It had never been my propensity to keep any records of anything." He left record-keeping to subordinates. He had always worked sixteen hours a day down the station. (This was a shameless exaggeration: father was almost always home for dinner.) Had he been less attentive to his duties as a law-enforcement officer he might easily have kept up with his records, might have taken papers home with him to pore over through the small hours of the morning, but in the interest of his family life he declined to do this.

When father read Speed's letter his self-esteem increased. The more he contemplated his past, as Speed had expressed it for him, the greater his optimism for the present. His plan was to mail copies of his letter at once to police bureaus in two hundred cities. Mother offered a strategic modification of this plan. She urged him to mail copies of his letter two or three a day, not all at once, so that negative responses, if any, might always be balanced by the reassurance of later letters just beginning their journey.

Neither Speed's text nor mother's strategy gained an immediate job for father. But every reading of his letter, as he folded it again, sealed the envelope, licked the stamp, renewed his self-respect.

When as weeks passed and the response to his national letter produced nothing he began increasingly to describe himself as the blameless victim of *Daily Argus* publicity, although in reality nobody read the Mount Vernon *Daily Argus* beyond Bronxville and Pelham. He mistook his own situation for a national scandal on the scale of Teapot Dome.

I clearly recall a long telephone conversation he initiated with a prospective employer far away, and his hanging up knowing he hadn't stood a chance from the beginning. He had spent more money on that call than he had ever spent on a telephone call. People in those days didn't pick up the phone and talk all over the country, as they do now.

Responses from some of his recipients were brutal, like some of the responses to my phone calls searching for Champrain. After several weeks of disappointment father added a handwritten postscript to his letter reiterating in the strongest terms his commitment to begin again as a cop on the beat if anyone anywhere asked him, but nobody asked him. Nobody asked him to come in at the top, either. A city official out west scrawled beside father's postscript, "Still too old."

Eventually father began to blame this slow progress on Speed, whose letter had not been "practical," not been "realistic." Speed as usual, said father, had "raced off half-cocked into the wilderness." Father had begun to discover that the honorable chief of Speed's letter was not regularly the kind of chief for whom departments were on the lookout. Departments were not seeking outstanding chiefs dedicated to the due process of law. They were looking for high-scoring tallies in arrests and convictions, and impeccable record-keeping to document these triumphs. They did not admire "great policemen" and they were definitely put off (this of course was father's lie, not Speed's) by policemen with law degrees from New York universities. Speed had placed father's future in jeopardy, Speed had been reckless with facts, etc. Father used some hard language against Speed for "overdoing the truth."

He had a few nibbles. Nibble a Nab for a nickel. For those six words the National Biscuit Company had once paid grandfather a hundred thousand dollars. When somebody nibbled, father's spirits rose to a state of excitement, but when the possibility collapsed his spirits collapsed with it, and his excitement thereafter became increasingly cautious. Mother was his support. She was with him all the way. She sat on the arm of the living-room easy chair stroking his head, listening with him to dance bands on the radio, and when we boys left the room she tumbled down from the arm of the chair into his lap.

CHAPTER NINE

BEYOND ME lay my life of work. "Beyond him lay the gray Azores . . ." So we sang in school. The hero of the song was Christopher Columbus, and the Azores was the tiniest little mid-Atlantic dot the teacher located for us (who cared?) with a long wooden pointer on the map on the wall. Columbus discovered it and I had to find work in it. Columbus Avenue intersects Lincoln Avenue in Mount Vernon, New York. Many's the bus I waited for on that corner. Many's the bus the Revolvers waited for on that corner, too, on our way out of town for a game. Out of town, ten or fifteen miles up the line, play the game, and back again, sometimes on the same bus, same driver, two hours later for hamburgers at the Columbus Diner. That's what Columbus meant to me.

I had no more idea what I wanted to do or what I was fit for doing than I had had when I was a pupil in Mrs. Packard-Steinberg's class in Occupational Guidance. All my relatives in Mount Vernon knew I was looking for a job, and many of them came forward with free advice, phoning me, dropping over with hints and clues and pointers and tips, things they had "learned the hard way." To hear them tell it, nobody in our family ever did it the easy way. I was going to be the first person who ended up doing it the easy way. Watch how easy I got my first job.

Father and I were simultaneously unemployed. Mother spoke of going to work, but father would not hear of it, and grandfather said he'd "kill her" if she disgraced him by taking any sort of job. "Women don't work," grandfather said. (Four black women worked for him as servants in Walk a Mile House.)

Things were tight. Speed wanted to quit school to "help out." Mother opposed his quitting school on the grounds that *three* of us would then be unemployed. This was funny logic and we laughed at it.

When Coach Cabot heard rumors that Speed was thinking of quitting school he persuaded Speed not to ruin his life so rashly, at least not until after basketball season. He loaned Speed his car. It was a good car but Speed preferred a motorcycle, and Mr. Cabot got hold of a motorcycle for Speed and let him keep the car, too. The motorcycle was a "moron bourgeois Harley-Davidson," as Speed called it, but it was better than nothing and he made plenty of use of it. Coach Cabot's car sat idle in front of the house.

Speed worked for a few days at the Bean Pot on Gramatan Avenue. I remember his coming home one night and taking his money out of his pocket and tossing it on the kitchen table. He was flushed with pride. He looked from mother to father expecting words of commendation. He felt as if he had rescued us from starvation in our snowbound shack in the Klondike. Father was moved by Speed's gesture but he would not tell him so, he only scowled and curled his lip because he was angry at Speed for having muffed the national letter. The money was only nickels and dimes and one pitiful dollar bill and it was not going to help us much. When Speed looked down at the money and up again into father's face he knew it. His hour of pride was over. We were a demoralized family.

Speed took days off from school and sped all around the county on his borrowed motorcycle looking for a newspaper job. He was determined to be a reporter, a writer. He would consent to be nothing else. He was confident that he would earn his living writing. It seemed so reasonable to him. He was a superlative writer—therefore people should be eager to give him a job writing.

He began his search right at home in Mount Vernon, but the

178

Daily Argus had no vacancies, and he sprang to his motorcycle and raced up one side of the county and down the other, and around again a second time, maybe a third, and even up a little into Putnam County, I think, and over into Connecticut, trying every newspaper in existence and a few that almost did not exist—these little weeklies that weren't really papers: they carried paid advertising sprinkled with a few social notes.

Pelham, New Rochelle, Scarsdale, Mamaroneck, Rye, Port Chester, Tuckahoe, Hartsdale, Tarrytown, Ossining, White Plains, Scarsdale, Larchmont, Yonkers, all those towns where the Revolvers had played basketball. He wanted to write. He didn't want to do anything else. He didn't want to be a printer or a truckman or any of the other things people on the newspapers seemed to be telling him he was fit for. It was his stuttering got in the way.

His stuttering was dooming him. People at the newspapers told him he couldn't write for newspapers if he couldn't speak. He showed them the manuscript of *Love Never Surrenders*, which he was then close to finishing. Couldn't they see the logic of it—he had written this wonderful manuscript without having had to speak a word to *anybody*, speaking and writing were different activities. Well, yes, they understood that, they said, and they took hold of his manuscript and admired the bulk of it and sometimes read lines or paragraphs and raised their eyebrows and nodded and said yes, indeed, that was beautiful writing—powerful, forceful, strong, effective, clear, dramatic, etc., etc., etc., but didn't he see how it still wasn't the same thing as newspaper writing? A person could write a novel without ever talking to anybody, unlike a newspaper reporter who had to talk to people to get the scoop. A reporter had to be able to talk on the phone and get out there on the street and go places and meet people and talk it all over. Speed replied to this that he could get anywhere in town in a minute or two on his motorcycle, even on this old piece of moron bourgeois middle-class Harley-Davidson merchandise. On his motorcycle he could get around town faster than the telephone, he said, but of course he knew this was not true, and so did the people who were trying to be as kind to him as they could even while saying no. People took a deep interest in my brother Speed. People loved him. People wanted to take him under their wings and counsel him.

Who then were the criminals in all this? I'll tell you who the criminals were in all this. Father and I were. We were different from everybody else. We were not offering him our wings or our counsel. Why didn't we step in at this point and do something for Speed?

Oh, father and I were "busy," we were "looking for work." Like hell we were looking for work. Every morning father walked up the Sheridan Avenue hill to the mailbox in front of the Esplanade Gardens Apartments and mailed three more copies of his national letter to three more dead-end police stations, and that was his day's work. He also considered it his exercise, "keeping in shape" walking up the Sheridan Avenue hill. It wasn't a hill, it was an incline.

I did as little. I made no effort to find work. I played basketball with the ninth-graders in the William Wilson, Jr., Junior High School schoolyard. I walked by myself in the black ghetto staring at girls who looked like Champrain. I walked up and down Fourth Avenue—Mount Vernon's shopping street—staring at black girls who looked like Champrain. I loafed around the high school staring at black girls who looked like Champrain. Apparently I expected some sort of job to come to *me*.

Father and I didn't know enough to know that we were blowing our lives before our eyes. We couldn't see ahead. We did not understand that the big problem in front of us was not my getting a job or his getting a job but Speed's getting a job. Speed's whole life was at stake and we didn't know it. Strangers were calling Speed on the phone with advice while father and I sat moping, feeling sorry for ourselves, unable to get ourselves going.

We never once—never for a moment—considered pooling our talents and our energies and going into something together, all of us. Maybe Speed and I. We should have gone into something together. Two guys as smart and as good-looking as we were could have made a big go of it at something. I had the gift of speech and Speed had the skills. I was the mouth and Speed was the hands. Even in Depression days with money so short I could have sold ideas and Speed could have carried them out. We could have renovated houses. Speed could have repaired cars and I could have sold them. Speed was the labor and I was the bullshit, and that wasn't so contemptible, either, that was what a lot of partnerships were made of. Speed could have been a fabulous mechanic, a builder, master electrician, for he could wire anything, connect anything, figure anything out, he was a master puzzle solver. There was no end to the things we could have done to get Speed started. He did not need practical advice. He needed simply total support.

But he saw that we weren't thinking about him, we were thinking about ourselves. Father and I agreed that Speed wouldn't have accepted total support even if we gave it to him, he was too independent, he wanted to go it alone, do things himself. We didn't know for a *fact* that Speed would have rejected our help. Maybe he would really and truly have responded to our putting our heads together, all four of us, but we will never know now because we never tried.

One evening came a turning point of my life. The telephone rang. It was a woman named Sheena Camuto Strutz calling for Speed from Port Chester, one of the many places Speed had gone job-hunting. Sheena was In Charge Of Everything Nobody Else Did at the Port Chester *Daily Item.* Her husband, Peter, was foreman of the *Daily Item* printers. He was the best-natured man in the world, and he in turn thought his wife Sheena was the most beautiful woman in the world. He referred to her as "my beautiful wife." Not to argue. He did believe it. It was a religious thing with him. He was an ardent church man. For him, Sheena brought him every day closer and closer to God who had perfected her.

God's idea of beauty may not be mine. Once I knew her I knew that if she was not beautiful she was nevertheless an angel, a person of boundless generosity who made her own causes of other peoples' needs. She told Speed on the phone that she knew of a way to send him to printers' school, that she and a bunch of people at the *Item* who had met him when he was there could tell at a glance that he was smart and honest and sincere and good-looking and idealistic and highly motivated and wholly and absolutely the kind of a person everybody at the *Item* wanted to have around the paper for a long time: they all lived closely together, the newspaper business was a tight-knit business, everybody had to be one big family.

True, she understood, he had gone there for a reporter's job, and they still needed a reporter there, and they wished they could have slipped him right into that job, but they had talked it over and they felt he wasn't quite right for it. But what they had in mind was a related idea, something that would very likely sooner or later *lead* to the reporter's job. It was a terrific deal they had. He'd learn to be a printer, that was the deal. He'd go awhile to print school, they'd pay his tuition, pay him a salary while he learned printing. If he didn't want to begin right away he could wait to start when basketball season was over, or he could wait and graduate from high school first. They weren't hurrying him into this.

When Speed did not reply to her she must have started over— the people on the *Item* knew he had gone there for the reporting job but when they talked it over they realized he just wasn't quite—

"On account of my imp-p-p-p-p-p-p-p-p-p-p-p . . ."—on account of his impediment, right?

Well, yes, said Sheena Camuto Strutz to Speed on the telephone, you could put it that way, but you never know, things were definitely likely to develop, she and Peter and a lot of other people at the *Item* saw him working his way *into* a reporter's job *in time to come*. Meanwhile, why not try starting at the printing end and see how it works out?

No.

When Speed hung up the phone he snapped his fingers. He had taken his manuscript to the *Item* for the editor to read. He should have asked for it back. I said Hey, don't knock yourself out, I'll pop up to Port Chester in the morning and retrieve it. I'll take the train. No, give me the key and I'll take Coach Cabot's car.

I left about ten in the morning. I wasn't one of those unemployed people that sprang from bed at dawn. I'm sure I've told you I *hated* dawn. I hated it from *Saturday Evening Post* days and I learned to hate it again on the farm. Off I went in Mr. Cabot's car, through

Pelham, where father and I straddled the Mount Vernon boundary line on Sunday mornings and stood in two places at once. What a miracle kid I was then. Now I was unemployed. Things were tight at home, father's money was running low. New Rochelle. In those days when you drove through Westchester County you didn't think in terms of parkways and interstates. You drove through the towns. Larchmont, Mamaroneck, Harrison, Rye, Port Chester.

Port Chester was about half an hour north of Mount Vernon, still in Westchester County, close to the Connecticut line. On the front of the *Daily Item* building was the big *Item* clock, and inside the door a long counter where people placed advertisements and made other inquiries and threatened to kill reporters who had written lies about them. People were terribly sensitive to their names in the paper. They begged you to write them up and then they got sore when you did. In my year in Port Chester I learned everything there was to know about human nature.

At the counter a goofy, wild-looking woman with her hair flying in her face asked me if she could help me. That was Sheena Camuto Strutz, who had phoned Speed last night. I perceived her as an "older woman." She was thirty. I told her I had come to retrieve my brother's manuscript of his novel *Love Never Surrenders*.

"Speed," she said. "Oh, what a lovely brother you have. I was awake all night thinking about that silence on the other end. We had a conversation on the phone."

"I know," I said. "I was there."

"He hates me," she said. She had been hurt by his rejection of her. I tried to smooth things over. "He hung up the phone," she said.

"I think you misunderstood something," I said. I said what I could to restore her good memory of Speed. "He was deeply, deeply appreciative of what you were trying to do for him. He was so moved he couldn't get his gratitude out. All he could do was hang up. He went in his room and—"

"What?" she asked. I let her imagine Speed's helpless remorse, although I didn't think that that was what it was. "He wanted so much to be here," she said, "but we don't really have anything for

him. The reporter's job isn't for him, but we'll always need printers. Are you by any chance a printer?"

"I used to be a printer," I said—Eureka! her eyes lit up—"but
when I was in fourth grade the teacher made me stop printing and
start writing in the cursive style." This was apparently more wit
than she had heard in ages, for she reached across the counter and
held my arm for support, as if she was about to fall to the floor with
laughter.

"If you're not a printer maybe you're a reporter," she said.

"I doubt it," I said.

"Are you being too modest?" She had sized me up as a reporter-
type, a person of words, a word-slinger, a wit. "What are you doing
now?" she asked.

Compelled to live up to my witty reputation, I said, "Standing
here talking to you, and then I'm going to grab a bite of lunch
someplace and then I'm going to drive back to Mount Vernon."

"I mean what work are you doing? What job?"

"I'm unemployed," I said.

"What do you think you want to be?" she asked.

"I'll be anything," I said.

The employment situation at the *Item* was just as I had heard it
from Speed. The main thing the *Item* needed right now was a
reporter. A job in Circulation was also "going begging," Sheena
said, and another in Advertising, but the *Item*'s big need was for a
reporter, "we're going crazy until we get him," she said. *Him* of
course. It never occurred to the *Item* to try a *her*. "For some reason
or other we're having the hardest damn time forgive my French
filling the reporter's job," Sheena said, "although we've raised the
salary from seventeen to nineteen dollars a week for a five-and-a-
half-day week." That was a company lie. It was never a five-and-
a-half-day week. It was a seven-day week. It was an eight-day
week. There was no end to the work of gathering the news of the
coming and going and birthing and dying and business and finance
and marriage and honorable or heroic activity and fire and mayhem
and charity and religion and social calendar and religious agenda of
the diverse people of Port Chester, New York.

The Circulation or Advertising jobs would have paid me a small salary and a lot of commission if I sold a lot of newspapers or a lot of space. But I saw myself riding around trying to persuade neighborhood kids to deliver the *Item*, like John Didakis riding around in my memory, the back of his Essex loaded with the *Saturday Evening Post*. Circulation and Advertising meant I'd need to hustle if I were to make any money. I didn't want to hustle for commission. I wanted a sure-thing salary. And you know, the thought clearly crossed my mind that I could work a couple or three weeks as a reporter, do a lousy job, get fired for incompetence, collect two or three weeks' salary and go home for a while and walk the streets and haunt the high-school corridors staring at black girls who looked like Champrain Johnson.

"I've always wanted to be a newspaper reporter," I replied. Sheena told me afterward that what she had liked so much about me was my honest face. Honest face, lying mouth.

She bid me go to lunch and come back in an hour to see the boss, Mr. Cornwall, whom in fact I already *was* seeing, sitting at his desk in a glass-enclosed office drinking from a wax-paper container and striking his typewriter at a furious clip with his two straight index fingers. His eyeglasses were falling off his face. He pushed them up. They fell again. He pushed them up again. He did this five hundred times a day. His nose was too big to accommodate glasses. His telephone was ringing but he was not answering it. He was smoking cigarettes and writing an editorial for which the presses were waiting.

As I became acquainted with his habits I learned that his wax-paper containers contained milk. His diet of milk and cigarettes nauseated me, but once the day's paper was out he revised his nutritional program—he abandoned cigarettes for the leisure of cigars. He seldom lit his cigar but more or less sucked it and licked it like a lollipop. Cigarettes with milk, cigars with milk, his breath was putrid. I noticed that visitors who began by sitting close to him soon backed off. Had he never heard of my lovely Champrain's wonderful Listerine habit?

I strolled out into the street. Behind the *Item* office the famous

Paul Arnold Brick Oven Bakery sent out its fine aroma. Port Chester was a city of aroma. A few blocks away the Life Savers candy plant sweetened the air with its variety of flavors. Later in life wherever I went in the world I bought Paul Arnold Brick Oven bread and Life Savers candies. But when Paul Arnold deserted Port Chester I deserted Paul Arnold bread, and when Life Savers deserted Port Chester I deserted Life Savers.

I was terribly excited that day. I believed I would get the job. I saw ahead of me a new life all my own, free of mother, father, grandfather. During the lunch hour allotted me by Sheena Camuto Strutz I fell in love with Port Chester. Here was inspiration for grandfather—"Good bread, good candy, and a free press." He could have made a million with a clever slogan like that, built another house, hired half a dozen Negro girls to cop feels from at breakfast.

In a greasy shop a block from the *Item* I ate a bad sandwich and drank a bad cup of coffee. That is to say, the food and coffee were delicious to me on that day, but when I re-evaluate them fifty-five thousand meals later I know they were poisonous slop.

I smoked a couple of cigarettes and returned to the *Daily Item*. The building shivered and trembled. The presses had begun their run. But the tension of deadline had dropped away, and Mr. Cornwall in his glass office leaned back in his swivel chair drinking his milk, sucking his cigar, still attempting to line up his vision through his obstinate eyeglasses. He could not make them perch stably on his big nose. I have made rather a deliberate point of his big nose. Listen and you will hear why.

Sheena led me to him. Through those eyeglasses he was reading my name on a slip of paper she had presented to him. "This son of a bitch was here before," he said.

And still my wit shone. This was my witty day. I said, "No, sir, I'm sorry to disagree with you. This son of a bitch was never here."

"Somebody by your name was here," said Mr. Cornwall.

"That must have been my brother."

"Oh, yes." He tossed the piece of paper bearing my name onto his desk among many other pieces of paper. He viewed me sympathetically. "The boy from Mount Vernon, so that was your brother. He had a terrible stutter."

"A very bad stammer," I replied.

"We couldn't live with that. He couldn't be a reporter. He wanted to be a reporter. How could he be a reporter—a reporter's got to be talking all day long. I was urging other things on him."

"He's a wonderful writer," I said. "He doesn't want to do anything else but write. It's his ambition to be a writer."

"That didn't come across," said Mr. Cornwall. "The best I could make out his ambition was to own a motorcycle. I didn't follow everything. You can see how difficult it could be, if I couldn't follow what he was saying. It wouldn't work, I tried to get him interested in something else, we need a man to drive a vehicle. I tried to urge him to learn printing. Linotypers are like pulling hen's teeth. A reporter's got to be able to talk to people. If you're going to be a reporter you're going to spend your life on the phone much of the time. How much reporting have you done?"

"I haven't done any, sir," I said. "I'm just starting out."

"He's just so modest," Sheena said.

"Don't be modest with me," said Mr. Cornwall. "Don't waste our busy time. We can't take on a reporter just starting out. I don't know why she brought you in here. She knows that. I need a son of a bitch with experience." He rose. The interview was over. His belt buckle was unfastened. He tightened it, yanking angrily at it. He had had the hope that a reporter had walked in his door, for he needed a reporter badly. I was a disappointment to him.

"This young man can do it," Sheena said. "He has the equivalent of experience, I can see it in his eyes."

Mr. Cornwall considered what Sheena had said. "What makes you think you want to be a reporter? I suppose you wrote poems in school. We don't publish this paper in poetry. I don't want you to think it wasn't nice of you to drop by, but when you've got some experience behind you drop by again and we'll talk it over. I'd think from Mount Vernon you'd go down to New York instead of up here."

"I thought I'd rather work in the county," I said.

187

"If I were a boy starting out I'd start in the city," he said. "Get some city experience. You've got to be realistic about yourself. You can't start out reporting. If I were you I'd start out selling advertising. I can find a place for you selling advertising if you don't mind making a lot of money for yourself. I wonder why you chose Port Chester of all places."

"My brother said you had a job open," I said.

"Your brother must be hard living with," the editor said.

I gave him our standard family reply. "It's a lot harder on him than on us," I said.

He saw that I had spoken sensitively, and he nodded his head sympathetically. "I don't see what you'd want to come up here for, this place is beginning to deteriorate, it's getting more and more like the city every day anyhow, we're filling up with the flotsam and jetsam of Europe and there's no way of stopping them. The Roman Empire rose and declined but this part of the county is declining without ever rising. We're not the Roman Empire, we're the Jewish Empire, look around you and you'll see what you'll see. Look at Main Street now, look at all the shops. I was talking to a distinguished citizen day before yesterday"—I soon saw how Mr. Cornwall employed this "distinguished citizen" to whom he had always been talking the day before yesterday: the distinguished citizen was himself—"Every shop on Main Street is owned by a Jew or it's vacant. If it's vacant there's a new Jew on the way over from Europe to start up a shop in it. These damn big-nosed Jews . . ."

"I'm a Jew," I said. I had to speak up. I could not remain silent. Speed and I had a policy position in this matter. If Speed had been there he would have spoken up.

"You don't look Jewish," Mr. Cornwall said. He was embarrassed but he cleverly hid his embarrassment. He laid down his unlit cigar. One seldom saw him empty-handed. He sat down. Our interview, which I had thought was over, appeared now to resume. "You brother didn't look Jewish, either, at least not to me and I'm an expert on the subject. Some of my best friends are Jews."

Oh, God, *now* who was in a pickle? But give him credit, he knew

188

the pickle he was in. He had made a terrible slip of the tongue and mind. He had said a bad thing about the Jews and he did not want it to get out among the Jewish merchants of Port Chester who even then were becoming influential in town. "It's not a Jewish name," he said, finding the piece of paper on which Sheena Strutz had written my name. "Why the hell does she think you need all that experience to be a reporter? You don't need experience to be a reporter. I learned to be a reporter in one day. You'll start right out as a reporter right here. It would be sensational if your brother was to become a printer. I never met a Jewish printer but I've always believed Jewish people would make your finest printers." There was nothing the Jews weren't best at, according to Mr. Cornwall. Mention anything, he'd have said the Jews were the best at it, at least when I was in the room. You could have tried him on parachute-jumpers—"the Jews are the world's best parachute-jumpers, no question about it."

There he was, scheming with himself, talking it out with the self-appointed distinguished citizen the way he talked out his editorials. Planning his editorials he walked round and round the newsroom talking to himself. Then do you know how he knew he was ready? His two index fingers went stiff, he'd look down at them and see they were ready to write, and off he'd go into his little glass room and bang away. He could talk himself out of anything.

He knew he had said a very bad thing to me and maybe he saw or suspected that I was the kind of serious kid that might go around town telling everything I knew about him. Now he'd turn his slip of the tongue to the best of all possible uses, he'd hire a Jewish reporter on a newspaper where no Jew had ever worked, and in that way he'd win the friendship, confidence, love, admiration, and adoration of the Jewish merchants of Main Street and the future Jewish occupants of Main Street stores and shops now vacant, all of whom would buy space in his pages to advertise their goods.

"You'll learn fast enough. If I learned in one day you'll learn in half a day, I never met a Jew who wasn't twice as smart as me. You inherited brain from your people. I'll teach you to be a reporter by lunchtime your first day on the job." He was correct about that. He

taught me between eight o'clock and eleven o'clock on the following Monday morning.

Do you believe all this? I'm not exaggerating. I'm not an exag-
gerator. I am a responsible man.

"I'll make you a great reporter. By the time you leave here and
go down to New York you'll know the business inside out. Talk to
Sheena about a rented room. She may have one in her own house.
You can't go back to Mount Vernon every night, you'll be covering
things later than the last train down. You'll work hard and long
here but you'll be happy you did. Give Sheena your Social Security
number. This job pays nineteen dollars but I'm going to pay you
twenty-one, we publish six days, we work half a day Saturday, it's
not a big-city newspaper salary but you're not primarily interested
in money, you're an idealist, Jews are idealists with their heads in
the clouds, you want to learn to write and this is where it'll happen.
Right here."

Fifty years after the event I once again reassure myself that I did
not go to Port Chester for a reporter's job, that I did not go there
for the malicious purpose of getting something Speed couldn't get.
I had gone there to retrieve his manuscript. It lay beside me on the
seat of the car as I drove home.

This was the first and last job that was ever offered to me. I had
not made a phone call or written a letter or read the Help Wanted
columns of any newspaper. I would not have heard of it if Speed
had not been turned down for it.

I was in joyful spirits as I drove, and I began to laugh. I was eager
to tell Speed how I had put down Mr. Cornwall's anti-Semitism,
how he made a 180-degree turn and became the world's best friend
of the Jews. Speed and I had a policy position on anti-Semitism and
I had carried it out.

Me a Jew. This was going to make Speed and mother and father
laugh, too. Aunt Ember would get a terrific kick out of it. It was
also going to raise a lot of merry laughter in the Sheridan Gardens
Apartments, A wing and B wing and C wing and D wing all floors
upstairs and down inclusive. You know, more and more tenants in

the house were being joined in those days by relatives, refugees from Hitler Europe. These relatives sat in lawn chairs in the court-yard. When Speed and I walked past we could feel them looking at us, sizing us up with intense curiosity. They couldn't believe what they were seeing—the sons of the police chief! In the old country nobody they knew had ever lived at peace in the same apartment house with the chief of police.

I was late for dinner. Mother and father and Speed were at dinner when I walked in. I tossed Speed the key to Coach Cabot's car. It was a lovely autumn night, the windows were open, and "The Star-Spangled Banner" came to us on the evening air from the Wartburg orphan asylum band. The music was a beautiful portent, happy days were here again, everything was looking up, I felt myself at peace with all existence, I was in high humor, the future was clear, I had a job now, father or Speed would have a job next, millions of people were a lot worse off than we were. Hey, twenty-one dollars a week!

I sat for dinner. My shining plate was at my place. I remember that plate and some sort of bright reflection in it. Speed saw how exuberant I was, and he waited with happy expectations for my good news. "Twenty-one dollars a week," I said. Nobody my age was making that. It was a lot of money then. In two months of farming I'd only made fifty. I was rich. We were rich. We were saved. I had saved us.

"Twenty-one dollars for w-w-w-w-w-w-w-w-w-w-w . . . ?"

"I got a job," I said.

Father asked me where.

Port Chester.

"What's in Port Chester?" father asked.

"On the newspaper," I said.

"Doing what on the newspaper?" father asked.

Mother saw the awful thing that was coming. "Dear," she said, "don't talk business now, eat your supper and tell us about it later," but that did not register on me, the terrible word was already out. "Reporter," I said.

Speed's mouth was filled with food. He could not empty his

191

mouth fast enough. He spit out his food. The food went flying everywhere. I had landed the job in Port Chester he had gone for. He was as good a writer as I, he'd applied for the job before me, and yet it was I who got it.

"You d-d-d-d-d-d-d-d-d-d-d-d-d-d-d . . ." he said.

I don't know what he meant to say. I don't think we heard it, but we knew what he meant. Dirty something, dirty bastard, something along that line. He sprang from his place, toppling his chair behind him, and ran from the room in despair. Father stood to follow him, but mother urged him to remain, and father saw the wisdom of that. "Dear," she said, "he'll be all right," but for once in her loving life she was wrong. That was the last time we dined as a family.

CHAPTER TEN

NEVER WAS a promise honored so completely as the promise
Mr. Cornwall made to me. He taught me the art of writing
the newspaper report, how to write with the speed of light. He
addressed me at eight o'clock sharp the following Monday morning without salutation in the following manner: "You,"—as if I'd
been around so long he'd forgotten my name—"get on the phone
and call these crooked sadistic morticians and find out who died
and what they died of and who they were and how old they were
and where they lived in life and who their relatives are now and
how long the sons of bitches lived and write them up. As soon as
you have written up all the dead get on the phone with the firehouse and find out about any little blazes they might have ex-
tinguished over the weekend and write them up giving due
praise to all volunteer firemen who were brave and risked their
lives in the searing flames of the latest cigarette smoldering in
the sofa. Don't praise the paid firemen, they get paid for being
brave. Get all your facts right. I want errorless performance from
you at the speed of light."

"Sir," I said, "I'm sure I'll learn how to write as fast as you need
me to after a while, but this is my first day on the job. I've had no
experience at it. Frankly, I can't understand why you hired me."
(He hired me because he believed I was a Jew.)

"This is the day to do it," he said. "If you can't get the hang of it in one day you never will. Learn or starve. Pick up that goddamn telephone and get to work. I'm going to teach you writing like I taught all these other sons of bitches"—he swept his hand around the newsroom. "Get your facts and condense them all together logically. That's all that writing is. Don't be too particular. Remember you're not writing history or art like your brother, this is not a museum but a newspaper, get the minute facts and spell the people's name correctly and don't commit libel or slander."

"I'll get to work right away," I said.

"You damn well better or you're fired."

"But I have one question, sir, I'm wondering when you want this material in completed written form."

Dear reader, please understand that this was Monday morning at eight o'clock of my first day as a reporter. When I asked him "When?" I expected him to reply "Friday at the latest" or "Next Monday, that'll give you the weekend to work on it," but that was not what he replied at all. He replied, he *thundered*, I might say—thunder to go with his lightning—"It's five minutes after eight, this gives you two hours and fifty-five minutes to complete a perfect job. Eleven o'clock absolutely, noon at the risk of your life. I am not asking much of you today because it's your first day. Tomorrow you'll do the police in addition to the dead and the fires, and after you've got the knack of the police and the fires and the dead we're going to put you to actual work like these other sons of bitches here."

Sons of bitches besides me at newsroom desks were the sports editor, the society editor, the city editor, the wire editor. I became good friends with the sports editor ideally named Jack Dempsey, less intimately with the others. Mr. Cornwall had told them all, *warned* them all, that I was Jewish. It really didn't matter to any of them, nor did it matter to them when they learned otherwise. The only person in the office to whom it mattered was Mr. Cornwall, who called everybody a particular *kind* of a son of a bitch—an *Italian* son of a bitch or a *Polish* son of a bitch—but who steeled himself to avoid calling me any sort of son of a bitch lest he call me the one variety he could not afford to let slip from his tongue: a Jewish son of a bitch.

Me a Jew. I never got over it. I can't get over it yet. Nobody in Port Chester ever thought I was a Jew but Mr. Cornwall.

But I tell you I adored him with all his faults. I'll demonstrate how much I loved him by telling you my constant daydream during the years I worked for him: a bunch of bad fellows from the slums of Port Chester race in through the front door of the newspaper office and attack Mr. Cornwall, and I rescue him and beat up all those bad fellows. Of course this has got to be the day's big story in the *Item,* and Mr. Cornwall says to me, "Kid, you've got five minutes to write it up." I write it up, it appears on page one surrounded by photos of Mr. Cornwall and me arms upraised in victory. I am the hero and the bylined author of the day's top story and I am publicly seen to be beloved of Mr. Cornwall.

Once he told me I was "brilliant." I don't know if I was brilliant, but I was certainly tireless, and I think that was what he meant. I who had hid from work beneath the shade trees of Brookside Bough now happily worked twelve or fourteen hours a day without complaint and asked for more. Mr. Cornwall always knew where I was, I never hid from work, and on the job I was always sober, too, which could not be said of all of my fellow reporters.

On my first day of labor I telephoned the morticians and I telephoned the firehouse, I collected all the data and I wrote them up. When Mr. Cornwall saw what I had done he congratulated me. "You can always write faster than you think you can. I don't want to see you just sitting there *thinking* at your machine. Don't pause. Don't cerebrate. I want to hear that son of a bitch going all the time"—the typewriter, he meant—"and if I don't hear you typing I want to hear you on the phone and if I don't hear you typing or phoning I'll assume you're out on the street looking for news. I want Port Chester news all over this newspaper. I don't want A.P. or U.P. or I.N.S. news, I don't want New York and Europe news. The people who buy this newspaper live in Port Chester. We are the only newspaper in the world that gives a damn about Port Chester, East Port Chester, and vicinity."

Everyone in the newsroom had heard all this before, but I was hearing it for the first time and I was amused, and my colleagues were amused at my amusement and smiled to see me smile.

I became a fabulously swift writer. I was the Jesse Owens of newspaper reporting, the Seabiscuit and the War Admiral of newspaper reporting. Nothing could stop me. I could sit down at my desk and bat things out so fast everybody thought there must be two or three of me. I reported fires and police and the dead and the Boy Scouts and Girl Scouts and Campfire Girls and the cookies they sold and the Community Chest and the Salvation Army and Kiwanis and Rotary and Knights of Columbus and the schools and the churches and the synagogues and above all—this became my specialty, for I was a latent novelist, not a factual reporter—the human interest feature stories, sad stories to make you cry, for that was what I was best at, the success stories of every kind, stories about people who had succeeded in raising dogs or orphans, people who had adopted children, people who built their own houses with their own hands, people who had accumulated immense collections of things such as coins or hubcaps or smoking-pipes, people who had strange or unusual jobs, people who had large families, people who had just received a letter from an aunt or an uncle in a foreign country from whom they had not heard in twenty years, and *funny* things, yes, I was good at writing up all sorts of funny things that happened to citizens of Port Chester, people finding long lost things and where they found them, such as a hat in an ice-cream vat, a long-lost document behind a wall, people involved in fabulous coincidences, people setting records for marriage and longevity, people nursing sick children, people raising money for tender causes. I wrote my heart out and cried my eyes out. I rewrote the weather from the wire services and the tides from *The Byram River Almanac:* with my lively swift-flowing torrential meteoric prose I made the weather sound as if I had run out into the open air and measured it myself, as if I had run down to the river and clocked the water.

I became emotionally involved with all my subjects overnight. Our involvement ended when the paper came out the next day.

Then new involvements flourished. I became famous from one end of Port Chester to the other, from the Rye line to the Greenwich line. When people saw me coming they thought to tell me something newsworthy, "Here's something your newspaper should have written up a long time ago." I took notes of what everybody said, scribble, scribble, scribble, direct quote, names and addresses and ages and the meat of the story. I folded my notepages and thrust them into my pocket and raced to my next subject, and when the day's deadline began to press me I raced back to the *Item*, under the clock, through the door, to my desk, and wrote four five six seven eight ten articles a day for the Port Chester *Daily Item*.

Of course I never wrote anything with the craft or care with which Speed and I had once composed two sentences to deliver to Miss Boland, the girl with crutches on the high stool at the high table in the Mount Vernon Public Library. We had spent a half-hour deciding how to ask her to roller-skate with us. But we had not been working for Mr. Cornwall.

During my first week at the *Item* I had envisioned myself carrying my paycheck home to mother and father, twenty-one good old solid United States dollars to rescue them from straits, tossing my money on the table, like Speed the night he came home from the Bean Pot, but when payday came my resolution evaporated and I looked around instead for a bank to put my money in.

The bank I chose to put it in gave another new direction to my life, like the phone call from Sheena Camuto Strutz ten days before.

The Port Chester Savings Bank was one of several banks in Port Chester. Why PCSB and not another? I know very clearly why. The bank had a doorman named Ty, as in Ty Cobb the baseball player. Later he became my friend for life. He was a Negro man about ten years older than I, tall and strong, standing out there guarding the bank in his gold-buttoned greatcoat and his black chauffeur cap with shining peak, and to me the most gorgeous thing about him was that he was unfriendly, that he declined to smile, that he offered anyone a mild "good day" if anyone offered him one first, but that was all. He treated everyone with equal discourtesy, men and women, rich and poor, the wealthy man pulling up at the curb in a limousine, the kid in an apron running over from the food market with a money-sack for change.

Presumably Ty held the door for bank customers coming and going, but he did not hold it for long. If you did not move quickly he let it swing shut. He took charge of your umbrella, more or less *grabbing* it from you before, like the clumsy oaf you were, you dripped it all over the bank. He was one of my favorite people in Port Chester and of course I soon wrote an article about him. Because I was so fond of his surly independence and his negative style I chose his bank.

Inside the bank a young woman named Ruth sat at a desk in New Accounts waiting for me or for anyone else to walk over and say to her, "I'd like to open an account." Compared to Ruth, Ty was jolly old St. Nick. If you think Ty the doorman did not smile you should have seen *Ruth* not smile.

It wasn't that she couldn't smile. There was nothing wrong with the muscles of her face. But she was a critical person, very serious about the world. Everything counted deeply and intensely with her, and so she would not smile just to be smiling. It's a wonder the bank hired her. As I came to know her better I criticized her for never smiling and she offered me a sensible reply. "Tell me something to smile about."

The first words she said to me were, "May I help you?" and I smiled but she did not return my smile. "I want to open a new account," I said. "Sit right down," she said, indicating her slightly private area (this is no double entendre) where she asked me several questions regarding my identity, with emphasis on the kind of bank account I thought I might prefer.

She asked me my birthdate, and when I told her she looked narrowly at me, as if to ask, "Is somebody putting you up to this? Is this an office joke?" We were born on the same day in the same year, she in the morning and I in the afternoon. "I've always been fond of older women," I said, but she did not smile at my witticism. Sheena Strutz at the *Item* would have rolled on the floor. Champrain Johnson would have laughed for a minute and kissed me for my mighty brain.

This first meeting was hardly a meeting. I'd call it a sighting. She described the account I would have and she mentioned several convenient additional features, and when I said I did not care for any of the additions she said she did not blame me, they were really worthless junk.

That night at midnight when I lay on my back in my rented room in the house of Sheena and Peter Strutz I could think of nobody but this girl at the bank. My bed was old and noisy and I worried that I was going to have the hardest time keeping things quiet if ever I brought a young lady to my room. I could not remember the name of the girl in the bank. I could remember only her unsmiling face. I wished I had been more observant. Yes, perhaps I had missed something about her, perhaps I now understood why she did not smile: she was crippled, I thought, her crutches were lying close by, not quite in sight. I remembered when Speed and I were entrapped, as it were, by Miss Boland the librarian at the Mount Vernon Public. I did not want to begin a flirtation with a disabled girl.

She had begun, "May I help you?" I wish I had dared to reply *Yes, you may come to my rented room tonight and lay your body down on my noisy bed.* But she had no humor, she'd have summoned that big doorman Ty to throw me out on my ass. She never smiled once. The thought came to me that the reason she did not smile was that her teeth were bad, completely rotted away. Maybe she had no teeth at all.

Speed would have said, "Better no smile than a fake smile." I had been one week on the job in Port Chester and twenty girls had smiled fake smiles at me. Well, so what, what was wrong with fake smiles for starters? Maybe she was more the type for Speed than for me. He hated fakery more than I did. I could put up with it better than he. Port Chester was heavily populated with ravishing girls smiling fake smiles. Why was I torturing myself with insomnia over a girl who did not care enough for me to smile at me, even in the line of banking. Hard as I tried, I could not remember her name. I ran

199

up and down the alphabet. I knew her name had four letters, but that was as much as my retrieval system would do for me.

I felt that I must either soon fall asleep or go mad. If only she had fallen instantly in love with me I could be asleep by now. Was she thinking of me tonight? After all, we had the same birthday. But what good was our common birthday doing me? It had not brought us together in passionate embrace. One person in every three hundred and sixty-five had one's own birthday. Tonight nothing was possible, I could do nothing about anything, the night was slipping away and tomorrow night would be worse. I foresaw no future. I mulled her over. She had forgotten me already. Where was she now? Where did she live?

These were my thoughts in the night after my first sight of Ruth. Tomorrow I would revise my schedule of life in order to pass old PCSB for a glimpse of her through the glass. Possibly I could find out something about her from Ty the doorman. Tonight, however, would be a long restless night stretching interminably forever and ever. Sleep was out of the question. Tomorrow I would be exhausted. So I thought. Actually I was soon asleep and slept the night soundly through.

Every day I clipped my writings from the *Item*. About two weeks after I began my job I bundled up everything I had written, including the tides and the weather, and sent it home to Speed. He did not react. When I sent him a second batch I enclosed a self-addressed penny postcard so he might let me know he had at least *received* the material, but he did not return the postcard to me. I next saw the postcard twenty years later in the Sheridan Gardens Apartments Authors Memorial Shrine.

When I told Mr. Cornwall of my brother's indifference to me he said "Your brother is a jealous son of a bitch. Jealousy rules the world."

But I knew Speed was not jealous of me. "There's no reason for him to be jealous of me," I said, "because he writes as well as I."

"Does anybody pay him twenty-one dollars a week for writing?"

"Nobody pays him anything for writing," I replied.

"That's what he's worth then."

That was unfair. Perhaps I said so—surely I thought so, knew so. Of course Speed could never write as *fast* as I. He could never have sat down and batted out eight newspaper articles while talking to fifteen people on the telephone by eleven o'clock in the morning. Noon at the latest. However, he could write far better than I, his words were elegant, his sentences were large and long and rounded and I held my breath while reading them, wondering if he could possibly manage to bring this divinely graceful formulation to an end, or whether he would nosedive into the earth. He always landed smoothly.

I loaned the manuscript of *Love Never Surrenders* to Mr. Cornwall. He did not read it. One day he began it. Then he threw it on his desk on top of everything else. I retrieved it. "Good but slow," Mr. Cornwall said. "I can tell by the way this proceeds that the writer struggles and sweats over every word. If I didn't already know he was a stutterer I'd ask you if your brother was a stutterer. The only trouble with slow writers is that they're a dime a dozen. I can get all the slow writers I need. I don't need any. This newsprint we send by the truckload has got to be covered with words or people aren't going to read it. We haven't got time to wait for your genius sons of bitches with their breathtaking aeronautical sentences."

For Mr. Cornwall my brother became a synonym for the most detestable kind of person in the world—the slow or artistic writer. When Mr. Cornwall saw me slowing down on an article he shouted at me, "Don't emulate your brother, I'm getting out a daily newspaper here, we're jobbing out Holy Bible assignments to Matthew, Mark, Luke, and John."

Mr. Cornwall's rough treatment of my brother's writing dismayed me. It was sacrilege. My brother's writing was moving to me. Nothing I wrote for the *Daily Item* could ever have moved anybody like *Love Never Surrenders*. Only two months before, Speed had been working hard on his manuscript at Brookside Bough—yes, in struggle, in sweat—sitting up half the night in the hayloft after laboring all day on the farm. I never worked as hard at the *Item* as Speed had worked on that book. And yet for a time I loved my work. I sat with the phone at my ear in imitation of Mr. Cornwall, smashing away at my machine while somebody out there in Port Chester spouted hot news and fresh facts into my head. I felt powerfully important. I wished Speed could see me.

The day after I opened my new account at the Port Chester Savings Bank I went again to see if I could get an idea of the rest of Ruth's body. As she sat at her desk I looked for rings on her fingers. None. I was relieved. I felt she should not commit herself to anyone before giving me a chance to talk more with her.

I stood at a distance filling out spurious bank forms at a table. She talked to a succession of customers at her desk. She did not rise from her desk. She looked over once in my direction and permitted her gaze (as we novelists say) to rest on my face for a moment, but I had no idea whether she remembered me from yesterday. She gave no sign. Had she tossed and turned in her bed last night with my face before her? Maybe so, probably not. Somehow it struck me as unlikely. She was too classy for me, too sophisticated. Yet I remembered how Champrain had once mocked my hesitation, saying to me, "You fool, you drown me for six weeks in that tub full of water before you knock on my door."

I peered all around Ruth's desk for crutches. I did not see any. I tried to see beneath her desk whether she was wearing leg braces, but it was not that kind of desk. Why didn't she ever get up from her desk? Obviously something was wrong with her or she'd have been up and down several times by now. She did not rise to greet new accounts when they came, or to bid them goodbye when they left—

But then—just then she rose from her desk and walked to her filing cabinet and selected a folder and returned to her desk without looking toward me. I saw that she was able-bodied. She was not crippled. On the contrary, she was the sturdiest healthiest girl in the world.

I remember her at that moment in the language of Aunt Ember recalling Champrain, "tall and slender, with long black shining hair flowing down her brown body like waves of darkness." Ruth, too, was tall and slender and black-haired, though her hair was short, not long, nor was her body brown, of course. As for "waves of darkness"—I don't know. Ruth's darkness was interior. I was in fact blinded for a while by the prospect of the whiteness of her body, and a little afraid of it, as I had been repulsed during the summer by all the *whiteness* of the girls at the Perkinsville public pool. I worried whether so much whiteness might be too much for me. I was not used to it. On the other hand, she had not asked me, had she?

On the third floor of Sheena's and Peter Strutz's house I lived in a furnished room though it wasn't furnished *much*. It was only a bed and a chair and a table with wobbling legs. The table was steady enough for me to load it up with newspapers and notebooks and many of the tools of my reporting trade, but now and again I came home from work to find that the table had tipped over and spilled everything to the floor.

Sheena established rules for her roomer to live by, but she did not enforce them. One rule seemed to be that I was to freeze to death. She hesitated to start up the furnace when cold weather arrived. She kept it off all day because she and Peter and I were down at the *Item,* and she kept it off all night because we were all presumably sound asleep under our toasty blankets. And there was to be no heat on Sunday because we were in church. I did not attend church, and the blankets with which Sheena provided me were not toasty but threadbare.

My room had no closet. It had no hooks on the wall, either. I felt like a savage throwing all my clothes on the floor. I bought hooks and a hammer. In that room of Sheena's I began to realize why God invented closets and shelf space and an extra chair or two and wall hooks to hang your hats on and ashtrays and wastebaskets and other humble luxuries.

My bathroom was unclean. It had a tub but no shower. Since I was not about to lie down and soak in that rusty tub I bathed less frequently than I should have. I took my sheets to the laundry every week. I could not close my window. My electrical wall plug had only one outlet—I could not simultaneously light my room and play my radio. I kept my shaving gear and my toothbrush in the men's room at the *Item*, where there was plenty of hot water.

This was a happy period for me. My rent was two and a half dollars a week. I could have done better elsewhere, but I was fond of Sheena and Peter.

I bought a broom and a mop and a pail and soap and swept the floors and scoured the toilet and tub with a powerful disinfectant whose odor improved my own, too. Mother would have smiled to see what a conscientious housekeeper I had become—I who had always thought the house kept itself. To enjoy the luxury of a big wastebasket I bought one for twenty-nine cents.

Then everything changed between Sheena and me. One chilly October night when I returned to Sheena's house she was waiting inside the door for me, her finger to her lips. Silence. Peter was asleep below. She studied me as if she had never quite seen me before. I was not the boy or young man to whom she had rented a room. I had become someone or something else. What had I become?

In the cold house Sheena was wrapped in a vast robe, revealing nothing of herself but her face and her toes. She was barefoot on those cold, cold floors. Perhaps beneath the robe she was bare, too, but that was nothing that occupied my mind, for Sheena, the world's most beautiful woman, was Peter's, not mine. "I was in your room today," Sheena said. Damn it all, here came trouble. No doubt I had broken house rules. Criminal that I was, I had purchased a wastebasket, I kept a live broom, a mop, a pail. But no, it was not that I had broken a rule. "I saw something beautiful and inspiring in your room."

"You've been into my laundry again," I said.

"Something even more sublime than your laundry," she said. "I read your writing on the table."

The writing on the table. What could she mean? She meant Speed's manuscript of *Love Never Surrenders* lying among so many documents on my wobbling table. "It's odd you were in my room," I said.

"Forgive me."

"O.K."

"I was cleaning," she said.

"Cleaning?"

"You're a wonderful writer," she said. "I saw those pages there and I began reading them, turning page after page, I couldn't stop. It's so chock full of beauty it breaks my heart."

"Those aren't my pages," I explained. "Those are my brother's pages. That's the manuscript I came to get when I got the job. Do you remember?"

She did not want to remember. "I don't care," said Sheena. Her attitude was that no difference existed between Speed and me, that if my brother had written a great thing I deserved equal praise, I had distinguished myself by being my brother's brother.

She began to tell me the story of *Love Never Surrenders*, beginning with Deeps's arrival in search of employment at the home of the rich Brookside family in Verne Mountain, New York, the revelation of his ferocious interior beneath his obsequious outward appearance, and his encounter with Thiwest, daughter and weaver, whose beauty overwhelms him.

She followed me into my room, gazing upon me with admiration, squinting at me in the dim light as if the harder she peered at me the sooner she might resolve this case of mistaken identity. "You need a better light in here," she said. She seized Speed's manuscript from my table and held it close to her. She sat on the edge of my noisy bed. "I'm telling you the story of this book," she said.

"I know the story very well," I said, but she hardly heard me speak. I sat on the floor, leaning against the wall, trying to remain awake, as if courtesy demanded it. That was silly, the author was not present, Sheena was lost in the tale, I needn't have worried about courtesy. And yet, in deference to Speed and his manuscript I could not allow myself to sleep.

"Let me read you a page," she said, searching for a page, finding a page, and beginning to read to me. By "a page" she meant a passage, and one passage suggested another, and other passages suggested still other passages, for everywhere she looked she was reminded of moving passages. The simplest thing for Sheena to do, finally, instead of searching out memorable passages, was to begin to read the whole book to me, although I had already read it countless times in the making. Yet now I heard it again, one more time, from Sheena Camuto Strutz sitting on the edge of my bed in the middle of the night in Port Chester.

The manuscript excited Sheena as she had never been excited by a literary work. Because it was so pure, so idealistic, so utopian, so generous in spirit Sheena was emboldened to look upon me as a holy figure, a saint. After that night she sent heat to my room all winter, and blessed my bed with first-class blankets. She would have bathed my tired feet at day's end if in the biblical way I had asked her. She scrubbed my tub. Her worshipful husband Peter also took a new elevated view of me, I think, for he repaired my window and reinforced the legs of my wobbling table.

Often her greeting to me was a question, "What do you hear from your brother?" and when I said I'd get her and him together when he came up for the Port Chester-Mount Vernon football game (as I then thought he would) she replied, "No, oh my no, it was enough to meet him once, I'm too bowled over now." As for Speed's brother, she attributed to him inner knowledge of life, saintliness by association.

On several occasions I lurked outside the PCSB, talking to Ty the doorman, trying to get a glimpse of Ruth inside the bank. I said to Ty, "There's a girl inside the bank I'd like to meet."

He replied, "If you're talking about the New Accounts girl you already met her."

"I'd like to meet her again," I said.

"How many times do you want to meet the same girl?" he asked.

"I'd like to spend more time with her."

"Open another new account," he said. "A rich man like you needs two."

I smiled, thinking he was kidding me, but since he did not smile I could not be sure.

One afternoon I stood in front of the bank at closing time, hoping to place myself in her path when she emerged, but bankers don't always leave the bank at closing time. I was learning things. Once while I was waiting in front of the bank she left by the rear door. I hadn't known banks had rear doors.

And then one happy day, after all my fruitless planning and scheming, I encountered Ruth quite by accident, almost bumped into her, one might say, on the sidewalk down the street from the bank, where I smiled at her and said to her with perfect truth, "I didn't expect to meet you here." She did not smile back at me, and for a moment I was discouraged. She said, "I didn't expect to meet you here, either, but now that I've met you I don't mind. Pardon me for forgetting your name."

"I'm a new account of yours," I said.

"I sign up many new accounts," she said. "I don't pretend to remember them all."

"We were born on the same day."

"Ah yes," she politely said. "Same year, too."

"That's what I meant. Aren't we having wonderful weather?"

"The weather doesn't change from year to year," she said. "It's an average day, nothing special about it. I don't like to talk about the weather."

"My brother doesn't like to talk about the weather, either," I said. "He feels it's a bourgeois evasion of the real issues."

"What are the real issues?"

"I don't know. You'll have to ask my brother. Which way are you headed?" I asked. "If you're going my way maybe you won't mind if I just walk along."

"You may," she said.

"I'm a big walker," I said, as if to stress that I was more interested in the walking than in her companionship. This was a stupid thing to say. Why be so circuitous? Why not just speak the truth? Ruth rhymes with truth. She was a rapid walker. I had a difficult time adjusting myself to her way of walking, trying to talk in a

207

leisurely, friendly, introductory way, and at the same time trying to keep up with her businesslike pace. Her fast walking encouraged serious conversation. Then, however, suddenly she slowed. Speed up and slow down, that was how she walked. She did many things that way, rode a bicycle that way, she set the pace and you'd better follow, nobody was setting *her* pace. I did not want to touch her, did not want to graze her with my hand, my wrist, my elbow, I was not yet ready to touch her and she was not yet ready to be touched by me, either. On this first little walk with her I learned the meaning of the phrase *keeping your distance*. She kept me at my distance.

When she walked slowly we talked small talk—how long had she been working at the bank, how long had she lived in Port Chester (all her life). I suggested to her that I might write an article about her for the *Item:* Girl banker, youngest banker, Port Chester girl banker chalks up many new accounts daily, etc., something along those lines, get her picture in the paper, too, impress her friends. "There's no telling where such a thing might lead," I said, and she said that was fine, she'd love to be written up, but when I tried to get hard information from her she would tell me nothing. She would not tell me where she lived. Her first enthusiasm melted away.

She asked about my family background. I told her about grandfather's career as an advertising writer, author of "When it rains it pours," for Morton Salt, "Taking the cracker out of the cracker barrel," for Uneeda Biscuits, and so forth. She was impressed. I told her that father had been the chief of police of Mount Vernon and was now moving on to greener pastures. I told her that Speed was our high-school basketball star. "He broke a lot of records last year." She was interested in Speed's versatility, his being both a basketball star and an enemy of bourgeois triviality. When she said she would enjoy meeting him I promised to arrange such a meeting.

"Are you also athletic?" she asked. I told her about my life in sports, and especially about the Revolvers, whom I had organized and managed. She was interested particularly in the Jewish character of the Revolvers, for she had been (perhaps still was; this was unclear) in love with a Jewish boy at Port Chester High, and she was pleased to hear, she said, that I was "democratic," she despised undemocratic people, she demanded of her associates that they be democratic from "the tips of their toes to the tips of their fingers." To this she added, "I could never marry an undemocratic man." She also demanded that her associates be exercise enthusiasts, she herself enjoyed tennis, swimming, and bicycling and had been a member of Port Chester High School Girls Field Hockey.

"We can bicycle, we can swim, we can play tennis," I said. "Get a bunch of girls together and I'll play field hockey, too."

"Possibly we'll do just that," she said, "as time elapses and I get to know you better."

Then very suddenly she said, "Here's where I go my way and you go back." This seemed crazy to me. Where were we? Why here? We were at a street corner about a mile up Westchester Avenue several blocks beyond the library.

"This is an odd destination," I said.

"I live nearby," she said, pointing into the distance. I said, "Why don't I just walk along with you, just to your door, you don't need to feel any obligation to ask me in," but she had made herself clear enough, she did not care to have me accompany her. My heart sank. "Are you married?" I asked her.

"Not a bit of it," she said.

"That's good news," I said. "Do you have any imminent plans to get married?"

"I intend to marry a democratic man when I find him," she said.

"I consider myself a democratic man," I said. I saw that this was a matter she had already been turning over in her mind, she had been sizing me up for my social philosophy. "Now that we've walked ten or twelve blocks together," I asked, "how am I shaping up as husband material?"

"You're athletic," she said, "and you're democratic, you come from a law-abiding family, you seem to be intelligent."

"My grandfather was recently tried for fraud and embezzlement," I said.

"We'll consider that as we come to it," she seriously replied. I had still not seen her smile. She mulled me over, as if I were applying for a job. "I hope I see you soon again."

"Why not see me some more right now? I'll walk you to your house. Why are we separating at this meaningless, pointless street corner?"

"You have a good vocabulary, too," she said. "Goodbye," and abruptly she pivoted on her heel and continued briskly on her way. There was no possibility of my going farther with her. She meant what she said, and I turned around and went back the way we had come.

I tried in several ways to discover where she lived, beginning of course with the telephone book and with various directories at the *Item*. She was not listed. I followed up with a few words with Ty the doorman. "I'm growing rather friendly with Ruth in New Accounts," I said to Ty, "and I'm wondering where she lives."

"In a house," he said.

"Where?"

"On a street," he said.

"This bank advertises itself as a courteous bank," I said.

"That doesn't mean we give out the girls' addresses. Maybe her husband told her to not give it out."

"She told me she wasn't married. I didn't see any ring on her finger."

"She wears it on her toe," said Ty.

Why was I pursuing her? I decided to allow myself to cool. I resolved that I would make no motion toward her for at least two weeks. Perhaps two weeks would stretch forever. I had met a number of girls in Port Chester I liked very much, including a red-haired girl with blindingly fair freckled skin. I began to see myself getting used to her skin after a while. She and I went to the movies one night, and once to a firehouse dance.

And then, one morning to my surprise, just as I was beginning to dismiss Ruth from my mind, she took the matter into her own hands. As I returned to the *Item* from the tour of my beat I found a message in my In basket: "Go to PC Savings and have your new account reviewed." This alarmed me. I was a novice at banking. I had probably filled out the wrong form and blown my money. After the paper went to press I hustled over to the bank and waited my turn for New Accounts. There she was.

As soon as she noticed me she left the customer she was serving and came to me, rising from her place at her desk and striding swiftly and in the most businesslike manner to the bench where I was waiting, and she said to me, "Did you receive my message?"

"My account needs reviewing," I said.

"Your account doesn't need reviewing. You just opened it, it was only my clever ruse to get you here." One never dangled in suspense waiting for Ruth to get to the point. Her expression was always serious. Nobody observing us would have suspected we were not talking bank business.

"You don't have to use clever ruses with me," I said. After a couple of weeks of cooling I was now all heat again. "Just haul out any old tired, stale, weary, dull, unimaginative ruse and I'll come running and throw myself at your feet." I thought this was amusing, but she did not smile. She took it under consideration. "And what do you want to do with me now that your clever ruse has got me here?" I asked.

"I thought you said we were going bike-riding," she said.

"Great," I said. "When?"

The Port Chester *Daily Item* owned four bicycles in poor condition parked in a shed between the newspaper and Paul Arnold's Brick Oven Bakery. The bicycles had night-lights but only two of the night-lights worked, some of the tires were flat, and everything squeaked. I switched the lights and tires and used an oil can generously, doing in a week the job Speed would have done in an hour. I got two bikes into shape.

They were called Speed-o bikes. Every time I saw the name on the top-tube I thought of Speed. He never mentioned receiving the clippings I had sent him. I telephoned him twice. Father was still out of work. Perhaps for this reason Speed was downcast. For whatever reason, he was curt, still mad at me for taking the job he had applied for. I assumed he would soon forgive me.

Over the bike rack hung a sign, "Bikes To Be Used for Staff on Official Business Only." I asked Mr. Cornwall if I might use them socially, and he said of course, of course. "You worry too much about these things," he said. What things? These moral things, he meant. "You pay too much attention to anything that's written down," he said.

One evening Ruth came over to the *Item* after work. She wore pants. Lots of people in Port Chester were mildly shocked to see a woman wearing pants, but that was a chance Ruth was willing to take. We rode a good distance out into the country. She set the pace. We started in a leisurely way, but after a while she quickened it, sprinting out ahead of me, and just as I caught up with her she slowed down and I went racing past her. We stopped and sat on the rail of a bridge awhile, and we returned to the *Item*.

We met Mr. Cornwall, who frowned at Ruth's trousers. I introduced him to her. To help disabuse him of the idea that she was a prostitute in trousers I mentioned that she worked at PCSB. He became friendlier. He praised us for biking. He said everyone should bike for health.

"Do you bike?" Ruth bluntly asked him. "You talk so enthusiastically about biking I assume you're a biker." She nailed him, didn't she? It was characteristic of Mr. Cornwall to talk enthusiastically about many things he was not prepared to invest himself in. "I would if I had time," he said, "but keeping this town in line is the busiest job in the world."

We stood talking together under the lamplight in front of the *Item*. Ruth kept backing away from Mr. Cornwall's bad breath. "I'm truly delighted you don't mind our using the bikes," I said. "They're supposed to be for official business only."

"You go ahead and ride these bikes to your heart's content," he said. "Don't worry so much about these things, don't overwork your moral senses. You have too much moral sense about things. I've seen other people use these bikes once in a while but nobody was ever worried about defying the rules. It's one of the

212

wonderful things about the Jewish people, it's a Jewish trait to worry about a thing like that, to worry about the rules, the Jews as a group are the most law-abiding citizens here or anywhere else. What do you care? Why do you worry about a thing like that? If the bikes are there why can't you two kids go out and have a good time on them? For all I care you can ride them home and bring them back in the morning. What sign are you talking about anyhow?"

We walked around to the back of the *Item* and he read the sign above the bike rack in the shed. I don't think he had really ever seen it before. "Well, staff on official business, you're staff, aren't you, and this young lady is your business. Just because a thing is written down doesn't sanctify it."

He was starting to rattle on a bit like grandfather. I felt a long Cornwallian speech coming, and I did not think Ruth would care for it any more than I did, but I was wrong, she was listening attentively to him, giving him her "undivided attention," to use Mrs. Packard-Steinberg's well-worn phrase, nodding her head as he spoke, inviting him to continue, which he did. "There was a time when we were thinking about giving every reporter a bike so he could get around a little easier, but it wasn't the obligation of the paper to supply its employees with vehicles. Give a son of a bitch his own bicycle, the next thing you know he wants his own car. You've got to be careful what precedents and principles you estab-lish. I've got the habit of principle-building, and I'll tell you where I learned it, I learned it from the greatest people of principle that ever lived—"

"Who are those?" Ruth asked.

"The Jews," said Mr. Cornwall. "You can't live from case to case. You've got to abide by principle, as the Jews did throughout the ages and are doing at the present time in Port Chester and every-where. Now, if everybody *did* ask for permission to borrow a bi-cycle we'd have to put a stop to it by applying the principle, but meanwhile we'll just roll along on our bicycles on the assumption that you are the only person asking for permission to borrow a bicycle, or to be accurate two bicycles, one for you and one for the girl, but the important thing is finally the principle, sticking to the principle, and that's what the Jews have taught mankind."

I have offered here only the smallest sample of Mr. Cornwall's tiresome lecture. I don't know *how* long we stood there under the lamplight. But to my surprise Ruth had not found him tiresome at all. After we parted from him she said, "He seems to have the idea you're Jewish."

"I thought you'd pick up on that," I said.

"What makes him think so?"

"Because I blurted it out when I came for the job interview," I said, "because he was making anti-Semitic remarks and my brother and I have a policy position on that. We deplore prejudice and speak up against it when we hear it."

Ruth stopped walking. "I'm glad to hear you say that," she said. "It's one of the things that's important to me, *essential* to me in a husband, he can't be a prejudiced person. It's very fine for a husband to be athletic and intelligent and law-abiding and a hard worker, as you say you are, but in addition to those qualities any husband of mine has got to be free from undemocratic prejudice."

"Are you thinking of me for a husband?"

"I intend to marry a good man when I find him," she said, not for the first time. That was *her* policy position. She was not in the least bit kidding. She intended to marry soon, to remain married forever, and to become the mother of four children. These things were firm in her mind that night and had been so for "many years." She asked me, "Would I like your brother?"

"Anybody who ever liked me liked my brother twice as much," I said. "Except grandfather, who doesn't like him because he stutters. Would that stop you—his stuttering?"

"Is it very bad?"

"It couldn't be worse."

"Of course I haven't heard him," she said, "but if I liked him twice as much as I like you he'd be on my list, he'd be a ranking candidate. A democratic person has no prejudice against a stuttering person. I hope I'll meet him soon."

"He's a year younger than I. He's really only a kid."

214

"A year doesn't make much difference in a long-range agreement like marriage."

"*Agreement!*" I said. "That's a peculiar way to think about marriage, as an *agreement*. You've got everything too doped out, like finding a husband is some kind of a contest, a scavenger hunt. You make me think of brownies and greenies. When I was a kid selling the *Saturday Evening Post* we won vouchers, brownies and greenies, we got prizes from Philadelphia. Brownies and greenies were vouchers. Sell so many *Posts* and you get brownies, this many brownies, that many greenies. When I get a hundred brownies you'll send me a marriage certificate."

"Everything you say keeps improving your position," she said. "I like your exceeding intelligence."

"Fine," I said, "but I might end up not caring about winning. You know what Coolidge said. 'If nominated I will not run, if elected I will not serve.' "

"You're already nominated," she said.

I wished I had been able to see her face, but we were beyond the shops and the lights now, and I think I probably knew, too, what it would have revealed had I seen it. She would not have been smiling. She would have been contemplative, deliberative, pleased to have discovered someone with *qualities* she liked. I was not a person but a collection of qualities. "Coolidge was a fool, I'm sure," she said, "but you're not a fool. Everything about you is on the positive side."

"I sexually molest little children," I said.

"No you don't," she said.

"This past summer I proposed marriage to a girl in Mount Vernon," I said.

This time she did not reply so quickly. I had given her something to think over, you may be sure. "I suppose that could be," she said. "Why haven't you told me this?"

"I didn't want to make you unhappy. You have me up there so high on your list."

"I'll take you off. I don't care for men who are engaged, married, or divorced. I want nothing to do with them. Has this Mount Vernon girl accepted your proposal?"

"She never answered my letter. She disappeared from the face of the earth."

"I would have answered your letter. It doesn't sound to me as if she cares for you."

"She cares for me and I care for her. Sometimes I think grandfather may have had her kidnapped."

"My goodness," she said. "Do you mean the grandfather who's a fraud, an embezzler, who almost went to jail—he's also a kidnapper? I wonder what kind of a family I'm getting into."

"I'm not forcing you into it," I said.

"No, you're not," she said. "What's the name of the girl you proposed to?"

I was prepared for this question. I had given the matter some thought. *Champrain*, I had learned, was definitely a Negro name. As I informed my reader many chapters ago, during the decade of the 1920s a fad raged among Negroes for naming children for cities and lakes of the Northeast and Upper Middle West. "Charlotte," I said. I wondered something. My mind began to challenge Ruth. How would her democratic convictions stand up if she met Champrain? What would she think of me? Would she really deep down think less of me for my lover's being black? In theory, of course, a girl who thought herself so democratic ought to fight for love between the races. But things break down. In Ruth's mind the two ideas might not come together in the way they came together for me, might not add up as logically as they'd add up for Speed. It might come awfully hard to Ruth to discover that the boy she had high up on her marriage list had spent so many hours of his life lying in bed with an untutored unschooled poverty-stricken poor possibly unhealthy or diseased Negro girl domestic servant in the attic.

I told her something about "Charlotte." I did not tell her everything. I told her that "Charlotte" was somewhat older than I (true enough; three months older), and that she worked for grandfather, also true enough in its way, but of course I knew Ruth would see "Charlotte" not as grandfather's housemaid but as his chaste Manhattan assistant. I did not mention that she was black. I debated with myself whether to mention that "Charlotte" and I had "made love," as people say, "slept together," had "engaged in intimacies," as the newspapers phrased it. I decided to say nothing on this score at the time.

I had hardly spoken when I began to regret my lies or omissions. I had deformed poor Champrain, mutilated her, changed her name, concealed her race, falsified her honorable occupation. She had become, instead of Champrain, a pale, chaste girl named "Charlotte" for whom I was unable as I talked to express any true emotion. Ruth shrewdly perceived my absence of feeling, saying to me, "It doesn't sound to me as if you even *like* her, much less love her."

"She's changed," I said.

We had reached our intersection. Here we had parted the other afternoon. Again we stopped walking. This was the point from which she had started down the side streets without me. I was fed up with her secrecy, her methods. She demanded that I pass all kinds of tests of character, meet all kinds of requirements before I could even come close to her.

Greenies and brownies were not enough for me. I wanted more. I had not yet touched her. I thought to myself, *Who wants to? Is it worth all this trouble? Is it worth going through all this inquisition? Go back to the girl at the firehouse dance.*

"These are the limits allowed to me by the laws of Ruth," I said. "I'm not permitted to go farther."

"Some day the law might change," she said. "I thank you for the bike-riding and the lovely evening. I enjoyed meeting Mr. Cornwall. I've always heard a lot about him but never met him. He's a mighty power in Port Chester."

My mind had rejected her but my body did not agree with my mind. I moved toward her, even as I had moved toward Champrain in the dark night of the electric storm. Now, however, things were different. Ruth backed away, saying with faint humor, "Don't come any closer or you'll lose greenie points."

My body was raging with fluids, inflicting on me a terrible case of poor old Speed's "blue balls." My pain was mounting. I would be unable to walk all the way back to Sheena's house. I would need to lie down along the way on grassy lawns for rest and recuperation—I who had thought I was past that infantile, inexperienced, virginal blue-ball stage of life!

She turned abruptly and began to walk at a good pace into the dark. I was so awfully sorely tempted to run after her I very nearly did so. I caught myself in time, seized control of myself, because her mind was really made up, she knew what she wanted. If anything was yet to happen between us it would happen in her time at her pace, we'd love at her pace, as we walked at her pace, as we biked.

I called after her down the dark street, "Ruth, goodnight, goodnight, I love you," and after a slight delay her answer came back to me through the darkness, "Thank you, that's another brownie voucher for you."

All right, those aching juvenile blue balls were not *my* idea of bliss, but I enjoyed other rewards. The blue balls went away overnight, after all, and the rewards remained. We were making progress. She knew my intentions and had not rejected me. I had really advanced well enough with the tall, slender, grave young woman who only three weeks before had seemed too suave for me, too mature for an awkward young fellow just out of high school. Yet she, too, was just out of high school, however sophisticated and unattainable she appeared behind her desk in New Accounts.

Autumn was cool—*crisp*, we writers call it. I could not believe I had so recently lived through so hot a summer as our summer at Brookside Bough. It had been one of the high points of my life, and I told Ruth a good deal about it.

We went to a Halloween party at the house of a friend of Ruth's from high school. Her friend's family was extremely rich, or so it seemed to me by the size of the house. We dressed as a bat out of hell and his friend. When Ruth and I danced she danced very well but at a distance from me, leaving a lot of space between us, holding me off. I said, "Do I have bad breath like Mr. Cornwall or maybe I'm contagious, maybe you want to sign me up for a leper

218

colony." Why did I put up with this? Look around, the house was filled with delightful girls, half of whom thought a newspaper reporter was glamorous. By the end of the evening Ruth and I were snarling at each other. I felt certain our little bat family had come to the end of its hellish life.

But when I dropped by the bank the next day she was as cordial as ever in her unsmiling way. I tell you, she was serious. She had a plan of life. She not only intended to find a good man and marry him and become the mother of four children, but she intended to make this happen *soon*. Her plan was so rigid and detailed it required every ounce of her concentration. Nothing was left for a smile.

In November the Maroons of Mount Vernon High School came to Port Chester for the annual football game, and Ruth and I were there. I thought Speed might come. Several motorcycles decorated in maroon were parked in the visitor's spaces, but none of the riders was Speed.

Speak of your cool, crisp, clear, cloudless autumn days, there had never been a day like this. We sat half the game on the Port Chester side and half the game on the Mount Vernon side and I saw lots of Mount Vernon people I knew, and lots more whose names I had already forgotten, and many Mount Vernon students so young I could not believe they were in high school.

I was of it all and apart from it all. I did not know which side of the field I preferred. All my memory lay in Mount Vernon, all my present devotion in Port Chester. But what was Port Chester? It was Ruth, that's all. And yet I was baffled to understand why I was sitting here with someone so loveless and touchless and unsmiling. All around me the girls were laughing and shrieking and cheering, but Ruth was silent.

On the Mount Vernon side of the grandstand I heard several black girls laughing, and I could have sworn Champrain was among them, but when I turned around and looked she was not there. How could she have been there? Wherever she was, she had only Thursday and Sunday afternoons off, and this was Saturday.

That evening I ran to my desk at the *Item* to compose an inspired article. I described my heart and soul divided between one city and the other. I thought it was an unrealized article finally. It had not wholly captured my feelings. I had begun by trying to reveal my sensations of past and present, last year and this, loss and gain, Mount Vernon and Port Chester, but my prose wasn't up to it. My piece kept demanding a light or humorous direction, and in the end I went with it. I let it have its way.

One of my fellow geniuses at the *Item* gave it the obvious head-line: A TALE OF TWO CITIES. Monday morning, when Mr. Cornwall read it, he shouted out, "Tell the score for Christ's sake, stick it down at the end," and I obediently added the following paragraph:

What was the score of the game? Oh yes, happiest of days for my divided non-partisan heart, the score of the game was tied, 13–13.

He featured it on the front page of Monday's paper. From the point of view of the public it was the most memorable piece of writing people had read in years. People telephoned Mr. Cornwall all day Monday and into Tuesday telling him how marvelous it was. I think that was the occasion of his calling me "brilliant."

I recall very well one detail of the day I tried without success to work into my story in our family newspaper. I offer it to a more sophisticated public now, fifty years in the ripening. Ruth had worn a conspicuous white or silver coat to the game. She called it her "furry coat" to distinguish it in her honest, precise way from real fur. I had not brought gloves to the game with me. My hands were cold. She permitted me to keep one hand at a time for warmth in her coat pocket not far from her warm body. I remember the warmth of her pockets as I remember the warmth of Champrain's apron pocket from which I once stole a quarter.

One night not long afterward as Ruth and I were sitting in the *Item* office she said to me, "My family and I want to have a very special sociable day, just for you. They want to meet you and have you meet them and see how we all like each other." She was sitting in Jack Dempsey's chair. Jack was the sports editor.

"I'm glad you asked me," I said. I think I was somewhat sarcastic. I had often complained that I had never been to her house, never met anyone in her family, did not know where she lived. I never even knew her home phone. Usually the first thing you knew about a girl was her phone number. "I'm assuming you'll tell me your address so I can get there."

"We want to make it Thanksgiving," she said.

"I'll be there," I said.

"I do hope we all like each other," she said.

"I'm sure I'll like everyone in your family," I replied.

"We may not be so easy to like," she said.

"I may not be so easy to like myself," I said.

"My family is full of opinions," she said. "They want to know if you and I are spiritually compatible."

"You know," I said, "another thing we ought to know is whether we're *sexually* compatible. Spirituality isn't the whole works. I have a noisy bed in a wonderful room going to waste right this minute. I should think you'd want to have sexual relationships with your prospective husband ahead of time to see if we're really in tune. It's only normal."

"We're in tune," she said. "I've thought it through."

"How do you know? How do you know I'm not some kind of a freak, a medical case, maybe I'm actually a female in disguise." I bounded out of my chair and flew to the sports editor's chair, where Ruth was sitting, and I tried to kiss her, but she resisted me, pushed me away, stuck her hand up between my mouth and hers. I kissed her fighting hand. But that was no fun, it was no fun kissing someone resisting, and I went back and sat in my own chair at my own desk. I was angry. I was furious. "I'm not going to marry an unknown quantity," I said.

"After all this time you can't consider me an unknown quantity. We've been acquainted since September."

"We've never *fucked*," I said.

I think this surprised me more than it surprised Ruth. I had never spoken that mighty word in her presence, but now that I had used it I thought I might as well go on, and I said, "That was one of the wonderful things about Champrain, it was the great thing that made our life together so simple and so wonderful. Right in the middle of one of grandfather's state dinners she'd come running upstairs in her uniform—"

"Who's Champrain? Charlotte?"

"I call her Champrain, gave her a little nickname. I like it better than Charlotte."

"Running upstairs in what uniform?" Ruth asked.

I had blundered. "In her formal dress," I said. "Not uniform. We fucked and fucked nine thousand times a day."

"One hour after you and I are married you can fuck me nine thousand times," said Ruth.

"I look forward to it," I said, back in my sarcastic mood.

"But first Thanksgiving," she said.

"She's so much easier to be in love with than you. She isn't after me to marry her all the time, she just wants to be with me and me with her, she doesn't go in for all these calculations about the future, all this comparison-shopping for compatibility. We just got together and worked it out. She laughed and smiled all the time."

"Apparently she has laughed and smiled her way right out of your life—disappeared. She can't really care very much for you if she disappeared without a word."

"She cares plenty for me," I said. But of course the evidence was all against me.

"She could have been back in touch with you by now if she really cares for you," said Ruth.

"If everybody likes me on Thanksgiving I'm supposed to marry you. That's what it sounds like. That's what you've got in mind. I've got more brownies and greenies than anybody else you know. I'm trapped. I'm too young to marry." I wished I was back at the controls of the Walk a Mile Railway and Champrain was in her room next door. My mind flashed on Mount Vernon, going home, getting a job with the *Daily Argus*, living the rest of my life in the place where I was born. I wanted to go back to Walk a Mile House to see who *was* up there now in the room beside my railroad. If not Champrain then Champrain the Second.

I knew such a thing could never happen. A great thing had been before me and had somehow been lost to me, somehow taken away, never to be recovered.

If so, I ought to learn something from the experience. Here now, right before me, sat another woman great in her way, this lovely woman Ruth, so brilliant, so strong, so wise, so clear in her desire. She knew what she wanted and there'd be no changing her. I had better start acting intelligent before I lost her, too.

She was terribly moving to me. Her face filled with sorrow. Her shoulders drooped. She gazed at me with imploring eyes, asking me, *How is it possible for you to love me so little when I love you so much?* She was weak, empty, vulnerable, all her strength gone from her. She would not cry. She sank low and confused in Jack Dempsey's chair. She said, "I know you're not madly in love with me the way you're madly in love with Charlotte—" but she could not go on, she had nowhere to go, she helplessly knew that nothing she could do could separate me from my vision of a woman perfect in retrospect.

Now, there, then, a thought invaded my mind, a memory, or at least a memory of a memory of an incident I had never got absolutely straight. At midnight, in the city room of the Port Chester *Daily Item*, mother appeared to my mind. My mood at this moment must have been mother's mood at her moment, too. Her bargaining position had been good, like mine. It would never be better. Father was convinced she was the perfect wife for him. He was prepared to marry her on any terms she might have presented to him. I said to Ruth, "I don't know how I can marry you as long as I know that Champrain is somewhere out there in the world. Suppose she comes back. I once heard of a similar case. A certain woman was mad for a certain guy, desperately, desperately in love with him. Then the war came and the guy was lost in the war, shot, poison-gassed, tortured by the Huns, probably plastered all over the beautiful French countryside. Then along came the second guy. He had actually been a friend of the first guy—college classmates for a year. Fordham University. The woman allowed the second guy to marry her with the agreement that if the first guy ever came back from the battlefield the second guy would step down from the marriage and leave the house."

"I don't think they could have legally done a thing like that," Ruth said.

"They thought they could," I said. "They had a verbal contract."

"You and I can have a *written* contract," Ruth said.

"A very simple one," I said. I reached for my notepad on my desk, coolly, as if I were interviewing someone for a news article, and I wrote at the top of a blank page the word "Contract" and drew a line beneath it. "The contract will go like this," I said. I did not write. I spoke it. "If Champrain comes back from wherever she's gone she's going to be my wife. I'm going to marry her even if I'm already married to you. You'll release me, no arguments, no backing out."

"Who'll get custody of our children?" she asked.

"You can have them," I said. "They're nothing but trouble anyway."

For the first time in my life I saw this determined girl smile. Her smile thrilled me, it seemed to promise so much of her I had not even begun to imagine. "Go ahead," she said. "Write it out, I'll sign it, we can get it notarized free at the bank." She wasn't afraid of it.

"I'll write it up in the morning. You don't know how wonderful it is to see you smile," I said. "It changes your whole face. It makes me love you more than ever. It's as if I'm seeing you for the first time."

"There's more to me than meets the eye," she said.

"Champrain smiled all the time, except when she was laughing."

"Champrain?"

"Charlotte."

"I'm smiling thinking of being married to you," Ruth said. "I'll make you forget Charlotte." She smiled yet again.

"Two smiles in one night," I said.

"I'll smile all night when we're married," she said.

We put on our coats and left the office. She took my arm. She had never taken my arm before. We walked up the street to the diner by the railroad and toasted ourselves with coffee. We were too young to be admitted to bars. I walked her up Westchester Avenue to our own personal parting corner, and she disappeared down the dark side street.

On the following morning—*the following morning!*—when I arrived at the paper mother was on the phone from home. "Mental telepathy," I said, "I was just thinking of you right at this desk last night. What's up?"

Father had been appointed chief in a place called Sentinel City, Florida. Mother wanted me home for Thanksgiving. Before me, on my desk, was my notepaper with the word "Contract" underlined. All night I had dreamed of Ruth's smile. "You've got to be sure to come home for Thanksgiving," mother said.

I couldn't come, I replied, I'd just been invited elsewhere by my—by my what? My fiancée? *Finacée?* I supposed I'd learn to say the word, but I wasn't ready yet.

"Dear," she said, "you must come home. You must come home now and join us. The moving men are coming right after Thanksgiving. We might not see each other for a while. It might be a long, long time. It might be—Florida is a long way away, you know. Maybe you could even come down a couple of days early."

She was speaking to me as if I were a little boy. "Mother, dear mother," I said, raising my voice so Mr. Cornwall could hear me sounding firm and robust just like him, for I was then still in my somewhat worshipful stage. "I can't just run off. A couple of days early is out of the question. I've got a paper to get out here." Wow! How was that for bigshot Cornwallism! "But I'll come down Thanksgiving morning."

Oh, I could have gone down Wednesday. I wanted mother to see how necessary I was, how adult and independent—couldn't get away, couldn't be spared by these news-hungry sons of bitches in Port Chester.

I thought Ruth would never believe me, but she did, she seemed to believe it very easily. I phoned her at the bank. She spoke in an impersonal, unsurprised voice. She said, "If I sound awfully businesslike for somebody who just got engaged last night it's because people are lined up three deep for new accounts."

"You got engaged?" I asked.

"Didn't I?"

It hadn't registered. In the past I had heard of people's becoming engaged, but I did not now recognize this thing as something happening to me. "I wasn't sure we went that far," I said. "I thought it depended on your family's looking me over on Thanksgiving, passing judgment on the turkey, you know, thighs, breast, intelligence, employment prospects, sense of humor. But it's all sort of a moot question right now. Mother just called." I explained the circumstances. "I hate to spoil your Thanksgiving," I said. "I know you were counting on me."

"Oh, no," she said, it would be a big day at her house nevertheless, many relations were coming—"hordes of family" all the way from the Bronx and Jersey. I was disappointed to hear her say that. I had thought Thanksgiving at her house was to have been a very special sociable day, just for me. She took command. "Let's count on you for Christmas then," she said, "a very special sociable day, just for you."

CHAPTER ELEVEN

EARLY THANKSGIVING morning I caught my train to Mount Vernon, reading yesterday's *Item* as I rode. Much of it I had written. It was already stale. Port Chester news sounded irrelevant by the time the train rolled south of Rye. By New Rochelle it was ancient history. By Pelham it was prehistoric. Across the Pelham line into Mount Vernon.

Father was jubilant, overflowing again with jokes and confidence and Irish expressions and good words for everybody. He felt that his being hired in Florida cleared him of all the local accusations. Years down the station had taught him it was never enough to win in court—you must also win in the eyes and minds of your neighbors.

His recent life had been difficult. Disaster had almost destroyed him. The responses to his letters of application had ceased. Nothing was coming in the mail. Sentinel City, Florida, was his last hope. Money was low. Grandfather would not help—to help would have been to admit his own guilt. Father sold our car. He had spent a lot of money taking trips to cities where he had been almost employed—not quite. He had not been able to afford those trips, but he had been unable not to make them, either. His five-thousand-dollar "enabling fee" had gone mostly to Messrs. Church and Dagger who, after all, as Mr. Dagger frankly put it, had saved him not only from jail but even from death. "You know yourself an incarcerated police chief is target practice for his fellow convicts."

Father had made the trip to Sentinel City without optimism, and after he returned home the city council which had raised his hopes so high kept him dangling unaccountably for weeks. He fretted all day and went sleepless at night. He feared that perhaps they had found him in a lie, found inaccuracies or exaggerations in the curriculum vitae he had prepared—Speed had prepared—and when his mood was lowest he blamed Speed for the disaster about to occur. When disaster turned to triumph he hugged the credit to himself. At one point he had considered withdrawing himself as a candidate, rejecting himself before Sentinel City could reject him, but mother steadied him, told him all along he'd get the job, and Aunt Ember's palmist confirmed this with felt sensations of "new-life deep-South vibrations winging north."

Thanksgiving Day father was much on the telephone with old friends wishing him well. Acquitted at law, once more an honorable chief, he continued nevertheless to argue his exoneration. "An up-and-coming place like Sentinel City, Florida, is not going to rush in pell-mell with a new chief that has any sort of blemish on his record. They checked me out thoroughly, that's what took the time. But I knew from the first minute I'd get the job. They're honest people down there." Of course he'd rather not be leaving Mount Vernon, he said, "and especially the *wife* would rather not be leaving Mount Vernon, but this is what circumstances brought us to." ("This is what *grandfather* brought us to," mother said. She had not spoken to grandfather since the day of father's indictment. She would never speak to him again.)

As late as Thanksgiving morning father was still borrowing money from friends to hire the long-distance moving company. But two of the three men of the family were now employed.

Speed had had an accident on the "moron bourgeois middle-class Harley" Mr. Cabot had borrowed for him. He skidded on wet pavement at the foot of the Lorraine Avenue hill in front of the

Columbus Avenue station, was hurled from his machine and knocked unconscious. The moron bourgeois Harley parked itself against a tree. When Speed awoke in the hospital he found himself cured of his stuttering, but the physician told him not to get his hopes up. Six hours later his stuttering returned with everything else. Coach Cabot drove him home.

When I arrived home for Thanksgiving Speed was cool to me. I thought I might thaw him by expressing an interest in the motorcycle. I said, "I'm hoping you'll take me for a long spin around town over the weekend." "Some time," he said. He never did. Thus I have never ridden on a motorcycle, have never particularly regretted missing the experience, and have grown too old to take it up.

The moment I arrived home I became a boy again. I had forgotten that a man at nineteen is really only half-man, half-boy, a wild freak. I reverted to my Sheridan Gardens Apartments self. Hardly had I kissed mother and embraced father than I saw from the window Speed and many neighborhood boys playing Touch in the sandlot. I was like a little kid. With shaking hands I changed from shoes to old sneakers and dashed out of doors. I could not wait to get there. I ran, I jumped, I shouted with joy. What had become of the dignified reporter for the Port Chester *Daily Item*?

When I dashed onto that field and held out my hands for the ball the boys greeted me with exclamations of delight. If you've been away they love you when you come back. It doesn't matter who you are. Hey, where you been? Hey, home again! Back now! "O.K. now"—my brother's voice in the huddle—"you fuckin shook hands enough, c-c-c-c-c-c-c-c-c-c-c-c-c-c . . ."—cut the shit, third down—"Go f-f-f-f-f-f-f-f-f-f . . ."—go far out and cut right, my powerful powerful powerful brother flinging footballs like baseballs, like missiles, hitting his receiver downfield with force and accuracy exactly where he said he would. I was back in the game again, this was where I belonged. On this vacant lot, among others, I had learned to sling a football, whack a baseball, learned to catch my brother's mile-long football passes on the run. My brother's arm was a neighborhood legend.

These boys welcomed me as if they had not seen me for centuries. Oh God, months were glacial ages in those long days! Where had I been? Between plays they gasped questions, asking me for details of my recent life, telling me about theirs. Froo Gross was home from his first term in college. I forget where. Many games in all sports Froo and I had played together. Today was the last game, our last sight of one another. After this day he would be lost to me forever. I envied him the college, but I instantly reflected that I was out ahead of him, ahead of everybody, ahead of all of them, I was the sterling reporter, newspaperman, covering everything, associating with cops and firemen and politicians and rich merchants and members of the board of education and every distinguished celebrity, politician, lecturer, athlete, author, entertainer passing through Port Chester. Fuck Froo Gross's college wherever it was and fuck my brother's haughty silence too.

There they were, a couple of my beloved Revolver teammates, Froo, Phil Shopsin, and then too (though never exalted Revolvers) the Schwartzman brothers, the Schwartz brothers, and one mere Swartz for luck, new kids unknown to me, old kids who had lived in the neighborhood for years, kids who the last I looked had been those most pitiful of creatures—somebody's baby brothers—grown in my absence into hefty deep-throated arrogant upstart menaces to respectable society (like me), dirty-mouthed kids of the rising generation, I'd show them some rough stuff before the day was done, I'd put them in their places.

It was a miracle! Before my eyes, though I had been gone an eternity, Mike and Archie Mullen savored the game as if Time had stood still. They played their rough dangerous bloodletting brand of football more like Tackle than Touch on this treacherous turf of stones and holes and tangled weeds and brush. The Mullens were one of the few Irish families in the Sheridan Gardens Apartments. How many are a few? I don't know, three or four—the Mullens, the Greeleys, the Evanses, the Cochranes—and for that reason I had always felt a bond with the Mullens. It was Mrs. Mullen years before who had referred to Speed as "the handsomest idiot who ever lived." Once more the brutal Mullen brothers flinging this old football around now for one day only, one long day, and I, too, home for the day soon to return to the journalistic pursuit of truth, gathering in my brother Speed's long long passes, cutting in, cutting out, risking myself, wrecking myself to make the play. The play's the thing.

On that Thanksgiving day that furious football game began at mid-morning and lasted till dusk. Running that ball, passing that ball, falling back on defense, dodging and twisting and turning, sweating and shouting and calling and yelling, we produced loud screaming directives I had not heard in ever so long, "Hey, for Christ's sake let's have some blocking . . . don't go out so fuckin far my arm's not iron . . . rush that fuckin Speed, don't let him get his fuckin pass off, kill him," and at the top of his voice "Holy fuck"—a younger boy's oath meaning in translation, "I don't know how to swear but I'm trying"—scoring touchdown after touchdown and then again being scored upon; and even as we played the game we announced it, imagined it, taking the parts not only of the football players on the field but of the radio announcers up there in the stadia of America, Fordham, Notre Dame, Colgate, Army, Navy, Holy Cross, Bowdoin, Penn State, Pitt, Purdue, Minnesota (professional football was still a sport of the future), big-time college stars, that's who we were out there behind the Sheridan Gardens Apartments in Mount Vernon, New York. As the day progressed some boys left the game and others joined it. Speed alone remained from first to last.

Of that day I retain one vivid memory equal to others—of father having sauntered out of the house standing with his arms folded, watching us boys at play. Like old times. Like here we'd be next week, too, Sundays and holidays, autumn and spring. Here he was joined now and again by one father or another, out for the air, walking the dog. Father shook hands all day with neighbors he had known a long, long time, who had always liked him and respected him, who wished him sweet farewells now, telling him they'd miss him. He was the only police chief they would ever know. He was the only police chief ever to live in the Sheridan Gardens Apartments, as Speed was the only All-County basketball player, as Mrs.

Packard-Steinberg was the only teacher, and as Aunt Ember was the only transcontinental *demimonde*. We were proud of them all.

Praise the Lord, I'd never again as long as I lived be required to endure father's Sunday morning sidewalk conversations. Those endless dialogues now had ended. Now he no longer needed Mount Vernon good will. His new constituency lived way down south in Sentinel City, Florida. Watching us romping all day out there, he wore a big frozen smile. He turned and went back indoors, and I saw him once or twice watching from the window, too.

This was more fun than I had had in months and months. Nothing I was doing up in Port Chester was as much fun as this, nothing was as bracing, as exhilarating. Why couldn't life stay this way? Once at a moment between plays I said to Speed, "My God, I haven't felt this great since the brook at Brookside Bough," and Speed scowled at me and said, "Play, don't talk, you t-t-t-t-t-t-t-t-t-t-t . . ."

Talk too much. I was the brother of words and Speed was the brother of silence. He who could scarcely utter words loved them and knew how precious they were. I on the other hand was a waster of words. I was profligate. Six days a week I filled my newspaper with fast language and sent it home to Speed with a self-addressed postcard. It might as well have been garbage. It *was* garbage, not garbage wrapped in newspaper but *newspaper* wrapped in newspaper, it came to the same thing. What had I expected him to write me on the postcard? If he had written what he felt he'd have written, "This is sentimental corporate word-shit, keep it," and sent it back, but he was kinder than that, and this hatred at least he kept to himself. "Don't talk," he said when I tried to talk to him between plays in this Thanksgiving game of Touch, and again, "Shut up," and again furiously, wildly, "Just do. Play, don't t-t-t-t-t-t-t-t . . ."

Even so, I wished I could remain there playing football all my life instead of returning to my job in Port Chester. How happy I could be if only I were a boy forever playing Touch all day every day with Speed and the Mullen brothers and the Schwartzman brothers and Schwartz and Swartz and Phil Shopsin and Froo Gross and all the other boys who came and went all day that sacred day, all that old gang of mine dropping in and out.

Oh, ouch, hey, holy Christ, the soreness and stiffness of my body when that immortal eight-hour game was done! These were muscles I had not used for at least a year, so fast was time flying away. After I played all day I sank gratefully into the hot tub and soaked my body for an hour.

At another time, in the past, Speed would have come into the bathroom with his towel wrapped around him and chatted, sat on the edge of the tub, shaved, splashing water everywhere, chewed the fat and talked about everything. As recently as last summer we were loving friends. Then what had happened? Was it my fault he lost his two hundred dollars in Rexall Drugs in Perkinsville? Was it my fault I'd been made accounts payable manager of the corporation? Was it my fault that life had been better to me than it had been to him? He had not won the job in Port Chester—why should I not have taken it? I intended to make it back to him. I intended to include him fifty-fifty in the corporation. Six months ago we'd have been screaming in the bathroom like savages, replaying the great moments of today's classic game of Touch.

I had come home prepared to describe to him the marvels of my job, how I ran all over Port Chester covering every sort of story, knowing everything about everybody. This guy's own brother was the intimate friend and confidant of rich merchants and school principals. I spread the news. I took everybody's facts and figures and hurried breathless back to the newspaper office where my desk was covered with telephone messages and memoranda telling me to call this person, that person, hurry, urgent, now, hot tips pouring in. So many people wanted my ear. Some of my stories went out on the Associated Press wire. His own brother's byline around the nation! Didn't all this count for something? Didn't this tell him our family was making its way in the world? Wasn't I making us proud?

Speed, however, did not join me at the bath. It was as if we were no longer brothers, as if we had become not strangers but worse

233

than strangers, as if I had ceased to exist for him. I wondered if I would even be able to drag myself back to work on Monday.

The game had taken my mind from Ruth. I had forgotten that I was to some degree engaged, committed. I intended to back out, but it was going to be delicate. So this was how society did it, this was how it tied you up! The moron bourgeois middle-class fuckers had it rigged. Lying on the back of my neck in the bathtub I thought of Ruth. I imagined her one hour after our marriage. Her promise was keeping me in line. *Don't worry, Ruth, I'll have my body back in shape in case we marry.* Young men recover quickly. If not Ruth somebody else. My aching body glowed with ease, for beyond this happy pain lay prospects of pleasure, rejoicing, health, serenity, delight.

Mother's brother Uncle Wilhelm and his wife Louisa, and father's brother Kevin and his wife Margaret Ann came to us for Thanksgiving dinner. At table I observed that we were history, that eleven years earlier, during my first week as a salesman of the *Saturday Evening Post*, I sold five copies, three of them to persons here at table this day—to father, to Uncle Wilhelm, to Uncle Kevin. My other customers were grandfather and Aunt Ember.

It occurs to me now, sixty years after the fact, that Speed could have sold the *Post*, too. We could have been partners. Why had this never occurred to him or to me? Why had it never occurred to father or mother? Surely it should have occurred to our socialistic Aunt Ember. How clear to my memory the day John Didakis started me out with five copies! He had refused Speed a chance, for Speed stuttered, Speed could not have "delivered the spiel." What rot! In all the years I delivered the damn magazine I never delivered the spiel. The spiel was superfluous. Every balanced adult in America knew without help from me what a blessing the *Saturday Evening Post* was. Speed could as easily have held a copy high, as I did, and sold it by its cover. Norman Rockwell, ain't he cute? And the ladies of the house for the same nickel had earned the privilege of pinching the cheek of the cute little salesboy. I liked that, and Speed would have liked it, too.

Speed did not dine with us. Mother had known he would not dine with us. Yet she had set a place for him. We were seven at table and an eighth setting untouched on the penultimate night of our lives in that apartment where we had lived so many years. "I'll never forgive him for this," father said, and mother replied, "Oh dear no, dear, you'll forgive him, I know you will, he's just a boy."

I don't know where he dined, if he dined at all. He went somewhere on his motorcycle and he returned some time after midnight, still wearing the shredded shirt and trousers he had played football in all day.

He had no job, no money. He had a borrowed motorcycle. His plan once mother and father were gone was to live at a friend's house, but who the friend was he did not say. Coach Cabot would "help out," at least through basketball season.

I invited Speed to Port Chester. He had a printer's job waiting at the *Item* any time he wanted it. He knew he was welcome in Sentinel City. He was popular all over Mount Vernon. He was a basketball star. He was physically handicapped, yes, he could not speak well, but he could run, jump, drive any kind of vehicle, build anything, repair anything, paint anything, write anything. He had never had a steady girl but he was tall dark and handsome and he would have a girl soon, one girl if it was one he wanted, ten girls, twenty girls if he wanted many girls.

He was sullen, surly, resentful, he'd been pretty much that way since summer, and all his life he'd been "moody"—we all agreed to that—but he had had many triumphs, too, the basketball, the honor roll; he had triumphed at farm work and triumphed at beautiful book-writing, having written *Love Never Surrenders;* some things came harder for him than for boys with normal speech; but it was my belief that for Speed as well as for me good health and success would surely prevail.

I felt that this winding down of our family life was not the end of things but the grand beginning. I do not recall feeling even a moment's sadness as we began to clear our home of almost everything in it. Time to move out, ship out. I was employed elsewhere at exciting work. I was beginning to feel professional in my writing. I was "involved" with a beautiful young woman, had got myself in deeper than I had meant to, resented her, discovered love was sweet and painful, and vowed I'd manage love better in the future as soon as I got out of the present. I felt not betrayed but uplifted, challenged, and I thought that Speed too saw the matter clear. He had the keenest eye for the world of anyone I had ever met or would. He may have known too much too soon. He was a one-handed basketball shooter two generations ahead of his time. He knew the life of America was false and true. He wasn't fooled. Possibly, however, he had not quite yet grasped the liberating idea—I was just coming to it myself—that our moron bourgeois middle-class society was a paradise for those of us who could flourish in it with humor, see it undistorted through our tears.

At dawn Jim & George Movers arrived. Jim and George were brothers or cousins of the family named Boccheciampi. They were not of an Italian-American family, as people supposed, but of Corsican people. An elder Boccheciampi had worked for father down the station. Father pronounced their name "Bochampy." Two women arrived with Jim and George. They were their sisters or wives or cousins, who set to work packing a thousand items of small stuff in cardboard boxes—dishes, clothes, everything loose—leaving for their men, of course, the great objects of furniture to be lifted from the settled places where for fifteen years they had dug in.

Speed worked hard. He always worked hard. He carried objects from the apartment to Jim and George's van. He trudged back and forth in silence. Everyone remarked on his strength. Awed neighbors watched him labor. He had the muscles. He carried things alone. He wouldn't help or be helped. As for me, I was terribly sore from yesterday's football, but I, too, carried objects as I could.

By mid-afternoon the Boccheciampi women had completed the packing they had come to do, and I was asked by Jim (or George) to telephone his home to ask for transportation for them. Our telephone had been disconnected. I popped upstairs to the apartment of people named Greenfield, and made the call from there.

The Greenfields were new. I had never met them. Soon a car came for the Boccheciampi women.

By day's end we had carried all the furniture from our apartment except the secretary. I have mentioned it earlier—that outsized monstrous object we had used sometimes as desk, sometimes as chest of drawers, sometimes as bureau, sometimes as all three at once. Years before, on the writing surface of that secretary, Speed had deposited the essay "My Occupational Life Intention," to be presented to Mrs. Packard-Steinberg in the morning. In that essay I had committed myself all unaware to a life of sharing the wealth.

When Speed and I were schoolboys mother and father had always tossed into the desk space of the secretary bills, correspondence, pamphlets, booklets, newspaper clippings, and hundreds of items of family history—any piece of paper nobody could think what else to do with—and rolled the roll-top down to hide the sight of it all. After their Sentinel City decision they tried to sell this secretary. They'd be living smaller in Florida. But this freak of furniture was not so easily sold, it was nothing anybody was dying to own, no takers, not even nibblers nibbling a Nab for a nickel, it was too vast and awkward and crazy.

They could have sold it to a madhouse. Could have given it to the Salvation Army. Instead, they performed a small action for which I have been extremely grateful: they left in the drawers and desk space of the secretary every piece of paper which had accumulated over the years. Father turned the key in the roll-top lock and engaged the Boccheciampi men to haul the whole mess crosstown to Walk a Mile House. There it stood safe, dry, and abandoned for twenty years in the warm basement of the house occupied finally only by grandfather in his dark bitter solitude, and Mary Washington his servant.

That night about eight o'clock nine o'clock half-past nine (dear reader, this was half a century ago, don't hold me to the minute) we sat as we could in the dim light of naked bulbs in naked rooms drinking cold liquids from glassware mother intended to abandon—mother, father, Jim Boccheciampi, George Boccheciampi, and I. I don't know where Speed had gone. The Boccheciampi men were excited to think of driving to far-off Florida. They had never hauled a load so far. All week they had been studying the road map. They'd have preferred February to November for the relief from winter, but beggars couldn't be choosers, and we emptied our glasses to that. They left.

Instantly they returned. They had locked themselves out of their van. They were pink with humiliation. How could they have done such an incredibly stupid thing? They turned their pockets inside out, they dug into their trouser cuffs, they examined their path foot by foot from our apartment to their van. They accused each other. They assured father that nothing like this had happened before, that they were ordinarily alert and responsible. "It's been a long day," father said.

They walked around and around their van. In their minds they retraced their actions during the final hour of their work. One of the Boccheciampi men climbed to the roof of the cab, attempting in the dark to learn by peering through the windshield whether he or his brother (cousin?) had left the keys in the ignition. Yes, in the dark interior of the cab they saw the precious keys. No, not the keys. Well, perhaps. Maybe yes, maybe no. In chagrin, one of the Boccheciampi men in self-abasement slumped across the fender of the cab, arms outstretched—*Crucify me, crucify any man that locks his key in his truck*. Then they recovered. Suddenly it was really no big problem. Here's what they would do. They would return home for a good night's sleep and come back at dawn to-morrow with another man of the family who in fourteen seconds could jimmy their cab door—could jimmy any door in the world. They looked hopefully at father. Would father the chief of police grant immunity to this jimmy expert in their family? "Have him do it," father replied. "Only don't let me see his face in Sentinel City, Florida." He meant it.

Again I popped upstairs to the Greenfields to call for transportation for the Boccheciampis, but when Mr. Greenfield overheard my business he said, "Hell, kid, I'll drive them home myself, let's all take a ride in the night air." We drove the Boccheciampi men home. Then father felt obliged to ask Mr. Greenfield along to dinner at the Bee Hive. Greenfield had dined, but he would join us, sip a cup of tea. From among the hundreds of people mother and father knew in Mount Vernon they would have chosen to dine their last night with someone not a stranger. But his kindness had trapped us.

We slept that night on old mattresses on the floor. We were roughing it. Father hated roughing it. Mother hated roughing it, too, but she did it with better nature than father. The beds were in the van—well, for Christ's sake, everything in the *world* was in the van. I slept in my own old room.

I was awakened at dawn to the most terrifying circumstance of my life. Father stood above me bellowing, moaning, keening, roaring, an unspeakable misery of soul rising from within him, his fists above his head, calling to God above and to me below, *"What the fuck is going on here? What are you and your brother up to? Are you trying to drive me crazy before I can even get to Florida? Is this a plot against me? Didn't your grandfather do enough to me?"*

Behind him strange men ran back and forth through the rooms. The men were Jim and George and the jimmy expert. Yesterday there had been two Boccheciampi men. Today there were three. One of the Boccheciampi men was at the telephone. When he realized the phone was disconnected he hurled it to the floor, swearing Corsican oaths. He ran from the house.

Mother alone was silent and seemingly composed, but she was not truly in her right mind, for if she had been wholly composed she would not have sat there in her nightgown among strange men. She sat on a suitcase in the center of the living room. Her head was bowed and she was praying.

I shouted up from the floor to father at his great height. "I haven't been up to anything. I don't know what you're talking about. For God's sake what's wrong?" I must have awakened to myself in my role as a newspaper reporter. Whatever was wrong I'd report it, write it up. Father remembered later that I had struggled from my mattress crying, "What's new? What's new? What's going on?"

The moving van was gone. Speed and his motorcycle were gone. At first I did not put the elements together. The van was one thing. Speed and his motorcycle were another. It was father as police-man, not father as father, who knew the elements for what they were as soon as he saw the walkboard plank in the gutter: Speed and his motorcycle and the van were one.

Jim and George had used the walkboard yesterday to wheel heavy objects onto the truck from the sidewalk. When they were done they had stowed the walkboard in the van. They were certain of that. They had now regained their certainty and their self-respect. They had not locked their keys in the cab. Their keys had been stolen from them, obviously by Speed. Another aspect of their certainty was that unless they recovered their van they were wiped out. Father and mother had no insurance, either. They, too, were wiped out. The jimmy expert Boccheciampi felt himself in his own way cheated. "I can't open a door of a vehicle gone," he sadly said.

In the dark dawn the police arrived. Lights went on in the courtyard windows. Mrs. Davidoff, on the third floor, on her way from bed to bathroom about three o'clock in the morning, had seen from her window Speed wheeling his motorcycle up the walkboard into the van. She had thought nothing of it—she had watched us moving all day, why not a last-minute motorcycle in the night? Was she certain it was Speed? "Of course certain," she said. She pro-nounced it "soytn." Mayor Boig of Mount Voinon. How come so soytn? "Because I know the boy from the day he moved in this house on his three-wheel bicycle."

Father made a quick decision and a good one, the best one, the only one. "I'm going to clear out of here," he said.

"You, dear, not you and me?" mother asked.

"You and me," father said. "Understand," he said to me, "I'm leaving you all alone in the middle of this mess. You're a man. You've got to take it on your shoulders for me because I better get down there and get on that job. I was lucky to get it. I stretched my credentials. There'll never be another. How an honest man like me ended up covered from head to foot in all your fucking grandfather's shit I can't tell you. Tell Speed I don't know if I can ever face him again. Everything we own is in that fucking truck."

"Dear," said mother, "he may only have driven it off for a joy-ride. He might be right around the corner coming back."

"Don't be taking bets," father said, "I don't understand him anymore."

"When we show up at the doorstep in Florida he's going to be waiting there with the van," said mother.

"It would have been convenient if he let us in on his plans in advance," said father. "Maybe you're right but then again you might be wrong. Maybe not. I don't know anything any more. I only know I better be on the job down there before they hear down there about this up here. A whole van gone. I'm some kind of a police officer. You know what they're going to think down there? They're going to think the same thing they're going to think all over Mount Vernon—they're going to think this missing van is another part of the conspiracy embezzlement case. That's what they're going to think if I don't get down there and do their thinking for them."

I carried the suitcases to the front of the courtyard. Mother and father had three or four suitcases and the clothes on their backs. That was all they had in the world. "People left Ireland with less," father said.

"It's true, dear," mother said, "and not by the Orange Blossom Special either." In sudden alarm she opened her purse to see that their tickets were there. "Thank God," she said. They had tickets out of New York on the Orange Blossom Special. It was the same train mother, Speed, and I had traveled between New York and Florida ages before, when Babe Ruth or Doc Duffy dropped by our tiny rented winter cottage in his naked skin, when Speed jumped, fell, dived, or was pushed from the kitchen table.

We stood at the curb. "I'm sure that the reason he took the moving company's van," said mother to me, "was because you didn't sign your half of the corporation over to him. He's waiting for that. Aunt Ember agrees with me in this. You can ask her if you don't believe me. Speed's playing this little joke on us until you sign the paper. You promised to sign, dear. Sign it as soon as you can and he'll come back. Call Mr. Dagger the lawyer, get his number from grandfather, have him write up the paper and send it to you to sign as soon as you can and Speed will come back with the moving company's van and everything in it safe and sound."

"I thought you said he was on the way driving the van to Sentinel City," said father.

"I may be confused," said mother. She took father's arm. A Mount Vernon Police Department car drew to the curb. I loaded the suitcases. Mother turned and blew kisses to the people hanging out of the courtyard windows. Then mother and father were gone from the Sheridan Gardens Apartments.

Part Two

I too was gone from my old life into my new life. My life entered a second phase both continuous with the first phase yet separate and different. My new life began in shock and continued forever in waiting. I awaited a resumption of my old life, a return to that wholeness which could be produced only by the single event of Speed's return from his dark act to the light of contrition and explanation. My lifelong vigil became my life. I lived every hour on the lookout for my brother.

As soon as Speed returned our lives would resume—all our lives, his life, my life, mother's life, father's life. Until he returned we existed in catastrophe. I do not know how we survived. I do not think we could have survived had we known from the beginning how long we were to wait, and with what outcome.

Every day of my life I imagined Speed's return. Something happened every day to present him to my mind: the ring of a telephone, the arrival in the mail of an unfamiliar envelope. Every telegram certainly, in that old familiar yellow envelope whose color was trouble. During the war I expected to hear almost every day of a telegram to father and mother from the War Department, telling them that Speed was dead, wounded, missing in action. I wonder whether we would have preferred his certain death to the mystery of his flight, his voyage behind the steering-wheel of a moving-van to silence and eternity.

In the beginning I knew or felt that any minute Speed would show up on my doorstep—to be accurate, Sheena and Peter Strutz's doorstep. I had no doorstep. I was gone from home. I waited for him. I imagined him. I awoke in the morning saying to myself, "The van is in the street outside the window," and I sprang from bed and looked out of the window and the van was not there.

I could see him parking that big van on the street below. He'd have mastered it by now. No street had ever been too narrow for Speed, no parking problem too difficult, he'd wheel that big thing around any way he pleased. Hell, Speed could drive things sideways if he wanted to. There he came, old Speed, good old Speed, my brother Speed, climbing down from the cab of the van with a silly sheepish smile on his face holding up his hand, signaling me not to speak, he'd explain everything, why he did it and where he went, he'd give me his answers before I asked the questions. We'd always known each other's answers before we heard the questions. "Why did I do it? Just because."

"I see."

Just because he took it into his head to do, and now he was ready to take his punishment. He'd face the consequences. We were a police family and we'd been taught by father that if you broke the law you risked the penalty, take your choice.

Here's what would happen, he'd turn himself in, he'd go to court, he'd plead guilty, father could recommend a good lawyer, he'd draw a light sentence from a sympathetic judge—Your Honor, the young man took a joyride in a van, got carried away and carried the van away with him, boys will be boys in the bubbling brook by Brookside Bough. Sorry, Judge, this is a first offense, honor-roll student, All-County basketball star, his father was police chief—you remember his father. The kindly old judge would consider Speed's case. Speed would agree to finish school, play his last year of basketball for Mr. Cabot, and after he graduated high school we'd go into some business together, we'd set up a print shop, a motorcycle shop, we'd write for a living, we'd do anything Speed wanted to do, but that wasn't what happened.

When Speed returned, Champrain would be with him. Almost from the hour of Speed's flight I had the idea that Champrain was its cause, that Speed had continued the search for her and found her and fallen in love with her and felt the need to show her the greatest kindness to compensate for my having, in his opinion, abandoned her. I saw it all. I saw her waiting for him on a street corner. In her arms she carried her worldly goods as she had carried them down from her room and out of Walk a Mile House forever when grandfather or Mary Washington discharged her, her Bible, her scratchy Philco, her pitiful possessions, her worldly goods.

What street corner? I squinted hard at the screen of my fantasy to see where she was. There she was, she was waiting, it was three o'clock in the morning. *It's three o'clock in the morning* grandmother sang to me on her lap in the chair beneath the chestnut tree. It was a business street, it looked familiar, oh my yes Champrain was waiting at the corner of First Street and Fourth Avenue, heart and center of Mount Vernon, at ten minutes after three on the Saturday morning after Thanksgiving.

Then along came Speed, having wheeled his motorcycle up the walkboard into the van and locked the van (in his haste left the walkboard in the gutter) and fired the engine and glided away under the observant eye of Mrs. Davidoff, who returned to bed thinking nothing of it.

By prearrangement he met our dear Champrain. Climb up, jump in. We're off. When Speed and I had been searching for Champrain he had imagined her traveling west, riding high in a great big cross-country truck to Denver, Yosemite, Pikes Peak, Albuquerque, the Rocky Mountains, maybe shoot north to Alaska, maybe marry a cowboy, maybe marry a fire warden. But now Speed himself had become the man of his own fantasies. I wished him well. I felt nothing like jealousy. Possibly I was falling in love with Ruth while Speed and Champrain were setting up life in a little mountain cabin. How they laughed, how they played, how they spoke of me! I wanted them safe, and I granted them their secret for a while. Sooner or later they'd be back in touch with me, for they both loved me, they'd send me a penny postcard.

I could never explain in my dreams how he drove the van all that way without ever being apprehended. The Mount Vernon police sent bulletins all over the country. Nor was it a small family truck you might easily miss in a traffic jam. A white guy and a black girl in a big truck were conspicuous. Yet there they were, one moment at the corner of First and Fourth, the next moment living in bliss high up in the wind-whipped Rockies.

My head ranged everywhere. Speed was in the West, Speed had crashed, Speed was dead, Speed sold the van and everything in it and emigrated to the Argentine, Switzerland, Ireland. Drove right across the water to Ireland, did he? No, signals off, he was pulling up right this minute to mother's and father's little house under the citrus trees down there in Sentinel City, Florida, climbing down from the cab with a silly sheepish smile on his face, holding up his hand, telling them not to ask, he'd give them his answer before they gave him the question: "Why did I do it? Just because." *Just because he took it into his head to do, and now he was ready to take his punishment. He'd face the consequences. We were a police family*, round and round my fantasies went, round and round at all hours amidst whatever duties.

For at least the first year of Speed's being gone I was a much-distracted reporter. I did a rotten job for the paper. My fantasies had taken possession of me, my mind thought of nothing all day but Speed's fate. A reporter's job was to ask questions, but the questions on my mind were not the questions the *Daily Item* was interested in my asking. Where was he? How could he have done this to me? To mother? To father? To Aunt Ember? To grandmother? Where had he gone? Was he safe? Would he return? Was he trying to reach me? What was he doing for money?

I could not believe my mind would ever rest, although I was told that it would. I was given to understand from several learned people that what I was suffering was grief, quite as if Speed were dead ("Not that he is, of course," people quickly assured me), that my grief would last for a certain period, and then end. No man's life sustained grief forever.

Indeed, after about a year, my grief which had been acute lightened itself, diminished, lessened. The pleasure of my relief from grief was the first true pleasure I had enjoyed since the night of Speed's leaving.

One day at my desk at the *Item* I realized that Speed at that very moment was pulling up to the door of the newspaper, climbing down from his cab, glancing up at the *Item* clock on the front of the building and saying to himself, "Just in time for lunch with my brother," but when in a kind of craziness I leaped up from my desk and hurried as if I were in my right mind (though in my right mind I knew I was not in my right mind) out the front door like a whirlwind to greet him he was not there.

I became horribly ill. I had "the grip." In our family the devil's gift of chills, fever, muscular aches and pains, miserable nausea, diarrhea, headaches, and melancholic spiritlessness in combination were the symptoms of an affliction we called "the grip." As a boy I assumed "the grip" derived from the black bag the doctor carried. Years later in France I encountered *la grippe*. Whatever its name, father always said it would go away in seven days or one week, whichever came first, and it always did.

Ruth purchased medicines and spooned them to me. She sat beside my bed. She kept me abreast of the news of Port Chester as she read it in the *Item* and as she heard it in the bank. Sheena and Peter filled my room with flowers.

As I began to recover from my "grip" I was able to enjoy the radio I had brought home from Perkinsville for Champrain. During this week of my life, listening more than ever to radio news, I became increasingly aware of reports about missing persons. I listened attentively. I had never realized how many people were missing, the varieties of ways they contrived to disappear, the unique signatures of their departure. I recall from my siege of "the grip" the account of a man missing for fifteen years who had set out in his shirtsleeves for the corner grocery store singing "Goodbye Forever."

Ruth lost a week's salary sitting by my bed. Once in terror I awoke calling the name of Doc Duffy. In my dream he returned from the battlefield in France, eyeglasses glittering, to claim his bride, our mother. He had not been killed. He had only had a case of "the grip."

Ruth said I'd do my best thinking about Speed by not consciously thinking about him, by allowing my mind to drift its own way. "Your subconsciousness will tell you the things you want to know," she said. At that time of my life I knew nothing about such things as the subconscious. Ruth was ahead of me in this, and all she said proved to be right. My best thoughts came to me at moments I was not attempting to think about Speed. At other times when I tried in my mind to track him to his hiding place I got nowhere. Once, half-dreaming, half-awake, I owned a huge van similar to the Boccheciampi van, and when Speed drove away in the Boccheciampi van I attempted to follow in mine, but I could not shift the complicated gears and Speed looked back at me and laughed.

Sick or well, for a while I dreamed only feverishly. I dreamed I was the hero of Speed's epic, first Americus the Modest, afterward Amiel Melvin, first horseman, afterward motorcyclist. In my dream I accurately recalled that some of the action of the poem occurred in Pittsburgh, where Amiel—Amiel the deaf; Speed the stutterer—had gone to rescue the heroine from the lecherous steel magnate. When I awoke I told Ruth I was convinced that Speed had gone to Pittsburgh. She promised we would look for him there. She promised to go with me anywhere I thought he might be found.

In another feverish dream I recalled Speed's speculation on Champrain's suicide. He believed she had sailed into the ocean and tossed herself overboard to prevent her body from being found. Now, in my dream, Speed sailed to the same location. He had always been a map-reader. They had arranged their rendezvous. With his usual disregard of the elements he leaped into the chilly

water, dived to the bottom, and found her resting on the sandy
floor of the sea. It was three o'clock in the morning and she was
listening to "Amos 'n' Andy" on her radio. I said to him, "But if you
were thinking of suicide why steal mother's and father's furniture
they so much needed down south?" His reply filled me with hope—
he said he would return it.

One moment occurred worse than all others—I went mad for a
moment. I was at my desk at the *Item*. I heard a voice, as if it were
coming to me on the telephone, although I had no telephone to my
ear. "Go home and look in your mailbox for news of Speed," said
the voice.

I dashed from the paper to Sheena Strutz's house and saw mail
in the box, but I had no key and I was in too great a frenzy to go
back to the paper and get the key from Sheena or Peter. At that
juncture I could have employed the Boccheciampi jimmy man,
couldn't I?—given him a chance at last to show his stuff. I tried to
pick the lock with a nail file, as I had heard of such things being
done, but I had no skill at it. Speed could have opened it in three
seconds. I ran for a screwdriver and tried to pry the lock, but by
that procedure I succeeded only in ruining the lock without opening the box. Therefore, since the lock was ruined anyhow I finished
the job with a hammer and opened the box and withdrew a single
envelope, Sheena's electric bill.

I felt that this was not something I had done. I said to Sheena
Strutz, "The hammer did it." Sheena wept into her hands and said,
"Why in the world did you let the hammer do such a thing, it can't
be fixed, I'll get Peter to fix it, you poor, poor boy, it's your
brother's being gone that makes you do these things. You're crazy
with grief. Luckily as soon as he comes back you'll be well again."
She saw that I was in danger of cracking. I was behaving peculiarly.
What was I doing running home for the mail in the middle of the
day?

My unhappiness made Sheena unhappy, too. She and Peter
prayed for Speed's return. She asked me often, "Any word yet?"
She spoke of Speed as if she had known him well, although actually

she had known him only for a few minutes, when he applied for the job at the *Item*. That night when she telephoned him in Mount Vernon I overheard her call, and my life began to follow a new course, not all for the better. For this she felt some responsibility, as if her generosity in trying to help Speed had caused my mind to jump the track.

The day after I smashed the Strutzes' mailbox I came to my senses. I realized that the voice I had heard as if by telephone had meant by "home" not Sheena's and Peter's house in Port Chester but the Sheridan Gardens Apartments in Mount Vernon. I had gone to the wrong house. It could have happened to anyone. I felt that I must go back to Mount Vernon. Ruth, too, agreed with my interpretation of the message I had received. I must go—we must go—and so we set out on the following Saturday on a journey.

Ruth had never been to Mount Vernon. We alighted at the Columbus Avenue station. We strolled past the site of Speed's recent motorcycle accident at the foot of the Lorraine Avenue hill. I pointed out the tree at which his motorcycle had miraculously parked itself. We walked in the glorious cloudless December day up the hill and down to the Sheridan Gardens Apartments, where I opened our old mailbox with my key. It was simpler than screwdriver and hammer. For my trouble I found nothing, although I had expected a great deal, a good message, even a letter from Speed himself. I had misinterpreted the voice I had heard, but I was certain I would hear it again, that I would receive a third chance, and I remained alert.

Mrs. Davidoff, coming down the hallway stairs, greeted me strangely. "I'm glad they found you. They were looking all over for you," she said, and then sarcastically, "Congratulations on coming home." She thought I was Speed. It was Mrs. Davidoff who, as far as we knew, was the last person to have seen Speed—saw him from her window wheeling his motorcycle up the walkboard.

Ruth and I entered the bare apartment. I was dazzled by its brightness—it had never been without curtains at the windows. My lifelong home, 2–D, was an echo. Nothing remained. The

Boccheciampi men had moved the secretary to Walk a Mile House. Poor fellows, they had anticipated a big haul to Florida and ended by carrying one piece of furniture crosstown. "I smell the lovely odor of my mother," I said. Ruth smelled only scouring powder.

We crossed the courtyard and sat with Aunt Ember awhile by her window in the sun. She had for a while lingered in melancholy to think of the mad thing Speed had done, but now she was in improved spirits, having heard from her palmist that Speed would "probably" return home in twenty-one days. "Twenty-one days from when?" I eagerly asked. "From yesterday," Aunt Ember said. Ruth disparaged palmistry, saying "I can't see how you can really believe in it," and Aunt Ember replied, "I wouldn't believe in it, either, if it weren't always so accurate."

"What does your palmist mean by *probably*?" I asked.

"If Speed doesn't come home in twenty-one days he won't be home for twenty-one weeks," Aunt Ember said.

"Is everything divisible by twenty-one?" Ruth somewhat scornfully asked.

"Only time," said Aunt Ember, studying Ruth as closely as courtesy permitted. Aunt Ember had heard from Mary Washington about Champrain and me. I did not then know she knew. She must have thought Ruth, too, was a wild one like Champrain, and she admired daring young women. How surprised she would have been to hear that Ruth and I had never kissed.

On the other hand, Aunt Ember had always been prepared to believe anything about love, and she believed now that Speed had absented himself to search for love. "He's trying out his freedom in the company of a girl," she said. "But even now he's growing tired of her and thinking of heading down south to join mother and father in Florida."

"In twenty-one days or twenty-one weeks," I said.

"Yes."

"Why does he need a whole moving van to try out his freedom with a girl?" Ruth skeptically asked.

"Maybe she's a very big girl," said Aunt Ember. "Speed is a big boy." Ruth did not smile. "You don't smile," said Aunt Ember. "I'd

251

be smiling if I had such an attractive boy as this one squiring me around," and she glanced up and down my body for a moment. Once she had spoken to Speed and me of our "handsome, sturdy bodies," and it had been a revelation to us that a woman, not merely a woman but an *aunt*, should speak to us of our bodies in that abandoned way. Her speaking so had also been extremely useful and educational, for we learned for the first time that our bodies were important to girls, to women.

"I do find him attractive," Ruth said, "and I love his squiring me around."

"Wait until you meet his father," Aunt Ember said.

"I want to meet Speed, too," said Ruth.

"He was the handsomest boy in Mount Vernon," Aunt Ember said. Ruth thought she was speaking of Speed, but she was speaking reminiscently of father. "One sight of him and you knew why you were born. The smile on that boy's face was sunshine. Let me advise you to marry both of them if you can bring yourself to bend the regulations." Speed and me, she meant. "He and I"—back to father now—"discovered this apartment house together when it was brand new and we all moved in among the Jews."

Ruth challenged Aunt Ember, who had aroused her democratic conscience. "What are you trying to say about the Jews?"

"He disliked the Jews," Aunt Ember said. "But he overcame his prejudice. The boys taught him better."

"With some help from our Aunt Ember," I said.

"That's nice of you to say," Aunt Ember said, "You boys were always each other's teachers, you lifted yourselves by your mental bootstraps. He wasn't a person of the world"—now it was father she meant. "After all, he was a cop, he'd only been carried off the boat a babe in arms. He didn't have all those advantages you young people have nowadays. He could throw a ball to the top of the Esplanade. He was a mighty man. He laid his gun on the sidewalk and heaved the ball eight stories up."

I corrected her. "Seven stories, Aunt Ember." I had known from age four that the Esplanade Gardens Apartments was seven stories high. Aunt Ember knew the streets of London and Paris but she did not know how high the Esplanade was.

I asked her if it were true, as mother said, that Speed ran away because I'd neglected to sign over to him half my share of the corporation."

"I heard of your promise," she said.

"I did promise, yes I did."

"What you must do is have the document ready for him the day he walks back in the house, hand it to him and tell him you're sorry about being late."

"What house?"

"Wherever you live he'll think of it as being your house and he'll go there. I can't answer your question. Nobody knows why Speed has run off. Speed's run off because Speed is Speed," Aunt Ember said. "He was oppressed by everything in general and nothing in particular. If there was anything in particular that oppressed him it was the lack of justice, cruelty. Your grandfather's crazy corporation—it's not the loot Speed misses, it's the stupidity that gets him down, the injustice, it's the *principle* of things. He raises everything to principle. He's not like you. You're just a practical American boy, but Speed's an old-fashioned dreamer for all his motorcycling. Everybody low-rates him. People cut him off before he gets to say his say. People are in too much of a hurry to wait around while he stutters through."

"I look forward to meeting Speed," Ruth said. "I'll listen."

"You will," Aunt Ember said, "you're a listener. He'll be back in twenty-one days or twenty-one weeks."

Aunt Ember walked to the corner with us, eyeing the Esplanade Gardens Apartments up the hill. We counted. Of course it was seven stories high, as I knew. "I've only lived in the neighborhood twenty years," Aunt Ember said.

Ruth and I walked from the Sheridan Gardens Apartments to Walk a Mile House, about which I had told her so much so often. Suppose we met Champrain! Champrain, the Doc Duffy of my marriage contract! This thought must have occurred to me—it could not *not* have occurred to me. Suppose we three met on the

253

street in front of Walk a Mile House! But of course that was impossible: Champrain was out west, she was hiding with Speed in Yosemite, she was at the top of Mount McKinley in Alaska, she was lounging at the bottom of the ocean listening to music on her scratchy Philco.

At moments I loved Ruth, too. Her mind was much better than Champrain's. Ruth was a learned person. Champrain was barely literate. Ruth's democratic convictions appealed to me, just as mine so much appealed to her. Democracy was our shared religion, our faith. Perhaps I could have two wives, one black and one white. Why not? My black wife would be my love wife and my white wife would nurse me through "the grip."

Just as I had been bursting at Brookside Bough to tell Speed about Champrain so was I bursting now to tell Ruth about Champrain's blackness. When I'd finally got the word to Speed, and he had taken it so joyfully, I was enormously relieved, pleased. It had been a good thing in spite of all my hesitation.

We stood across the street from Walk a Mile House. She said she'd love to see it from the inside. Yes, I said, some time, not now. From the street I gave her a good sense of it, I think. I identified the windows for her—living-room, dining-room, kitchen, butler's pantry, upstairs bedrooms, and the railroad room in the attic suite and the maid's room beside the railroad room, and over there beyond the chestnut tree grandfather's sun parlor where the big deals were made, and the corresponding wing at the other end of the house where the maids lived. Ruth inquired about the welfare of the maids. She defended maids as she defended Jews. She asked me whether the maids at Walk a Mile House were well-treated or abused. "Not one extreme or the other," I said, mainly well-treated, sometimes abused. I told her I had heard that grandfather made sexual advances to maids. I told her the story of *a certain cousin* of mine who had once stolen twenty-five cents from the apron pocket of one of the maids, which grandmother had repaid. Ruth liked what she heard of grandmother and hoped to meet her some day. Yes, some day, I said.

I told Ruth I had once heard grandfather insult a black maid in her very presence—heard him refer to her as a "smelly dirty nigger girl." This shocked Ruth, she gasped, she clenched her fists, she turned to me eagerly hoping to hear that I had gone to the rescue of the maid. "What did you do? Did you speak up for her?" I confessed that I had not spoken as directly to grandfather as I should have, certainly I did not speak right up to him as Speed would have done—not *directly*, no—but I did make known to the maid herself that I was on *her* side, that I deplored grandfather's evil tongue, and forever afterward, whenever I saw that maid, I expressed my friendship to her in the clearest terms and was kind to her and assisted her to know beyond all possibility of doubt that I held her much higher on the scale of love than I held grandfather.

Ruth saw that I was moved by my memories, and so I was, by grandmother, by the train room especially, by the attic suite, by the painful remembered sensation of my hand closing on the quarter in Champrain's apron pocket. Ruth, too, was moved by my being so moved, and impulsively she seized me there on the street in the shadow of Walk a Mile House and for the first time enthusiastically kissed me and said to me, "I can tell you everything is going to be all right." She admired my having befriended the Negro maid. She admired the version of me she had heard from Aunt Ember—how as a mere boy I had cleansed myself of my heritage of anti-Semitism. I was the man for her. I fit right in with her vision of her life. Since she was not likely to find another man meeting her steep requirements she was not going to let me get away. She had hooked me and she would keep me. I was attractive, I was intelligent, I was special, and the thing that was so special about me was that I was a democrat like her, loving all races and religions and classes and stations.

Things had turned around. The tide had turned, we novelists say. I was triumphant. I saw myself beginning to get my way with her now. She who had been so aloof from me, who had kept me dangling since September, who had kept her body from mine, who believed she had granted me the paramount erotic favor by allowing me to warm my hands in her coat pocket at a football game, was now at last heating up herself. The North Polar iceberg had begun to drift south, to thaw. Now came my turn to appear cool. In the most businesslike manner I disentangled myself from her and looked at my watch and said, "Our time is getting away from us."

We had lingered too long gazing at Walk a Mile House. Briskly we set off for the New York Central station. I purchased two tickets to Perkinsville. On the station platform I sat beside her on a bench. We had decided to take a trip to Perkinsville to look around. I had some hunches that Speed was there.

Ruth held out her hand to me. She wore a diamond solitaire. I believe I made some comment about her "sporting" the ring, for she said, "I'm not *sporting* it, this is not sport. This is the game of life."

"Whom are you engaged to marry?"

"You."

"I was afraid that's who it was," I said.

"You and I are perfectly mated," she said.

"So are two shoes," I said.

"If you don't want to marry me you don't have to by any means. I'm certainly not eager to marry someone who's not eager to marry me."

"It's not that I'm not *eager*," I said.

"Then what are you?" she asked, answering her own question. "I know what you are. You're just a cheap conniving person like your aunt says you are."

"I didn't hear my aunt say that," I said.

"You're not principled. Your brother's the idealist. You aren't," she said, "and I think the best thing for me to do is leave you right here where maybe some old Mount Vernon girl friend will show up and show you the kind of good time you think you're looking for."

We were at a parting of the ways. Was this the end of us? She crossed the tracks to the southbound side. She'd go down to New York on the Central and back to Port Chester on the New Haven. I wanted her to do that. I offered to buy her a ticket. I wanted to lose her forever. Yet I wanted to keep her. The southbound train came into view. I'd race it across the tracks. But then I decided I was a fool to risk my life racing a train to catch up with a girl I never wanted to see again.

She walked briskly back across the tracks. "All right," she said, "now that I've given you the fright of your life I'll go to Perkinsville with you because you're not really well yet, you're still in a bad mental state. You bought the ticket and I'm not a wasteful person. But you might as well make a note of the fact that when we get back to Port Chester it's all over. This is the first and last train ride you and I will ever take together."

"The ticket wouldn't be wasted," I said. "I can cash it in. Don't marry me to save the price of a railroad ticket."

We had come to town on the New Haven side, we left on the Central side. I was not to set foot in Mount Vernon again for twenty years—drive its outskirts on the insane parkway, yes, now and again speed through on the train, yes, and though I would be gone for twenty years, come home for a day, and leave again for thirty more, I should never forget the order of the streets or the features of hundreds of people who had lived there with me in the time of our lives, from the night father taught me to tie my shoelaces to the night my brother vanished in the moving-van. I have lived in many cities, and I am everywhere lost except in Mount Vernon, New York. Spin me around a hundred times on the least street of Mount Vernon and you cannot confuse me.

In Perkinsville, in a burst of extravagance ($2.50 an hour), we hired a city cab to carry us about. I had been trying to think as I thought Speed might think. I knew he would soon discover his folly in stealing the van. Of what use could it be? Therefore he would want to dispose of it. Where? A moving-van is rather a burden. Thinking along those lines I concluded that I would hide the van in an orchard, in a grove of trees, a spacious meadow somewhere along the lovely country road between Perkinsville and Brookside Bough, and ride away on my motorcycle.

I had in mind a certain meadow. Our hired cabbie drove us slowly out of Perkinsville toward Brookside Bough, and all along the way we peered left and right into the depths of meadows for an abandoned moving-van. The driver said from the beginning that we would find no such thing, and he was correct.

My conviction had risen absurdly in my mind. In my privacy I had felt certain that we would spot the van near Brookside Bough, but now that we were here I realized how foolish I must appear to Ruth. She said nothing of that, however. She knew I was under a strain.

Now I followed up on another idea. I had thought that once Speed had disposed of the van he might find a job at Cameron's Wheel Shop. Our cabbie drove us to Cameron's Wheel Shop and I spoke to Mr. Cameron himself. I reminded him of the day I had waited with him while Speed roared to the farm to borrow deposit money. Mr. Cameron did not remember that occasion—or so he said. I think he thought I had come to reclaim the twenty-dollar deposit.

Then of course I knew where Speed was. He would have returned to Rexall Drugs where his labor of weeks had been robbed from him in a single second, where justice had abandoned him. In front of the drugstore Ruth and I dismissed the cab. We stood where I had stood that terrible morning. We strolled inside and looked about. We saw Speed nowhere. I asked for him at the register. No, nobody by that name was known there. Ruth and I strolled in Perkinsville until train time, when we started home to Port Chester.

On the following Thursday the *Daily Item* poured from the press, as usual. The saucy printer's devil in his ink-stained apron and baker's hat whirled around the newsroom with a copy of the paper for everyone, as usual. One development, however, was not the least bit usual, it was once-in-a-lifetime-only: I saw by the paper that I was engaged to be married.

I was deluged by congratulations. Mr. Cornwall behind his fresh newspaper called to me from his glass office, "Is that the girl from the bank? I didn't know your case had advanced that far."

"I didn't know it, either," I replied with a jovial loud shout. But I did not feel my joviality.

"I noticed who was wearing the pants," Mr. Cornwall exulted.

"It's a press report, you never know what to believe in this newspaper." Everyone laughed at my witticism. Oh, what jollity!

Christmas was coming. I was bowling them over. I was a howl. Sheena Strutz came running into the city room to congratulate me. "That's Ruth who took care of you when you had the grip."

"She took care of me all right," I bitterly said, and again my colleagues laughed, but I was not really feeling funny or clever or witty. This was the kind of thing Ruth did. She took matters into her own hands, bought her own ring, announced her own engagement. Let her go marry herself. I did not believe I had ever consented to become engaged. I wanted to get out of this. This must have happened to men before me. I had heard of such things in song and story, of men fleeing west, of men confronted by the brothers of the bride, forced to marry, shotgun weddings, men fleeing pregnant brides. Ruth was not pregnant, at least not by me. No, of course not, a person could not become pregnant without the touch of passion. I understood why men fled west. Perhaps Speed himself was fleeing some alliance of which the rest of us were ignorant.

Everything was explained to me by this event. I saw the whole system of the world with wondrous clarity. This fanatical woman was tracking me down, aided and abetted by all society. No wonder it was called the *society* page, for on that page society committed men to their fates, announcing their marriages ready or not, hurling them into captivity.

How unfair it was that I should pay so great a penalty for having carried my small business to New Accounts! Why her? Who was she? Where did she live? What was her telephone number? Everything about her was concealed from view, especially her body. This was an unfair sentence, a lifetime sentence, although I had not to my knowledge committed any crime.

I was to be deprived of all the girls in the world before I had exhausted even Port Chester. In Port Chester I had fallen in love with girls everywhere, on their jobs at counters in every shop, I was in love with seven girls at the *Item*, six girls in the public library, eight girls up and down the street where I lived with Sheena and Peter, with the cashiers outside the moviehouses and the ushers within, with secretaries to rich and important executives, with flour-covered girls at Paul Arnold's Brick Oven Bakery and sweet-smelling candy-factory girls at Life Savers.

Ruth was neither more nor less exciting to me than other girls—many girls, more girls than most boys cared for. I had a greater selection to choose from in view of my drawing no line at skin color. With Ruth everything had to be tested against the democratic standard. Why? This voracious person was imposing upon me an exorbitant price. No wonder she worked at a bank—she had a banker's mentality—I was condemned to mortgage my whole life to her before she'd reward me with interest on my investment. She had given me one kiss—in public, in Mount Vernon on the street before Walk a Mile House, and that was the end of it. One kiss and then engaged! At that rate the world would be in chains in sixty days. One smile late at night in the *Item* office, and nothing more! Oh yes, after the smile she took my arm and we went for coffee, and now the next step must be—how perfectly apt the brilliant expression now appeared!—*the tying of the knot.*

That was a knot I'd slip out of. Under the cover of night I'd leave Port Chester, and Ruth would awaken to a busy morning of informing her friends that her prisoner had escaped, he was some sort of wild disappearing man like his brother. Hear behind her back her snickering friends!

That afternoon I left the *Item* office on the pretext of chasing down stories. I wanted to be out of there, unreachable, incommunicado. I did not want to receive a telephone call from Ruth. I did not want to see her. I wanted to hurt her by ignoring her. I wanted to humiliate her, embarrass her.

I decided to flee Port Chester. Mr. Cornwall had been surprised I came here in the first place. I would bury myself among opportunities in New York City, and I would enjoy a variety of young ladies, too. I would find Champrain and produce her and nullify my marriage contract with Ruth. What contract? Where was it? She had said we could notarize our contract at the bank, but in some way she tricked me into forgetting to do so. She was furtive. (To do her justice, how could we notarize a contract I had not yet written?)

I intended to avoid her bank. I would transfer my account else-where. I had one hundred dollars in my account. The more time I spent with Ruth the less money I saved. I was always treating her to food and entertainment, while behind my back she was making announcements to the society editor, in effect an advertisement revealing to all and sundry the withdrawal of my pleasure-loving body from the public marketplace of love and lust. The goods were sold, the shop was closed, the merchandise was disposed of, the job was taken, no more girls need apply.

I fulfilled my resolution to keep my distance. I did not telephone her. She left no message for me at the office. If she had I would have ignored it. I refrained from phoning her at the bank on Fri-day. Now I could not be tempted to reach her all weekend. I did not know her home phone. We had been acquainted for three months, the newspaper reported us engaged to be married, and *I did not even know her home phone.*

Saturday I was again unwell. I feared I was relapsing from "the grip." After the paper went to bed I went to bed myself. I had promised to join Jack Dempsey, the sports editor, and some of his friends for a game of Touch, but I was too ill. I begged off. "Under the weather," I told Jack. I slept from Saturday afternoon until Sunday afternoon, awakening feeling slightly better.

Nobody in the world knew I had been ill except Dempsey, from whose mind the information would have evaporated in three sec-onds. It was possible for me to die and rot on Sheena's and Peter's noisy bed unnoticed until they stuck their heads in the door to see what the silence and smell were about.

It occurred to me I had no family. Where were they? Mother and father were far away in Florida and Speed was—gone. All the girls I was in love with all over Port Chester from the public library to the Life Savers factory were flying hither and yon on their Sunday business, their church business, their cake-baking busi-ness, their fudge-making business, their pre-Christmas business, their cleaning and scrubbing and sewing and sweeping. Not one of them was thinking of me.

I who from the hour of my birth had had a family to care for me had had none yesterday when I fell ill, had none today, and probably had better begin forming a family for myself before my condition went backward from Sunday to Saturday. This had been a narrow escape, no telling when I'd fall sick again. I left the house and stopped at the Westchester Diner for a bowl of broth and continued to the deserted paper, silent but for the news flowing on the teletype. On my desk lay a message from Ruth. Now that our engagement had been announced in the daily newspaper she had consented to honor me with her telephone number.

One evening soon after she announced our engagement Ruth appointed me to meet her at Main and Westchester—Liberty Square, it was called—the heartbeat of Port Chester, as Fourth and First was the heartbeat of Mount Vernon. Snow had begun to fall. This would be our first time in snow together. Everything was a first time.

We walked to her house. She did not live, as I had supposed, down a tree-lined street near the intersection where we always parted. Our parting at that intersection had been her trick. After she left me she had always circled more than two miles to make her way home.

Her home was in a small brick apartment house far south on Main. This apartment house was more modest even than the Sheridan Gardens Apartments, and yet not modest by choice, either, but modest by age and condition, necessity and neglect. It appeared to me from the outside, in the darkness. to be falling down, coming apart, listing, a house not on the level.

"I bet you didn't expect to land in such a dump," said Ruth.

"It's no dump," I said. "It's lovely," but of course it was not lovely, it was a dump.

"Try to be honest," she said, "it's not even a lovely dump. It's ugly, it's hideous."

"That's why you never invited me," I said.

"That's partly why," she said.

"This is where you live," I said. I hoped she would say no, it was a practical joke, she didn't live here, she was just testing my love, her true home was a fine house next door to the fine house where we had gone to the Hallowe'en party. I had had a fleeting expectation of—even a hope for—a residence of bankers. I wouldn't have minded marrying rich into a banking family living somewhere in grand circumstances. I could handle it.

But that was not to be. The entrance to her apartment house was unlocked. My experience of the Sheridan Gardens Apartments had taught me that all apartment houses were locked up front. Adults needed keys. Children knew how to run around to the back. But perhaps what was true of Mount Vernon was untrue of Port Chester. Beyond the door we paused, and in the shallow light of the hallway Ruth spoke earnestly to me, "This is your chance to change your mind," she said. "If you want to change it you should change it now before everything goes too far."

"We're already engaged. How far can everything go?"

"You can break your engagement," she said.

"I didn't know I was allowed to do that."

"Then I'm sorry I told you."

"What would you do if you were I?" I asked.

"If I were who I think you are I'd be happy about the whole thing, but if you're not who I think you are you're in for the biggest disaster of your life."

"It's hard for me to know if I'm who you think I am," I said.

"Once we go upstairs the whole picture is going to be totally different. You may decide you're not in love with me. I don't exactly have a normal everyday run-of-the-mill family. Things aren't going to be exactly what you expected them to be."

What could she be saying? She was extremely nervous. Her life was at the edge, she was departing an old place and entering a new place. She seemed to expect that within the next sixty seconds a change would occur so profound that I would never be the same again. I felt that she was suffering a delusion, that she was advertising more than reality would dare to deliver, like the barker at the peep show on 42nd Street advertising naked girls run through with long knives. Speed and I knew it could not happen. Yet we paid our precious money to see. "I'm ready to take my chances," I said.

"You'll be amazed," she said.

"Your father grew breasts and your mother grew a penis," I said.

"It might be worse than that. This is the test of your life. You might not be making jokes in a minute," she said, "unless you're the right kind of person."

We ascended the stairs toward the sound of the party. I was excited, I was in suspense. I was grateful the term of suspense would be short. In a few seconds it would be over, in a few seconds we would know if I were the right kind of person. We approached the sound of the party, not so much the sound of music or dancing as of quiet conversation, of people waiting in their own suspense for Ruth and me. The hallway smelled rancid, as of fish frying, not tonight's fish, not even yesterday's fish, but last week's fish, last year's fish. The building was poorly cared for, if cared for at all. Where was the super? Faced with these conditions at the Sheridan Gardens Apartments the tenants would have been marching in a rent strike by now.

When Ruth opened the door to the apartment all conversation ceased, silence engulfed us all, everyone stared at me as I stood in the doorway, perhaps to see if I would enter when I saw what I saw. It was as I had suspected, the party had not yet become a party, it could not begin until its waiting was over. The person everybody was waiting for was me.

In that moment in the doorway it was as Ruth had predicted, the direction of my life was altered. Before me waited three generations of her family, twenty or thirty people, I think, not yet drinking though the tables glittered with punchbowls and bottles and silvery glasses of Christmas cheer, creamy eggnog briskly spiked with rum, brandy, bourbon. Choose your punchbowl. Choose your delicacies, too, meats and sausages, baked breads, pickles, and sauces.

Of the people before me, waiting for me, gazing upon me now in suspense, half were black and half were white. I saw one man who appeared familiar. I could not place his face. Where had I seen him? Somewhere in town. If only he would jump back into his context I would know him. He was a large man, a dark black man, casually dressed for this Christmas party, and I knew that in the context I knew him he was differently dressed, he wore some sort of uniform, yes, uniform, gold buttons down his coat, chauffeur's cap, and he did not smile, even as he stared at me unsmiling now. I knew. He was Ty the doorman at the Port Chester Savings Bank. He was the only banker in Ruth's family. I thought, *Dear God, please make Champrain white,* my old prayer answered at last, good old *Prayer Four for the Future,* Dear God, You did it.

Ty the doorman was watching me closely, filled with interest, to see how I was taking this. He remembered my coming to the bank for a glimpse of the nice white girl in New Accounts. Well, what did I think of her now that she was not white but black? He spoke in a big voice and he did not smile. "How are you tonight?" he asked me, holding out his hand to me, "I'm Ruth's Uncle Ticonderoga," and I seized his hand. Now was the time for all my wit to come to the aid of the party, and I spoke up in the crude loud boisterous good-time voice I had heard at lunches of Port Chester men's clubs, "Any uncle of Ruth's is an uncle of mine," and the tension of the silence snapped open into laughter, and the party began.

God had made Champrain white, He'd delivered a miracle instructed by my prayers, turned Champrain into Ruth whose true name, I learned, was not even Ruth but Duruth—she was named for the Minnesota city on Lake Superior, in the manner of black families in the twenties who named their children for cities and lakes of the Northeast and Upper Middle West. Ruth was Duruth or Ruth or she was black or she was white, she was what she chose to be. Her relations were black and white. Some, like Ruth, lived optionally, white or black as their hearts chose. Some of these faces I had seen around Port Chester. "Merry Christmas, merry Christmas, merry Christmas." They filled their glasses, wishing me joyful life. I was an important object of their attention, I was Ruth's young man, her husband-to-be, her future and theirs, too.

The eggnog was too strong for me. It wasn't the egg, it was the nog. But at this hour drinking was right for me. A crisis of my life had come and passed. Now I knew Ruth's secret of home and family, now I knew everything, even her telephone number. Everything was beautiful. The smell of fish was gone. I kissed her. It was a perfectly natural thing to do, as if I were accustomed to kissing her. I put down my glass and held her, and I said to her, "You know that I love you whatever color you select, I love you more than anyone in the world except Champrain and my family, I can see already that I'm going to fit right in with your family, and you and I are going to live happily ever after no matter how unhappy we are."

I toured from person to person and from mouth to mouth, too. Before the evening was done I had kissed many of the women more than once, among them Ruth's gorgeous sister Niagala. I kissed Pracid, who was a cousin of Niagala and Ruth/Duruth, and I kissed two wonderful women named Adilondack and Lacine, who were related to Ruth in some way, and Salanac, Elie, Toredo, Tolonto, possibly others. I nibbled all the luscious goodies (the foods, I mean). There I was and feeling very comfortable, warm and toasted, as if I too were a tasty sausage. I felt myself belonging, merging, melting in.

At a card table in a corner of the living-room Ruth and others were playing a popular game called Spare Me: dice on a board. The longer they played the more they drank and the more they drank the louder they laughed. They invited me to play. I did not know the rules of the game, but it did not seem awfully to matter, and I learned as I went.

Ruth's father and mother asked me many questions about myself. We stood talking for a long time leaning against the refrigerator. People came by, opening and shutting the door in our faces, but we were absorbed beyond interruption. Their names were Jim and Lynn. I was pleased to notice how slim Lynn was. I hoped Ruth would learn from her mother the lifetime lesson of slimness.

Ruth's father was a Million Mile dining-car waiter. Had he traveled *actually* a million miles? "Many many more," he told me. On some railroad runs he was a steward, a high position not ordinarily granted to a black man, but although he was black he was also white. He "passed." That was a word I had first heard from Champrain.

I told Lynn and Jim about Walk a Mile Railway. "I ride the real thing," Jim said. I told him grandfather had written the famous advertisement, "A hog can cross the country without changing trains. Why can't you?" I told him grandfather had invented the Chessie cat for the Chesapeake ads, and the catchy national slogan "Santa Fe all the way." But the fact that amazed them most of all was my telling them that grandfather was the author of "Nibble a Nab for a Nickel." Their eyes shone and they congratulated me on his triumph as if it had happened yesterday. Jim said to Lynn, "Duruthie might have fallen into something good after all," for he assumed that the grandson of the author of such famous slogans was certainly rich.

"We're taking a chance with you," Jim said. "We all have a secret here and we've got to be able to trust you. We worry about a man who's a newspaper reporter. We don't want to see any stories in the newspaper about how many people are working around town white by day and going home Negro at night."

"Why would I put such a fact in the paper?" I asked. "I'm in love with your daughter, she's going to be my wife, why would I betray her family?"

"It's been done," said Ruth's mother.

"We worry about naming names," Jim said. "You might do it in your cups. You might do it in anger."

"You do drink with enthusiasm," Lynn said.

"I do everything with enthusiasm," I said. I set my glass on the top of the refrigerator to show them that I could take it or leave it. I intended to drink no more, and in fact for a few minutes I drank no more. I was happier than I could have imagined. My importance impressed me, everyone depended on me, I was a hero. My being on the inside of their secret made me feel sophisticated. The place I occupied served as a powerful bond between Ruth's family and me.

In spite of Jim's and Lynn's doubts about me I saw by their faces that I had got off to a good start with them. I was overwhelmed with gratitude toward Fate. Think what an unfailing good friend Fate had been to me! I had been walking down Main Street in Port

Chester looking for nothing more than a bank to put my meager money in when Fate delivered me to Uncle Ty. I liked his discourtesy. I liked a face that never smiled. I loved it when he slammed the bank door to keep people hopping. Uncle Ty masquerading as doorman had known all the while that I adored his niece. He kept her informed of my inquiries. Ty had told me once that she wore her wedding ring on her toe. He and I laughed about that now.

Lynn and Jim were especially interested in Speed's having— what? run off; disappeared; dropped out of sight; taken himself out of the game for the moment. I had a hard time knowing what to call it, I hadn't found words yet for explaining what he had done and how long he was likely to be—well, to be *what*? That was the problem. Gone? Away? Missing?

On this issue Ruth's father consoled me. "Your brother hasn't entirely left home, he'll be better for it when he comes back, he'll learn something out there on the road. There's no place like home. East or west, home is best. Boys might run off for a bit, but I'd advise you not to worry, don't lose sleep. Duruthie tells me you've been under a strain regarding your brother, and I can see it in your eyes right this minute. Your brother will be home by spring."

"Spring," I said.

"It's such a common pattern, we see it on the trains all the time, boys going off here and there."

"The track comes back," Lynn said.

"Yes, that's an old railroad saying," Jim said. "The track comes back. Out you go and back you come, same for everybody. He'll be back."

Later in the evening he took me aside. "I'm trusting and praying to the Lord above that you're not a wanderer like your brother," he said. "You've got to stay home and be as serious about Ruth as she is about you. It would deeply pain everybody in this room if we saw her hurt in any way, and her mother and I especially."

"I would never never never hurt her," I said.

"Never say never," he said. "We've got to help and protect each other. We're all in this together, you know. We've got to keep things out of the newspaper. We want to live our lives without attention. Nobody at the Port Chester Savings Bank need to know that Ruthie is Ticonderoga's niece."

"Nobody will know from me," I said.

"Duruthie talks about you all the time. She never stopped talking about you since the day you showed up at New Accounts. She came home. She couldn't sleep all night. You were born on the same birthday. That's pretty much of a rarity, isn't it? Of course you've got to remember that colored girls are different."

"In what way are they different?" I asked him.

"They're just not the same," he said. "They're not as free and unrelaxed as white girls, they're more restrained, they were brought up more strictly. Colored girls are inhibited, they're not as sexual as white girls, they're not as full of joy and song as white girls are."

"I knew a wonderful colored girl once in Mount Vernon," I said.

"How do you mean you knew her?"

"Only that she worked for grandfather," I said. "Her name was Champrain."

Ruth's father laughed hard at that. "Nobody would ever name a kid Champrain," he said.

Aunt Ember's palmist had said Speed would return in twenty-one days or twenty-one weeks, and twenty-one days came and went and Speed did not return. Twenty-one weeks came and went and he did not return. Ruth's father Jim had said Speed would return in the spring, but spring passed and Speed had not returned.

In July I prepared a document giving over to Speed half of my interest in the Mount Vernon Venue Investment Corporation (MV-VIC). Ruth arranged for me to have the document notarized free of charge at the bank, and I sent it for safekeeping to mother in Sentinel City. One year ago this month we had been farming.

The following summer grandmother died. For several weeks I sang incessantly to myself the song she had sung to me when I was a small boy my nodding head on her breast in the garden of Walk a

Mile House beneath the chestnut tree. *Willie, Willie, oh so silly, smoked a big cigar. Took a puff, that's enough, silly boy you are. They had to call the doctor in because it made him ill.*

Even so, I now smoked cigars as well as cigarettes and never fell ill. Grandmother was sixty, I was twenty. In a tender moment on one of the most significant nights of my life—the night grandfather insulted Champrain—grandmother had reached for my hand at the dinner table and said to me, "I wonder what will become of you, my dear child, when I am dead and gone." Now she was dead and gone and nothing much seemed to be becoming of me one way or another. My salary at the Port Chester *Daily Item* was raised from twenty-one dollars to twenty-five-fifty. I moved up in the corporation from accounts payable manager to vice-president, replacing mother, who moved up to president, replacing grandmother.

As father became known among the police chiefs of the South the tale of his missing son reached many ears. One day he received a call from the police chief at Waycross, Georgia, announcing the presence of an unidentified body that might be Speed's. Father drove from Sentinel City to Waycross and saw at a glance that the boy who was dead was somebody else, not Speed. When father returned from Waycross to Sentinel City he received a report of an abandoned moving van in Springfield, Missouri, but the van proved not to be the Boccheciampi van.

A flurry of activity also stirred things in Mount Vernon, giving me the feeling that something was about to happen. Father heard from the Mount Vernon police of "new information." He telephoned me, telling me not to get excited, but he was himself rather excited. Everyone had uncritically assumed that Speed had driven away in the van. Mrs. Davidoff said she had seen him from the window wheeling his motorcycle up the walkboard, into the van. No reason existed to doubt her. Now, however, after more than a year of inexplicable reticence, Mrs. Zorn came forward to say that from her window not less advantageously situated than Mrs. Davidoff's she had clearly seen Speed's taking flight not in the van but on his motorcycle; she had seen a second "young person," at the same moment, climb into the van and drive away "in the opposite direction from the boy on the motorcycle." Upon this version of events Mrs. Zorn insisted.

Mrs. Zorn was the grandmother of Norman Hirsch, who had been one of my Revolvers. He was left-handed. She was silly and erratic. She baked good cakes. A Mount Vernon Police Department detective named Billy Whittler, whose work father respected, after talking at length with her and with her acquaintants, informed father that she was not reliable, that her unlikely testimony was probably motivated by her well-known rivalry with Mrs. Davidoff.

Ruth fell in love with Speed without ever having met him. When she read the manuscript of *Love Never Surrenders* she was genuinely moved. At first she could scarcely discuss it with me. She declared it to be as beautiful a book as she had ever read, it was generous, it was sensitive, it was sympathetic, it was wise. Sometimes when she discussed *Love Never Surrenders* I could not be certain whether she was talking about the book or the author. She talked with such evident emotion I was sometimes afraid of Speed's returning and stealing her from me.

Ruth adhered to the theory that Speed had run off with Champrain. From Ruth's point of view it was a no-lose theory. If Champrain returned and I left Ruth to marry her, according to the terms of our (as yet unwritten) marriage contract, Ruth would marry Speed. Speed was a back-up for her. My wife would become my sister-in-law.

Ruth established a professional contact with an hilarious young man named Abner Klang, who commuted from Darien, Connecticut, to a literary agency in New York. Abner Klang encouraged me to write novels. He believed I had it in me. He cited the fact of my brother's having written a novel. "Scientists say talent is in the blood," said Abner. Science always says whatever Abner wants it to say. As Mr. Cornwall had assisted me to believe in myself as a fast-writing reporter so did Abner Klang persuade me I could become a fast-writing novelist. He urged me to write "history novels" set in distant places, which, by offering readers "bonus sensations" of facts and data, appeared to be "true."

He suggested I begin with an historical novel about farming. I had worked with Speed on the farm. "I hated farming," I said.

"You rebelled against farming. Write about the agrarian rebellion," he said. "Specialize in rebellions. People love to read about rebellions as long as nobody is rebelling in their own neighborhood. Read twelve farming books as fast as you can and never look at them again. Throw them away. Give them to the poor children. Write your own novel based on what you remember from the books and from your miserable experience farming and we'll make a pack of money."

We met frequently with Abner, usually at the Port Chester railroad station. He arrived on the southbound train from Connecticut, jumped to the platform in his glittering pointy-toed shoes, and concluded our business without delay. If our business was brief—a mere exchange of documents—he re-boarded the train before it resumed its trip to New York. More often our business was sufficiently complex to detain him until the next train, or the train after that. For the rest of our careers (we have worked more than forty years together) he has measured our tasks in commuting terms, "We need a one-train meeting . . . a two-train telephone conversation . . ."

In Port Chester I wrote *The Agrarian Rebellion, The Whiskey Rebellion,* and *The Rebellion of Anne of Austria.* I never meant to be a writer. Speed was the writer. I had gone to Port Chester to retrieve my brother's manuscript and remained to discover I was a born reporter. Now I discovered I was a novelist. Abner took my manuscripts to Apthorp House, which published them with pleasure and profit.

Five years from the day Mr. Cornwall ordered me to connect myself with the morticians and the firefighters I resigned from the newspaper. I had risen in my career from cub reporter to star writer for the *Item.* At my farewell party my colleagues presented me with a bronze facsimile of page one reproducing my article about the Port Chester-Mount Vernon football game I had attended with heart divided. Ruth and I moved to Manhattan.

Ruth was persuaded that Speed's novel should be published. She urged Abner Klang to urge Apthorp House to do so.

My own thought was that the publication of *Love Never Surrenders* would bring Speed from his hiding. He would recognize at last his freedom from his helplessness. He would see that he was neither mute nor voiceless.

Not as much enthusiasm existed for Speed's manuscript at Apthorp House. I confess it was a boy's book, awaiting its author's growth. Mainly as a gesture of good will toward me, I think, Apthorp House published *Love Never Surrenders*, which received several short, generous notices from reviewers. Speed earned in royalties about six hundred dollars, which I placed in his name among the funds of our family corporation.

From the early days of our tragedy my persistent idea had been that the clue to Speed's whereabouts was motorcycle-connected. A year after his flight I composed a letter addressed to motorcycle shops and factories everywhere, describing Speed in the most relevant way, and offering a big reward for information leading to him. I had no money for a reward. I did not have even the money for postage. Are you aware how many motorcycle shops and factories there are in the country? Does the number one hundred and fifty thousand surprise you? And do you want to talk Mexico and Canada, too? The cost of printing and mailing one hundred and fifty thousand letters was rather more than I could contemplate on twenty-five dollars and fifty cents a week.

Therefore I was compelled to defer my project until my wealth increased. When in time it did, Ruth and I mailed one hundred and fifty thousand inquiries in the innocent expectation that we would be deluged with responses, but the proprietors of motorcycle shops and factories, it would appear, are people not of the pencil but of the wrench. They do not answer letters. They do not drop their tools and wipe their hands and pick up pencil and paper and start writing a letter. No, they prefer the grease on their hands. The longest letter I received was this jovial communique from a man in Michigan on a leaflet advertising his wares: "I have a stuttering person working in my shop for awhile but being as she is sixty years old and is my wife I can tell you she is not your brother."

My name was joined to many motorcycle lists. I received hundreds of leaflets, brochures, pamphlets, and advertisements offering varieties of motorcycles wholesale or retail. Now and again, sometimes after the passage of years, a copy of my circular letter drifted home to me smeared with honest grease, carrying a message in the margin. Here is one: "Sorry no sign of your brother. Selling the shop."

One day as I was walking with my children in New York a glimpse of a horse and a motorcycle pausing side by side at a red light made me think of Speed's epic hero, Americus the Modest on horseback, afterward Amiel Melvin on motorcycle rescuing abused young women from steel magnates on "screened porches" in the city of Pittsburgh. I became persuaded that Speed had settled in Pittsburgh. It must have held a fascination for him, city of steel, smoke, heavy manufacture, where the sheer labor of the body exceeded in purity the deceptions of speech.

We moved to Pittsburgh. We were then four in our family. We found a good house in a Jewish neighborhood. The real-estate agent assured us—reassured us—as Aunt Ember had once reassured father, that a Jewish neighborhood was a positive place to raise a child.

Every day after the children had gone to school I toured Pittsburgh for the sight of my brother. I stood at factory gates to watch the men come and go. I was able to gain permission to study employment lists, and to interview personnel managers who might recall that just such a fellow as my brother had applied for work at their plant or shop. Inevitably I described his principal characteristic as his stuttering. Many men stuttered. Some of the personnel managers stuttered. They told me many jokes and anecdotes about stuttering.

The social center of the district called Squirrel Hill, where we lived, was the public library, as in another district the social center might have been a church. At the library I met several writers whose books then or afterward interested me. One of them had written an autobiography in which the following passage startled

me into such a painful state of self-recognition that with Ruth and
our children I soon returned to New York:

> Barriss Mills . . . mentioned a certain fellow—a student, a poet. . . .
> This fellow had a brother six years older than he who, a few years
> earlier, simply disappeared from the face of the earth. Our student—
> the poet—could never as a consequence settle down, he'd stop
> awhile somewhere, but then he'd suddenly get the idea he'd find his
> brother in Alaska, or San Antonio, and off he'd go.

On or about the tenth anniversary of Speed's departure the song
"Joe Hill" drummed through my head. "Says I, but Joe you're ten
years dead . . ." Dead, dead, dead, I could do nothing to stop the
song in my head. For weeks it impaired my concentration. I had
had a similar experience after grandmother's death, when *Willie
Willie oh so silly* marched in my head as her memorial.

But Willie soon passed from my head, while Joe Hill remained
to harass me. I discovered that I could relieve my system for a day
or two by a vigorous program of singing the whole song repeatedly.
I sang and sang in the garden, in the basement, in the car. Some
days I could not work, some nights I could not sleep. A thousand
times I saw myself in all my wakefulness striding in a dream of the
past down the country road near Brookside Bough arm in arm with
Bob and Marianne Chakerian and Speed singing that old song
whose altered words now conformed to the logic of my disorien-
tation.

> I dreamed I saw ol' Speed last night,
> Alive as you and me.
> Says I, but Speed you're ten years dead,
> I never died, says he.
> I never died, says he.
>
> The copper bosses killed you Speed,
> They shot you Speed says I.
> Takes more than guns to kill a man,
> Says Speed, I didn't die,
> Says Speed, I didn't die.

Says Speed, what they forgot to kill
Went on to organize,
Went on to organize.

Where working men defend their rights
It's there you'll find my Speed
It's there you'll find my Speed.
I never died, says he,
I never died, says he.

In my thirty-fifth year I revised my prayers. I had for most of my life offered four prayers for the future and two for forgiveness. With my first prayer—*Prayer One for the Future*—I had sought to end grandfather's blindness. "God, please see to it that my poor grandfather may have sight and not have to live the rest of his life in darkness." I now perceived this as a lost cause. Grandfather was never going to regain his sight, he was quite accustomed to his "darkness," quite resigned to it, wholly adapted to it.

My second Prayer for the Future, as my reader may recall, had been a kind of daily (nightly) reminder or memorandum to God never to relent in the matter of my mother's one-time lover, Doc Duffy. "Dear God, please make sure Doc Duffy stays dead as we do not want him here in this apartment." This memorandum now appeared to me to be spiritually negative. God as I preferred Him was the agent of life, not of death, the agent of resurrection, not of continued absence. Moreover, my prayer was obsolete: "we" no longer lived "here in this apartment."

Prayer Four for the Future—"Dear God, make Champrain white"—was also obsolete. Champrain's reappearance was an event as unlikely as the restoration of grandfather's sight or the return of Doc Duffy from World War One. At any rate a higher degree of sophistication now enriched my idea of race. I saw that the sensible objective was not to hope for the whiteness of black people but to create a society of colors harmoniously mingling.

Thus I agreed with myself to drop from my prayers my petitions for grandfather, Doc Duffy, and Champrain, leaving myself with the question of how to manage *Prayer Three for the Future* ("Dear

God, fix Speed's stuttering so he could talk normal like the rest of us"). This prayer for Speed I easily amended by simplification, replacing the long-term demand with an emphasis on short-term urgency: "Dear God, please deliver Speed to us," as if we here at home would attend to the stuttering. Simple, direct, brief, let him come home first. Bring Speed back and we'll live with the stuttering.

From my repertoire I deleted my two forgiveness prayers. *Prayer One for Forgiveness* was ancient, composed on the night I also composed my prayer for grandfather. "Dear God, I don't really know if I pushed Speed off the table in Florida. Maybe he jumped or fell or was pushed or dived. If it was an act of God it was Your fault, right? If it was me that pushed him off please forgive me forevermore."

This plea for forgiveness, like *Prayer Two for Forgiveness* ("Dear God, please forgive me for stealing Champrain's quarter from her apron"), impressed me now as obsolete or nullified, a law or regulation in disuse or never noticed—"Bikes To Be Used for Staff on Official Business Only." One of those improper actions for which I sought forgiveness had been committed if at all when I was an infant, the other in an impulsive moment which I had always regretted and for which my victim Champrain had long since forgiven me.

Mrs. Packard-Steinberg established the Sheridan Gardens Apartments Authors Memorial Shrine in Apartment 2–D. One day I drove a long distance to see it, and to visit with Mrs. Packard-Steinberg alone among the memorabilia of the two boys she had enshrined. (To have enshrined only one person would have endangered her tax exemption: a tax-exempt shrine must embrace not one person but a class of persons. Did you know that?)

She had chosen to enshrine Gifford Gimbel and me. Who was Gifford Gimbel? I do not think I ever spoke to him. I saw him pass through the courtyard. He was four years older than I, according to data in the shrine, a whiz at school studies, a Certified Public Accountant, author of *How to Get a Job in Civil Service*, the second volume of which was *How to Get a Job in Civil Service Second Edition,* the third volume of which was *How to Get a Job in Civil Service Third Edition,* and so forth through many volumes standing erect now between bookends on a small table in that corner of our one-time living-room designated the Gifford Gimbel Wing.

"What do you think of Gifford Gimbel's writings?" Mrs. Packard-Steinberg asked me.

"Oh, I worship them," I said. This did not please her. She did not worship *him.* She worshipped me.

Mrs. Packard-Steinberg's shrine was so infrequently visited that she had expected no one that morning. She was surprised to see me—that is to say, not so much surprised to see *me* as surprised to see any man dressed for the city in the middle of the week in the middle of March. She assumed when she saw me that I was some sort of official visitor, perhaps yet one more tax examiner. She seldom had visitors, her shrine was almost never patronized. Now and then a few teachers, energetic, effervescent, enthusiastic, as she had once been, came wide-eyed to the shrine of live writers, trailing a few pupils behind.

I too was surprised, not to see her, whom I had known I would see, but surprised not to be recognized by one of the few people from whom, after all, I had reason to *expect* recognition, from her whose shrine implied indeed that the whole world ought to recognize me.

She asked me, she *demanded* of me, that I sign the guest book. I thought to sign a name other than my own. For a moment, though my head was filled with forty years of names, I could think of nothing, nobody, no name. But soon I confidently named my temporary self by combining Ruth's uncle Ty, to whom I had recently spoken on the phone, with Speed's basketball coach Mr. Cabot, who had crossed my mind as I drove through Mount Vernon: Ticonderoga Cabot, that was who I chose to be today, and scribbled my new name with Mrs. Packard-Steinberg's pen. And then when I had done it she did not trouble herself to look at it.

The room was furnished with display cases and the comical secretary she had retrieved from the cellar of Walk a Mile House. No chairs—I was not expected to waste my time sitting. In the featured case two copies of *Love Never Surrenders* lay embalmed, it seemed, one copy held open at the title page by a metal clip—a kind of large barette—the other exposed to reveal the passage of the book in which Deeps goes forth in life with Thiwest at his side to reclaim the goods of the world for "the people." Appropriately the copies of his book shared the case with his treasured essay, "My Occupational Life Intention," also attributed by Mrs. Packard-Steinberg to me. The only works of mine Mrs. Packard-Steinberg truly admired were not mine: the essay Speed had written to help me out, and the novel he had written for the world.

Mrs. Packard-Steinberg's opinion of my "rebellion" books was reflected in their being assigned places not in glass cases but on bookshelves, exposed, touchable, like ordinary books anywhere, my *Agrarian Rebellion*, my *Whiskey Rebellion*, My This Rebellion, My That Rebellion.

"But I'd really like to be able to say," I said, after I had surveyed myself enshrined, "that you've got a bit of historical confusion going here. Your enshrined fellow wrote the rebellion books but he certainly didn't write *Love Never Surrenders*. His brother wrote *Love Never Surrenders*."

"He had no brother," said Mrs. Packard-Steinberg turning away from me to avoid dispute. She had heard this argument before, notably from Aunt Ember, and she did not care to hear it again, she was weary of it, as Baconians are weary of Shakespeare.

"But I knew his brother," I said.

"People say he had a brother," she said. She seemed about to capitulate, as if so many people's saying so might even make it true, but if it were it was irrelevant, and if it was irrelevant why should anyone mention it?

In other glass display cases Mrs. Packard-Steinberg preserved souvenirs of my existence haunting to see again. I saw old familiar pocket notebooks in which I had kept my magazine accounts. At the top of each page I had written "Owes me" and below those words the name of the hateful person who owed me five cents, ten cents. Through most of these names I had drawn a line, the debt collected. A three-by-five card perched atop these old notebooks explained, "These subscriber notebooks were maintained by the famous author who, as a boy, sold the *Saturday Evening Post* from door to door throughout this neighborhood he loved so much."

That was accurate enough. She was not always accurate. I had not been, as she described me, "a star athlete" in high school. She may in this matter have been confusing me with Speed, or she may have drawn her conclusion from her display of my collection of Mount Vernon Revolvers game books—three years, three books, recording all our games and all our individual scoring achievements, sometimes to my own advantage.

The most amazing thing was this—she made me also a star student. On my high-school report cards, especially those issued when my Revolvers were at their heights and my school marks at their depths, Mrs. Packard-Steinberg upgraded me by forgery, altering every *F* grade to *A* with clever strokes of her matching pen.

In my shrine I was to appear for posterity as a collectivist genius, a world-saver, a boy of good character. She believed every great writer must have earned good report cards. She viewed my social concerns as having begun almost in infancy: here I saw exhibited my letter as a child to father from Florida reporting the lawlessness of drivers driving with only one license plate. Here was the letter to grandfather from Henry Ford—odd fellow to endorse a socialistic boy—its allusion to me encircled: "your promising grandson." Here was the letter to Speed and me from Mr. Kyrene of Brookside Bough, outlining our summer arrangement. "Dear Boys," it began . . . "Then who are these boys if not brothers?" I demanded of Mrs. Packard-Steinberg.

"The other was his friend," she confidently said.

"What friend?" I calmly asked.

"Name unknown," she said.

"Easily found out." I said.

"This shrine is closing for lunch," she said.

"I'll come back after lunch."

"This shrine is closing for the day."

"You should make some effort to find these things out," I said.

"Many many people in Mount Vernon must remember his brother."

"This shrine is closing," she said. She cared nothing for evidence. Evidence confused her. "We don't know," she said.

But she did not close her shrine. She forgot she had said she would. Her span of memory was short. As if no sharp words had passed between us she urged me to continue my "study." I passed from display to display. I saw again the manuscript of Speed's unfinished epic poem composed at Brookside Bough on Durable Tablet, soon abandoned for *Love Never Surrenders*. I read again, with the most intense personal interest, you may be sure, Speed's Durable Tablet essay "Intermarriage," written to serve as my assignment for Current Events.

Until the day of my visit to the Sheridan Gardens Apartments Authors Memorial Shrine I had forgotten that during the last months of our family life we had broken our boundary, expanded our space from Apartment 2–D to Apartment 3–D, connected by Speed's arched doorway. The arched space had now again been obliterated, the wall restored and made—I was about to say like new again, except that it was not like new, it was stained, mottled, dirty, soiled, Speed's fine art sloppily plastered over.

Once, during a single week, Ruth and I attended two memorable public dinners, one at each end of the country.

When father retired after twenty-five years as police chief of Sentinel City, Florida, the city sponsored a farewell dinner for him, to which Ruth and I were invited. We happily attended. One of our daughters accompanied us.

Here was a heavy-drinking crowd. In the procession of speakers the thread of the occasion was often lost, but the presiding toastmaster brought it back again and again to father's distinction, cueing each speaker, who in fact, to begin with at least, stuck to the point, which was father's distinction, his service, his having helped to make Sentinel City a safe and sane place after rugged beginnings.

Father himself at last was introduced. I thought the applause for him would never cease. Mother wept. The toastmaster brought the applause finally to an end by setting off a firecracker. The hall became silent.

I recalled from his remarks a few intriguing words about his being a man "with my own terrible disappointments in my own life, like anybody else." I thought he must have had Speed in mind, but when I asked him afterward "Was it Speed you were thinking of?" he replied no, no, not that, he was thinking of the stupid toastmaster setting off a firecracker in "a crowded hall full of drunken rednecks and trigger-happy deputies." As for Speed—speaking resentfully, I thought, as if Speed were the sole calamity in a serene life—he, father, had been an awfully busy man for a quarter of a century in a greedy, corrupt town, he had no time to admit Speed any longer to his thoughts.

Mother, on the other hand, had not been so busy as father. She told me that for twenty-five years not an hour of her life passed without her thinking of Speed.

In California a few days later Ruth and I attended a public literary dinner at which I gave a speech or listened to others speak but in any case was to have been seated at the speakers' long table. At cocktails beforehand, however, my old Revolvers teammate Ed Selkowitz presented himself to me. I had not heard of him since high school. I rejoiced to see him, we embraced, he asked if he might sit at table with us. "Of course, of course, there's nobody we'd rather be with," I said.

But no, that was not to be permitted by the chairman of arrangements who had worked out the speakers' table to the last butter knife. Very well then, I said, my wife and I would sit below with the strong-wristed Ed Selkowitz, once of the Esplanade Gardens Apartments, once of the Mount Vernon Revolvers, now a California businessman in plastics or computers or I-know-not-what. Ed sat between Ruth and me. We began our meal. He unfolded his napkin and asked, "How's old Speed?"

I thought he knew. I thought everybody knew. But how should everybody have known? "Speed is gone," I said.

"Gone?"

Ruth was more straightforward than I. "Not dead," she said. "We don't know."

"He's missing," I said to Ed Selkowitz. "We haven't heard from Speed in twenty-five years."

Ed Selkowitz became pale, distressed, doubled as if by the pressure of sudden pain. We did not mention Speed again. We talked Mount Vernon names and places until he abruptly asked to be excused for a moment. He left the table with his napkin tucked into his belt and he never returned.

Thus I had seen him for fifteen minutes after twenty-five years. Now twenty-five more have passed. What had caused his distress? In the years gone by I have been able to speculate only that his distress had been caused by his inexpungible memory of my having tried to keep Speed from joining the Revolvers. It was Ed Selkowitz who for the sake of the team had rallied our teammates against me for Speed's sake. My character revived in his mind. I saw in his face a memory of outrage, of unfairness, which I could interpret only as his comparing Speed with me, his considering the proposition that if one man and not the other were to be missing from this earth it should be me, not my brother, that Speed was fine, Speed was one whom the world could not lose, Speed was essential.

He remembered me as the irrational ball-hogger, and he therefore perceived my present alleged celebrity as a cover-up of my tarnished past. I was misleading the public. His sense of fairness was offended. In that way he resembled Speed, sensitive to offenses against justice. Ed Selkowitz could recall games lost we should have won, his having been forced to play the game the wrong way, not Revolvers against opponents but Revolvers against *me*, keeping the ball from me lest I monopolize it to the zero-zero end while he screamed at me *pass, pass, pass, don't hog the fuckin ball you fuckin maniac, feed it to somebody, let it go let it go let it go.*

Grandfather, who had always hated Negroes, bequeathed Walk a Mile House to Mary Washington, who cared for him for thirty years after grandmother's death. Mary Washington converted Walk a Mile House to apartments. As landlady she flourished. On her one-hundredth birthday she was the subject of a feature article in the Mount Vernon *Daily Argus* composed at a furious clip by a rapid young reporter twenty years old smoking a cigarette. Aunt Ember sent me the clippings.

Aunt Ember died. Father died. Mother died. Ruth's mother Lynn died. Ruth's father Jim had dropped dead bearing a tray of break-fasts down the aisle of the dining care *en route* from Chicago to New York on the Twentieth-Century Limited. Speed had been gone for thirty-five years. I no longer said even my one remaining prayer for him. Ruth and I were grandparents nine times over.

One day in a supermarket I saw a sign.

SCIENTIFIC COMPUTER PALMISTRY 50 CENTS

It was a machine. Aunt Ember's palmist was routed by technology. I slid two quarters into the slot and laid my palms flat on the warm metal of the machine, as I was instructed to do. The machine soon released for my information a little square ticket the size of the little square passenger tickets issued by the New Haven Railroad. The ticket said to me, "You must go abroad to find the person you are looking for."

Ruth and I lived abroad for fifteen years. The names of the streets of London and Paris became as familiar to us as they had been to Aunt Ember, nor did I forget the height of the Esplanade Gardens Apartments, either. Wherever we went I dreamed up rebellions to write books about, *The French Rebellion, The Royalist Rebellion, The Scotch Rebellion, Rebellion in the Hebrides, Rebellion at Scapa Flow, Rebellion in the Var.*

My mission abroad was to "find the person you are looking for," and wherever we went I was sharp-eyed. People remarked upon my intensity. I became a student of faces. For all I know I saw him. How would I have known what he looked like?

Ruth and I would have remained in Europe forever, but we heard of a continuing dispute between our two sons and we came home and I said to each of them, "Love your brother, you'll be sorry if you don't."

Our children and grandchildren celebrated Ruth's and my forty-fifth wedding anniversary with a party for two hundred and seventy-five guests in the Grand Ballroom of the Arizona Biltmore.

At one point the orchestra played the song "Joe Hill." The conductor of the orchestra must have asked to know my favorite songs and been told "Joe Hill" among others. He dragged it along. His corruption of the historic tempo drove the words from my memory. The song I'd been singing off and on since Brookside Bough was lost to me, elusive, impossible to seize. My imagination failed. I was growing old. *Dear God, deliver Speed to us.* In the spirit of the tune at its right tempo I might have imagined Speed walking through the ballroom door, but on this day the odd irregular unfamiliar tempo of the old song released me from my obligation to visualize Speed's presence. I no longer required myself to imagine his walking through the door. He was gone.